THE DARK RECKONING

THE COLD WAR LEGACY SERIES
BOOK THREE

SARAH HAMAKER

ISBN print: 978-1-958375-04-4

Cover design and interior layout by 100 Covers.

Edited by Liz Tolsma.

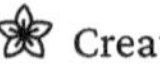 Created with Vellum

Let the favor of the Lord our God be upon us, and establish the work
of our hands upon us; yes, establish the work of our hands!
Psalm 90:17 (ESV)

CHAPTER

ONE

Isana Thomas adjusted the focus on the Leica M-A Rangefinder, peering through the viewfinder at the glistening drop of water clinging to the cherry blossom petal. Fog swirled around her, creating an atmosphere much like the ones evoked in the 1940s noir films she loved. Blowing out a breath, she depressed the shutter, then lined up another shot. Thirty minutes later, satisfied she'd captured the photos she envisioned, she lowered her camera. The fog had intensified, shrouding the cherry trees in a thick, soupy mist as it rolled off the Potomac River and into the Tidal Basin.

Footsteps echoed, the weather shrouding their exact location. A bicyclist buzzed by on the paved pathway circling the basin, the bike's taillight blinking rapidly. Isana shook her head at the folly of biking in this weather with its low visibility. She sure wouldn't risk a tumble into the cold, dark Potomac. A car door slammed, then an engine started. Voices drifted in her direction, and she caught a glimpse of a pair of joggers moving through the fog, headlamps illuminating the predawn darkness. Something brushed against her sleeve. She stumbled back, her heel sliding on the wet grass and sending her careening into a cherry tree.

Wrapping her hand around one of its damp branches, Isana stood very still, sucking in deep breaths to calm her racing heart as panic clawed at her like a monster from a B movie. *Get a hold of yourself. Don't let your imagination run away with you.* Not for the first time, she vowed to stop watching suspenseful movies before bed. No doubt last night's viewing of the 1945 film "Escape in the Fog" contributed to her sense of unease this morning. Probably should have stayed in her nice, safe apartment rather than venturing out to take photos of the early cherry blossoms in the mist. But she'd awakened with a jolt at four and couldn't chance a return to slumber— and the vivid dream that had haunted her since childhood.

A quick glance at her phone revealed she needed to pack up and head home to change for work. Her camera snug in its case, she slung it over her shoulder and paused to get her bearings in the thickening fog. She should walk to the right to catch a bus at the West Basin stop. Her Next Bus app showed the incoming bus would be going in the direction of her apartment and arrive at six-twelve. Five-fifty-eight. Plenty of time to make the short walk. Flipping up her jacket hood against the drizzle, she set out.

She'd only taken a few steps when the sound of an old-fashioned ringing telephone sent her heartrate back into the stratosphere. Her hand on her chest, she cocked her head as the ringing continued, then stopped. She strained to hear the voice of whoever answered the phone, but only the faint rustling of something in a nearby tree reached her ears. Shaking her head to clear it of fanciful imaginings, she turned, but the return of the ringing halted her progress. This time, the sound was louder, more insistent. After six rings, the sound ceased only to immediately start again.

Someone must have lost their cell. Turning on her phone's flashlight, she shone the beam onto the pathway around her feet as the ringing continued. Nothing there. To the left, the Potomac slapped against the retaining wall of the Tidal Basin. No phone there. To the right, a line of stately cherry trees, their budding blossoms blobs of white in the mist. For once, the arborists had timed Washington,

DC's Cherry Blossom Festival perfectly. When the events kicked off in three days, the trees would be in full bloom.

The ringing persisted. The Next Bus app buzzed, reminding her the bus would arrive in five minutes. Drat. She'd miss it because she couldn't abandon the phone. She'd lost hers once and had been so grateful when a Good Samaritan had recovered it. Stepping off the path, she directed the flashlight to the ground. No phone. The fog swirled, and the beam reflected off something shiny. There! She reached down and plucked the still trilling phone from the ground. The device immediately went quiet. Using the sleeve of her jacket, she wiped the muddied and cracked screen, nearly dropping the phone as it rang again in her hand. Hoping she could answer without unlocking the screen, she hit the accept button and raised the phone to her ear underneath the jacket hood.

"Hello?"

Silence, then a male voice said, "I'm sorry, I must have dialed the wrong number."

"Wait!" She listened hard, hoping he hadn't hung up. "Have you been calling this number over and over this morning?"

Another pause, then the man answered. "Yes. What's going on?"

Isana shifted as the coolness of the late March morning sank into her bones. "I found the phone by a cherry tree."

"Cherry tree?"

"By the Tidal Basin." She frowned. Something about the man's voice sounded familiar.

"Where exactly?"

"Near the Japanese Lantern."

"And no one's near?" The fear in the man's voice registered.

"I don't think so. I had been looking for it because it wouldn't stop ringing." She glanced around, using her phone's flashlight to pierce the mist near where the other device had been.

"It's my mother's," the man said, his voice catching. "I've just returned from being out of town and have been trying to reach her."

"And you're worried." She ducked under a low-hanging branch

to peer deeper into the stand of trees between the Tidal Basin and Independence Avenue.

"Yes."

"I'm not finding anything or anyone in the vicinity of where I found the phone." She turned back to the path, holding a tree branch out of her way as she passed.

"I should probably introduce myself. I'm—"

Isana sensed someone near her seconds before being shoved hard. The phone flew out of her hand as her knees hit the ground. She tried to get purchase on the wet grass, but something walloped her on the head, and she sank down into the fog.

Cyrus Hillam nearly dropped his phone when the woman grunted. He gripped his cell tighter. "What's going on?"

The only answer was . . . nothing. His concern ratcheted up to nuclear when she didn't speak. "Hello?"

The phone disconnected. Cy grabbed his car keys and hustled out the door. Little traffic clogged the roads as he drove from Arlington, Virginia, over the Roosevelt Bridge into DC. If only his mother hadn't refused to activate the Find My Phone app on her device, he would have been able to locate her and her phone.

Turning onto the Rock Creek and Potomac Parkway, he slowed as thick fog blanketed the road. Flicking his hazard lights on, he checked that the crossover vehicle's fog lights were on. As he inched his way slowly down the parkway at below the posted 25 mph speed limit, he again berated himself for going out of town for a bachelor party weekend with his former college roommate. His mom had insisted he go on the trip, even though his instincts said to stay. The anniversary of his father's death had happened over the weekend, but Lillian Hillam had always determined to not let her grief interfere with her only child's life.

When he hadn't been able to reach his mother by phone upon his arrival back home yesterday evening, he'd driven to the small house in Falls Church she and his father had purchased on their return to the states from their final overseas assignment with the State Department. But the house had been empty, no sign of Mom and no clue as to her whereabouts. Her Mini Cooper sat in the garage. An empty bowl evidence she'd fed the cat that morning, which indicated she hadn't been away from home long. Her purse and phone were the only things he could tell were missing.

He should have continued to live with her instead of getting his own condo in Clarendon. In the three months since he'd moved out, he had relished the independence. While he could have afforded his own place years ago, he'd stayed because his mother had appeared too fragile emotionally to survive without him. Only lately, she'd been more assertive and had actively encouraged him to move out, telling him thirty-five was much too old to be living with his mother.

His GPS directed him to turn onto Ohio Drive SW. Just past West Basin Drive SW, he swung into an empty parking space and cut the engine. Pocketing his keys, he crossed Ohio and jogged up West Basin Drive before leaving the road to cut through the cherry trees to reach the path circling the Tidal Basin. The woman on the phone had indicated she was near the Japanese Lantern. A jogger's headlamp nearly blinded him as the man ran by. Using his phone's flashlight, he slowed as he neared the location where he'd last spoken with the woman.

"Hello?" Cy stepped off the path and almost tripped over a tree root. "Ma'am? Are you okay?"

Silence greeted his questions. Moving deeper into the stand of cherry trees, the fog swirled around his body like a dancer. The unease hugging his shoulders now encased him like a straitjacket. His finger trembled so much it took him three tries to hit the right button to redial his mother's phone. A ringing phone echoed around him. Lowering his own phone, he cautiously stepped forward until he spotted the device lying against a tree trunk.

He picked it up, his heart dropping to his stomach as he recognized his mother's case, bright gold with the outline of a black cat. *Dear God, let her be okay.* The fog pressed around him tighter, disorienting him. Where was the woman who had answered his call? And more worrying, where was his mother?

Cy turned in a circle, shining his light around him, but could see nothing except the trunks and limbs of cherry trees. Moving at a snail's pace, he headed back toward the path, his eyes downcast to avoid falling over the uneven ground. Then his foot bumped into something pliable. His pulse jumped as the beam revealed a figure lying on the ground.

CHAPTER

TWO

Cy dropped to his knees beside the fallen person, illuminating the scene with his flashlight. The shape resolved into a woman lying on her side wearing leggings, sturdy hiking boots, and a jacket. The woman's head angled away from him, the jacket's hood obscuring her features. Relief coursed through him as he studied the slim figure. Not his mother. This was the body of a younger woman.

The woman moaned.

"Hey," he said softly. "Are you okay?"

At the sound of his voice, her shoulders tensed.

"I'm not going to hurt you. I think you were talking to me on a phone you found when something happened." He laid a hand on her shoulder. "May I help you up?"

Without answering directly, the woman pushed her upper body off the ground, gathering her legs underneath her. Cy assisted her to rise to a seated position, her back braced against a trunk. A light drizzle joined the mist, creating a soupy mess that coated them quickly and lowered visibility.

Her hand touched her hair as a groan escaped her lips. "My head hurts."

Her soft voice told him she had been the woman on the other end of the phone. "Do you remember what happened?"

She grasped her temples with both hands, rocking a little bit forward. "I think I'm going to be sick." Then she leaned away from him and vomited in the grass, her body heaving.

Concern inched up his spine. While a small part of him wanted to continue grilling her about finding the phone, she needed medical attention stat. He phoned 911 but when he gave his location, the dispatcher informed him it would be at least thirty or more minutes before an ambulance could arrive due to a massive traffic accident. He relayed the info to the woman, then added, "We should get you to a hospital."

The woman didn't acknowledge his statement. She stayed hunched over, her hands on the ground.

He calculated the distance between their location and his vehicle. While he could move it a little bit closer on West Basin Drive, he wouldn't be able to get it near enough to load her in easily. "Do you think you could walk if I helped you? My car is a little distance away."

The woman slowly reverted to her seated position. "I don't know. The world is spinning right now. I think if I move, I might throw up again."

It was a chance he'd have to take. She needed medical help. He rose and secured both his and his mother's phone, zipping his coat pocket to ensure he didn't lose one along the way. The woman had a small backpack still looped over her shoulders. A quick scan of the area with his flashlight showed a second device a few feet away. "I found your phone." He tucked it in the outside pocket of the woman's backpack. "Come on."

Cy held out a hand toward the woman, who took it, her cold fingers curling around his. Gently, he tugged her to her feet. She staggered against him, then she twisted away as she heaved again off to the side. He slipped an arm around her waist to keep her upright as she dry-heaved. She must have hit her head, given the symptoms. He'd experienced a concussion once during a pickup football game, and the nausea had been terrible right after it happened.

"Did you fall and hit your head?" He kept his arm around her middle when she straightened.

"No." She tried to take a step and nearly collapsed against him.

"Steady." Cy hugged her closer. "Put your arm around my waist."

She did as instructed, tucking her body closer to his. "Someone . . . pushed me . . . hit me . . . on the head."

Her words, spoken softly, at first didn't make sense to Cy. "Someone attacked you?"

"Yes."

They made it to the pathway, and he turned to the right, matching his steps to her faltering ones. He didn't grill her further as he concentrated on keeping to the path in the heavy mist. The drizzle had morphed into a light, steady rain. Then out of the mist, he spotted the Martin Luther King Jr. Memorial with its large chiseled depiction of the Civil Rights icon in an airy setting. "We're at the MLK memorial."

Cy took more of her weight as her strength flagged. She wouldn't make it to his vehicle, and much as he liked to think he was in good shape, there was no way he could sweep her in his arms and carry her the rest of the way. "You're tired, and my car's down along Ohio Drive. Would you be okay for a few minutes resting on one of the benches by the memorial while I get the car?"

"If . . . I . . . can sit . . . down, . . . yes." She sagged against him, her head flopping on his shoulder.

He supported her to one of the backless slabs that functioned as seats, now wet with rain. She immediately laid down on the wet marble, her eyes sliding shut.

Touching her shoulder, he said, "I'll be back as quick as I can." He took off at a jog, praying God would protect both his mom and this young woman.

～

Isana shivered as she lay on the cold marble slab on the perimeter of the memorial. Driving rain pummeled her body. Her head ached. If she opened her eyes, the nausea returned. Better to keep them closed so she could inhabit the dream that had sustained her ever since the man had touched her shoulder.

It had been *his* voice she'd heard, even though she knew it couldn't possibly be true. Had to be a distortion of the fog or perhaps her head injury making her think so. She allowed herself the luxury of pretending it was. It had been easy enough to avoid looking directly at his face since every movement of her head brought a wave of nausea. Pretending the man was her secret office crush, Cyrus Hillam, gave her the strength to walk beside him, tucked close to his warm body. She put her hand at her waist where his had supported her.

His voice had been so kind and gentle, urging her onward, telling her it would be okay. Worry for his mother lent an urgency to his actions, leading him to find Isana. Who knows what might have happened had he not come along.

Isana breathed deeply, trying to stall the pounding in her head. Other memories banged on the door of her mind, but the padlock she'd put there years ago held steady. Better to think about Cyrus, the new public relations and marketing director at The Heritage. Cy, as he preferred to be called, had only been at the private museum for a few months but already had all the single—and some married—women's hearts aflutter with his blond good looks. If his lean, six-foot-one height and green eyes weren't enough to make him the museum's most eligible bachelor, the hint of a tattoo on his upper bicep sealed the deal. With her job as a researcher and authenticator for the museum's acquisitions of twentieth century objects, she had very little interaction with the public face of The Heritage, and so had ample opportunities to gaze at Cy from afar.

Late last year, the museum had received a substantial donation to expand its mission of interpreting the major and minor events of the 1900s, leading it to acquire a larger building near the National Mall in downtown DC and hire a new marketing and PR director. Already, Cy had endeared himself to both the museum staff and its board with his innovative ideas on generating both publicity and paying customers.

But it had been the kindness in his eyes that had caught Isana's attention. Usually, she kept her head down at work. Interpersonal interactions made her so nervous, she sometimes broke out in hives. Her job required limited speaking to her coworkers, which suited her just fine. She sensed they thought her quiet and a little strange, but mostly they left her alone in the museum's basement, where she had a spacious office and few interruptions.

A crack of thunder brought her back to the present with a jolt. The rain increased its temper. Had the man simply left her here? Panic seized her heart and squeezed. Surely he wouldn't leave her to freeze to death at the memorial. Maybe she could make it to the bus stop. She still wore her backpack, into which the man had tucked her phone, plus a backup SmartTrip card just in case her phone app decided not to work. But where was her camera case?

Her heartrate accelerated like a plane's jet engine during takeoff. *Please God, let my rescuer have it.* No way she was leaving without it. She'd just have to retrace their steps until she found the camera.

Placing her hand on the slippery marble, she eased to a sitting position with her eyes closed. While her head ached something fierce, the dizziness had passed. She counted to three, then opened her eyes. Nausea swept over her, but she resisted the urge to close her eyes and lay back down. Several slow, deep breaths countered the feeling. Glancing around to get her bearings, her heart stuttered when she caught a glimpse of a figure standing slightly behind one of the stone walls.

She blinked rain out of her eyes. The figure vanished. It couldn't be the man who'd rescued her, as he was getting the car. Maybe it was whoever had attacked her. Every fiber in her wanted to head back to the Tidal Basin path to search for her missing camera, but to do so would mean moving past where the person had gone. Indecision kept her frozen to the bench for a long, shivering moment. Which way to go—forward or backward? That was the story of her life, her inability to make decisions about her future because she kept looking to her past. But this was one decision she could make. She would go back for her camera.

Isana rose, her legs nearly giving out. Was this a smart idea? Bracing a hand against the slab, she managed to keep her feet. She would need to pass the statute to get to the Tidal Basin. She could do this. Walk purposefully like you know where you were going, her self-defense instructor had said. Squaring her shoulders, she took her first step, grateful her legs held steady. Half a dozen steps led her to the center of the memorial. Her breathing hitched, and she paused to rest her cheek against the cooler stone of the upright slabs. No time to rest. She mustn't stop but keep her momentum going forward. She ignored the voice in her head telling her she should have stayed put.

Time to get moving. Isana took another step. A bit of stone struck her cheek. A whizzing sound sent another small chunk of King's statute flying inches from her head. Her heart squeezed inside her chest as a third bullet hit the slab to her right. Someone was shooting at her!

THREE

Cy pulled the SUV to the curb in front of the Martin Luther King Jr. Memorial entrance and hit the hazards button. The rain had intensified during his short drive up West Basin Drive. The early morning hour and the weather kept other drivers away, easing his conscience about illegally parking at the curb. After turning off the engine, he dashed into the wetness, chirping the vehicle locked as he jogged to the towering stone pillars marking the memorial entrance. The cold rain increased the fog, making it difficult to see clearly. By the foot of the stone statute of King, he spotted a figure wearing a familiar blue jacket. Why was the woman there and not on the wall bench where he'd left her?

Something whizzed by his head, thunking into the pillar over his left shoulder. Instinctively, he dropped to a crouch as another bullet buried itself into the stone. His mind registered someone was shooting at them, but he couldn't believe it. This kind of thing only happened on crime shows or superhero movies, not to a PR professional for a private museum. A siren pierced the rain and fog, bright lights flashing by on nearby Ohio Drive. Once the emergency vehicles had passed, Cy counted to sixty. No more bullets were fired. Perhaps the sirens had scared off the shooter.

The woman had collapsed against the statue. He shot God a fervent a prayer for safety and darted across the open expanse, flattening himself against the stone in front of the woman. "Hey, are you okay?"

"Someone was shooting at me." She raised her head, a rivet of blood mixing with the rain on her cheek.

"You're hurt!" He used the edge of his jacket sleeve to wipe away the blood. "Were you shot?"

She shook her head. "A piece of stone hit me in the face." A shiver rocked her body. He needed to get her out of the rain and to a hospital pronto. He'd call 911 to report the incident once he got her in his SUV, but given the rainy conditions and the fact emergency vehicles had zoomed past with lights flashing a while ago, he would stick to his earlier decision to transport her himself rather than wait for an ambulance.

"I thought you weren't coming back for me."

Her lack of faith in him cut to the quick, but he ignored the hurt. Not a time to focus on himself. "I'm sorry it took a little longer to fetch my car than I thought. I'm parked at the curb." He glanced around but saw no one else. "I think the shooter's gone. Can you stand?"

With a nod, she rose, using the statue as a guide. He got to his own feet and steadied her, once again tucking her close under his arm with a hand at her waist. He moved as quickly as he could, praying the shooter had vanished. Their progress to the SUV was unhindered by any additional shots. He unlocked the doors and eased her inside the vehicle, buckling her in as if she were a child.

Hurrying around to the driver's side, he slid into the seat and pushed the ignition button, turning the heat on full blast. "How are you feeling?"

"My head hurts. I'm so cold." Her body shook.

"Let's get you to the ER."

"No!"

Her vehement response startled him.

"My camera's missing." Despite her bedraggled appearance, the determination came through loud and clear. "We have to go back and look for it."

"You need to see a doctor. I don't want hypothermia to set in." Cy put the car into gear and pulled away from the curb.

The woman placed a trembling hand in his shoulder. "Please, I need my camera. It's in a case. It was around my neck when I was on the phone with you."

He ignored her pleas and headed toward George Washington University Hospital. "You need medical attention first."

She slumped into the seat beside him, her arms hugging her small frame. He didn't pepper her with questions during the short drive to the hospital, as the lifting fog and continuing rain made traffic conditions less than ideal.

He found a parking spot close to the ER entrance and helped the woman from his car and into the brightly lit waiting room. After lowering her into a chair close to the check-in counter, he approached the desk.

The lone male at the desk made eye contact as he stepped forward. "May I help you?"

"Yes, this woman was hit over the head by the Tidal Basin and got caught in the rain," he began. "She threw up at the scene, and I think she might have a concussion."

The employee pushed his glasses further up his nose, then signaled a young man wearing a maroon blazer. "This woman needs a wheelchair and a thermal blanket. Then get her back to cubicle fourteen."

Cy returned to the woman and updated her on what was happening. Within minutes, the young man had the chair next to Isana. Cy assisted him in helping to transfer her. Snapping open the silver blanket, the hospital employee tucked it around Isana before wheeling her through the double doors. Cy followed, not wanting to lose this link to his mother and out of concern about the young woman's health.

In the cubicle, a nurse who introduced herself as Kayleigh assisted the woman into a bed, wrapping a second blanket around her and checking her vitals. That completed, the nurse shooed Cy into a chair, then addressed her patient. "Let's get some info from you. Name and date of birth?"

"Isana Thomas."

The name rang a faint bell in Cy's mind, but he couldn't immediately place her. The woman continued to shiver as her body slowly warmed. Kayleigh asked Isana more questions.

Cy tried to tune out into her answers, not wanting to eavesdrop on sensitive information, but when the nurse asked where she worked, he thought he heard Isana say, "The Heritage Museum."

"Where?" The question burst out of him before he could stop himself.

Isana raised her gaze to lock with his. "The Heritage Museum."

"That's where I work." He studied her pale, wet face for any clue he knew her.

An emotion he couldn't label flashed across her face before she dropped her gaze. "We've only met once, during an all-staff meeting."

Kayleigh cleared her throat. "So you're not related to Ms. Thomas?"

Cy shook his head.

"Then you'll need to leave."

"Please let him stay." Isana's voice trembled. "He saved my life."

Kayleigh eyed Cy. "Only if he doesn't get in the way."

"I won't."

Isana relaxed against the bed. Her voice still shook slightly, but she answered the remaining handful of questions as she clutched the silver blankets.

After Kayleigh left the cubicle, Cy tugged the plastic chair closer to the bed. "I'm so sorry I didn't recognize you. I'm Cy Hillam."

"I know." A faint blush added a touch of color to her cheeks. "No need for an apology. I work in the basement, so don't mingle with the public or other staff much."

Cy frowned, trying to recall what happened in the basement of the museum from his brief tour after starting six months ago. "Forgive me, but I'm still putting together all the pieces of what goes on at the museum. What exactly do you do?"

"I'm a researcher and authenticator for the donations and objects the museum acquires." She tucked the blanket tighter around her legs. "I make sure everything we display has been properly documented and its provenance established."

"Ah, I see." He smiled. "You have the most important job in the entire museum."

Surprise flickered in her eyes for an instant, bringing out gold flecks among the green. Eyes like that could mesmerize a man. Then she dropped her head. "No, I don't."

Cy leaned toward her. "Not the way I see it. If the museum didn't have you, we wouldn't have anything to display."

"Then it's a good thing there's a few of us in the department."

"Isana Thomas?" A woman with white coat and tablet in hand stepped into the cubicle. "I'm Dr. Zenner. What's going on?"

"I'll go to the waiting room." Cy gave Isana a reassuring smile as the doctor approached the bed, then slipped out of the room.

He found a seat and pulled out his phone. For a moment, he held the device as he tried to think of what to do. Now that Isana was safe, his next step would be to see if he could file a missing person's report on his mother.

"It's a Leica M-A Rangefinder film camera in a hard cover carrying case." Isana added to the description of her missing camera as DC Metro Police Officer Jenson jotted down the particulars. She held a Styrofoam cup of steaming black coffee in her hands as she sat on the edge of a bed in an ER cubicle. A CT scan showed no fractures on her skull, and the doctor had determined she hadn't suffered from a concussion, although she had been prescribed rest for the remainder of the day and over-the-counter pain relievers for the headache.

"You think your attacker took the camera?" Officer Jenson huffed the question, as if he couldn't wait to get back to real policing instead of taking notes about an ordinary mugging.

"I don't know who else it could have been. The strap was around my neck." She'd already been over the events of the morning several times with both the ER doctor and Jenson. "Has anyone checked the scene for my camera?"

Jenson snapped his notebook closed. "We have a team going over the memorial to recover any bullets from the shooting. I'll stop by to see if they're also searching along the path for the first attack." He extracted a business card from a pocket on his uniform. "In the meantime, if you think of anything else, please give me a call."

She accepted the card. "I will."

He moved toward the curtain.

"Office Jenson?"

The officer turned back, tapping his fingers lightly against his thigh.

She swallowed as butterflies took flight in her stomach. She hated to assert herself. A lifetime spent adhering to her mother's adage to not bother people was hard to overcome. But she desperately wanted the camera back, so she ploughed on. "The camera was a gift from my late grandfather, so it's rather special to me. I really appreciate your help in finding it."

His features relaxed into the first genuine smile she'd seen during the fifteen-minute interview. "Sure thing. I'll be in touch as soon as we have any news."

After he'd gone, she battled the urge to sink onto the bed and close her eyes. Her symptoms of hypothermia had subsided as her body warmed under blankets and a dry set of scrubs, and she felt nearly human again.

The wall clock ticked to eight-thirty-nine. Technically, she wasn't late for work until nine, but since she always arrived a little after eight, she should let HR know about her absence. Quickly, she made the call, saying she'd been in an accident and wouldn't be coming into work today, grateful to get Faith Gibbons's voicemail and not the woman herself. Then she waited for the nurse to bring her discharge papers and wondered how she'd get home.

The nurse bustled in with a sheaf of papers and a tablet. Isana signed her name on the electronic forms, nodding as the nurse reviewed the diagnosis and prescription.

"Let me check on your ride." The nurse switched the curtain back to reveal Cy standing a foot away, his hands jammed into the front pocket of his jeans. "She's all yours."

Isana's cheeks warmed at the words, hoping Cy hadn't noticed the wink the nurse gave her as she exited the cubicle.

"Ready?"

She slid off the bed, wobbling a bit as her sock feet hit the floor. "Yes." She shoved her feet into hospital slippers, the thin material not much of a barrier against the cold tile.

Cy picked up the clear plastic bag containing her wet clothes while she shouldered her backpack. "Do you want a wheelchair?"

She bit her lip, not wanting to ride but unsure of walking on her own.

"Maybe if I provide some assistance?" He cocked his elbow toward her as if about to escort her to a ball.

Slipping her arm through his, she mumbled her thanks. This was going to be a very long walk to his vehicle, one she would relive over and over in her mind later. For now, she would bask in the fantasy that a handsome man desired her company.

CHAPTER

FOUR

Lillian Hillam lay still, keeping her eyes closed as she gathered all possible intel about where she was. Her head ached, leading her to surmise she'd been conked out with a heavy object. How long she'd been unconscious was something she'd try to discern later. First up was an inventory of her body.

With as little movement as possible—she didn't want to tip off anyone watching about her being awake—she ascertained her hands were bound behind her, but her legs and ankles were not secured. A blindfold covered her eyes, but the scratchy fabric felt loose. Other than the fierce headache and her shoulders because of how her arms were positioned, nothing else hurt. She moved her head against the floor to push the blindfold up enough that by casting her eyes down, she could catch a glimpse of the room without removing the entire covering.

By moving her head slowly, then pausing for several minutes, she was able to check out the room. Concrete floor splattered with old paint. No artificial lights on, but there must be a window, as the room wasn't bathed in darkness. Listening hard, she heard nothing but the sound of her own breathing and the pitter-patter of rain.

After waiting a while, she decided to remove more of the blindfold and maneuvered the cloth toward her forehead on the right side, allowing her more visual of the room. The bright grayness of the light told her dawn had broken but the sun was hiding behind clouds. A crack of thunder affirmed her conclusion.

Lillian closed her eyes to recall how she'd arrived at this place. Yesterday—assuming she had only been unconscious for twenty-four hours or less—had been the anniversary of her beloved husband's death. The date always hit her hard, especially because Greg had shot himself in their home where she would be sure to find him. The horror of coming in from grocery shopping and seeing him sprawled over the kitchen table still haunted her. Lillian forced her thoughts away from the question that would plague her the rest of her life and refocused on mentally retracing her steps.

She'd visited his grave in the predawn hours, having woken at three and been unable to return to sleep. Despite the late March chill, she'd sat on the dew-covered ground for hours, talking to her dead husband about Cyrus and her worries he wouldn't find love because of the tragedy of his father's demise thirty years ago. Then she'd gone home, taken a hot bath, and brewed a cup of tea before tackling the next item on her annual pilgrimage through the past. She'd spent the rest of the morning pouring through photo albums and talking out loud as if Greg were merely in the other room and not six feet under the ground. Those reminiscences ended like they always did—with her sobbing into a pillow on the couch, one of Greg's old cardigans wrapped around her like his arms used to do. She'd fallen asleep and awakened several hours later, cold and stiff.

Washing her face, she'd stared at the middle-aged woman she'd become, her fingers tracing the tired lines of her once flawless complexion. The words of her counselor during their final session several days earlier drifted across her mind. *Only you can decide when you've had enough of the grief, enough of living in the past and the what-ifs and the maybes. You've been grieving for Greg half your life. Is this how you want to keep living? I can't help you when you're unwilling to move past the thing that's holding you under.*

Had she really been mourning Greg for three decades? In some respects, it seemed like only yesterday when she'd met the handsome, self-assured man at a State Department orientation course for those going overseas for their first assignment. To her surprise, Greg had been attending as a student, not as an instructor as she had assumed. Something about him didn't lend itself to being a first-time diplomat. But, as she later discovered, Greg's friendly, outgoing demeanor hid the hard steel of the real man very well.

Lillian shifted on the cold cement, her bones aching. She was no longer that starry-eyed college graduate who'd recklessly agreed to marry a near stranger and go off on the adventure of a lifetime. Greg hadn't lied about that. They had done some good, had a lot of fun, and maybe even saved the world a time or two.

The door hinge creaked, alerting her to someone else's presence seconds before the person entered the room. For a moment, no other sound reached her ears except her own steady breathing. The door closed with a bang. Lillian couldn't control her body's jolt at the sudden noise.

"I thought you were awake." The man walked toward her, his shoes making only a whisper of sound.

She tensed as he squatted next to her. He jerked off her blindfold in one, quick movement, sending her head crashing back to the cement before she had time to react. A single bulb dangled from the ceiling, casting yellow light into the small room. With the man's back to the light, his features stayed in shadow, but she could see the smile curving his lips.

"You're still a beautiful woman, Lillian." The man's voice was almost a caress. "Here, let's make you more comfortable."

As he turned her onto her side, she forced her body to stay limp and relaxed, even as her pulse accelerated at his compliment. He knew her, had *known* her. The man inserted a knife blade in between her bound writs and slit the plastic zip ties without nicking her skin.

After he removed the pieces of plastic, he leaned back. Only then did she bring her arms to her front, her shoulders screaming with pain. She allowed her hair, which had escaped its tidy chignon at the base of her neck, to fall in front of her face, obscuring her reaction from his view. Slowly, she raised herself to a seated position, scooting backwards to rest against the cement block wall.

"Better?"

She nodded, not trusting her voice would sound steady if she spoke. Whoever this man was, they had history together. While she desperately wanted to know why she'd been taken, Lillian kept her mouth shut. Silence, she'd learned early in her diplomatic career, could unnerve even the strongest man.

Her captor rose, pacing to the far side of the room. Lillian measured his stride. He wasn't taking long steps, as one would when walking outside, for example. The average man's step was thirty-one inches. It took him six steps to reach the opposite wall. She did the math in her head and calculated the room had a width of approximately 200 feet. Without moving her head too much, she estimated the length of the room to be roughly the same.

"Do you know why you're here?"

"No." Lillian snuck a look at the man as he pivoted at the far wall. Shorter than her husband but taller than her, maybe five-foot-eleven. A full beard covered the lower half of his face. Bushy eyebrows dominated his forehead. Something about the eyebrows puzzled her, almost as if they had been added as a distraction. Then she spotted the thin scar running from his left temple along the hairline.

"You don't remember me."

"No." She could tell by the way the man's shoulders tensed a fraction her answer hurt him, but his eyes, when they collided with hers, blazed with fury.

"Funny you can't recall the man whose life you ruined." He crossed to her, his hand cracking across her face before she registered his intention.

The blow whipped her head against the wall, but she suppressed the cry of pain banging at her lips to come out.

"*Du siehst den Wald vor lauter Bäumen nicht.*" He spat inches from her foot, disgust written on the lines of his face.

Even after all these years, the German translation effortlessly came to her mind. *You can't see the forest for the trees.* She was missing the obvious connection. Then as if a logging company had cleared away the dead trees in a thick forest to allow more sunlight in, she knew. "Nathan Schmidt."

"Ah, so you do remember me." Schmidt returned to crouch down in front of her.

Lillian's heart raced faster, but she met his gaze without flinching, even as memories of what this man was capable of flooded her mind. "We thought you were dead."

He snorted. "You and your husband betrayed me."

She shook her head. "No, it wasn't like that."

"You told a Stasi agent who I was. I understand why, Frau Hillam. That was clear to me even back then. But I need the list."

Her stomach dropped to her toes. The list.

"Greg was most convincing, even with a gun to his head, that he had no idea what I was talking about. I truly believed him, which was why I walked away after killing him."

Fury stampeded over fear, catapulting Lillian into action. She lunged up, cracking her head purposefully against Schmidt's face. Warm blood spurted in the air between them, but she ignored the spray. Driving her shoulder into his, her movement toppled him over. He fell heavily onto the concrete on his back like an overbalanced turtle. Using his imbalance to her advantage, she straddled him. Her hands closed around his neck.

Revenge for taking her beloved husband's life coursed through her veins, leaving her with one thought only—to take his life for Greg's. His eyes bulged.

Then something pricked her arm. Schmidt's face faded from view as Lillian slumped forward into darkness.

~

"I LAST SAW MY MOM ON THURSDAY EVENING. WE HAD DINNER TOGETHER."
Cy pinched the bridge of his nose, worry about his mother's
continued absence consuming his thoughts. He'd managed to get a
little work done at the office after dropping Isana off at her apartment, but he'd left right at five to file a missing person report in
person with the Arlington County Police Department.

Officer Shattuck keyed in the info. "Was that also the last time
you spoke with her?"

Cy shook his head. "We spoke Saturday morning, and she texted
me Sunday, but I didn't get that text until my plane landed." He
explained why he was out of town over the weekend.

"Nothing alarmed you in that final text?" The officer, a middle-
aged woman with kind eyes, glanced up from her keyboard.

"No. Here's the text." He brought up the short message and
turned his phone for Shattuck to read the short missive.

Hope your flight is smooth. Have news about dad. See you soon.

The officer added the info to the form. "What about your father?"

"He died when I was in kindergarten." Even after all these years,
sadness washed over him.

"How did he die?"

A natural question, but one Cy always hated answering. "He shot
himself." Memories of a family friend picking him up from school
and taking him to stay with her and her loud, boisterous family for a
few days. His mother stopping by at bedtime to tuck him in and tell
him his father had died. The funeral with all those men in dark suits,
and his mother crying softly at his side through the entire service. It
wasn't until middle school that he learned the truth about his
father's death from a classmate who taunted him with being the son
of a suicide.

She met his gaze. He steeled himself for pity but found only mild
interest in her eyes. "What do you think she meant about your dad?"

He ran a hand through his hair. "Since she took early retirement

—she'd been an executive assistant to the CEO of a multi-million-dollar company for years—she'd been obsessed with finding out why he killed himself."

"He didn't leave a note?"

Cy shook his head. "No. She came home from running an errand and found him dead at the kitchen table."

"No work or financial troubles?"

Again, he responded in the negative. "Once they ruled his death a suicide, they stopped investigating, so I don't know how closely they looked into his work or finances."

"Where did he work?"

"State Department. He and my mother both did at that time."

The officer's fingers flew over the keyboard as she entered the information. "Anything troubling your mother of late?"

"No." Anger flared as Cy jumped ahead to the questions he thought the officer was leading up to. "And if you're about to ask if she'd been despondent and perhaps gone off somewhere to kill herself, then that's a hard no." He drew in a breath to grab hold of his temper. No need to bite off Shattuck's head. "My mom would never commit suicide, not after living with my father's actions all these years. She always said how surprised she was that he had done such a thing."

"In my experience, the family is often the last to know of a loved one's inner turmoil."

"I know. I've read all the books, listened to all the podcasts, visited a counselor myself for a time." And it had helped him move on, but he could see his mother never really had. Which was why Lillian Hillam would never take her own life and leave him to live with the guilt and uncertainty like she had. "I think something's happened to my mom. She wouldn't leave without telling me."

"Is there any evidence someone else was involved with your mom's disappearance?"

Cy pulled out his mom's phone. "All I have is her phone. Someone found it by the Tidal Basin early yesterday morning. Then she was attacked. A DC police officer took her statement at the hospital's emergency department. Isana Thomas."

The officer clicked some keys. "I'll request the report. Why don't you grab some coffee?"

She indicated an open break area with a Keurig as well as a more traditional coffeemaker with a half-full pot of java. He didn't want a cup but wandered over anyway. After examining the available pods —nothing decaf, which didn't surprise him, given police officers would want the full-strength stuff to power through their shifts—he made his way back to Shattuck's desk.

"Report just came through my email."

He waited while she read, trying not to let his hopes rise that this information would spur a full investigation into what happened to his mom.

"Says here someone shot at the two of you in the MLK memorial park."

He nodded. "Officer Jenson indicated a team checked the park for evidence, but I haven't heard whether they found anything."

She faced the computer screen. "The rain pretty much washed away anything left behind except for two bullets embedded in the stone. Those were extracted and sent to the forensics lab. No camera bag was recovered either."

Cy recalled Isana asking about her camera, but he hadn't seen it near where he'd stumbled upon her in the grass. For Cy, the bullets and Isana's injuries pointed to someone else involved in his mother's disappearance. However, he could tell by the officer's bland facial expression the police wouldn't come to the same conclusion.

The officer added something to the file, then lifted her fingers off the keyboard. "I'm going to be honest with you. There's not a whole lot we can do without proof your mother met with foul play. We'll add her to the missing persons database and circulate her description to our patrol officers. Beyond that . . . " She shrugged. "I wish I could say more will be done."

"What about my mom's phone?" He held out the device to the officer.

Without accepting it, she said, "Have you checked the recent call list?"

"It's been cleared other than the calls I made trying to contact her. The only text messages are from people I know or myself. Nothing new from anyone the last three days."

"There's not much else we'd do with her phone at this time, but keep it in a safe place."

Although Cy had anticipated this response, disappointment still crushed down on his shoulders. He stood, holding out his hand to Shattuck. "I appreciate your candor."

"If anything changes, if you hear from her or find evidence pointing to an abduction or foul play, please call me right away." She handed him a business card. "This has my direct line on it."

He pocketed the card with thanks and threaded his way out of the police station and into the cool March air. Pointing his car toward the house he'd grown up in, he did the only thing he could do at that moment.

Please, God. Keep Mom safe. Help me to find her.

CHAPTER

FIVE

D o you have it?" The voice had lost none of its authority, despite the owner pushing seventy now.

Brenner Lorenz crushed the spent cigarette under the toe of his boot before replying into the phone. "No."

"But you have the woman."

The statement, spoken in a tone colder than an artic freeze, reminded Brenner of his failure to convince Lillian Hillam to give him what he wanted. "Yes." Something compelled him to add, "She insists she doesn't have it."

"That's what her husband said."

"Schmidt told her that." As soon as the words left his mouth, Brenner cursed himself for his stupidity. The man on the other end of the line hated any deviation from his plan.

"He always had a soft spot for that woman." The disgust over such a mundane emotion like desire or even love reminded Brenner sharply to whom he was indebted. Even after all these years, the thought of what the man could do sent a shiver down his spine.

"I don't think he will any longer. Lillian nearly strangled him when he told her he'd killed her husband. If I hadn't happened along, she would have succeeded."

The man grunted, whether in admiration or disgust, Brenner couldn't be sure. "What about the son?"

"He won't be a problem. He has no idea what his parents really did, and there's nothing in Lillian's house to contradict the story she's told him."

"You were thorough in your search?"

"Yes. Went through every book, nook, and cranny." The tedious job had taken his men nearly all night, but in the end, no list had been found. "If Hillam had the list, it's not in the house."

"We cannot take that chance. If it surfaces, things will not go well for either of us."

Brenner didn't reply, his mind whirring with the implications of such a document getting into the wrong hands.

"Make sure Lillian truly doesn't have the list."

"Yes, sir. And the son?"

"Does he still live with his mother?"

"I don't think so. There was a guest room, but it looked unused."

"Then you'd better search his house as well."

"Consider it done."

"And keep him under surveillance for now." The man paused, then asked, "What about the girl?"

Brenner frowned. "The girl?" Then he placed her. "Oh, the one who found the phone?"

"Yes. She works with the son at the museum. Could there be a connection?"

"I don't think she's anything but an innocent bystander. The son hardly speaks to her at work."

"So why did your man shoot at her?"

"He was new and wanted to ensure we recovered the phone." Brenner wasn't sure why he bothered with the explanation. The man on the other end only cared about results, not excuses for not completing a job. "He did get the girl's camera."

The silence stretched between them. He hurried to fill it. "It's one of those film cameras. We're getting it developed in case she saw something she shouldn't have."

"You're developing the film of a camera your man stole."

Despite the statement's benign meaning, the words sent a sliver of fear through Brenner's body. "Yes."

"Keep me informed."

The dead air hummed in Brenner's ear. He lowered his phone, then used a tissue to wipe the sweat dotting his brow. Time to put his contingency plan into action, after he cleaned up the mess the new guy made. He was definitely getting too old for this, but the ambitions of his younger self meant playing when the piper called.

Isana adjusted the magnifying glass to read the microscopic inscription on the inner side of a plain, gold band. *With love, May 22, 1935.* She noted the inscription in the computer field, then printed a label. Tucking the ring carefully into its box, she affixed the label to the container. Her shoulders ached, and her head pounded. 12:45. Time for more pain reliever and lunch.

In the ground floor staff breakroom, Isana refilled her water bottle and downed three ibuprofen. She shouldn't have lost track of time and missed her late-morning dose. Sidestepping one of the museum docents, she opened the refrigerator for her lunch, but the container wasn't where she'd put it that morning. Isana leaned into the fridge, moving various containers and insulated sacks around, but no soup container appeared. Someone had absconded with her lunch, despite her name written in Sharpie on the lid and bottom.

She closed the fridge with a little more force than necessary. Tears of frustration pricked at the back of her eyes, but she rapidly blinked to keep them at bay. Silly to cry over missing soup.

Carson Willoughby, one of the museum's curators, breezed into the room, a round plastic container in his hand.

Isana eyed the familiar container, a bit of leafy green stuck to the side confirming her suspicion. He'd eaten her kale-and-sausage soup. It wasn't the first time Carson had gobbled food he hadn't brought. "Carson, that's my—"

Cy entered with a mug.

"Oh, hi, Cy." Carson spoke as if she hadn't been addressing him. "I want to talk to you about the new special exhibit I'm working on for the summer."

Cy nodded in her direction as he moved to the sink and turned on the water. "What's the idea?"

"Weddings through the century." Carson's pleased expression snapped the last bit of Isana's control. First he took her soup, now he was trying to steal the idea she'd had for a June special exhibit. When she had come to him two weeks ago with the concept, he had dismissed it as not prestigious enough for The Heritage Museum to even consider.

Cy rinsed his mug, setting it in the drainer. "Do we have enough inventory in house to pull off a special exhibit?"

Isana opened her mouth to snap *We do, as I told Carson a couple of weeks ago when I proposed the idea to him,* but the words stayed in her mind.

Carson nodded. "I checked our acquisitions and believe we do."

"Have you approached the director with your idea? I thought the summer calendar was full."

"Usually that's the case, but the traveling special exhibit scheduled for June fell through."

"Keep me posted. I've been thinking we should incorporate more public interest with receptions for special exhibits, so this might be a good one to start with." Cy moved toward the door.

Berating herself for not speaking up when Carson co-opted her idea, she found her voice at last. "That's my soup." She pointed to the container Carson still held in his hand. Cy turned around, his gaze flicking from her to Carson.

"What?" Carson glanced down at his hand holding the dish. "No, I brought this."

"Labeled with Isana's name?" Cy pointed to her name on the bottom. "I think you owe Isana an apology and lunch money."

Surprise kept Isana's mouth shut as Carson's face flushed an unbecoming shade of red.

"I must have mixed it up with the bowl I brought." Carson looked everywhere around the room but at her directly. "My apologies."

Cy crossed his arms, his eyes fastened on the other man.

Under that steady gaze, Carson slammed the empty container on the counter and reached for his wallet. Extracting a five-dollar bill, he held it out toward Isana.

Before she could reach for it, Cy shook his head. "You can't buy a bowl of soup anywhere in DC for five bucks."

Huffing, Carson rifled through his wallet and pulled out a ten. Cy snatched both bills and handed them to Isana. Carson glared, his eyes promising revenge. For once, Isana didn't cower in the face of his displeasure. Having someone stand up for her had straightened her spine.

"Thank you," she said.

Carson huffed, then stalked to the door.

"Next time, read the labels before chowing down someone else's lunch," Cy called after the departing man.

Isana shifted on her feet, tongue-tied in his presence. The warm, fuzzy feeling his taking on Carson's theft made her like him even more. But girls like her didn't get the prince, no matter how many times he rescued her.

"How are you feeling?"

His question brought her gaze to his face. "Better. My head still hurts some." The medicine had eased some of the pain, but her stomach growled, reminding her food was a top priority. She clutched the money, wondering where she could go for a quick lunch. Her budget didn't extend to eating out, so she'd never explored any restaurants near the museum.

A trio of admins came in, their laughter reminding Isana of how disconnected she was from her colleagues because of where she worked and her own shy personality. The three pretty, young women fluttered around Cy, drawing him into their conversation as easily as a spider lured flies to its web.

Isana turned and slipped out of the room, not wanting to see him flirt back, further crushing her impossible dream of a future together. Hurrying to the staff entrance on the side, she stepped into the sunshine. A gust of wind nearly knocked her off her feet, its icy tendrils reminding her that spring hadn't quite arrived. She hugged her arms around her waist, wishing she'd thought to grab her jacket from her desk chair. No way would she re-enter the museum and chance to run into Cy. She'd make a quick lunch run and eat at her desk, like always.

"Can't decide where to go for lunch?"

She froze as Cy came alongside her. "I don't eat out much." Ever, but no sense in making herself appear more pathetic than she was.

"Mind if I join you? I've been dying to try the pho place around the block."

Join her? For lunch? Isana could only mumble, "Sure," and follow him as he took the lead to the restaurant. She scrambled to remember what exactly pho was. A Vietnamese soup. That would be okay, as long as it wasn't too spicy. Her stomach could never handle spicy foods.

CY SLURPED SOUP FROM HIS SPOON, WONDERING IF THE WOMAN ACROSS FROM him would ever settle down. Her jerky movements spoke of tension or nerves in his presence. He'd noticed a little bit of that yesterday when he drove her home from the hospital. Today, she'd barely taken a sip from her steaming bowl.

Resting the spoon in his bowl, he decided the blunt approach would work best. "Do I make you nervous?"

She nearly dropped her spoon into the soup. "What?" Her gaze fastened on the tabletop.

"Isana, look at me." When she didn't raise her head, he added, "Please."

Slowly, she lifted her gaze to his. Uncertainty warred with fear in the depths of her hazel eyes. "Why are you being nice to me?"

Her counter question confused him. "I don't understand."

"You've barely spoken to me in the six months you've been at the museum."

True, but he'd had no need to seek her out in her professional capacity, given how many other things demanded his immediate attention. He discretely swept his gaze over her, noting the loose business slacks and drab blouse covering what he knew from their encounter yesterday was a firm, fit body. She wore her hair in a bun and no makeup he could discern on her peaches-and-cream complexion. Compared to the other single women at the museum, under normal circumstances, he probably would not have given her a second glance. But now that he had, he could see beyond the external wrappings to an intriguing and attractive woman.

"You're right, I haven't. But Monday changed all that."

"Because your mom's missing." Compassion softened her face. "I take it there's been no news?"

He shook his head. "I filed a missing person's report with the police last night on my way home from work."

She swallowed some soup. "So they'll be looking for her?"

"They won't do much other than add her to the database of missing persons. As an adult, unless there's evidence of foul play, she's in danger from herself, or needs urgent medical attention, they won't do much to actively search for her." He shrugged away the rising frustration at the police inaction. "It's like a catch 22."

"I'm sorry. That must be hard on you." She glanced at the table. "You must be very close to your mother."

"She's all I have in way of relatives. My father died when I was in kindergarten." Even after thirty years, it hurt to admit that. His mom had talked about his dad often during Cy's childhood. Her stories of his father had filled his imagination of the man he only vaguely remembered.

"I'm sorry. I might not see my family often, but it's comforting to know they are out there."

"Where's there?" He grabbed hold of a natural way to turn the conversation from his loss.

"My father lives in South Dakota."

Given the tightness of her mouth, he guessed her mom might be a painful subject. He'd focus instead on the sighing way she uttered the state. "I wouldn't have pegged you as someone from South Dakota."

She dragged her spoon through the remains of her soup. "I'm not. My father worked for an international oil company, so we lived all over the place. I was actually born in Budapest."

"Really?"

Isana chuckled. "Yes, really. I've lived in," she held up her fingers, ticking off each country as she listed it, "Hungary, Brazil, Singapore, and Australia. Then when I was in college, my dad changed jobs. He's now president of an oil-and-fracking company in South Dakota."

So much for his opinion of her as a quiet mouse who rarely left her basement workstation. She'd obviously traveled more than he had. "Your passport must have needed extra pages for entry and exit stamps."

"I haven't done much traveling since high school when my parents divorced. Guess I got my fill during my childhood." She laid her spoon down. "This was delicious."

"Better than the soup Carson ate?" He teased.

"Since I made that soup, what can I say that's not self-promoting?" Her eyes danced with amusement.

He sucked in a breath at how gorgeous she looked when her body wasn't tense. He sensed any false move on his part would send her scurrying back into her shell, so he added with a wink, "Carson seemed to enjoy it."

She huffed, the light-heartedness draining from her as if someone bailed out all her joy with a rusty bucket. "What he enjoys is stealing other people's stuff."

Cy sensed she wasn't only talking about the soup. "What other stuff?"

"It's not important." She picked up her bag and scooted to the end of the bench.

He rose as well, gathering their empty bowls to deposit them in the dirty dish bin. Once outside, he touched her arm to halt her forward progress. "Isana, what did you mean about Carson stealing things?"

She shivered, reminding him she'd not brought a jacket. Cy buffeted her from the wind with his body as the lunchtime foot traffic weaved around them.

"The wedding exhibit."

Cy frowned at the mention of Carson's summer exhibition idea. "What about it?"

"It was mine." She met his gaze, misery darkening the light in her eyes. "I'd heard the traveling exhibit might be delayed and had been thinking of how we could showcase some of the wedding dresses and accompanying items in our collection. We've got a lot more stuff than people realize. A couple of weeks ago, I suggested it to Carson, adding that I would love to curate it since I handle the collection inventory."

"And what did he say?" Cy had a sinking feeling he knew exactly what the man had told Isana.

"That it was a stupid idea and I should stick to what I'd been hired to do." She broke eye contact, directing her gaze to the ground. "Now he's saying he came up with it."

Outrage on her behalf sizzled in his blood. "You should confront him."

"And what exactly would that accomplish? He's a senior employee and has been with the Heritage for a decade. I've only been here three years. He also has a master's degree from a fancy university and is in a doctorate program at Georgetown University, while I only have a bachelor's degree from a small liberal arts college." She shoved a strand of hair off her forehead. "Besides, I tried to say something to my supervisor the first time it happened and was told to stick to my job."

"I hardly knew you worked for the Heritage. Maybe if you mingled with the staff more . . . " He uttered the words before he realized how she might take the criticism.

"I'd be more likeable? Have more friends among my co-workers?" She swiped moisture from her cheeks, whether tears or eyes watering from the wind whipping around them, he wasn't sure. But his heart saddened to see her distress.

She sighed. "I do my job and I do it well. That should count for something, but apparently, unless someone notices you, it doesn't."

"Isana, I didn't mean to hurt your feelings. It was an insensitive comment." His words did little to erase the dismay rimming her eyes. "I'm—"

"I've got to get back to the office." After spinning on her heel, she charged down the block.

Frustrated that his bumbling attempt to help had exacerbated the situation, Cy hurried to catch up with her, but a bicycle messenger zipped by, cutting him off. He spotted her brown hair in a small crowd of pedestrians waiting to cross the street. Lengthening his stride to make light, he kept his gaze fastened on Isana.

His anxiety over his mother's disappearance had erased his good manners, something Mom would not be happy about. He would sincerely apologize for hurting her feelings. Ahead, the light changed, signaling it was safe to cross.

She stepped onto the pavement, along with a few others. A motorcycle roared around the corner, ignoring the *Yield to Pedestrians in Crosswalk* sign as it barreled straight toward those crossers.

And Isana.

SIX

Isana placed her booted foot into the white crosswalk, her mind replaying the conversation with Cy. Up until he'd implied her predicament with Carson was because no one liked her, she'd enjoy eating lunch with him. She'd even allowed herself to envision future lunches, perhaps morphing into after-work outings, but his latter words had doused that fantasy. That's what she got for thinking someone like Cy would look twice at someone as unassuming as herself.

A loud engine caught her attention. Her heart rate accelerated as a motorcyclist gunned his engine, seeming to direct the bike straight for her. Then strong arms encased her body, tackling her to the asphalt as the motorcycle roared by. The man cushioned the fall by positioning his body to hit the pavement first, so she ended up lying partially atop him. She struggled to catch her breath as she tried to process what happened. Then the subtle scent of the ocean tickled her nostrils. Cy.

He shifted her away from him, then scrambled to his feet before helping her up. "Come on, let's get out of the intersection." Cupping her elbow, he guided her to the opposite sidewalk and out of the flow of pedestrians. Gripping both her upper arms lightly, he searched her face. "Are you okay?" His voice held a note of concern.

She cleared her throat, willing her cheeks not to redden at the close encounter with the man she'd often daydreamed about. "Um, yes, I think so."

He moved his hands up and down her arms as if assessing for himself. "Are you sure?"

She mentally inventoried her body. Other than some new bruises from the fall, she didn't register any serious injuries. "Yes."

A grim look set his features into hard lines as other pedestrians passed them. "The motorcyclist wasn't slowing down, even when he saw people crossing the street."

Isana's mouth fell open, astonishment robbing her of speech for a few seconds. She snapped it closed. "You think he deliberately wanted to hurt someone?"

"Not someone." Cy glanced over her head, then returned his gaze to hers. "You."

"Me? Who'd want to hurt me?" Her phone trilled the theme song to the Indiana Jones franchise. She fished it out of her purse as it continued to ring.

He raised his eyebrows, but she ignored him as she registered the caller ID. Mom. Better answer it. She'd just keep calling if she didn't. "Hey, Mom."

"Why didn't you send me the money I asked for?" Her mother's shrill voice threatened to bring back the headache Isana had been keeping at bay with over-the-counter medications all day. "I told you why I needed it."

Not for the first time did Isana wish her mother would call to ask how her daughter was instead of berating her about not bankrolling her lifestyle. Her mother must be between men at the moment, or she wouldn't be hounding Isana about money. Her father had given her a generous settlement, finally having had enough of her mother's mercurial moods and refusal to seek medical treatment. Her mom never saw herself as needing help. "Mom, I told you I'm not sending you any more money."

Her mother huffed. "You want me out on the street, homeless?"

Isana turned her back to Cy and dropped her voice. "I don't. You could get a job."

Silence, her mother's answer to anything she didn't want to do. Isana sighed. "I've got to get back to work." She tossed out an olive branch to forestall her mother's tirade about Isana never calling her. "I'll call you tonight. Goodbye."

Before her mother could protest, she disconnected. Harsh, perhaps, but her mother would keep her on the phone for an hour if she allowed it.

"Everything all right?" Cy touched her arm.

"You seem to be asking me that a lot." She smiled to soften the words. Falling into step beside him as they walked in the direction of the museum, she added, "My mom can be a little intense."

She blew out a breath, frustration nibbling at her frayed nerves. She so didn't want to deal with her mother's neediness on top of yesterday's attack and this morning's near-accident. They reached the museum's staff entrance. "But that's a story for another day."

"Wait, please."

She halted, her badge outstretched toward the security pad. Lowering her hand, she turned. "Yes?"

"I'm sorry for what I said at the restaurant." His green eyes radiated sincerity. "I've been worried about my mom, and I let down my guard on my tongue. I'm usually a nice guy, and I don't want you to get the wrong impression about me."

Her heartrate, which had settled into its normal pace, kicked up a notch again. "Why not?" The question triggered upraised eyebrows from Cy.

"Because I need your help."

Not the answer she'd been hoping for, but she shouldn't be

surprised it wasn't a personal request. She hadn't had a date in ages. "Oh, with the exhibit."

"What?" Confusion clouded his face, then his expression cleared. "Not work related." His phone buzzed. "Argh, forgot I have a two o'clock meeting. Listen, I'll stop after work, and we can talk then."

He reached around her and swiped his badge, unlocking the door. He pulled it open, held it for her to pass through first, then moved by her. "See you later."

Isana trudged toward the stairs, descending the one flight slowly as her thoughts pinged back and forth between elation and disappointment. Elated Cy wanted to see her about something not connected to the museum, but disappointed it wasn't a date.

As consciousness returned, Lillian once more lay as relaxed as possible, keeping her eyes closed as she listened to her surroundings. Silence, the kind of silence formed from the absence of anyone else. The kind of silence she'd grown accustomed to in her home of late, since Cyrus had moved out. A stab of pain accompanied the thought of her only child. She'd never liked nicknames and had insisted on calling him Cyrus instead of the Cy he preferred. Being the dutiful and loving son that she'd raised, he tolerated her reminder of his full given name.

She slowly opened her eyes. Still the same four walls. The memory of Schmidt tormenting her with his vile statements about killing her beloved husband sent her pulse racing. Vindication of her rightness in believing Greg would never take his own life had been swiftly followed by a rage so deep, she'd hardly realized her intention until her hands had closed around his neck. The prick of a needle had put a stop to her quest for vengeance on the man who'd consigned her to a living hell for thirty years.

From where she lay on the cold concrete, she took inventory of her injuries. Her head ached, but otherwise, she was in reasonable shape. However, she needed water and food. Footsteps echoed in the hallway outside the door, alerting her in time to resume her posture of sleep, letting her lashes rest against her cheek but not closing her eyes all the way. The door clanged open, and a single pair of footsteps entered the room. The figure crossed over to where she lay against the wall. Lillian steadied her breathing, using a yoga technique to completely relax her muscles to give the appearance of sleep. He toed her thigh with his shoe, but she remained limp.

"*Sie ist noch draußen.*" The man spoke German like a native. Not Schmidt, but someone else whose voice didn't sound familiar to her.

Lillian mentally translated his words. Good, he thought her unconscious.

A short pause, then the man spoke. "*Ich lasse es dich wissen, wenn sie für Fragen bereit ist.*"

Her heartrate jumped at the thought of the man returning to question her. What did he want to know? Schmidt had mentioned something about a list, but she had no idea what he'd been yammering on about. A phone buzzed, and the man moved away from her.

"Brenner."

She filed the name away to ponder later, as she didn't immediately think she'd known anyone with that name.

"Tell me everything." The German words had a harsh edge to them.

She strained to hear more as his footsteps moved away from her.

"Someone else is after the list," the man hissed. The menace behind the words sent fear slithering through her veins. "You said she wasn't involved with her son."

Lillian bottled the gasp that wanted to release from her throat. Why was he talking about Cyrus? She strained to hear more.

"Follow the woman too, and search her flat. If she knows something, we need to find out before they do."

The man exited the room, pulling the door closed with a bang. She couldn't stop herself from jumping, ruining the illusion of sleep. But she didn't care as her mind struggled to figure out who was the woman involved with Cyrus and if she knew something about this mysterious list.

~

CY TOSSED THE PEN ON HIS DESK, NOT CARING THAT IT BOUNCED ONTO THE floor. He should have been finishing edits to the summer exhibit brochure, but he had no interest in correcting grammar. Instead, his mind replayed the moment when he'd realized the motorcyclist was deliberately aiming straight for Isana. Thank God he'd been able to get to her in time. His pulse accelerated as he relived how close a call it had been. Then his thoughts switched to how Isana had felt in his arms. Underneath her baggy clothes lay a slender yet curvy body. He'd noticed it Monday morning when carrying her into the hospital but hadn't fully grasped how attractive until holding her in his arms on the pavement. The urge to kiss her after the danger passed had nearly overwhelmed him. It had been too long since a woman had invaded his senses the way Isana had in so short a time.

The strange thing was, she was nothing like the tall, outgoing, and composed women he usually dated. His desk phone rang, dragging him back to work. The extension for the administrative assistant to the museum's director flashed on the readout.

"Hey, Marilyn." He liked the young woman whose bubbly personality masked her mad organizational skills.

"Cy, the director wants to know if you can come to his office."

He looked over his to-do list. Nothing that needed his immediate attention. "I'm assuming now?"

"You got it."

"I'm on my way." Cy replaced the receiver, grabbed his company tablet, and hustled down the hallway to the spacious corner suite occupied by Baxter Umbel, the museum's long-time director.

"Go right in." Marilyn waved him toward the closed office door.

With a short knock to alert the occupant of his arrival, Cy twisted the knob and entered the inner sanctum. A showcase illuminated by lights had pride of place in the room's center. Anyone approaching the director's desk had to pass by the display. The last time Cy had been in here several months ago, the display had held vintage Christmas cards. Now a reproduction of the Tidal Basin with flowering cherry trees and the Japanese lantern statue lay under the glass.

"Cy, glad you could join us." Baxter drew his attention to the curator seated in one of the club chairs in front of the massive desk.

Carson nodded as Cy took the other chair.

"Carson was telling me of his wonderful idea to replace the traveling exhibit that fell through," Baxter said. "Weddings through the centuries. It's going to be even better than the canceled painting exhibition."

Cy's stomach clenched. Carson had wasted no time presenting Isana's idea as his own. People who stole other people's things or ideas made Cy see red. "Actually, that was Isana's idea."

Carson's face took on a pinkish hue while Baxter's features appeared puzzled.

"Who's Isana?" The director's question threatened to push Cy's anger into the red zone. How could the man who recalled the name of every donor not know all of his employees?

"She works in the basement," Carson slipped in smoothly. "Logging in the donations and acquisitions."

Baxter's face cleared. "Then why would she make exhibit suggestions?"

"Look, I know where Cy is going with this." Carson offered an insincere smile. "Isana came to me last week to ask for help in getting more archive supplies, specifically for a new wedding dress that had been donated recently. Perhaps she misrepresented the conversation to Cy in an effort to make herself sound more important, but I can assure you I most certainly did not steal her idea. Why would I, as the museum's senior curator, need to co-opt the ideas of a junior employee who doesn't even work directly with exhibitions?"

Cy glanced from one man to the other. The director had the bored expression of someone losing interest in the conversation, while Carson's self-satisfied visage made Cy want to punch something. Preferably the other man's nose.

"Now that that's settled, let's get down to how we'll publicize the change in the exhibitions." Baxter's tone brooked no argument, and Cy tamped down his indignation on Isana's behalf.

"Sure." Cy opened the notes app on his tablet. "What will the exhibition consist of?"

"Wedding dresses throughout the twentieth century." Carson folded his arms.

"Okay," Cy said into the void when it became apparent both men expected him to run with that short description. "I'm going to need more than that to craft publicity materials."

"Like what?" Carson frowned, as if he shouldn't have to help Cy do his job.

"Like how many dresses for starters?" Cy rapid-fired other questions. "From which decades? Are they dresses somebody famous wore? By well-known designers? Why did you choose these particular dresses for the exhibit? Will they be exhibited on mannequins? What special events will be tied to the exhibition?"

Carson's smugness faltered, then dropped away entirely as Cy added several more questions to the list.

Cy waited for the other man to answer. Carson opened his mouth, then shut it again with a snap.

"I haven't picked the dresses yet," Carson said.

"Then it's a little premature to talk about publicity." Cy's phone buzzed, and he used that as an excuse to rise. "If you'll excuse me, I need to take this call." He didn't care if the director found his actions rude, he couldn't spend another second in the room with the smug Carson.

As Cy strode out of the room, he hit the accept button without noting the number. "Hello?"

"Cyrus Hillam?" The unfamiliar voice had a husky timber, as if the caller suffered from a bad cold.

"Speaking." He nodded at Marilyn and headed to his office.

"If you want your mother back alive, listen carefully."

CHAPTER

SEVEN

Isana grabbed her temper with both hands and held on tight as Carson waltzed into her windowless office. His email—sent an hour ago—had pushed her blood to the boiling point, with his directive for her to get a selection of the best wedding dresses in the collection ready for his immediate inspection for *his* June "Weddings Through the Twentieth Century" exhibition. Like she was going to do his job curating the exhibition and let him take all the glory. She might have kept her head down before, but after being attacked, shot at, and nearly run over by a motorcyclist, she was done being a doormat.

"What do you have for me?" He rubbed his hands together, probably not realizing the gesture brought to her mind a parody of a screen villain.

Without bothering to rise from her desk chair, she held out several sheets of paper in his general direction. "Here you go."

He frowned but took the papers. "What's this?"

"A detailed inventory of what wedding items we have in our collection." An easy database search Carson could have done himself. "I organized it by decade." She had wrestled with doing even that bit

51

of work but hadn't wanted Carson to complain she wasn't being helpful.

He dipped his head and shuffled the papers too quickly to read much on any one page. "There must be dozens of items listed here."

"Two hundred and fifty-four, to be exact. You'll have lots to choose from for *your* special exhibition." Snide of her to emphasize *your*, but she couldn't help herself.

"This isn't what I asked you to do." He slapped the papers on the corner of her desk.

With a smile to keep the edge out of her voice, she replied calmly, "No, it's not."

He pointed a finger in her direction. "See? Even you agree you did not deliver what I told you to. So I expect your dress selections for the exhibition on my desk by the end of the day."

Carson swiveled, but before he'd taken one step, she spoke. "I'm sorry, but that won't be possible."

He slowly turned back to face her. "The director himself has greenlighted this, which means it's all hands on deck to get the exhibition ready in two months. What's the problem?"

She stood, feeling at a disadvantage to remain seated. She could do this. She had to do this. No more doormat. "Because it's not my job."

A red flush crept up his neck, invading his cheeks like a conquering army. "What's that supposed to mean? You're in charge of the acquisitions. You know what's in the collection."

"I do."

Her short answer only fueled his ire. "Then do your job!"

His raised voice made her tremble, but she stuck to her guns. "But you're not asking me to do my job. You're asking me to curate the exhibition. That's your job."

He threw up his hands. "I see what's going on here."

"Good."

"The director knows the wedding exhibition is my idea, despite Cy's attempt to push your claim that you brought the idea to me."

She stayed silent, part of her not surprised Carson had manipulated the facts to his advantage. The larger part of her did a happy dance at the news Cy had stood up for her, had believed she'd told the truth about the wedding exhibition. Despite the unfavorable outcome with the director, the thought of Cy's support warmed her.

"We good here?"

His question intruded on her happy thoughts. "What?"

He crossed his arms. "You'll bring me a list of wedding dresses and photos by the end of the day."

She shook her head. "I really wish I could help, but like you said so yourself, curating exhibitions is not in my job description."

"I don't have time for this, but since you insist, let's go see what Baxter has to say." He spun on his heel and marched out of the room.

She scrambled to catch up, arriving at the director's office a little breathless.

Carson barely paused after confirming with Marilyn the boss was in. "Baxter, I'm sorry to bother you, but we have a slight hitch in the wedding exhibition plans."

Isana skidded to a halt to the left of the curator. She'd had very little interactions with the director, preferring to stay away from a man whose professional smile reminded her of the Cheshire cat in *Alice in Wonderland*. Like that fictitious feline, he too changed according to his surroundings.

Director Umbel tapped his fingers on the smooth desk surface. In the few times she'd been invited to the corner office, she had never seen any papers cluttering his desk. "I thought we'd settled this matter earlier."

"I thought so too, but apparently not." He nodded toward Isana. "You remember Isana in acquisitions."

She suspected Carson had deliberately referred to her like that to ensure the director knew her place wasn't as exalted as a curator.

Umbel waved a hand as if to say get to the point.

"She's refusing to help with the exhibition." Carson's tone turned wheedling, "You know we need everyone's cooperation to pull it off in time."

"Is that so, Ms. Thomas?" Mr. Umbel narrowed his eyes.

"No, sir." Best to keep her answers short and on point with this man. Less chance of misinterpretations.

At her answer, Mr. Umbel shifted his gaze to Carson, who hurried to explain. "I asked her to send me a list of wedding dresses for the exhibition, and she flat-out refused."

As if watching a tennis match, Mr. Umbel returned his attention to Isana. She summoned her courage. "I gave him a printout, organized by decade, of all wedding dresses and related items in our collection."

The director waited for Carson's response. When the other man didn't immediately reply, he prompted, "Did she provide you with such a list?"

"Well, yes," Carson admitted. "But that's not what I asked her to do."

Director Umbel didn't respond for a full minute. Isana counted the off the seconds in her head. She needed this job, but she was tired of Carson's attempts to fob off his work on her without giving her credit. When he'd first approached her for assistance in curating an exhibition shortly after she'd joined the staff, Isana had been flattered and had eagerly provided him with her suggestions. With his praise ringing in her ears, she'd walked through the exhibition during the staff and donor preview and realized he'd taken every one of her ideas for staging and grouping the items but never once acknowledged her assistance in public or private. When she'd confronted him about it, he'd said he'd tried to include her name, but the director had said only one curator could be mentioned. During the intervening years, Carson had frequently come asking for her help with pieces to other exhibits, but last winter, she'd finally realized Carson would never admit he needed help with a key component of his job and therefore all her behind-the-scenes work would stay behind the scenes. Her dream of moving into a curator position with these exhibitions documented on her resume crashed and burned, and she vowed Carson would take advantage of her expertise no more.

"You applied for the vacant assistant curator position, didn't you?" Mr. Umbel asked Isana.

"Yes." The junior curator worked closely with the two senior curators, of which Carson was one. The position had been advertised nearly a year ago, when the woman holding it had decided not to return to work after having a baby. Instead of filling it, the museum had decided to hire a marketing and media relations person instead, bringing Cy Hillam on board. She figured her resume had been filed into some black hole and perhaps would be dusted off if the funds became available for the position.

"Cy tells me you came up with the idea for the special weddings through the century exhibition. I know you've also helped Carson on his exhibitions in the past."

Isana nodded, unable to find words to respond to the revelation the director had noticed her contributions.

"She provided minimal assistance on a handful of exhibitions over the years," Carson spluttered. "It hardly warranted a mention."

"You've been with us three years now?"

"Yes, sir." She wasn't sure where this was going, but she wasn't about to derail the train with too many words.

The director slapped his hand on the top of his desk, the movement echoing in the spacious room. "Carson, since it appears you're having trouble figuring out exactly what to put in this exhibition, Ms. Thomas will find the items."

Carson preened, throwing Isana a predatory smile. "Thank you, sir." He turned to leave.

"I'm not finished." The director's words halted Carson's progress, and he faced the desk once more.

"Ms. Thomas, I see from the excellent reports you provide each week as to the status of our acquisitions that you only have a few outstanding items to review and log into the collection," Mr. Umbel said. "Therefore, am I correct in assuming your desk could be cleared for a larger project?"

"Yes, sir." Her heart pounded, but she told herself not to jump to conclusions.

"Good." He speared Carson with a look. "I'm handing over the entire Weddings Through the Twentieth Century exhibition to Ms. Thomas. You will, of course, assist her in any way she requires."

Carson's jaw dropped. "But that's my special exhibit."

"Not anymore." Mr. Umbel's desk phone buzzed, and he hit the intercom button. "Yes, Marilyn?"

"Your wife is on line one for you."

"Tell her I'm finishing a meeting and will be with her directly." He punched off the intercom. "Ms. Thomas, please brief me at the end of the week. Marilyn will find space for you on my calendar." He picked up the receiver, dismissing them both.

Isana moved quickly to the door, slipping out ahead of Carson, who brushed past her. After confirming a time for Friday on the director's schedule, she stopped by the restroom to compose herself. Never in a million years did she think she would get a chance to curate and stage her own exhibition. Her mind whirred with all the things she'd need to do in a compressed time frame. Most exhibitions took years of planning. She had six weeks. But since Weddings Through the Twentieth Century had been in the back of her mind for a couple of years, she would hit the ground running.

Back in her basement office, she removed the unlogged acquisition boxes off her worktable. First she would highlight the dresses from each decade she wanted to examine for possible inclusion. Then she would—

"Who do you think are?" Carson's angry voice broke into her mental to-do list. He stalked into her space, his face flushed, and his fists clenched. "Do you think you can steal my special exhibition?"

Isana rounded her desk, putting a barrier between them. "The director said—"

"I'm not going to let some lowly acquisitions staffer horn in on my territory." Carson hissed as he leaned over the desk.

She'd heard about how cutthroat the museum world could be but had never experienced it firsthand. Seeing the blazing fury in his eyes jacked up her own pulse. A heated response pummeled her mind. However, she refused to fight fire with fire. Instead, she meekly lowered her head, clasping her hands together. "I understand."

Her soft answer did little to derail his tirade. He paced in front of her desk, hurling invectives at her, but she tuned it out, keeping her gaze on her desktop. After all, she'd had years of practice ignoring the filth others dumped on her head. Instead, she continued planning the steps necessary to pull off the special exhibit in the compressed timeline.

A crash, followed by breaking glass, jerked her attention back to Carson. He'd slammed her desk lamp—a Tiffany reproduction she'd purchased at a flea market with her own money—onto the floor.

"Guess you'll be buying her a new lamp too."

She sagged with relief at the sound of Cy's voice from behind Carson. Cy stepped closer to the desk, his eyes briefly meeting hers before focusing on the mess of broken glass on the floor beside her desk.

"It was an accident." Carson's eyes darted around the room like he was a cornered animal seeking escape.

Cy held up his phone. "I'm afraid I have recorded evidence to the contrary."

Isana thanked God Cy had the foresight to record the encounter. Carson's verbal assault had her feeling decidedly unsafe. Having proof of his actions would mean human resources would have to address the situation.

The color drained from Carson's face. "You had no right to record our discussion."

"Discussion?" Cy's eyebrows rose. "I don't think you understand the definition of discussion if that's what you think you were doing."

Carson brushed past Cy, knocking into his shoulder as he did so. "She's the problem. Watch out. She'll be after your job next."

Cy shook his head as the door swung shut behind Carson. "Are you okay?"

Isana drew in a breath. "I think so. I can't tell you how relieved I am at your timely appearance."

"Happy to help." He surveyed the busted glass. "Your lamp's totaled."

"It's only stuff and can be replaced." She didn't mention how long she'd saved to purchase the light. Maybe the museum would buy her a new one since an employee destroyed it on museum property.

"What set him off?"

She recapped the series of events, but even as Cy appeared to follow the story, she had the distinct feeling his mind was elsewhere. "But then a unicorn came along and told me where to find the missing pot of gold," she finished, testing her theory he wasn't tracking her words closely.

Cy blinked. A smile started at the corners of his mouth but dropped before it fully formed. "Sorry, have something else on my mind."

Her heart dropped as she considered what that could be. "Did you hear from your mom?"

"Not exactly." Misery and panic flared in his green eyes. "Someone's kidnapped her."

EIGHT

Cy twisted his glass on the coaster in a slow circle. The noisy café provided the perfect buffer for his inner turmoil. The kidnapper, a man who called himself Schmidt, said he had seventy-two hours to find a list of names his father had in his possession before he died or else his mother would die too. Naturally, Schmidt had informed him going to the authorities would result in immediate negative action against his mom. But Schmidt hadn't said a word about roping in a colleague for assistance. So he sat in the restaurant waiting for Isana to arrive because he had no earthly idea how to proceed and fear of losing his mother was mudding his thought process.

When he turned eighteen, his mother had handed over two boxes containing his father's papers and books, saying Cy could be the keeper of the past from now on. He'd poured over the items, both delighted and pained to have something his father touched. But never had he come across anything resembling a list.

He sipped his drink, replacing it on the coaster to begin another circuit with the glass. Why now? His father had been dead for thirty years. What had precipitated the search for this list three decades later? If it hadn't surfaced after his father died, then it probably never would. If Mom knew the whereabouts of the list, she would have said so.

Cy glanced up at movement heading toward his table. Isana gave a little wave as she weaved her way toward him. He still didn't know how to broach the subject of the list and ask for her help in finding it. Maybe the entire thing was a bad idea, pulling an innocent bystander into this mess. But then again, with her finding his mother's phone, she was involved.

"Everything okay?" Isana settled into the chair opposite him, placing her beverage on the table. "You look worried."

He attempted a laugh. "Have a lot on my mind."

Her face sobered. "I'm sorry, I shouldn't have…"

Impulsively, he covered her hand with his, squeezing gently. "You're right. I was thinking of more than my mom's, er, disappearance."

A fleeting smile crossed her face, then she smoothed her expression. "I don't understand why someone would kidnap your mom."

"That's why I wanted to talk to you."

"I have the butternut squash soup with flax seeds and the grilled steak-and-blue cheese panini." A perky waitress, her blonde hair sporting purple and blue streaks, raised the dishes aloft as she glanced from Cy to Isana.

"The lady has the sandwich," Cy said.

The server chuckled as she placed the correct dish in front of each of them. "Usually, it's the woman who has the soup and the guy the sandwich. Need anything else?"

At the head shakes, she departed with a bouncy step.

"Think she's been hitting the espresso machine too frequently during her shift?" Isana smoothed a paper napkin on her lap.

"Or maybe she's just one of those annoying people who is always bubbly." Cy reached for her hand. "Would you mind if I ask a blessing?"

She hesitated for second, then took his hand while he uttered a short prayer. Her discomfort radiated across the table. Perhaps she didn't like to pray in a public setting.

Picking up his spoon, he delayed taking a bite to say, "I'm sorry if that made you uncomfortable."

Her eyes widened as she chewed, sipped her iced tea. "I was surprised by the request, that's all." She hesitated, a faint blush coloring her cheeks. "So you go to church?"

He swallowed his mouthful. "Yes, Redeemer Church near the Courthouse Metro."

"Ah, I see." She didn't add anything else, and while he wanted to press her about her faith, he didn't, instead shifting the conversation to small talk while he discarded several ways to approach the real reason he'd asked her for a quick bite after work.

The waitress came to clear their dishes and left the bill after both had declined dessert or coffee. He laid his credit card on the slip, worry about his mother worming its way to the forefront of his mind again.

Isana leaned across the table, her hazel eyes fastening on his. "Are you ready to tell me why I'm here?"

Her soft question drew his attention outward. "I think I'd better show you."

Twenty minutes later, Cy inserted his key into the deadbolt lock of his condo, Isana at his back.

"So this is how the other half lives." A smile lit her voice. "I've always wanted to see the inside of one of these condos."

"Glad I could accommodate you." He disengaged the lock and pulled out his key. "After you."

She slipped around him as he pushed open the door, then followed her into the darkened space. Strange. He usually left a living room lamp on to avoid this situation. "Let me get the lights on."

He flicked the switch, but nothing happened. Beside him, Isana had turned on her phone's flashlight app, shining it into the living room. "Cy?"

"Must have blown a fuse. I'll check the utility box." He stepped to the right to go around her, but she snagged his arm. "It's okay, I'll be right back."

She held on. "Look."

The quaver in her voice registered, and he turned to see what her flashlight illuminated. Overturned furniture, broken lamps, and other detritus lay in a jumble on the floor. Someone had broken into his apartment and trashed the place. "We'd better leave and call the police."

"Yeah," she agreed.

Cy took her hand, and they slowly backed out of the apartment. He closed and relocked the deadbolt. He caught her eyes on him. "Force of habit."

"It was locked when we arrived?"

"Yes, both the deadbolt and handle." He dialed 911, his pulse pounding in his ears. The flicker of hope fanned by Isana's willingness to help him find the list and save his mother whooshed out at the realization the information might already be in the hands of someone else. After relaying the pertinent details to the dispatcher, he and Isana waited in the hallway for the police to arrive.

"Do you think it's related to your mom's kidnapping?"

Her question echoed his own. "I don't know." He scrubbed a hand over his face. "This place is pretty secure. It seems too much of a stretch for this to be a random burglary."

"Does appear too coincidental to not be connected somehow." She wrinkled her nose, the childlike gesture almost bringing a smile to his lips. "But why would the kidnapper ask you to bring him a list, then break into your apartment to look for it?"

"Are you reading my mind?" Her expression turned puzzled at his attempt at levity. "I meant you're voicing the very question rattling around in my own brain."

She held out her hand toward him, her eyes seeking his own. When he slipped his into hers, she squeezed it. "My *oma* always said, '*Tragen Sie die Lasten des anderen und erfüllen Sie so das Gesetz Christi.*'"

The German, spoken with what sounded like an authentic accent, startled him.

Isana smiled. "You probably know it is as, 'Bear one another's burdens, and so fulfill the law of Christ.'"

"Galatians 6:2." When he'd prayed over their meals, he'd gotten the distinct impression Isana was uncomfortable. But here she was, quoting Scripture in German of all things to comfort him. The elevator dinged, announcing the arrival of the car to his floor. Two uniformed police officers rounded the corner and headed their way. Cy would explore this anomaly later, just one of the many things he wanted to find out about the lovely woman standing beside him.

LILLIAN SHIFTED HER WEIGHT TO NO AVAIL. THE UNYIELDING MATTRESS STILL bruised her bones, while the thin blanket did little to ward off the chill. At least Schmidt had left her hands and ankles unbound. The anger that had propelled her to attack him had dissipated, along with her physical strength. She'd long since drained the water bottle he'd left. Her stomach weakly protested its emptiness, and her bladder screamed for relief. She would put off using the bucket in the corner for as long as possible. The darkness outside the window told her it was night, but whether it was evening or the wee hours of the morning, she hadn't a clue. Hours ago, she'd overheard Schmidt call Cyrus, demanding the list in exchange for her. Lying here had given her ample time to think about what list and why Schmidt and his cronies thought she had it.

In mining the past for clues as to the list itself, her mind kept circling back to why the urgency now. If her husband could have taken such a list, what made it so valuable to locate thirty years after his death?

A key rattled in the lock, and the door swung open. She didn't bother to hide her wakefulness, not when the scent of chicken broth teased her nostrils. Light flooded the room from the single, unshaded bulb. The light switch could only be accessed outside the room, leaving her with the small, dingy window to illuminate her surroundings. Frankly, she didn't mind not seeing the blank, cinderblock walls and dirty concrete floor.

"I brought you some soup," Schmidt barked.

She pushed to a seated position, expecting him to place the tray on the mattress beside her. Instead he put it on the floor near the door.

"Come." He followed the command with a hand gesture.

Lillian stayed put. "Where?"

"Don't make me come get you, woman." The growl in his voice jolted her into movement.

She gained her feet, staggering a bit after lying prone for so many hours. Following Schmidt out of the room, he led her down a short hallway, pausing before an open door. "You have five minutes."

Relief poured over her at the sight of a dingy bathroom. Without acknowledging the parameters he'd set, she closed the door and flipped the handle lock before taking care of business. Washing her hands with a sliver of soap, she glanced in the cracked mirror above the sink. Sunken eyes stared back, hair lank and flat against her head. No one would recognize the carefully coiffured woman of two —or was it three?—days ago. Her rumpled clothing had a slightly sour smell, but that couldn't be helped.

Schmidt pounded on the door. "Time's up!"

She dried her hands on a ratty towel and opened the door. Back in her cell, Schmidt left the light on. Peeling back the kitchen towel covering the tray, she surveyed the bowl of chicken noodle soup, a piece of crusty bread, a bottle of water, and a pink-tinged apple. The soup, now lukewarm, was surprisingly tasty. Homemade if she had to guess, given the subtly of the spices and the freshness of the broth. She devoured the entire bowl, stopping herself from licking it to get every drop. Finishing the rest of her meal, she set the tray by the door, keeping the water bottle with her. She'd drank only a little with her meal, wanting to preserve the water for as long as possible.

Schmidt returned to collect the tray. His phone buzzed as he picked it up, and he answered as he maneuvered out the door. "*Hallo.*"

The door clanged shut, the lock snicking into place. Schmidt's voice didn't fade. The tray rattled as if the man placed it on the floor. Lillian crept off the bed and to the door, pressing her ear below the top hinge.

"*Was? Natürlich nicht!*" The emphatic German denial made her shift closer. Something unexpected had happened.

Amazing how easily her German had returned to her. She mentally translated the phrases nearly as fast as Schmidt spoke them.

"We went through his apartment. It's not there."

It must be Cyrus's condo they were discussing. She'd known they had searched her house and wasn't surprised to learn they'd done the same with Cyrus. Wherever the list was, it wasn't in their possession.

Schmidt snapped out a goodbye. He must have dialed someone else immediately because he began a new conversation. "*Ja,* it's me. Someone broke into the son's apartment and trashed the place."

Lillian managed to keep her gasp of surprise from escaping. The rest of the conversation consisted of Schmidt getting assurances from the other person they would find out who was behind the break-in. Schmidt finished the short conversation, turned off the light in her room, and picked up the tray, the dishes rattling as he made his way down the hallway.

She made her way back to the bed in near-total darkness, her heart aching with the thought of Cyrus in danger. She'd already lost her husband because of this list. She wasn't about to lose her son too. There wasn't anything she wouldn't do to keep Cyrus safe.

CHAPTER

NINE

Isana entered the police station on M Street and queued in line behind a man wearing at least three coats. Granted, the temperature at 7:00 a.m. hovered in the low forties, but she suspected it wasn't the chill in the air that had him bundled up. The shopping cart stuffed with plastic grocery bags parked at the foot of the stairs leading to the building's entrance probably belonged to him.

"Next!" the burly desk sergeant called, his tone laced with impatience and boredom.

The homeless man shuffled forward to speak in a low voice to the officer, who, to his credit, listened attentively to the older man. The two conversed for several minutes while Isana shifted from one foot to another. Her muscles ached after a restless night, and her early morning run had done little to relieve the tension coursing through her body. She'd barely spoken to Cy since the break-in at his apartment two nights ago, when he'd insisted she leave after giving her statement to the police. His haggard appearance had been the topic of gossip in the breakroom among the single women, but from what she'd overheard while heating her lunch in the microwave, the circles under his eyes didn't detract from his overall appeal.

She agreed with them. Even exhaustion looked good on Cy Hillam. His blond hair swept back from his forehead and haunted green eyes gave him the appearance of a tortured artist. Too bad she knew exactly why he looked like he had just lost his best friend. She couldn't imagine the difficulty in keeping his mother's kidnapping a secret while hunting for a mysterious list. In the days since, her attempts to engage him in conversation at the office had been met with one-word replies and a distracted smile.

"Next!" The sergeant's booming voice yanked her back to the present.

She stepped up to the counter where the officer sat behind bulletproof glass. "I'm here to pick up my camera. Isana Thomas."

His fingers pounded the keyboard. "May I see some identification?"

She dropped her driver's license into the well under the window. The sergeant fished it out, propping it against his keyboard as he continued typing. She waited patiently until he met her gaze. "I'll send someone to lost and found to fetch it. Please wait over there." He pointed to a row of backless benches rimming the room.

"Thanks." She retrieved her license and headed to an unoccupied bench. She had no sooner sat down on the cold surface than her phone buzzed. Her heart gave a little leap of joy at the caller ID. Cy.

"Hello?"

"Hi." He cleared his throat. "It's Cy."

"How are you?" With effort, she modulated her voice to convey concern, not eagerness to speak to him.

"Not good." Despair hummed over the line. "Because of the break-in, I got an, um, extension."

What did one say to that? Perhaps best to stick to the facts. "Until when?"

"Friday."

Given today was Saturday, he had a week to locate the list. "Were you able to speak to your mom?"

"Yes."

Her heart contracted at the pain in that one word. "What did she say?"

"That she loved me." His voice broke on a sob.

Isana clutched the phone tighter as she waited for him to continue.

"And that she knew I'd do my best to find what they wanted."

"When did she call?"

"Thursday evening."

"Ms. Thomas?"

Isana glanced up to see a female officer striding toward her, a bulky bag and tablet in her hands. "Can I call you back?"

"Where are you?"

"The police station. Someone found my camera."

"Could you meet me at my mom's house when you're finished? I'll text you the address."

"Sure. Bye." She ended the call just as the officer reached her. "I'm Isana Thomas."

"ID please." The officer waited while Isana showed her license. "Here's your camera."

Isana took the package and broke the seal. "Where was it found?"

"Some Good Samaritan found it in the fountain at Robert Latham Owen Park on 20th St NW and turned it in to the police."

The camera bag appeared undamaged, as was the camera itself. A quick check revealed the film was missing. Relief at having her prized possession back flooded her body. "Good thing the fountain hasn't been turned on yet, or this would have been ruined."

"That's an expensive vintage camera. I'm surprised someone didn't try to hawk it for cash." The officer shrugged. "Anything missing?"

"Just the film." She tucked the camera back into its case.

"Strange someone would take the time to remove the film but leave the camera."

Now it was Isana's turn to shrug. "I'm grateful that's all they took." She slipped the strap over her shoulder.

"Sign here and you'll be on your way."

Isana finger-signed the space on the tablet. "Thanks again."

The officer nodded and disappeared through the door. Isana checked her phone for Cy's text. His mother lived in Falls Church, Virginia. Opening a ride-sharing app, she ordered a pickup and went outside to wait for her ride.

Cy PULLED THE BATCH OF BLUEBERRY SCONES FROM THE OVEN, THE SCENT filling his mother's kitchen. If he closed his eyes, he could picture her tsking him about using frozen blueberries instead of fresh ones. Tears pricked the backs of his eyelids. He needed to get a hold of himself and stop mourning his mother as if she were no longer among the living. Her voice, though weaker than he'd remembered, conveyed her confidence he'd figure out where the list could be. But how could he do that in only six days when he hadn't a clue where to begin?

The doorbell rang, and he slid the second tray of scones into the oven, setting the timer before hurrying to answer. Isana stood on the porch, her short brown hair covered with a bright blue bandana.

"Hi, thanks for coming." He held the door open for her. As she passed him, a light floral scent filled his senses. Somehow the aroma made his heartrate accelerate even as a sense of calm permeated his body. Strange combination he would examine more fully later.

"What smells so good?" She drew in a deep breath. "Blueberries?"

"Blueberry scones. I'm impressed. Most people wouldn't be that precise on first sniff."

She unwound a scarf from her neck. "I've been blessed—or

cursed—with a heightened sense of smell. It's both annoying and wonderful."

"Let me take your coat." He helped her out of a thigh-length peacoat, hanging it in the foyer closet. "Right this way to warm scones and coffee."

"Sounds divine." She followed him into the kitchen, setting the camera bag on the kitchen table as he plated the scones.

Soon he'd poured coffee and joined her. He kept his eyes on her face as she bit into the scone smothered with real clotted cream.

"These are delicious." She laughed as a bit of cream clung to the corner of her mouth. She flicked her tongue out and licked it away.

The back of his neck itched, a sure sign of flushing. He yanked his attention away from her lips and sank his teeth into his own scone. For a few minutes, they ate and drank in a companionable silence.

Her scone finished, Isana blotted her lips. "The scone was amazing. Better than the ones from Panera."

"Thanks. I'm told it's an old family recipe."

"Wait, you made these?" Her eyes widened.

"I like to bake." He tried not to be overly wary of her reaction. While the idea of men in the kitchen had become more commonplace, some of his male friends still ribbed him about his love of creating edible delights from flour, sugar, and eggs.

"How long have you been baking?" She leaned back in her chair, apparently at ease with his whipping up biscuits, cookies, and cakes.

The kitchen timer went off. "Gotta get the last batch from the oven." He placed the sheet on a hot pad and turned off the oven. "My mom loved to watch cooking shows, so I grew up seeing Julia Child and other chefs making magic in the kitchen. Mom didn't bake often enough for me, so one day, when I was around ten and begging for homemade chocolate chip cookies, she put all the ingredients on the counter, opened the cookbook to the recipe, and told me to make them myself." Even now he remembered the feeling of accomplishment when he pulled the first batch from the oven. "I was hooked."

Isana smiled, but he detected a sadness behind the gesture. "Let me guess. Your favorite cooking program is *The Great British Baking Show*?"

"The lady got it in one." He returned her grin, then placed the scones on a cooling rack before joining her at the table. "Need a coffee warmup?

"Sure." She pushed her mug toward him.

Once they both had hot cups of coffee, he plunged into the reason he'd called her. "Thanks for coming over on your day off."

"And I didn't even know about the homemade blueberry scones."

"You're saying you would have been here even earlier if you'd known about my baking?"

"Maybe." She hid another smile behind her mug as she took another sip.

"I wish I could say it was merely for the pleasure of your company." The truth burst out of him. "But I need your help. I have six days to find this blasted list and have no idea where to start."

"I'm happy to offer whatever assistance I can." She met his gaze, her hazel eyes steady. "Were you able to determine if anything was missing after the burglary?"

"I spent the last two nights cataloging everything." He shuddered at the memory of the destruction. Dishes broken, books ripped, and pillows and couch cushions slashed. Whoever had broken in had been extremely thorough in their search. "Nothing was missing, not even the two tubs of my dad's things, although everything had been destroyed." He drew in a breath, letting it out slowly as the pain of losing the only tangible tie he'd had to a father he barely remembered.

"Oh, Cy. I'm so sorry." She covered his hand with hers.

Without thinking, he turned his over and grasped her hand tightly, needing a physical connection with someone else. If he were being honest, not just anyone, but this lovely woman sitting across from him. The urge to pull her into his arms and kiss her gobsmacked him like an armored tank. Much as he would have liked to act on the impulse, he couldn't. Not when his mother's life depended on him focusing all his attention on finding the list. He squeezed her hand, then let go, picking up his coffee cup to give himself something to do. "Obviously, the list wasn't with my father's things, so where could it be?"

She glanced around the cheerful kitchen with its glossy yellow cabinets and stainless steel appliances. "I take it you've searched this house?"

"Top to bottom." He shoved a hand through his hair. "I figured if Mom knew where the list was, she'd have told by now."

"Do you have a pen and paper?"

"Yes." He hustled out of the room to his mom's study, grabbing two yellow pads and pens. Returning to the kitchen, he handed one of each to Isana.

She clicked the end of the ballpoint pen and poised it over the tablet. "Now we jot down what we know about the list."

"Not much." Despair threatened to overtake him, but he tamped it down. He couldn't fall apart. His mother needed him to be strong.

"More than you think." She wrote something down on her pad. "First, we know the list has a connection to your family, specifically your father. Second, we know more than one someone is suddenly looking for it."

"Wait, why do you think more than one person is seeking the list?" He'd hoped the coffee would jumpstart his brain, but three late nights in the row were taking their toll on his ability to think clearly.

"Whoever has your mom and whoever broke into your condo."

Understanding dawned. "Because whoever took my mom already knew there was nothing of interest in the condo."

"My guess is they searched your condo and this house before snatching your mom." Tapping the pen against the pad, she continued, "The trashing of your condo seems to be the work of amateurs."

He wasn't following. "Sorry, too many late nights. Explain, please?"

The sympathy in her eyes warmed his heart. "Why else would they destroy everything and let you know they were there? They could have searched your condo without breaking dishes and ruining everything. It looks like they had a massive temper tantrum after not finding the list."

"Perhaps." He sighed. "I'm staying here until I can sort out the insurance claim."

"Do you think that's wise? What if they come back?"

"I don't think they will, since they've already searched it."

She stared down at the tabletop. "Maybe the answer to where the list might be is in your father's past. What do you know about him?"

"He died when I was in kindergarten." Cy could barely recall what his father looked like. His memories of a tall, clean-shaven man with dark blond hair and blue eyes were fuzzy around the edges like an old photograph. "He worked for the State Department."

"Doing what exactly?"

He searched his memory but came up blank. "I don't know. Mom was always evasive when I asked, which wasn't often. I do know they were stationed in West Germany when the Berlin Wall fell."

"Was your mom a civil servant as well?"

"I think she was a secretary or something like that." He frowned. "I thought I knew things about my parents, but I really don't. Mom talked about Dad a lot, but not about his work. More along the lines of what he liked to do or the music, books, or movies he enjoyed. She told me the story of their courtship and what she loved about him, but now that I think about, she didn't share many facts."

"Then that's where we'll start—with the facts of your father's life."

Despite the ticking clock and the concern for his mother's safety, part of Cy buzzed with anticipation at finally raising the curtain on a man whose shadow had loomed over him his entire life. Maybe Cy would even learn why his father committed suicide.

CHAPTER

TEN

Gina Sanders struggled to close the clasp on the diamond tennis bracelet. *Calm down. He doesn't know the full story.* But her self-talk did little to steady her nerves.

"Darling, let me," her husband crooned. His fingers brushed the skin of her wrist as he made short work of the clasp. "There."

"Thank you." Gina lifted her lips to kiss the air above Gil's cheek, not wanting to muss her lipstick. "Ready?"

"I think so." He adjusted the bowtie of his tuxedo, still a handsome man after all these years. But instead of moving toward the bedroom door, he grasped her hands. "It will be all right."

His allusion to their troubles sent a spasm of fear and worry through her body, but she managed a lightness to her voice despite of it. "Will it?"

He squeezed gently. "It will. I said I'd take care of it, and I am."

She nodded, wanting to believe him, but knowing there were things beyond his control, things he didn't know because she hadn't told him. Couldn't tell him without destroying the life they'd built together.

On their descent to the main floor of their spacious home, her phone buzzed. She ignored it as Nigel, her husband's assistant, met them halfway up the stairs to say the car would be arriving in ten minutes because of an accident on the Capital Beltway.

"My dear, I should return Senator Eaton's call." Gil patted her hand as she smiled in understanding.

Parting ways at the bottom of the wide, curving staircase, she gazed after him as he disappeared into his study, Nigel nipping at his heels like a yipping dog. Her phone vibrated again, and she slipped into the morning room she commandeered for her office. The text simply read *Call.*

Closing the door and flipping the lock on the handle, she hurried to her desk. The deep bottom drawer had a keypad lock. Her husband thought it was to secure her laptop and tablet, which it certainly did, but it also held a collection of burner phones. If only they'd had access to this kind of technology forty years ago, think of how they could have outsmarted the Stasi even more.

Gina selected the one on top and dialed the number from memory. It rang only once before a voice barked, "Yep."

"It's me." She paced the room, straightening a framed photo of herself, her husband, the President of the United States, and the First Lady at a party in the East Garden of the White House. How happy they had been that day last May.

"We've been through the papers Hillam left behind."

She firmed her lips to stop from asking the question burning on her tongue. His tone of voice told her they found nothing.

"The list wasn't there." He answered her unspoken question anyway.

"What's next?" They had to find it, or the very bright future dangling within their grasp would disappear in a poof of smoke.

"Someone else is looking for it too."

She couldn't hold back the gasp. "Who?"

"Unknown at this time."

Something about the pause that followed made her stop her circuit of the room. "What aren't you telling me?"

"Lillian Hillam has been kidnapped."

"What?" Disbelief sharpened her voice. "How do you know?"

"We're monitoring the son's phone and intercepted a call from the kidnappers."

"Tell me everything." She fumbled in the top drawer of the desk for a packet of cigarettes she kept for emergencies. She'd quit years ago, but sometimes the old craving overpowered her. Her husband would not be happy if he smelled smoke on her clothing, but she needed the nicotine hit. Shoving open a window before she lit up, Gina inhaled deeply as the man told her Cy Hillam had until Saturday to find the list or his mother would be dead.

"You have eyes on him?" She drew in another lungful of smoke, the nicotine calming her jumbled thoughts.

"Yes. He's spent late nights in his condo, we assume trying to figure out what's missing after the mess we left. By the layer of dust on the two plastic bins of his father's things, he hadn't looked in there for a long time, so we figured he won't know what we took. Not that it held any clue to the whereabouts of the list."

"What's he doing to find it?" She fished an ashtray out of the drawer, flicking ashes into it. What did this new wrinkle mean?

"Not sure. He was holed up in his mother's home with that girl from the museum all morning."

"The one who found the phone by the Tidal Basin?"

"Isana Thomas."

"What's her story?"

"She grew up overseas—her father worked for several international oil and gas companies. Her parents divorced when she was a teenager. She attended George Mason University for both undergrad and graduate degrees. First job was with a small museum in Bedford, Virginia. She moved to The Heritage three years ago in their acquisitions department."

"Dig deeper into her background and the son's."

"Will do."

Headlights swept over the house as a Lincoln Town Car purred to a stop in front of the door. She stubbed out the cigarette and shoved the ashtray into the drawer. "I've got to go. Keep me posted." She disconnected the call, putting the phone back into the drawer and securing it.

Gina met her husband in the hallway. "Got on your game face?"

"Always." He sniffed as he draped her evening wrap over her shoulders.

"Don't ask." She warned with a playful shake of her finger.

"I never do." Gil cupped her elbow as he escorted her into the waiting car. As the Lincoln glided down the long driveway, Gina made small talk with her husband about who they might see at the night's charity fundraiser and prayed a decision she'd made four decades earlier wouldn't come back to haunt their lives today.

FROST PEPPERED THE GRASS, CRUNCHING UNDER CY'S FEET AS HE CUT ACROSS the lawn to the driveway. Only five days left to find the elusive list. After church yesterday, he and Isana had grabbed Indian takeout, then spent the afternoon tossing ideas back and forth. While he enjoyed being with her, they had come up with no solid leads on how to uncover the list his father supposedly had taken. Given his mother's ignorance of the document, Cy surmised the list had come into Greg's possession shortly before his death.

Isana had voiced the question always hovering at the back of Cy's mind. Was his father's death a suicide or murder? At least that was one mystery he might be able to solve. His first bit of business before heading to work this morning would be to stop by the City of Falls Church Police Department to request a copy of his father's autopsy and any notes related to his death. According to his mother, a detective had initially investigated but stopped when the medical examiner ruled cause of death as suicide. His father's death certificate noted that as manner of death, but Cy wanted to read the report for himself.

He hadn't told Isana of his intention, sure she would dissuade him from viewing potentially gruesome photographs and text about his father. But with nothing else to go on, maybe he'd glean a vital clue as to the whereabouts of the list from reading the report.

Entering Falls Church City Hall, he made his way to the police department. The sergeant on duty took his name and request, then directed him to have a seat. Cy settled in one of the plastic chairs haphazardly grouped in clumps of two and three in the open lobby and pulled up his work email. Might as well get a head start on the day while he waited. Thirty minutes later, someone called his name.

He rose as a middle-aged woman, her close-cropped hair studded with silver amidst the black, approached. She held a large brown envelope in her hands, and his stomach churned with anticipation and dread. Now that his goal might be achieved, he questioned his decision to read the report and see the autopsy photos.

"I'm Detective Chalmers. May I see some identification?"

He showed her his driver's license, which she studied for several seconds before returning it to him. "Thank you. I understand you're interested in reading what we have on file concerning Greg Hillam's death in July of 1992."

"That's right. He's my father."

She nodded. "Since it's a closed case, I received clearance to give you a copy of the investigation file, including the autopsy report and photos." Her gaze softened. "Are you sure you want to see this?"

No! But he steeled himself. "Yes, I have to. I've lived my whole life in the shadow of his death. I need to understand what happened, what drove him to take his own life."

She handed him the envelope. "Then here you go."

"Thank you."

"Good luck. I hope you find what you're looking for." With those parting words, she retreated through the door into the department.

Cy gripped the envelope, staring at its blank surface. His phone's reminder bell chimed. 8:48. He'd better fly if he was going to make the 9:30 all-staff meeting. As he drove in rush hour traffic over the

Theodore Roosevelt Bridge, he prayed the report would provide the answers he needed to save his mother's life.

❧

Isana had hoped to talk to Cy before the staff meeting, but he'd slid into his chair mere seconds before the director called everyone to order. Notably absent was Carson, who the director said had sent in his resignation over the weekend. Ms. Gibbons, the HR director, told Isana privately Carson had been given a choice to resign or be fired because of his threats against Isana.

This week, the meeting went longer than usual, given last week's change to have her curate the Weddings Through the Twentieth Century special exhibit in June. She'd rarely had to deliver a report to the group, and her voice shook as she outlined her ideas for the exhibition and what support she needed from other departments. The enthusiastic response from her colleagues calmed her nerves, and by the end of her presentation, she had a good plan in place to make the exhibition happen.

Cy gave her a brief hello before slipping away at the meeting's end. Isana wanted to go after him, but several other staff members vied for her attention about details concerning the exhibition. Cy's office door was closed when she passed it on her way to the basement, and she didn't have the nerve to knock.

She pushed all thoughts of Cy and the list to the back of her mind as she examined the dresses she'd selected, making notes about any repairs needed to ensure the fabric would hold up on the mannequins. Then she had a light bulb moment. What if the exhibition had a wedding fashion show with live models? They could invite the public to submit photos of themselves in wedding dresses—their own or a family member's—and pick a variety of styles for an opening wedding extravaganza. She spent the rest of the morning formalizing her thoughts on the fashion show, then gathered her courage to seek out Cy. If she happened to catch him before lunch, perhaps they could grab a bite and she could tell him about her idea. They both had to eat, right?

His office door stood open, but when she peeked inside, it was empty. Disappointment made her shoulders slump as she turned away toward the break room. Heating leftover soup—with Carson gone, at least her food remained untouched—she carried the steaming bowl back to her office to dine alone as usual. Tears threatened to fall into the homemade chicken and rice soup, but she refused to give in to the hurt roiling inside, telling herself how ridiculous it was for her heart to ache just because a man who'd barely spoken to her a couple of weeks ago had reverted to barely speaking to her again. She'd managed her secret crush just fine without falling apart because Cy wasn't seeking her out, and she'd wrestle her heart back into its box to carry on without drawing attention to herself.

Her pep talk, coupled with the boatload of work on her plate to get things ready for the exhibition, distracted her enough that Cy slipped to the back of her mind for the rest of the workday. But when she passed his empty office at the end of the day—much later than usual for her—the now-familiar ache returned to her heart.

The March wind kicked up as she tugged the outer door closed, tangling her hair and bringing tears to her eyes from its bite. At least now she had an excuse to cry. Ducking her head, she headed toward the Metro, her mind busy reviewing a list of things yet to do for the exhibition. With overtime, she might just make the deadline. Her stomach growled, reminding her how long ago lunch had been. A Thai restaurant beckoned up ahead, promising warmth and Pad Thai. On impulse, she went inside, asking for a table for one from the hostess.

Digging into the delicious noodle dish, Isana wished she'd have brought her e-reader. At the table to her right, the hostess seated two women, who immediately ordered cocktails.

"I can't believe his wife found out," a sleek blonde said, a predatory gleam in her eye.

"He should have remembered Ellen was good friends with the receptionist," her companion retorted, shrugging out of her coat.

"True," the blonde replied. "It can be hard to keep a secret from someone who can keep tabs on your coming and going."

"Ellen would never have known otherwise. After all, it's pretty easy to keep your work and home life separate."

"How is everything?" The waitress's question drew Isana's attention away from the other table's conversation.

Isana glanced down at her half-eaten dish. "Fine, but can I get a box for the rest? And the check?"

If her sudden request startled the young woman, her demeanor didn't show it. "Of course."

Isana took a final bite and blotted her lips. One thing she and Cy hadn't fully considered would be whether Greg Hillam's colleagues knew anything they hadn't said at the time of his death. People often shied away from revealing potentially damaging information about someone who had just died. Perhaps thirty years was long enough to make sharing those stories easier. After settling her bill and packing up the rest of her meal, Isana determined to try Cy at home. With the clock ticking, she hoped her intrusion and idea would be welcome. She ignored the tiny part of her that also hoped he would explain why he'd been so distant lately.

CHAPTER

ELEVEN

Cy shuffled the autopsy photos into a stack and placed them face down beside the photocopied pages. He probably shouldn't have viewed the gruesome images that showed his father's lifeless form slumped over the kitchen table, a bullet hole in his right temple and the gun resting in his limp hand. Even to his untrained eye, powder burns on his skin attested to the gun's proximity and bolstered the suicide theory. Nothing about the scene screamed of an intruder. The kitchen looked much as it currently did.

He pinched the bridge of his nose, his stomach reminding him he'd skipped dinner to dive directly into the police report. The antique clock chimed the half hour. Seven-thirty. No wonder he was peckish. He'd just risen to go to the kitchen for something to eat when the doorbell rang.

He wasn't expecting anyone, and especially not at his mother's house. Cautiously, he moved through the darkened living room to the foyer. Through the frosted glass on either side of the door, he caught a glimpse of taillights moving away from the house. His mother had no peephole, so he palmed his phone for easy access in case help was needed and opened the door.

Isana shifted on her feet, a takeout bag in her hand. "Sorry to drop by unannounced, but I had an idea about how to find out more information about your father and thought you'd like to know sooner rather than later." Her words came out in a rush, as if she'd rehearsed them.

His mind still reeling from the autopsy photos, he had trouble deciphering what she'd said. Something about a way to uncover details about his father.

"I've interrupted you. Sorry." She rolled her lips inward together, as if bottling up more words. Her eyes skittered away from his but not before he noted the hurt in their hazel depths.

"No, I'm the one who's sorry." He blew out a breath, trying to let go of his own pain. "Please, come in and tell me your thought."

She hesitated, as if weighing his sincerity.

"Right before you came, I was viewing my dad's autopsy photos." The confession surprised him, as he hadn't consciously intended to tell her that, but once the words left his mouth, something akin to relief seeped into his bones. What was that Bible verse about burdens shared? *Bear one another's burdens, and so fulfill the law of Christ.* Galatians 6:2. That's why he'd been so down. He'd had no one with which to share this heavy burden. Isana's unexpected arrival reminded him he didn't have to slog through this alone.

"Oh, Cyrus." Her soft voice, tinged with empathy, soothed his battered soul. "That must have been tough. You've never seen them before?"

He shook his head, stepping back and gesturing for her to enter his home without speaking around the clog in his throat. Cy led her to the kitchen, not quite ready to face the study and its grim documents. "Have you eaten?"

She nodded toward the takeout bag. "Stopped at that little Thai restaurant a block from L'Enfant Metro station on my way home. Didn't finish the meal."

His stomach took that moment to recognize the delicious smells emanating from the bag. "As you can hear, I haven't, so was going to make myself something." He pulled open the fridge, staring at the nearly bare shelves. A carton of eggs, a couple of single-serve yogurt containers, and a half a loaf of bread.

Isana peered over his shoulder into the refrigerator. "Not much there."

"I cleared out most of it after . . . " He couldn't finish the sentence with *my mother was taken.* Somehow, speaking the words out loud would make the nightmare unbearable.

She put the bag on the counter. "Where are your plates?"

He pointed to the correct cabinet as he struggled to bring his emotions under control. But seeing his father's dead body had affected him more than he'd realized. The tears threatening since learning of his mother's kidnapping burst over the dam he'd built. He turned away, his hands covering his face as silent sobs tore through his body.

Isana rubbed his back, the only thing grounding him in the moment as anger, fear, and loss battled for supremacy inside him. Her soft murmurings only exacerbated the situation, drawing out even more of the suppressed emotions. With a groan wrested deep from inside him, he turned blindly toward her, his arms crushing her body to his, the need to hold onto someone real overwhelming him. Still the tears came, falling into her soft, shoulder-length hair. Her arms encircled him, her hands once again moving up and down his back.

Gradually, his emotional storm spent itself, leaving only the feel of her tight against him. Stirrings of a different kind tingled in his body. How long had it been since he'd felt a deep connection with a woman? Guilt rose up that he would be thinking such thoughts when his mother was in the hands of unknown captors. He needed to get his mind off how holding Isana filled him with a sense of homecoming and back on how to rescue his mother.

But a small voice whispered his mother would call him a fool to deny his growing attraction to Isana, that the potential for love didn't come along every day. Lillian would want him to give her grandchildren eventually, and to do so meant falling in love with a suitable woman. Isana might be that woman, although he had the feeling after seeing her in church yesterday that her faith had been put on the backburner for a while. Which meant she would be off limits for anything long term.

She stirred in his arms, and he loosened his hold. Tilting her face up to his, she smiled. "Feel better?"

He gave into temptation and raised a hand to brush a strand of hair from her cheek. "Much." His gaze strayed to her lips, now only inches from his own. An easy distance to close.

Isana must have read his intention because she pulled out of his arms as he leaned down. His lips touched her temple instead of the intended target. Her abrupt movement after the emotional storm left him distinctly unbalanced. Had he misread her interest in him? Cy covered his confusion by grabbing a couple of tissues from the box on the counter and blowing his nose.

She slid a plate covered with a paper towel into the microwave. "I figured you'd might as well have the rest of my Pad Thai, since you need nourishment, and it doesn't look like you have many options."

He cleared his throat. "Thank you." He tossed the tissues into the trash. "And thank you for, well, understanding."

Her eyes met his, the empathy telling him she had her own story to tell about grief and loss, one he would push to explore another time. "It helps to let those emotions out every once in a while."

"The understatement of the day." But he didn't want her to think it was only an overwhelming need to unburden himself in general. Her presence made him feel safe enough to cry. "You're an easy person to be real with."

Isana's eyes widened, then she faced the microwave, her back to him.

He touched her shoulder. "Isana? Did I say something wrong?"

The microwave dinged. "Your dinner is ready." She took out the steaming plate. "Where's the silverware?" She pulled open the closest drawer but closed it after glancing at the hot pads. Moving around the dishwasher, she tugged another drawer handle.

"I'll get the silverware."

But his words had no effect on her actions. Isana continued to try drawer after drawer until at last she arrived at the one holding silverware. Extracting a fork, she laid it on the counter, then pushed the drawer in.

Cy stayed put, unsure what had upset her and not wanting to do the wrong thing. He'd only recently discovered he wanted to be around this woman, not for her help in finding the list to free his mother but because Isana made him feel alive again. He'd not realized how dead inside he'd become, slogging through life with a happy exterior but building walls in his heart to avoid feeling. A therapist would likely have a field day with that, but the truth was, he'd been living in the past for so long, he'd forgotten how to be in the present, looking toward the future.

His mother talked about his father all the time to keep his memory alive for Cy, who had few clear memories of the man who died when he was five. Hearing how much she missed her late husband all these years had made Cy wary of opening his own heart to love. If his mother could sound so shattered after three decades of widowhood, how could he chance bringing pain into his life by falling in love?

Meeting Isana had awakened his heart. Yesterday's sermon reminded him that God's faithfulness and love for his children meant believers didn't have to live in fear but in hope. The knowledge gave Cy the strength to overcome a lifetime of avoiding close relationships and pursue one with the woman who stood with her back to him in his mother's kitchen. But now he faced the perplexing problem of figuring out what he'd done. She'd been so nice earlier, comforting him as he worked through seeing his dad's autopsy photos, then had frozen him out.

"Isana?" He spoke her name softly, but she didn't turn around.

Lord, help me to know what to say right now. "I think perhaps I haven't been clear."

Her shoulders stiffened, but she stayed silent.

No time to worry about making a fool of himself. He didn't want to face this week without her by his side. "And I think I might have sent mixed signals as to my intentions." He paused, then added, "With you."

She half-turned, giving him a glimpse of her profile and signaling she was at least listening.

He blew out a breath. "I'm not any good at this. I don't date much—haven't wanted to risk my heart, if I'm being honest. But then I met you, and, well, I found myself twitterpated."

The reference from *Bambi* to being smitten brought Isana around to face him. "You know *Bambi*?"

"My favorite movie as a kid," he admitted. "I wore out the VHS tape."

Then her eyes widened as what he'd said before twitterpated must have registered.

He hurried on. "I like you, and I'd like to spend time getting to know you. Not because you're my work colleague or because I want your help with finding this list but because I'm interested in you. Romantically." There, that ought to make things crystal clear.

"Oh." Her brow furrowed. "I see."

He threw himself at her feet and that was all she could say? Then a smile blossomed across her face like the rays of the rising sun, its brilliance filling the kitchen. "I feel the same way."

She did? With a whoop, he lifted her off the ground, spinning a circle. Her hands rested on his shoulders, and her eyes sparkled. The shrill sound of the house phone ringing cut into their celebration. He wanted to ignore it. Probably a telemarketer, but the chance it could be the kidnappers calling had him setting her down.

"I'd better answer." He picked up the handset. "Hello?"

∿

Happiness infused Isana as she mentally reviewed Cy's words while he answered the phone. She, who had dated very little, had a handsome man interested in her. The warm glow of his words spread throughout her body. She had been feeling bereft earlier as he'd seemed to withdraw from nearly kissing her. Focusing on reheating her leftovers for him had given her something to do rather than beat herself up for yet again wanting something she couldn't have.

Lines of tension radiated from the corners of Cy's mouth as he listened to whoever had called. His entire body had gone rigid, his left hand clenched in a fist at his side. He caught her eye and pointed toward a darkened room across the hall from the kitchen. In a flash, she understood he wanted her to pick up another handset to listen in. She found it and lifted it off the base, punching in the green button as quietly as possible.

"Cy, I'm okay," an older woman's voice said.

Isana listened hard as Lillian Hillam tried to assure her son she was fine. Isana didn't buy the lie any more than Cy did, if his response was any indication.

"Mom, I know you're not doing well. How could you when you're being held against your will?"

"Any progress on finding what they want?" Lillian's voice sounded stronger, as if her son's gentle rebuke had given her license to speak her mind.

"No." The one-word answer cracked across the line.

"You'll keep digging." It wasn't a question but more of a command.

"I won't stop until I find it."

"I know you won't." Lillian drew in a breath. "But remember, God has us both in the palm of his hand. As his children, nothing can separate us from him. Not even death."

"Mom, don't say that." The anguish in Cy's words tugged at Isana's heart.

"I love you," his mother said before the line went dead.

Isana replaced the receiver and returned to the kitchen. Cy stood where she'd left him, the handset still in his hand. She took it from him and placed it in the base. Then she hit the one-minute button on the microwave to reheat the food and found two glasses that she filled with tap water. Carrying the glasses to the table, she retrieved the plate and fork. "Come on and eat."

He sank into a chair, bowed his head for what she supposed was a silent prayer, then dug into the food. While he ate, she recounted the conversation she'd overheard in the Thai restaurant.

"I started thinking about your dad and his colleagues from around the time of his death. If we could talk to some of them, maybe we'd get a better picture of his movements before he died and that might give us a clue as to where he put the list."

"If he even had such a list." Cy put his fork on his empty plate. "Thank you for sharing your leftovers. I didn't realize how hungry I was."

"It's hard to think clearly on an empty stomach." She hoped her words sounded light enough not to allude to the fact she had personal experience with concentrating while hungry. Isana loaded his plate into the dishwasher over his objection he could clear his own dish. Refilling the water in his Keurig, she found two mugs. "I think we're going to need some caffeine to get through the police report."

"I haven't read it." His eyes dropped from hers. "I got stuck on the photos."

She selected a pod of medium roast coffee and inserted it into the machine. "The police probably talked to someone at his office in the course of their investigation, so we will likely find a couple of names we could follow up on."

His eyes brightened. "I hadn't thought about that."

She added sugar to her mug. "Now tell me what kind of coffee you'd like, and let's get started."

CHAPTER

TWELVE

Three names. Cy stared down at the short list on his phone's notes app. The cursory interviews conducted by the Falls Church Police Department after his father's death yielded little information but did provide the last known addresses and phone numbers for three of Greg's co-workers, including the head of his unit at the State Department. With the way State employees moved around, he had little faith the two men and one woman listed would still be reachable by thirty-year-old contact details.

"Brayerton is dead." Isana sounded more chipper than he was after two hours of reading his father's police file, but that was because her emotions weren't roiling with each new piece of information.

"Was he the boss?" He rubbed the back of his neck, wishing he'd taken her up on the offer for a second cup of coffee.

"Yes, died of lung cancer, according to his obituary. Five years ago in Arlington, Virginia, so it appears he stayed in the area." Her finger swiped up on her phone. "I'm checking to see if his widow still resides here. Any luck with Johnston?"

Right, he was supposed to be Googling Harold Johnston, one of his father's colleagues. After entering the name with Silver Spring, Maryland—the city and state given with Johnston's address in the report—he skimmed through the results. His heart sank at the obit halfway down the page. Clicking on the link, he said, "He's dead too. Car accident."

"When?"

He scrolled to the top to find the date he'd read past at first. His pulse jumped. "Six weeks ago."

She put her phone on the table, her eyes troubled as she gazed into his. "Would you mind reading me the obit?"

"Sure." He cleared his throat. "Harold Franklin Johnston traveled the world, bringing back exotic trinkets and fabulous stories of the people he'd met and the places he'd seen during his four-decade career in the U.S. State Department. Harold's aptitude for languages —he spoke six fluently and another five passably—proved a valuable asset in his work on behalf of the U.S. government. Some of his duty stations included Istanbul, Tokyo, Seoul, Paris, Athens, and West Berlin. Colleagues described him as friendly and hard-working, while his family enjoyed his wicked sense of humor, which he often exhibited in the form of puns."

The obituary continued with a list of Johnston's various club and organization memberships, then concluded with a list of survivors, including his widow, Cecelia Maron Johnston of Silver Spring, Maryland.

"So as of six weeks ago, the Johnstons resided in Silver Spring." She caught her lower lip between her teeth. "Was there any news coverage of the accident?"

Her question brought him crashing back to their search. Shoving his growing attraction to Isana to the far recesses of his mind, he returned to the search results. "Let me see." He examined them more closely. "The *Silver Springs Gazette* ran a story a couple of days after the accident." He pulled it up. "It says the incident happened late at night at the intersection of Arlington Boulevard/Route 50 and Graham Road."

"That's only a few blocks from here." Isana turned her phone to show Cy a maps app with the intersection highlighted. "Did the police say why he was in this area?"

"No. It occurred around four a.m. with no witnesses."

"What about the driver of the other vehicle?"

"'Police found the second vehicle involved in the accident, a dark blue Ford SUV, abandoned in the Anacostia neighborhood of Washington, DC, a day after the incident. The SUV had been reported stolen hours before the accident.'" He glanced up from his phone. "The red-light camera caught the SUV running the light seconds before smashing into Johnston's car."

"Did the police say whether they thought it was a deliberate hit-and-run or an accident?"

"The office in charge of the investigation said it was 'ongoing.'" He once again returned to the search results. "Here's a small follow-up story a week later." He skimmed the two-paragraph item. "It appears the police labeled it as a hit-and-run and are still seeking information on the driver of the other vehicle, but there's no new information."

"What's the officer's name? We might want to talk to him before we stop by the widow's house."

He rattled off the name, then swiped the app closed. As he did, he noticed the time. 9:34. "I didn't realize how late it is. We should probably call it a night."

"Will you be in the office tomorrow?"

Cy nodded. "I have a couple of meetings, and since I started only a few months ago, I don't have a lot of vacation accrued." He wished he had, as it would be pure torture to concentrate on museum publicity when the clock ticked away the hours of his mother's life. "I'll see if I can track down the officer during my lunch hour."

"And I can contact the widow. Perhaps we can see her after work." Isana carried her mug to the sink. "We'll find the list in time."

He wanted to believe they would, but how could two amateurs

locate a missing list when they didn't even know what they were looking for? Or why?

~

Brenner Lorenz removed his headphones as Cy and Isana left his mother's house. The son insisted on driving the woman to her DC apartment. And here Brenner thought chivalry was dead. Knowing their plans thanks to several listening devices planted when he'd searched the house before kidnapping Lillian wouldn't help in the race for the list. He'd already spoken with every living co-worker Greg had had in the two years prior to his death. Johnston had been the most likely of confidants, since the Hillams and the Johnstons had been stationed together during Greg's last overseas assignment in West Berlin in the late 1980s.

But the interview with Johnston had yielded nothing. The man's visit to Lillian before the accident bothered Brenner, but Lillian obviously did not have the list, nor did she know its whereabouts. Of that he was certain, because if she did, she would have handed it over to ensure her son's safety. Cyrus was her weakness, the one thing guaranteed to make her do whatever it took to keep him safe, and he felt the same about his mother.

Cy and Isana wouldn't find anything new talking to Johnston's widow, but their conversation did remind Brenner he wanted to follow up on who had run that red light and smashed into Johnston's sports car. Johnston had expired at the scene. Schmidt noted someone else was searching for the list in a very sloppy, violent manner. The trashing of Cy's apartment and the hit-and-run accident pointed to amateurs on the trail of the list or someone with a grudge.

Better check on Schmidt. The man talked like he hated Lillian, but Brenner suspected it was a cover for his real feelings of affection toward the woman.

Schmidt picked up on the first ring. "Hallo."

"Anything to report?" Brenner didn't bother with a formal greeting, his irritation at how long this assignment was taking rising to the surface.

"No. The woman eats, sleeps, and whines about being cold." Schmidt coughed. "How much longer are we going to keep her?"

"As long as it takes to find what we're looking for." *Like I've told you a million times.* "How did the conversation go with her son?"

Schmidt chortled. "She was so pathetically grateful for the chance to talk to him, I think she might have kissed me, had I let her."

"Keep your mind on the prize, Schmidt," Brenner snapped. "Or do I need to find someone else for the job?"

"No, sir." Schmidt's voice had a conciliatory tone, telling Brenner he got the message loud and clear.

"Good. Call me if she tells you anything new." Brenner disconnected without waiting for Schmidt's acquiescence.

He'd pay a visit to the widow's house tomorrow morning while she was at her yoga class. Even though he thought that particular well to be dry as a bone, he didn't want to take the chance she might remember something significant when talking to Cy and Isana. A few strategically placed listening devices would allow him to eavesdrop from the comfort of his home.

Now to finalize plans for his exit from the game. He put the three flash drives into a padded envelope, along with a note he'd signed in front of a notary, then addressed it to his lawyer. The rather dramatic to-be-sent-to-FBI-Special-Agent-Raul-in-the-event-of-my-death letter wouldn't rattle the attorney. A quick trip to the twenty-four-hour shipping store, and the envelope was on its way. On the short walk back to his condo, he reviewed his plans. His accountant had moved his money to new offshore accounts. Brenner carried the key to a Swiss security box on his person at all times, along with his passport and enough cash to fly anywhere in the world at a moment's notice.

Back at home, he brewed a cup of decaf and settled in his favorite chair to read a biography of W.G. Sebald, an influential twentieth century writer, but even though he enjoyed the lively prose, his mind kept returning to what would happen when the list failed to surface.

TUCKING HER TABLET UNDER HER ARM, ISANA STACKED THE PAGES AND ROSE, glad her meeting with Cy, the curator staff, and the director about the wedding exhibition had gone smoothly. Based on their questions and encouragement, everyone seemed excited about the replacement show. Being in front of people usually required a massive internal pep talk, but she'd been so distracted with helping Cy find the list, she'd forgotten to be nervous. Cy's friendly face in the audience had settled her nerves as well. Too bad both of them had full days and had agreed the night before to meet after work to compare notes.

Chatting briefly with a junior curator, she tracked Cy's progress as he weaved his way through their co-workers and disappeared out the conference room door. *Do* not *be disappointed*. He'd told her his day was crammed with meetings, so she shouldn't be surprised he'd left without saying anything directly to her.

Her phone buzzed as Isana headed for the stairs. She glanced at the screen. A text from Cy. She paused on the landing to read it out of sight from other personnel.

> You did great. Sorry I couldn't stay to tell you in person. Next meeting starts in thirty seconds. C U after work.

A weight she hadn't known was there lifted from her shoulders, allowing her to breath easier.

> Thanks. I'm off to the clothing storage area to check my selections. Probably be there most of the day.

She hit send, then pocketed the phone. Her mind flitted from task to task as she clattered down the stairs to her basement office. Once inside, she dumped her papers and tablet on her desk, then found the list of dresses she wanted to bring out of the massive storage area one floor down from the basement. Slipping on a knee-length white lab coat with a zipper front to protect any garments from snagging on her street clothing, she put her phone and wireless ear bud case in her pocket to listen to music while she sorted.

The museum's climate-controlled storage area had eight separate rooms, four on each side off a central hallway. Each of the rooms had its own climate setting to ensure the objects stayed as pristine as possible. The clothing room occupied the entire back wall with a door in the center. Inside, two banks of various sized drawers for pieces to lie flat alternated with long, shallow closets for hanging garments. Scanning her museum ID badge on the pad outside the door to release the lock, she entered the clothing room with a cart in tow. The door closed with a soft click, the sound echoing in the quiet chamber.

Uneasiness skittered up her spine like a monkey climbing a tree. *Steady. You come down here all the time. Nothing to be afraid of.* The reminder relieved some of the tension swirling in her body, and she got to work. The quiet of the space usually calmed her, but today her nerves jumped at every creak of a hanger on the metal bar or screech of a drawer's runner as she tugged it open.

Enough was enough. Fishing her wireless ear pods out of the case tucked into her lab coat pocket, she scrolled through her downloads to select background music to create a more calming atmosphere. Soon the notes of Rachmaninoff's "Rhapsody on a Theme of Paganini," from the movie *Somewhere in Time* filled her ears. The sweeping piano and violins soothed her, allowing her to concentrate on the task.

Three hours later, she stretched. Time for a lunch break. Her cart held a dozen dresses, about half of the exhibition. She'd take them upstairs into the staging area and return in the afternoon to examine the other choices. Once she'd picked which wedding dresses would be in the exhibition, she'd add accessories, such as jewelry, shoes, and other artifacts a bride from that year might have had or worn. For half of the dresses, she'd decided to showcase a separate mannequin with the undergarments necessary to achieve the wedding dress's finished look. The director loved that part of her idea. Maybe she should apply for the now-open curator position, with Carson's departure. Turning off her music, she put her ear pods back into their case before heading to the door.

After maneuvering the cart to the left of the door, she twisted the knob, but her hand slipped around it without the knob turning. Drat. She'd accidentally locked the door. Isana touched her badge to the lock release on the wall, but the indicator light stayed red. She repeated the gesture several times, but the light stubbornly refused to turn green and release the handle lock.

No matter, she'd call for assistance. No signal. She frowned. Sometimes it could be tricky to get a cell signal on this level, which was why the director had wired routers installed in every room to provide reliable WiFi access. She glanced to the right, but the outlets were empty. To the left, she spied something lying on the floor near a corner plug. Maybe someone bumped into the router and disconnected it.

But when she squatted down beside the object, it was immediately clear this was no accident. Someone had smashed the router to bits, rendering it useless. *No need to panic. Cy knows you're down here. Someone will come along soon and rescue you.*

Then the lights went out, plunging the room into darkness.

CHAPTER

THIRTEEN

Cy stretched, his eyes gritty after a two-hour long virtual meeting with his counterparts with public and private DC museums, including the Smithsonians, the International Spy Museum, and the Museum of the Bible. The city was launching a DC museums campaign in May ahead of the summer tourist season and wanted buy-in on promotional language and images. The meeting had been more fruitful than Cy had anticipated. Fingers crossed no important emails had flooded his inbox while he was in the meeting and he could call it a day.

Thirty minutes later, he closed his office door and headed toward the stairwell. In her earlier text, Isana said she'd wait for him at work, and they'd head out together. Her office door was closed, and when he tried the handle, it was locked as well. Strange. He reread her text. Surely she wasn't still in the storage area, but he'd check there anyway. He punched the down button on the elevator and waited for the car. Inside the elevator, he held his ID up to the security pad to activate the panel, then punched the right button. Nothing happened. He tapped his ID against the pad again. The light stayed red. Exiting the car, he turned right to take the separate stairs to the storage area, but his ID wouldn't unlock that door either.

Cy crossed back to the stairs servicing the rest of the museum. Worry nibbled at the edges of his mind. His ID unlocked that door immediately. Senior-level staff had access to every part of the museum, including the storage area. Like all new employees, Faith Gibbons, the museum's long-time manager of human resources, had given him a walking tour of the sub-basement rooms on his first day. He clearly remembered her telling him his ID would allow him to access the rooms.

He tried texting Isana, but the text didn't register as delivered like usual. Her voicemail kicked in immediately when he dialed her number. His concern morphed from a simmer into a full boil. Something wasn't right. Returning to the main level, he headed to Faith's office, where he thought he'd seen a light spilling into the hallway on his way to the basement. He caught Faith as she was locking her office.

"Faith?"

The woman's hand fluttered to her neck. "You startled me."

"Sorry." He shoved his hands into his pocket as she adjusted the messenger bag strap across her body. "I was supposed to meet Isana after work, but her office is locked."

"I imagine she's gone home for the day." She glanced at her watch. "It is nearly seven."

He heard the implication behind her noting of the time—she was ready to head home herself. But he couldn't let Faith go without verifying Isana wasn't on the premises. "I know, but I'm worried."

Faith studied him. "Yes, I can see you are." Pivoting to unlock her door, she said over her shoulder, "You'd better come in and tell me why."

"Thank you." He followed her in and sank into the visitor's chair while she shed her coat and sat behind her desk. He quickly recapped their plans and his inability to connect with Isana by phone or access the storage floor.

"Let's check and see if she left that area." Faith booted up her laptop, then clicked keys while Cy silently prayed for Isana's safety.

"Okay, the system registered her clocking in at 10:36 this morning." She ran a finger down the side of her screen. "That's strange. It has her leaving the area at 10:25."

He frowned. "She left before she arrived?"

"That's what the system says." Faith's brow furrowed. "Obviously, it can't be correct."

"My ID wouldn't open the stairs or the elevator to the storage area," he reminded her.

Their eyes met over her open laptop. "You should have access to all areas of the museum."

"I didn't ten minutes ago."

"Give me a minute to look into that."

Cy tamped down his impatience, his worry for Isana skyrocketing with every passing second. *Please God, let her be okay.*

ISANA SHIVERED IN THE COOL ROOM. THE DEHUMIDIFIER HUMMED IN THE background. The electricity hadn't gone out, just the lights, which was strange. Her phone battery died not long after the lights went out, leaving the darkness to press in on all sides. After realizing she was stuck, she paced for as long as she could to keep warm, but lack of food and water made her head swim, and she ended up huddling on the cement floor next to the door. The fur coats in an even colder storage closet beckoned, but the preservationist in her couldn't use century-old pelts for warmth, not when she might inadvertently tear a fragile lining. Besides, the temperature was kept at 50 degrees Fahrenheit, hardly likely to cause frostbite.

It had been years since she'd had to worry about her blood pressure, which tended to plummet under extreme stress, cold, or heat, and an empty stomach. Eating at regular intervals, exercising, and dressing in layers helped to ensure she didn't experience an adverse reaction. Her doctor had agreed her condition didn't warrant regular medication yet, as long as she kept a close eye on her stress and ate at regular intervals. But with no food or water since breakfast and fear invading her entire body, she wondered how long before she slipped into unconsciousness.

Repeating Psalm 23 had helped at first, but now she could barely get the words past her lips. "The Lord is my shepherd," she whispered, her voice unrecognizable to her own ears. How often had she quoted those words in a closet devoid of light? Too many times to remember. Before when she'd recited the psalm, it was to the accompaniment of shouts and crashes as her parents fought after her mother locked her in one dark closet, light bulb removed and towels stuffed along the bottom of the door.

"I shall not want." The beauty of the King James Version of the Bible had been lost on her seven-year-old self, but as an adult, she could appreciate the simplicity of the words.

Sitting upright with her arms wrapped around her knees made the room undulate as if viewed through old glass. Dizziness came in waves like water on the seashore, drawing her into its depths only to spit her out onto the sand in the next moment. But her physical ailments had nothing on her mental state. The blackness of the room crept under her skin, like an inky microbe bent on consuming her body one inch at a time. "He maketh me to lie down in green pastures."

Her body slumped sideways, her aching head resting on the cold floor. "He leadeth me beside the still waters." Nausea pummeled her innards. Sliding her eyes closed, she concentrated on breathing in and out in as measured a breath as she could muster, leaving the remainder of the passage unspoken. Shivers vibrated her body. Curling up into a ball, her arms hugging her knees to her chest, she prayed for Cy and Lillian and for someone to come rescue her. The words jumbled together in her mind until nothing made sense. Then darkness draped over her like a blanket, covering her completely.

∿

"Mine's not working either." Outside the elevator that would access the sub-basement area, Faith's brows knit as Cy's worry headed for Mars. "Are you sure she's down there?"

He didn't have time for this. Isana was trapped in the sub-basement storage area and might be hurt. He refused to think about anything else but getting her out of there. "Yes. She texted me that was where she was going after the staff meeting. Her purse and coat are in her desk with her laptop still on." Faith had used her key to unlock Isana's office, where it became evident she hadn't left the building.

"She's not anywhere else in the museum." He let his fear clip his words.

She must have conceded his point because her next words alloyed a small portion of his concern. "I'm calling the director."

Cy fidgeted while she succinctly explained what had happened, then listened to whatever the director replied.

"This can't wait until the morning," she snapped into the phone. "Ms. Thomas is missing. I called you as a courtesy, not for permission. Protocol is clear in these situations. Remember what happened in 2015?"

Whatever had occurred in 2015 must have made an impression because she ended the call soon after, then immediately phoned someone else. "Tim? It's Faith Gibbons. We have a situation here and need your expertise pronto." This conversation was short and to the point. Tim would be at the museum within half an hour.

Faith tapped the phone against her hand, her expression troubled. "We'll wait to call the police until Tim arrives. There's nothing the cops could do that Tim couldn't do faster. Those doors are designed to withstand fire and bomb blasts, so there's no way we could break them down."

Her words made sense but didn't calm his fear for Isana. To

distract himself from his inability to do something to find her, he asked, "What happened in 2015?"

"A pair of young teens decided hiding in the museum overnight would be fun. Apparently, they'd watched all three of the *Night at the Museum* movies."

For a moment, Cy couldn't place the series, then he recalled the plot. "Where a night security guard realizes the exhibits come to life after hours?"

"That's the one. They thought it would be cute to spend the night here and somehow managed to get into one of the storage rooms behind an exhibit on Art Deco jewelry." Faith shook her head. "The stunt caused a big hullabaloo, but thank goodness the kids weathered the unauthorized sleepover okay."

"Was that when electronic lock pads were put on every door?"

"Yes, and we also updated our procedures in case of an emergency." She glanced at her phone. "Tim's here."

A couple of minutes later, Tim Duprey strode down the corridor toward them, unwrapping his long scarf. "Come to my office and walk me through what happened."

Without waiting for a response, he unlocked a door at the end of the hallway. Cy followed Faith inside the large space set up with several huge monitors and other computer equipment. Tim swiveled his chair to face the bank of monitors.

Faith explained what she'd found related to Isana's check-in and checkout time in the storage area.

"They didn't know when she'd checked in, so probably estimated it had been an earlier time than she actually did," Tim surmised, his finger flying over a keyboard. "And someone's hacked our system and removed access from everyone's ID to the storage area."

Cy's stomach bottomed out. He managed to voice the question burning in his brain. "This wasn't an accident?"

"Not a chance." Tim focused on a series of numbers and letters flashing the middle screen. "Also, the same person managed to nix the lights in the storage area as well."

The thought of Isana being trapped in total darkness made him feel even sicker. "Any idea who did this?"

"It looks like an inside job, but let me restore lights and access first. Whoever did it won't get away with it."

Hearing one of their colleagues could have done such a thing to Isana ignited anger in Cy. He bounced on the balls of his feet, a nervous habit he'd done constantly as a child and one he usually kept under wraps as an adult. But he had to do something with his body before he smashed something, as his anger at whoever would play such a vicious prank grew.

"There," Tim said, "you should be able to open the stairway door or take the elevator to the storage floor."

Cy didn't wait to hear what Faith said to Tim. He raced for the stairs, his heart pounding in time with his feet. *Please God, let me get there in time.* He refused to think otherwise.

CHAPTER

FOURTEEN

Something bright pressed on her closed eyelids. Isana fluttered them enough to see the lights had come back on in the clothing room. Maybe now the door would open. She raised her head, but the world spun faster than it should, so she rested it on the cement again.

A few seconds later, the door handle rattled, then scraped open. The sound echoed in the chamber, but she couldn't muster the strength to see who was rescuing her.

"Isana!"

Cy? A hand cupped her cold cheek, the blessed warmth triggering shivers throughout her body.

"Hey, it's okay. I've got you." He gently gathered her in his arms as her body shook. A female voice murmured something about an ambulance, but Isana focused on the man now cuddling her close. The steady beat of his heart thrummed in her ear as she laid her head against his chest.

"Your rescuing me is getting to be a habit," she whispered, leaving her eyes closed.

A soft chuckle rumbled through his body. "I don't mind if you don't."

She certainly didn't, but telling him would take more energy than she had at the moment. Isana drifted into a state of semi-consciousness as Cy carried her out of the sub-basement and into warmer air. When Cy sat down, she peered through her lashes to see they were in the reception area. Someone placed a space heater at Cy's feet, then tucked a blanket around them both. She relaxed deeper into his embrace as warmth invaded her bones.

"Isana?"

At Cy's insistent nudging of her shoulder, she forced her eyes open. "Yes?"

"The EMTs want to check you over." He stood, easing her onto the loveseat and stepping away as a man in a dark blue uniform and surgical gloves stooped.

Isana missed Cy's comforting presence. Now that she was marginally warmer, her shivers had eased. Faith handed her a steaming mug. "Chicken noodle soup. Figured you could use something hot and nourishing."

She cupped the mug and took a tentative sip. Hot but drinkable. As she slowly sipped the soup, the EMT asked her a series of questions as he checked her temperature, blood pressure, and other vitals. When she'd finished, Faith handed her another mug, this time with coffee made just the way she liked it.

"Cy told me how you take it," Faith said before Isana could ask how the HR manager knew her java preference.

Warmth of a different kind filled her from her toes to her head. She lifted the mug for a sip to cover any telltale signs of a blush she was sure covered her cheeks.

The EMT packed away his equipment. "Right now, your blood pressure is within the low end of normal, but I recommend following up with your primary care doctor if you are still feeling dizzy or lightheaded."

She thanked the EMT as he joined his partner and the pair left.

Faith talked on her cell a few feet away, her voice too low for Isana to discern individual words, but the HR manager's stiff posture radiated tension. Cy stood talking to a uniformed police office with Tim, the museum's IT manager.

Cy glanced her way, winking when he caught her staring at him. Her cheeks heated again, but this time, she didn't duck her head. Cy gestured toward her, and the trio came over.

"Isana, this is Office Lutz with the DC police," Cy said. "He'd like to ask you a few questions about what happened."

"Sure." She took another sip of the coffee, starting to feel more like her normal self. Cy dropped onto the space beside her, his closeness bolstering her courage to recount her harrowing day.

The officer walked her through the events of the morning leading up to her entrapment in the clothing room. "You didn't hear anyone?"

She shook her head. "But I wouldn't have. The doors to each of the storage rooms are fireproof, which means they're practically soundproof as well."

"Tell me what happened next." Officer Lutz had his pen poised above a slim notebook.

Her heartrate picked up speed as memories of being trapped in the cold and dark assailed her. For a moment, Isana couldn't separate her recollection of this morning from her childhood memories of similar experiences. Then Cy's hand took hers, his strong fingers gentle in their grip. Drawing in a breath, she recounted everything she could remember.

When she'd finished, the officer turned to Cy. "You and Ms. Gibbons discovered your ID badges wouldn't allow access to the sub-basement either, correct?"

Cy nodded. "Faith checked online where the computer logs each staff's whereabouts based on their ID badges. She found Isana had accessed the storage area at 10:36 this morning but left at 10:25."

"The system registered her as leaving before she'd arrived," Officer Lutz clarified.

Tim spoke up. "Faith called me when neither of their ID badges would let them use the stairs or elevator leading to the storage area. There's a separate set of stairs and elevator to that floor for both security and safety in case of fire, etc. I delved deeper into our security system and discovered someone had hacked in and deactivated everyone's access to that floor as well as turned off the lights."

The officer wrote something down, then tapped the pen on the pad. "Any idea who?"

"I need to do some more digging, but it appears it's an inside job," Tim said.

Isana gasped. "Someone at the museum did this to me?" Someone must hate her a lot to play such an awful trick. At least she hoped it had been intended as a prank and not to seriously hurt her. No one could have known such a situation might cause her physical distress beyond a little chill.

Cy squeezed her hand. "Tim will find out who it was."

Lutz handed a card to everyone. "Please call me if you think of anything else. Mr. Duprey, let me know what you find out."

"Will do," Tim said.

With a nod, Lutz took his leave.

Faith joined the group after saying farewell to the cop. "I've spoken to the director, and we've decided to ask staff to work from home tomorrow to give Tim time to figure out who's behind this."

"Wouldn't the person be able to erase his tracks?" Cy asked the question tumbling around in Isana's mind as well.

"I've already limited access to files and email only, so there's little chance the person will be able to cover what they did before I find out who and how." Tim rubbed the back of his neck. "I'm so sorry, Isana."

The misery in her co-worker's eyes surprised her. She hadn't thought she had many friends on staff, given her retiring nature and office being one floor down from everyone else's. "It's not your fault someone played such a nasty trick on me."

"It kind of is. I knew there was the potential for someone on staff to find a way into our security system, but I kept putting off checking it out thoroughly and patching the hole."

Isana wasn't sure how to respond, so she was glad when Cy interjected. "But you're sure it had to be someone on staff?"

"Positive."

"Could it have been a former staff member?" Cy pressed.

Isana knew exactly who Cy was thinking of. "Carson?" She pictured the former curator, his face livid with anger.

Tim shook his head. "I revoked his staff access as soon as Faith told me he was leaving." He stood. "Don't worry, I'll find out." He strode off down the hall toward his office.

Faith placed a hand on Isana's shoulder. "You look done in. Don't worry about logging in at the usual start time tomorrow morning." She held up a hand as if forestalling Isana's unspoken protest. "We will figure out how to get everything done for the exhibition on Wednesday when you return."

Isana nodded. "Okay." She set down the unfinished coffee, exhaustion pulling at her eyelids.

Cy rose, then tugged her up beside him. "Come on, let's get you home."

Faith held out her coat and purse, and Cy bundled her into her outerwear, then tucked her close to his side as he walked her to the elevator to the underground parking garage. As he drove to her apartment, Isana turned over and over in her mind who would do such a thing to her and kept coming up blank. She decided to put the thought of who aside and instead concentrate on how wonderful it had been to be held by Cy.

Lillian brushed her teeth. Never had she imagined the very act of cleaning her pearly whites would give her so much joy, but after days without access to toothpaste or a toothbrush, she enjoyed the sensation of washing away all the plaque buildup in her mouth. Finished, she placed the toothbrush on the edge of the sink. Time to do something with her wet hair, though without a comb or hair ties, her choices were limited. Thank goodness she wore it fairly short, so a vigorous toweling would have to suffice. Finger combing the strands gave them some semblance of order.

A sharp knock on the door intruded on her ablutions. *"Die Zeit ist um!"* Schmidt called in his guttural tone.

Time's up. She'd known her peaceful interlude wouldn't last forever, but it had been so delightful to shower and change from the clothes she'd been wearing for a week. The sweatshirt and sweatpants might be a size too big, but the thick fleece would keep her much warmer than her dress slacks and blouse had.

Unlocking the door, she stepped into the hallway, her clothes bundled in her arms.

"Gib mir die Kleider." He held out his hands.

She hesitated, then placed the clothing in them, reluctant to give away a tie to home.

"Zurück ins Zimmer." He shooed her toward the cold, familiar room.

Protesting would only anger her captor, so she shuffled in too large slippers back to her prison. The door clanged shut behind her, but the light stayed on. To her amazement, the room had been transformed in her absence. Sheets and thick blankets covered the bare mattress, now on an iron stand. A small table and chair stood in the opposite corner, while a round rag rug took up most of the open space in between table and bed. On the table lay a stack of books plus a small battery-operated reading light. Tears sprang to her eyes. Somehow she doubted Schmidt had done this—in his every glance, gesture, and tone, he conveyed his displeasure with her—but whoever her benefactor was, she whispered a prayer of thanks.

Feeling like Sara Crewe in *A Little Princess*—one of her favorite childhood books—Lillian examined each of the titles. A book of fairy tales from the Brothers Grimm in German, *The Stasi in East Berlin* by Dr. Henry Silverton, and several recent bestselling novels. The nonfiction book had been written by a local history professor who taught at George Mason University, one of a trilogy of books about East Germany leading up to the fall of the Berlin Wall. She'd start with this one, probably put there to jog her memory about where Greg might have hidden whatever list they were seeking.

Several chapters later, she closed the book, unable to continue as memories of her and Greg's time in West Berlin in the mid-1980s flooded her mind. They had been newlyweds in their mid-twenties, full of life and sure adventure lay around every corner. She'd been a secretary at the US embassy, while Greg had worked for the Central Intelligence Agency under the guise of an embassy employee. How happy they'd been, doing their part to help America win the Cold War. How she still missed Greg, his booming laugh so at odds with his thick glasses and normally serious expression.

He'd once told her he was good at spying because of his ordinary appearance and demeanor. "No one suspects the nerdy, thin guy with glasses." His brown eyes twinkled. "In fact, no one gives me a second glance."

But someone had noticed him, and that had gotten him killed. Hearing Schmidt admit to pulling the trigger on her husband's supposed suicide brought anger flowing through her veins again. She'd have to wrestle it back into a box, tucking it away in her heart until this was over because if she didn't, she'd never make it through her captivity. She stood, then took the Downward Facing Dog yoga position, moving through a series of poses, coupled with deep breathing, to calm her racing heart.

As she held each yoga stance, she couldn't blame Schmidt for his antipathy toward Greg and herself. But Schmidt had crossed the wrong person and exposed himself as someone who sold informa-tion to the highest bidder. Schmidt's loyalty lay only with himself, which made it strange he'd now be working for someone else. Maybe that person had purchased Schmidt's allegiance. Lillian sensed resentment on Schmidt's part for being tasked as her captor. He might have a debt to pay for failure to get the list from Greg thirty years earlier.

The overhead bulb went out, ending her yoga session. The light exercise had reinvigorated her, and she decided to read a little more before bed. She turned on the portable reading lamp, clipping it to the back cover of *The Stasi in East Berlin*. Midway through the book, she bit back a gasp as she read a name she'd never expected to see again. In the chapter on "Ordinary Citizens, Ordinary Spies," she traced the letters of *Marta Bauer* with her finger, then read the rest of the paragraph with close interest. Closing the book, she flicked the lamp's off button and placed both book and light on the table.

Under the covers, warm at night for the first time in days, she repeated the name Marta Bauer over and over again, wishing she could shield Cyrus from finding out who the woman was.

And why her name was important to their family.

CHAPTER

FIFTEEN

October 1987, West Berlin

Lillian twisted her wedding band round and round her finger, ignoring the now-cold cup of coffee sitting on the table before her. The coffeehouse's large picture window afforded her an ideal view of anyone approaching the café's entrance. Thirty minutes late. Did that mean she wasn't coming?

Then a lone woman wearing a multicolored scarf wrapped loosely around her neck veered from the sidewalk to the café door. Once inside, she paused, glanced around with a casualness that appeared practiced to Lillian. The woman smiled and nodded at Lillian before pointing to the counter as if saying she'd join her as soon as she placed her order.

Lillian picked up her own cup and sipped the bitter brew. Normally she didn't drink coffee, but not wanting to draw attention to herself, she'd ordered a cup of the house blend. The woman slid into the seat opposite her, setting down her cup and saucer with a slight tinkle of china. "Relax and smile. Remember we're just friends

115

meeting for a coffee," she hissed in English underneath her bright grin.

Lillian air-kissed the woman's cheeks, murmuring something about good to see her again. She forced her shoulders down and back and put her hands in her lap out of sight. "I was getting worried you weren't coming," Lillian said, affecting an unconcerned expression despite the worry lacing her words.

The other woman waved her hand. "I always come. Sometimes later than expected, but you can't control everything."

"I guess not." Lillian knew exactly what the woman referred to and took a deep breath to banish the shiver wanting to race up her spine. Crossing the border from East to West Berlin wasn't for the faint of heart, even for those officially sanctioned to make the trip.

The woman sipped her steaming coffee. "We don't have much time, so let's talk particulars."

Her words made the endeavor seem more real and less of a dream. Panic seized Lillian by the nape of her neck, its icy fingers squeezing. Could she really take this step?

Something in her expression must have alarmed the other woman, because she laid a hand on Lillian's upper arm. "If you change your mind now, there's no going back. This door will be forever closed to you."

Her tone held a casual inflection, as if they were discussing the weather, but Lillian caught the steel resolve underneath. She'd been over and over this, twisting the information this way and that. There was no other way. They'd thoroughly explored the normal channels and been told it would be impossible. No other options remained. Now Lillian nodded her understanding, and the woman released her arm.

Lillian lifted her cup to resettle her thoughts. Meeting the other woman's eyes, Lillian said, "My husband can never know."

The other woman smiled. "There will never be a question with my paperwork."

Lillian drew in a breath and cast her lot with this woman. "What shall I call you?"

"Marta will do," she said. "Now let's get started."

Isana opened her eyes, blinking away sleep as she turned to see the time on her clock radio, which she preferred to use as an alarm rather than her phone. But instead of the rectangle brown box, a seashell lamp stood on the bedside table. Panic flared as she sat up in bed, taking in the unfamiliar surroundings. Then she sank back as memory returned. Cy had insisted on taking her to his mother's house after stopping by her apartment for an overnight bag, not wanting her to stay by herself after her ordeal.

She'd agreed, mostly because she didn't want to be alone after spending the entire day trapped in the clothing storage room. Now the scent of bacon frying teased her out of bed. After a trip to the bathroom for a shower, Isana emerged dressed and ready to face the day. At least she wouldn't have to face her colleagues just yet. Even though it wasn't her fault, the humility of being locked in a storage room rankled.

"Something smells delicious." She paused in the kitchen doorway.

Cy stood at the stove, a plate of crisp bacon draining on paper towels on the counter beside him. He pointed to the table with a spatula. "Coffee's on the table, and the eggs are about done."

"Thanks." She took a seat, then poured hot coffee from a Chemex pitcher into a Mickey Mouse mug. Stirring in a dash of cream and a spoonful of sugar, she sipped. "Is this Starbucks's Pike Place or house roast?"

"Ah, a woman who knows her Starbucks's blends." He carried the bacon platter and a bowl of fluffy, scrambled eggs to the table. "It's the medium house roast."

"One of my favorites." Her stomach growled.

He raised his eyebrows. "I see I'm feeding you just in time."

She returned his smile, then took his proffered hand as naturally as if she said grace with him over every meal. Listening to him thank God for their night's rest and the food while asking his blessing on their day didn't make her as uncomfortable as it would have several weeks ago.

Cy kept the conversation light while they ate, regaling her with stories from his previous job doing PR for a family-owned zoo in Richmond, Virginia. On her second cup of joe, she brought up the topic of the list. "Did you get the text from Faith about the office being officially closed for the day?"

"Yes. Looks like we have the entire day to ourselves." He cleared the dishes.

She checked the time. Eight-thirty. "Too early to stop by Mrs. Johnston's?"

"By the time we get there, it should be closer to nine. I was going to drop by last night after work." He left the rest unsaid, but Isana shivered with the memory of being locked in the cold room.

"I'll go brush my teeth." She handed him her mug. Their fingers brushed, sending a jolt through her body.

Cy put the mug on the counter, then lightly rubbed his knuckles over her cheek. "I'm glad you're okay."

The intimate gesture sent tingles throughout her body. "Me too. Thanks for rescuing me." Her voice sounded breathless, as if she'd been running. No man had ever looked at her the way Cy was gazing into her eyes.

His hand slid from her cheek to the nape of her neck, gently tangling with her hair. His body shifted closer to hers, bringing a scent of cedar to her nostrils. She could definitely get used to that smell. He dropped his gaze from her eyes to her lips, then back again, a question lingering in their brown depths.

In answer, she swayed toward him, tilting her head slightly as if anticipating the kiss. A slight smile creased the corners of his mouth before he closed the distance between them. His lips met hers, a tentative contract like a butterfly's wings brushing her skin. Then his mouth returned to hers more firmly, yet tender, and she forgot to think at all.

Alarm bells rang in Cy's head as he deepened the kiss. The feel of Isana's lips under his own ignited a fire in his body he needed to get under control before he crossed a line. No kiss had ever impacted him the way this one had. Breaking contact, he rested his forehead against hers, his breath choppy. Her breathing hitched, telling him he wasn't the only one affected by their kiss.

"Is kissing always like this?" Her soft question told him she had very little experience with this kind of mouth-to-mouth encounter.

He cleared his throat to answer. "No."

Her hazel eyes widened, surprise stamped on the lines of her face. "You're sure?"

Cy chuckled. "I'm sure." He took a step back, shoving his hands into the pockets of his jeans. "This was something special."

A faint blush tinged her cheeks with pink. "Oh." Her arms went around her waist.

"Which is why I'm keeping my distance." He most certainly did not want her to think he wasn't interested in kissing her more.

The blush deepened. "I, um, see." A shy smile stole across her lips, still rosy from his mouth. "I think I'd better finish getting ready for our outing."

He didn't stop her when she scurried from the room, needing another minute to wrestle his emotions under control. He'd known he was attracted to Isana, but until their kiss, he hadn't realized how emotionally involved he'd become. But he must keep focused on finding the list, no matter how lovely Isana Thomas was. After finishing the dishes, he brushed his teeth and entered the Johnston's address into his phone's map app. Forty-five minutes to her house, given rush hour traffic conditions.

Fifty minutes later, he turned off Colesville Road onto Franklin Avenue. The mechanized map app voice informed them their destination was on the right. Pulling to the curb in front of number 315, he cut the engine. The home's exterior appeared well-kept but old, the once-white siding now dingy with age. Shrubbery hugged the house, the leaves beginning to awaken after their winter slumber. Cy stared as if mesmerized by the modest house, uncertainty about their intrusion into a woman's grief.

"Shall we?" Isana asked.

He caught what she hadn't voiced. Was he ready to face the widow of a man who'd known his father and who might give him some of the answers he craved?

"Maybe we should pray before knocking on the door."

Her suggestion grounded him, reminding Cy he wasn't in this alone. He reached for her hand and bowed his head, but the words wouldn't come. For a while, he simply gripped her fingers in his.

"God, please be with Cy." Isana's voice grew stronger as the words tumbled out. "You know how much he loves and misses his mother. Please keep her safe. Let us find some answers today that will help us free her. Amen."

"Amen." He squeezed her hand before releasing it.

Her eyes searched his face, then her fingers brushed wetness from his cheek. He hadn't realized he'd been crying. "Ready?"

After scrubbing his face with his handkerchief, he opened his door. "Let's do this." He headed around to help Isana from the car. Together, they climbed the stairs. But before he could knock on the storm door, the inner door opened to reveal a short, slim woman, her silver hair cut into a stylish bob.

"Who are you and what do you want?" the woman said.

"My name is Cyrus Hillam, and this is Isana Thomas. My father was Greg Hillam. I was hoping you could tell me a little bit about him."

The woman regarded him for a long moment, her faded blue eyes steady on his. "May I see some identification?"

Her question startled Cy, but he obligingly held up his driver's license to the storm door glass, which she studied carefully before nodding.

"I'm Cecelia Johnston. Come inside for a cup of tea." Without waiting for an answer, she disappeared into the house.

Cy held the door for Isana, then closed it behind them. The living room held an eclectic mix of chairs grouped in threes and fours. Woven and knitted blankets draped the backs of some, while colorful cushions and pillows graced others.

Mrs. Johnston reappeared with a tray holding a teapot nestled under a cozy—similar to one his mother used regularly—and three cups on saucers, along with a small pitcher presumably holding cream and a bowl with a spoon.

"What an inviting room," Isana said. "All the different styles shouldn't work, but somehow, they do."

Mrs. Johnston smiled as she set the tray on a low coffee table with a ceramic mosaic design on top and along the sides. "My husband and I traveled all over the world because of his work, and in each country, I bought a chair. When he retired, I decided I wanted to enjoy them all, so I ditched the couch and put them all in the living room." She slanted a glance in Isana's direction. "Not everyone appreciates the results."

"It probably wouldn't appeal to those liking things just so, but it makes me wish I'd brought my camera."

"Sit anywhere you'd like." The older woman sank into a brown leather chair with wooden arms.

Isana chose a chair with an embroidered seat and wooden back, while Cy picked one with chrome legs and an oval, fabric-covered seat and back.

Mrs. Johnston poured steaming tea into the cups. "I knew your parents when we were all stationed together for a time in West Berlin."

"When was that?" He accepted the cup and saucer after declining sugar or cream for his tea.

"In the mid-1980s." She stirred sugar into her tea. "My Harold got orders to head to Athens a few months after Greg and Lillian arrived in West Berlin. But we reconnected when Harold and Greg were both stateside in the early 1990s."

Cy sipped his tea, barely tasting it as his mind catalogued the fact Mrs. Johnston was telling him. "Your husband was interviewed by police after my father's death."

"Yes, it was a terrible shock." Her hand trembled, rattling the cup in its saucer. Mrs. Johnston put it on the table. "Harold didn't sleep for weeks afterwards, he was so upset."

"So your husband didn't notice anything different in my dad's demeanor before his death?" He tried not to put too much hope into his question, but he was beginning to think this had been a wasted trip.

"That was what bothered Harold. Something did seem to be troubling Greg, but Harold didn't chalk it up to being suicidal." Her mouth turned down. "Unfortunately, we both have had experience with a loved one taking their own life. Harold was adamant Greg wasn't contemplating killing himself."

"Why makes you so sure?" Isana asked.

"Greg loved Cy and Lillian more than anything in the world. There's no way he would have shot himself at home where you or your mother would find his body. If he wanted to commit suicide, he would have chosen a remote location to spare you both."

Cy heard her words but had couldn't quite comprehend their meaning. Isana spoke again while he wrestled with Mrs. Johnston's meaning with what he knew of his father's death. "Are you saying your husband didn't think Greg killed himself?"

"That's exactly what he told the police afterwards, but no one wanted to hear it." Mrs. Johnston gazed directly into Cy's eyes. "Harold thought Greg had been murdered."

CHAPTER
SIXTEEN

Isana gasped at Mrs. Johnston's words. Whatever they thought Mrs. Johnston could tell them about his father and the mysterious list, she could tell by Cy's raised eyebrows, he hadn't considered this either.

"Murdered?" Cy's voice shook.

Mrs. Johnston nodded. "I know it sounds shocking."

"My mother always believed my father's death had to have been an accident, not suicide, but she'd never breathed a word about suspecting murder. Why did your husband believe someone killed him?"

"Harold and Greg became close during the eighteen months they worked together at the State Department." Mrs. Johnston smiled. "You probably don't remember, but we were guests at your fifth birthday party. My youngest, Amanda, was close to your age, so she was invited to the festivities."

He shook his head. "I remember the turtle cake and playing pin the tail on the donkey, but I don't recall who was there."

"Not surprising, given what happened soon after to your father. At the party, Harold and Greg both seemed preoccupied, whispering together and ignoring the other adult partygoers. It vexed Lillian something fierce. I remember her grousing to me about it."

"Did you ever find out what they were concerned about?" Cy asked.

"I asked my husband about it on the way home, but he shrugged it off as something work-related."

Isana sipped her tea, listening while Cy asked Mrs. Johnston more questions about her husband in the weeks following his father's death, but the older woman recalled nothing else of significance.

"I wish I'd pressed Harold at the time, but shortly after your father's funeral, my mother broke her leg and needed my assistance. I haven't thought about it much since." Mrs. Johnston set down her teacup and saucer, as if putting a period on the end of the entire matter.

"There's no mention of your husband's suspicions in the police report," Cy said.

Mrs. Johnston shrugged. "Maybe whoever he told didn't include it for some reason, but I distinctly remember Harold telling me Greg had been murdered."

"Did he ever follow up?" Cy bit into one of the sugar cookies Mrs. Johnston had brought with the tea.

"I don't know." Mrs. Johnston's expression turned thoughtful. "Harold never mentioned it to me again and, well, as I said, taking care of my mother and our children pushed the entire thing from my mind at the time."

Isana jumped in with a question. "What exactly did your husband do at the State Department?"

"Oh, this and that." Mrs. Johnston smiled, but it didn't quite reach her eyes. "Harold never discussed his work."

"But you must have had some idea," she pressed.

"My husband served his country well. That's all I ever needed to know." Mrs. Johnston stood. "Now if you'll excuse me, I have another appointment."

Isana rose, gathering her coat from the back of a chair. "Thank you for your time, Mrs. Johnston, and please accept our condolences about your husband's death."

"Thank you." The older woman's eyes filled with tears. "I miss him more than I ever did when he was posted to places without me. I think it's because I know he's never walking through the door again."

Isana touched Mrs. Johnston's arm but said nothing. She and Cy walked to the door, saying their goodbyes as they started down the stairs. They'd reached the bottom when Mrs. Johnston called to them to wait through the open storm door.

She disappeared back into the house before they could ask what she meant. "She seemed in a hurry to get us out of the house and now she wants us to wait?" Isana tucked her hands into the pockets of her coat as the late March wind gusted around them.

"Maybe she wants to send us home with cookies. She did get rather prickly when you asked about her husband's job."

"I hope she comes back before I turn into a popsicle."

"I might have an extra scarf in the back seat of the car." Cy pulled his key fob from his pocket. "I can run down and grab it for you."

She glanced back to the house, but Mrs. Johnston hadn't reappeared. Another gust of wind, sharper than before, sliced through her. "If you don't mind, that would be lovely."

"Be back in a jiffy." He started down the sidewalk to the second set of stairs leading to the street. At the top of the stairs, he held his hand toward the vehicle, a soft chirp of the key fob unlocking it floating to her ears as another wind gust stirred up old leaves.

Then the world exploded, sending her tumbling to the sidewalk.

CY SLAMMED INTO THE GROUND, HIS CHEEK STRIKING THE RAILING WHERE IT met the cement steps. Pain radiated throughout his body. On the street below, flames engulfed his car while debris rained onto the asphalt and lawn. Smoke billowed up before the wind sent it flying in all directions. Everything moved in slow and silent motion, as if he viewed the world from underwater. He filled his lungs with air, drawing in smoke from the fire. Coughing, he rolled onto his belly.

Isana! She might be hurt from the blast or flying debris. He pushed himself up on all fours, but the sensation of spinning nearly made him lose his breakfast and the cookies he'd eaten with the tea. Closing his eyes stopped the spinning, but he couldn't see Isana.

Sinking back on his haunches, he pried open his eyes. The world stayed as it should. He was positioned to the right of the stairs. Isana wasn't directly in his line of sight, so he gritted his teeth and moved his head to the left. A wave of dizziness swept over him, then receded like water rushing away from a beach. There! She lay on her side, Mrs. Johnston kneeling beside her.

Cy crawled up the hill and over to them, sure he'd fall over if he stood. All sounds were muted, as if his ears were stuffed full of cotton. Mrs. Johnston glanced his way, her lips moving with no sound.

"Is she okay?" He wasn't sure Mrs. Johnston actually heard him or guessed his question as she pointed to Isana's alert eyes.

Blood smeared across her cheek, and her coat lay bunched underneath her. He touched her cheek, his fingers trembling. "I'm okay," he mouthed slowly.

"Me too." She made a circle motion with her finger and pointed to her head, letting him know why she still rested on the ground. She must feel as dizzy as he did.

He nodded in agreement, then closed his eyes to keep his stomach from heaving its contents all over Isana and Mrs. Johnston.

The flashing red and white lights of a fire truck snagged his attention. He took Isana's hand and held it tight while emergency responders swarmed the scene. EMTs arrived within minutes, separating him and Isana as they tended to their immediate injuries and loaded them into separate ambulances. Cy closed his eyes on the gurney, allowing himself to think the one thought he'd pushed to the back of his mind until he'd known Isana was safe. Someone had planted a bomb in his car while he and Isana sipped tea with Mrs. Johnston.

~

A CAR BOMB. BRENNER LORENZ CURSED UNDER HIS BREATH FLUIDLY IN German and English, not caring who heard him as he strode along the reflecting pond before the Lincoln Memorial. Anger set his shoulders stiff and firmed his jaw. Their mysterious opponent in the hunt for the list had proven to be truly stupid. And dangerous. He'd thought their competition wanted the same thing, the list itself. But now, his miscalculation might have cost the life of the one person who might actually be able to recover the list.

Taking the stone steps two at a time, he entered the memorial. The sharp March wind had driven away the tourists usually haunting Lincoln's feet, making it much easier to spot his quarry. He causally lit a cigarette, ignoring the disdainful glance a young mother with two kids bundled up like Artic explorers threw his way as she hustled her charges out of the memorial. Good, smoking usually drove away any potential listening ears.

Leaning against the wall, he blew out, ignoring the No SMOKING signs. Despite the smoke filling his nostrils, he caught a whiff of Old Spice cologne before the other man spoke from behind him.

"*Wer sind diese Leute?*"

The very question Brenner had been debating himself. "*Ich weiß nicht.*"

The truth that he didn't know wasn't what the other man wanted to hear. Brenner let him vent, then added, still speaking softly in German, "I think they must have also killed Harold Johnston."

"Ah, the car accident was no accident," the other man agreed. "Did the widow give them anything useful?"

"I don't think so." Brenner finished his cigarette, grounding out the butt on the polished marble floor before picking it up and tucking it into his pocket. It didn't pay to leave behind evidence of one's presence. "She did go back into the house but never said or gave them anything after the explosion."

"Has Schmidt been behaving himself with our caged bird?"

Brenner sighed. "As far as I know, he has, but he's not happy about it."

The other man chuckled. "He wants to squish her like a bug, but she's more useful to us alive and being treated well."

Brenner silently filled in what was left unsaid. *For now.* He had no doubt once Lillian Hillam's usefulness came to an end, Schmidt would be allowed to enact his revenge on the woman who had betrayed him. No matter that Schmidt had been playing both sides of the fence for years, he still believed it had been Lillian Hillam who'd outed him to the Stasi. In reality, Lillian had only confirmed what the Stasi already knew about Schmidt, who had been scheduled to be picked up even if Lillian hadn't offered his name as payment.

Schmidt would have been better served had he stopped to think about what Lillian had traded his name for, but that would have required too much thought on the part of a man whose greed had finally given him away. Brenner tuned back into what his contact was saying. Wouldn't do to miss something important.

"If we don't have the list, we can't put our plan into place." The man shifted, keeping to the shadows of Lincoln's knee.

Brenner schooled his face to remain impassive, but inwardly he chuckled at the man's attempts to be unknown to Brenner. As if he hadn't ferreted out the man's identity directly after their first in-person encounter. The other man had no idea Brenner's photographic memory had flipped through thousands of mental images before connecting the shape of the man's head and his posture with a name and face from the distant past. But he'd let the man think Brenner hadn't a clue to his real name and occupation. And why he so badly wanted the list.

"We are getting close," Brenner replied, his voice calm and

measured like always. "The car bomb today showed us the other side is getting desperate."

"Perhaps." The other man took another step deeper into the shadows as a group of Japanese tourists came into the memorial.

"I will check in with Schmidt in person tonight to make sure he understands the plan," Brenner offered. "I've pulled in more men to keep an eye on Mrs. Johnston's movements. If she contacts Isana or Cy again, we'll know about it."

"And put your best men on the pair of them. I don't want anything to happen to either one of them until we have the list safely in hand."

Brenner nodded as the other man faded into the background. He stayed where he was, contemplating the massive statue of the sixteenth president. He pretended not to notice the slim, young woman who had slipped out after the man. She would report back to him where the man went and with whom he spoke. Brenner might be taking orders, but he had long ago learned it paid to know the whole story, not just what was being fed to him directly.

CHAPTER
SEVENTEEN

Isana dragged her eyelids upward. A darkened room greeted her once her eyesight adjusted. A soft beep-beep and a whoosh as a blood pressure cuff tightened around her left upper arm. A hospital room then. At least her hearing had come back after the blast had given her a ringing in her ears, followed by the feeling she was inside bubble wrap that blocked nearly all sounds.

Lying still, not wanting to alert anyone of her wakefulness, she put her memories in order. The visit to Mrs. Johnston. Being cold and Cy offering to get a scarf from his car. He chirped it unlocked, then the ground shook, knocking her off her feet. The car in flames. Debris flying through the air. Something hot striking her right shoulder. The universe spinning out of control. Mrs. Johnston mouthing words she couldn't decipher. Cy crawling toward her, a gash on his fore-head. The firefighters arriving, then the EMTs applying first aid before loading her onto a gurney and taking her to the hospital. After that, things became blurrier.

How long had she been asleep? The shade in the room's lone window was down, blocking out sun or moon. She eased onto the pillow a bit more, her eyes scanning the room. A sink stood near the closed door, a wall mounted TV directly opposite her bed. A wardrobe hugged the left side of another door, presumably to a bathroom.

Sleep claimed her once more. The sound of her door opening penetrated her consciousness, but she didn't have the energy to acknowledge whoever came in. Probably a nurse to check her vitals. When no one approached the bed, she opened her eyes a slit to see a figure standing at the foot of her bed.

"Good, you're awake." The man spoke with a slight accent. German, if she wasn't mistaken. Sounded like her paternal German grandfather's English.

She didn't acknowledge his words.

"No need to pretend sleep now. We have much to discuss." His voice pitched low enough for her to hear but not loud enough to draw the attention of anyone passing the room.

Still, Isana kept silent, having long ago realized the effect not talking had on most people.

"Your boyfriend is running out of time to find the list," he said. "You must impress upon him the danger his mother faces if he does not find it in the next forty-eight hours."

His words broke her resolve, bringing anger to the surface at his implication she and Cy had been twiddling their thumbs instead of doing everything they could to find the blasted list. "We didn't plant a bomb in his car."

"*Wir auch nicht,*" the man said sotto voce.

Neither did we, Isana mentally translated, grateful for her paternal grandparents' insistence she learn German the summers she spent with them on their small farm. Now, however, she didn't let on she understood his aside. Instead, she went on the offensive. "Why are you harassing us? It's only making it more difficult to discover this mysterious list."

The door opened. Isana swiveled her head to see a nurse step into the room, only to lean back out and speak to someone Isana couldn't see. When the nurse came in again, she smiled when she caught sight of Isana. "You're awake. Let's get a little more light in here." The nurse crossed to the window, raising the blind to let in faint rays of sunlight. Isana couldn't discern whether the sun was setting or rising from the sun's position in the sky.

The man had disappeared, probably ducking into the bathroom. Isana should have told the nurse about the visitor, but something held her tongue. The nurse, who introduced herself as Cherry, bustled about the room, checking Isana's vitals, then filling the plastic drink jug with fresh water. "Breakfast will be here shortly."

"Breakfast." Isana frowned. "What time is it?"

The woman checked her watch. "Five-fifteen."

She'd been asleep for nearly fourteen hours. No wonder she felt a bit better. "I came in with someone, Cy Hillam. Is he okay?"

"I can't comment on other patients without their permission, but if you will give me yours, I could pass a message along to him." Cherry winked.

"Just tell him I'm okay," Isana said as Cherry finished her tasks and left with a little wave.

The man stepped out of the bathroom a few seconds after the door closed behind Cherry. "You didn't tell her I was here."

Isana shrugged. "Why are you here?"

"To make sure you're able to complete the task at hand. I suggest you get out of the hospital as soon as possible. Mrs. Hillam doesn't have much time left."

With that parting shot, he slipped from the room. Isana ran through the encounter again. The man had seemed sincere when denying he'd had anything to do with the bombing, which meant there were two factions at play. Were both after the same list? Or was one bent on keeping the list from coming to light?

Her stomach growled, reminding her how hungry she was. Maybe food would clear her head and give her a better path forward. She had to find one, or Cy's mother would pay the ultimate price.

~

"A car bomb?" Gina Sanders pumped her arms as she power-walked down the street. Sweat dotted her forehead but a chill settled over her body at the caller's words. "I wanted them stopped, not killed."

"You were not so squeamish before," the man said. "*Es braucht manchmal eine harte Hand.*"

Gina struggled to translate the man's words. Something about a hard hand. No matter the precise translation. She understood the gist of his comment. "The widow didn't give them anything?"

"No. She merely rehashed what her husband had mentioned long ago about Greg Hillam's death. Old news."

Gina turned into the long driveway leading to home. Time to wrap up the call. "Keep up the good work."

A soft chuckle. "But of course."

She pocketed the burner cell as the house came into view. Mounting the steps, she concentrated on taking several deep, cleansing breaths. In the foyer, she met her husband, his dark business suit and crisp, blue shirt telling her he was on his way to the office. "Hello, darling. Early start this morning?"

"Yes, back-to-back meetings I'm afraid." He bussed her cheek, then patted her arm. "I'll be home for dinner."

"We're dining at the Claytons' tonight."

He grimaced. "I thought we'd rescheduled that."

She smiled. He disliked the couple as much as she did, but the Claytons were a powerful Washington pair you needed on your side. "This is the reschedule. If we cancel again . . . " She left the rest unsaid, knowing he would grasp her meaning.

"Then overcooked roast beef and fake smiles it is."

They shared a conspiratorial glance as Cameron Eaton, Gil's assistant, came into foyer from the front door. "Sir, your car is here."

Gil checked his watch. "I might need to meet you at the Claytons."

"As long as you're not late. Sylvia Clayton is a stickler for guests arriving on time."

He saluted her. "I've been duly warned."

The door closed behind them, leaving Gina alone in the foyer. She deadheaded one of the roses in the large vase centered on the mosaic tile round table, then headed up the stairs to shower and dress for the day. She mentally reviewed her agenda. A luncheon of the Art League of Alexandria at a waterfront restaurant, then a tour of the renovated Torpedo Factory in the heart of Old Towne Alexandria.

Forty-five minutes later, she savored her second cup of coffee while sorting through the personal mail. Maisey Amory took care of the general invitations, bills, and requests generated by Gil's position as vice president of the United States, leaving only a handful of letters for her to read. Her grandmother commanded her presence at her eighty-sixth birthday party in June. Gina set that aside for Maisey to add to their official calendar. A note from the chairwoman of Gina's favorite charity, thanking her for a recent fundraiser. A save-the-date for the wedding of Gil's niece in November. She added that one to the Maisey pile. The final letter bore a Washington, DC, postmark of two days ago. The return address had been smudged, rendering it unreadable.

Gina slit it open and pulled out the single sheet of computer paper.

Grüße *Gina*,

She dropped the letter onto the top of her desk, her fingers tingling as if singed by heat. No need to be alarmed by the German word for greeting. A coincidence, since her mind had been thinking about the time she and Gil spent in West Berlin during the mid-1980s. She returned to the letter.

I'm sure you are surprised to hear from me after our promise to never speak of the matter again. However, recent events have me worried, and I thought it might be good to remind you of our agreement.

The paper shook in Gina's hand so violently, she couldn't read on. Steadying herself, she smoothed the letter on the desk and continued.

Someone is searching for the information only I was privy to and that alarms me greatly. Yours wasn't the only family I helped. You and I both know others will not understand, will misconstrue even, the nobleness of our quest, if the events of yesteryear are made known.

Meet me at eleven a.m. at the butterfly exhibit in the Botanical Gardens. I'll be there every day at that time until you come. We must discuss how to contain this threat to my livelihood and your happiness.

Sincerely,

Marta

Gina refolded the letter, tucking it into its envelope. Then she rummaged in the back of the drawer for her lighter. Rising, she opened a window and held a flame to the envelope. As the flame greedily lapped the paper, she steeled herself for what she must do next. Marta was right. Her happiness did depend on containing the threat.

Cy ran a comb through his hair, glad to be back in his condo after spending the night in the hospital. He and Isana had parted ways at the hospital entrance, agreeing to meet at his mother's house in two hours to continue their search for the list. She'd told him in hushed tones about her early morning visitor. Anger had pulsed in his veins at the audacity of the man to plant a car bomb, then act like it was their fault for not finding the list. Isana hadn't agreed with his assessment the man had tried to kill them, but it was too fantastical to think two different groups of people were after the same mysterious list.

He loaded a cooler with food from his fridge, then met his Uber driver for the trip to Falls Church. Once at his mother's, he scrubbed baking potatoes, wrapped them in foil, and put them in the oven set to start in several hours. Steaks marinated in the fridge and salad fixings rested in the crisper. Dinner preparations finished, he brewed a cup of coffee and carried it to the table to look through her mail.

He'd just sorted the stack into bills, junk mail, and few personal-looking letters to his mother when the doorbell rang.

A smile hovered on his lips as he went to answer it. Instead of Isana, a courier stood on the stoop, his van idling at the curb. "Sign here." He thrusted a tablet at Cy.

Cy scribbled his name with his finger, then accepted a padded envelope. The courier jogged back to his van and climbed in, roaring down the street. Cy started to close the front door when a dark blue sedan pulled up in front of the house and Isana got out of the back. She moved slowly, her muscles likely as stiff as his own after their adventure yesterday.

He waved as she came up the walk.

"How'd you know I was coming?" Her smile did funny things to his insides.

"I didn't." He held out the package. "Had to sign for this delivery."

"Not from Amazon, then?" She joined him on the stoop.

"No. Private courier service." He glanced at the label. "It's from Mrs. Johnston."

"Maybe it's what she wanted to give us yesterday."

His pulse jackknifed as she stepped closer to peer at the envelope, whether from the scent of her floral perfume or from finding out what the package contained, he wasn't sure. "Then we'd better get inside and take a look."

At the kitchen table, he pulled the envelope's open tab before tipping it upside down to pour the contents out on the table. A hardback book thunked down. The orange and gold cover had a rising sun in the bottom fourth.

"*The Pelican Brief* by John Grisham." Isana read the title and author aloud. "Is there a note from Mrs. Johnston?"

He peered into the package. "Yes, it got stuck to the inside." Unfolding the paper, he skimmed the words. "She says she came across this when cleaning out her husband's home office and realized my father had lent it to Harold a couple of weeks before his death. Thought I might like to have it back."

"Was your father a Grisham fan?" Isana paged through the book.

"I don't think so." He frowned, concentrating on his own meager memories of the man. "My mom kept most of his books in the study, so we can check."

Carrying the book, she followed him into the study, its built-in bookshelves spanning three of the four walls. He started at one end and she the other.

"Classic novels over here—the basic Western civ titles," Isana called out.

"Biographies of all kinds here." He noted recent books. "This must be my mom's area, because she loves to read memoirs and biographies."

"Nonfiction on this wall." Isana plucked random books from the shelf, opening them to glance at a page before replacing them. "These must be your dad's, as the publication dates are mostly in the 1980s and relate to the old Soviet Union and other dictator regimes of that era."

"But no spy novels or legal thrillers," he concluded.

"Nothing except this one." She turned the Grisham novel upside down, shaking it violently. "And no hidden pieces of paper stuck inside."

Cy crossed his arms. "There must be something significant about the book if my father had it and gave it to Harold, almost as if for safe keeping."

She opened it. "Let's see what chapter one has to say." She cleared her throat and began to read. She'd only been reading for a few minutes when she stopped.

"Want me to take over?" He reached for the book, but Isana didn't respond immediately, her gaze riveted on the page.

"M."

"What?" He moved closer to peer over her shoulder. Her finger rested on the *m* in the word *freedom.*

"Look at this." She moved her finger and underneath the *m*, a faint pencil dot appeared. "Do you see that dot?"

"Uh huh." He wasn't convinced it meant anything, but she scanned further down the page, turning it before pausing again.

"Here's another one, under an *a*." Their eyes met, excitement shining in hers, trepidation surely showing in his. "Maybe he left a message in the book."

"I'll get a pad and something to write with." He rummaged in the desk and found several sheets of notebook paper, as well as a pen. Dropping into the desk chair, he waited until she sat in a nearby club chair. "Okay, ready."

"M, A."

He dutifully wrote down the two letters, adding an R, T, and A. That was all chapter one revealed, but the faint dots started again on the first page of chapter two. "He must be spelling out one word per chapter."

"I think it's a name. Marta." She looked over his shoulder. "The first letter in chapter two is B."

He started a new word with that letter, then added four more to end up with the name Bauer. "Marta Bauer."

"Chapter three, V." For the next half an hour, Isana worked her way through the chapters, calling out letters as that formed themselves into names.

When she stopped calling out letters, he put the pen down. "Is that it?" He counted the names. "We have nineteen names here."

"No, there's one more." Her eyes met his. "It's L, I, L, L, I, A, N."

Lillian. His mother's first name. "And the last name?"

Pages rustled as she turned to the following chapter. "The first letter is H."

Heart heavy, he jotted down the rest of the letters to form his last name. "Lillian Hillam." Somehow, his mother's name was on this list. If only he could ask her what it meant.

EIGHTEEN

Isana wished she could have shielded Cy from finding out his mother's name was on this list, but they didn't have that luxury. They had to make sure this was the right list before handing it over in exchange for his mother's release. The agony of not knowing whether or not Lillian Hillam still breathed must be killing him.

"We need to figure out the significance of these names." She tapped the list. "I'll Google the first ten, and you do the same with the final ones."

He nodded, but his bleak expression told her his heart wasn't in the chase. She rose and laid a hand on his shoulder. "Cy, we've found the list, but we need to know why these names are on it." She didn't add *including your mother's,* but the words hovered in the air between them anyway.

"I know." He sighed. "I need a fresh cup of coffee."

She trailed him to the kitchen. He punched on the Keurig, then pointed to the oven. "I thought we'd have dinner here tonight."

"Sounds good." She eyed his jerky movements as he inserted a pod. "We'll figure this out and get your mom back safe and sound. You'll see."

"But if her name's on it, why didn't she just give the kidnappers the rest of the names?"

She couldn't answer that. Instead, she selected her own pod of coffee and booted up her laptop, which she had brought along with her. Ten minutes later, they sat opposite each other, steaming mugs at their elbows and their attention fixed on their screens. Marta Bauer turned up numerous hits, so she narrowed the search by adding "1980s" to the name. Still nothing that showed a link between Cy's mother and this woman. She needed to refine the search even more. "Where was the last duty station for your father?"

"West Berlin. They left a couple of months before the Berlin Wall came down in 1989." He smiled. "I was actually born there. At home, if you can believe it."

"Really? Seems unusual your mom would be comfortable giving birth at home in a foreign country." She added "West Berlin" to the search criteria and hit enter.

"My father was in another part of West Germany on a business trip when she went into labor in their apartment. The ambulance didn't make it in time before I came. A midwife was on hand for the actual delivery, and a doctor came by several times in the days that followed, according to my mom. My dad was miffed he'd missed the entire thing—didn't come back until I was a few days old. And back then, she had no way to reach him other than leaving a message at the embassy."

"That's a wild story." She scrolled through the list generated by her latest search. Something caught her eye, a mention of Marta Bauer in *The Stasi in East Berlin* by Dr. Henry Silverton. She jotted it down, noting the author taught at George Mason University in Fairfax, Virginia.

The two worked in silence until the oven timer beeped. Cy rose, stretching his arms above his head and giving her a nice view of his lean torso. Her cheeks heated with the memory of his lips on hers in this very kitchen.

"Time to light the grill for the steaks. Be back in a minute." He disappeared out the back door.

Isana drew her attention away from thoughts of kissing Cy to the name Virginia Sanders, the last one on her list. The first hit Google returned was for the vice president's wife. She nearly scrolled past it when she paused. Wouldn't hurt to read the woman's bio, even though it was preposterous the Second Lady could have some connection to Lillian Hillam and these other women. Not one of the other names on her list had been even remotely famous. From what she could tell, most had lived fairly ordinary lives at a surface glance.

She skimmed through Virginia's early years, her collegiate experience, her marriage to Gilbert Sanders at age twenty-three. Her following her husband on his overseas appointments with the State Department. Then her heart stuttered.

The Sanders's last diplomatic post was in West Berlin from 1985 through 1987. Mrs. Sanders gave birth to their only children, identical twin boys, during their sojourn in West Germany. Lyle and Logan Sanders were born at home during an early snowstorm on October 30, 1987.

There it was. A connection, however tenuous, to Lillian Hillam. The two women's birth stories were very similar.

"Grill's heating." Cy rubbed his hands together. "It's started to drizzle a bit, but the weather app says steadier rain will hold off until after our dinner is cooked."

"Hmm." She stared at the info on the screen, trying to make sense of it all. "Did you finish looking up the names on your list?"

"Yep." He pulled a package of steaks from the fridge. "Three of them are dead. And before you ask, their obits indicated things like cancer and other diseases. Nothing sinister." He wagged a finger at her. "I did jot down contact info for next-of-kin, so we can follow up to be sure."

She grinned. "Good. Anything interesting about the others?"

He removed the plastic wrap and shook salt and pepper onto the steaks. "The only common link between the women was their husbands' service with the State Department."

Her pulse kicked into high gear. "Did it say where they served?"

"Incomplete. We'll have to call to find out, but two of the obits mentioned the husband and wife lived in West Berlin for a time, but no dates." He washed his hands, then picked up the plate holding the steaks. "I'd better get these on the grill."

She tapped her fingers against the table. Other than Lillian and Virginia, she'd also struck out with finding pertinent information on exactly where these women's husbands had served with the State Department. Who did she know at the State Department? Ah, yes. Lena Hoffman, whom she'd met a few weeks ago when taking engagement photos of Lena and her fiancé, Dr. Devlin Mills. A friend of a friend had recommended Isana to the newly engaged couple, who had photographed the friend's bridal portraits as a favor, and Isana had agreed to the photo shoot at the botanical gardens. Lena and Devlin had been thrilled with the results and had been trying to talk Isana into photographing their June wedding. Dialing Lena's number, she hoped the other woman would be able to help them figure out what the connection was before it was too late for Lillian Hillam.

"Hello?"

"Lena? It's Isana Thomas. I'm sorry to call during dinner."

"Hey, Isana. I hope you're calling to say yes to photographing our nuptials."

Isana grimaced at the hopeful note in Lena's voice. "I'm afraid it has to be no." She quickly explained about the wedding dress exhibition. "So I'll be swamped."

"Oh, well." Lena appeared to take the news in stride. "I appreciate your letting me know."

"That's not the only reason I called." Isana gazed out the window at Cy flipping steaks on the gas grill. "I need your help with something."

"I'm all ears."

Isana outlined what they needed. "Any ideas how we can figure out where these couples were stationed from 1985 through 1989?"

"Hmmm, I do know someone in HR, but she's a stickler for following the rules."

Isana heard the hesitation in Lena's voice and hastened to explain further. "I know this sounds cloak-and-dagger, but it truly is a matter of life and death." A sob clogged her throat, and she swallowed before continuing. "Please. I wouldn't ask if it wasn't very important."

"I'll see what I can do. Text me the list of names, both husband and wife."

"Consider it done." Isana ended the call and quickly composed a text with the requested info to Lena, praying she would be able to find the information they needed before time ran out on Cy's mother.

At the sound of the lock rattling on the door, Lillian marked her place in *The Stasi of East Berlin* and rose to her feet. She'd learned it paid to appear composed and in charge no matter the circumstances. Standing when Schmidt delivered her meals or allowed her a bathroom break was her way of telegraphing she wasn't cowed by her captivity.

The door swung inward, but Schmidt didn't step through. Instead, a tall man with a regal bearing and highly polished shoes came inside. Lillian caught a glimpse of Schmidt hovering in the hallway, but the man dismissed his underling with a flick of his hand.

"Your time is running out." His words jogged loose a memory Lillian had forgotten she possessed but she schooled her face into blankness.

"I know you." The scene cleared in her mind like mist retreating from a mountain. "I saw you with Marta."

"Funny you should bring her up." He walked to the table, his fingers lightly grazing the small stack of books. "Did you know she was here?"

"What?" Lillian wasn't sure she'd heard him correctly. Marta in the United States? Surely that couldn't be true.

His cold blue eyes studied her face. "She didn't contact you?"

She shook her head.

"She must have contacted someone because she's dead."

Lillian groped behind her for the chair, sinking down onto it before her legs gave out from the shock. "Dead?"

"She was found in the botanical gardens around noon today with her throat cut."

She raised her hand to her own neck, the image of the vibrant woman she'd known briefly in West Berlin with a scarlet slash so similar to the brightly colored scarfs she always wore filling her mind's eye.

"You really had no idea she was in town." The man paced to the far wall, pivoting on his heel with military precision to face her again.

"No." Her voice sounded weak, like an old woman's, but at that moment, Lillian felt every one of her six decades. She met the man's steely gaze. "Who killed her?"

He didn't answer for so long, she was sure he would ignore the question. Then he approached her, stopping close enough that she caught a whiff of his aftershave. The spicy scent reminded her of Greg, and she lowered her eyes to study the floor, not wanting the man to see the sheen of tears in her eyes. Even after all these years, she missed her husband with an ache that physically hurt.

"Whoever's after the list."

His words brought her head up with a jerk. "But that's you."

"Someone else is sniffing around too, someone who has no compunction about using deadly force."

Fear wrapped its icy fingers around her throat, but she wouldn't let it take over, not when her son was depending on her to keep her wits about her. Drawing in a deep breath and letting it out slowly drove the fear into its cage . . . for now. She took several more controlled breaths before a few more pieces clicked together. "And you haven't a clue who it is."

The man's jaw muscles twitched, telling her she'd hit the nail on the head with her remark.

"You want my help to find out who else is looking." The knowledge of his need tipped the balance slightly in her favor. She might still be a pawn in the man's overall game, but she also held the key to uncovering a dangerous new enemy who could scuttle whatever the man's plan for the list might be. Lillian had had plenty of time to think about why the list was important now, but she suspected whoever was behind Schmidt and this man—his very mannerism spoke of taking orders from someone else—had only learned of the list's existence after all these years. The list must have a powerful name on it, one worthwhile to have in their possession.

Another thought popped into Lillian's mind, one that brought a smile to her lips, and she spoke without considering the consequences. "Your boss hasn't told you the entire story, has he? I wonder why he doesn't trust you."

The man's grin drove the smile from her lips. "Don't join the game if you can't handle the stakes, my dear. You have no idea who you're dealing with."

"Maybe not, but you also need something from me. What is it?" She crossed her arms to project nonchalance, but the man's quirked eyebrow told her he saw through her charade.

"A trip down memory lane." His eyes narrowed. "Schmidt will bring your dinner, then you will tell me all you can remember about your time in West Berlin."

NINETEEN

Cy took the dried platter from Isana. "Thanks for helping with the dishes." He put the daisy patterned oval plate in a cupboard with other serving bowls and platters. With the list in hand, all he had to do was wait for the kidnappers to contact him tomorrow when the deadline came due. In the meantime, he and Isana would find out as much as they could about the names in the hopes they would discover who was behind the attacks on them and his mom.

"It was the least I could do after the yummy meal you just threw together." She playfully flicked the kitchen towel in his direction, parroting his words when he served the grilled steaks, baked potatoes, and tossed salad.

By mutual agreement, during dinner they had discussed everything from the books they enjoyed reading to trips they'd taken and had not once brought up the list. But dishes done, it was time to return to the names.

Isana draped the towel over the oven handle, then retook her seat at the kitchen table, which had become their de facto worktable. He'd set the little-used dining room table for dinner, even lighting tapered candles his mother used mostly for decoration. He thought Mom would have approved of him pulling out all the stops for someone as special as Isana. And she had become special to him in such a short time. To think if his mother hadn't been kidnapped and her phone tossed from a passing car—which is what they'd deduced must have happened—he would never have gotten to know the young woman seated across from him. He doubted he would have ever gotten up the nerve to ask her out at work, not when their paths so seldom crossed.

"I think I know why the list is so valuable." Her words jerked his thoughts back to the problem at hand.

"I'm listening." *And thinking of when I might kiss you again.*

"Virginia Sanders is on the list."

It took him a moment to register where he'd heard the name. "The vice president's wife?"

"Yes."

"Are you sure it's referring to that Virginia Sanders?" He had a hard time believing Virginia and Gilbert Sanders, well-liked on both sides of the aisle and generous supporters of preserving American history, would have any connection to his parents and the rest of the nobodies on the list.

"They were stationed in West Berlin beginning in May 1986 and left in November 1987 shortly after the birth of their twin boys." She nibbled on her bottom lip. "West Berlin's the connection."

His mind whirred with possibilities as Isana continued. "I called someone I know who works for the State Department's translation division. She's asking someone in HR about cross-referencing all the names with the list of embassy staff stationed in West Germany in the mid to late 80s."

"Like my parents were." Frustration nibbled at the edges of patience as he couldn't see what the information meant. "Beyond your hypothesis—and I agree it's the likeliest thread tying them all together—I can't see why being in West Berlin during that time frame would be so important thirty-odd years later."

"I don't either, so I sent an email to the professor who wrote the book mentioning Marta Bauer. Dr. Henry Silverton teaches at George Mason University." She rested her chin on her hand. "Maybe with his expertise about East Germany, he'll give us some insight into what was happening that would help us make sense of all of this."

"If he bothers to get back to you at all." He fisted his hands on top of the table. "We're never going to figure this out before we hand over the list. I'm afraid . . . " He couldn't put into words his greatest fear, that despite their best efforts, his mother wouldn't be coming home.

Isana placed her hand over his fisted one. "I know." Her phone buzzed.

He removed his hand from under hers. "You'd better get that. Maybe it's your State Department friend."

She flipped her phone over to read the text. "No, it's even better."

"What?" He couldn't imagine anything better.

"Dr. Silverton has invited us over for coffee." Her fingers flew over the keyboard. "I included my cell number in my email in case he'd prefer to contact me that way."

"When?" Cy tried not to get his hopes up this history professor would know anything about the names, no matter his expertise.

"Get your coat. He's expecting us in half an hour."

Isana eyed the brick townhome in Old Towne Alexandria, Virginia. "Nice house."

"Being a history professor must pay more than I thought," Cy added. "I looked at a couple of listings in this area before buying my condo but quickly realized it was way out of my price range."

"He's a tenured professor as well as a best-selling author." She'd read the biography listed on Silverton's website to Cy during the Uber ride over.

"I'm trying not to get my hopes up he'll be able to shed any light on these names." He knocked on the door.

The door opened, and a pretty woman about Isana's age stood there, a hand on her round belly. "You must be Cy and Isana. I'm Violet, Henry's wife. Come in."

Isana stepped over the threshold, following Violet's instructions to leave their coats on the tree in the foyer. Their hostess led them to a cozy room at the back of the house with a roaring wood fire. A man sat in a recliner, a knitted afghan on his lap and a pair of crutches on the floor.

"Henry, Cy and Isana have arrived. I'll get the coffee." Violet smiled at her husband, then left.

"Forgive me for not rising to greet you properly," Dr. Henry Silverton said. "I had polio as a child, and sometimes this cold weather makes my legs ache something fierce. My lovely wife insists I rest whenever possible."

"Not a problem." Cy sank onto a loveseat and Isana joined him.

"Thanks for responding to my inquiry so quickly," she said.

"I wish I could say I had good news to share." Dr. Silverton tugged the blanket higher on his lap.

"Here's the coffee." Violet returned with a tray holding four mugs and a French press. After distributing the coffee, she settled into a club chair. "What did I miss?"

"Nothing," her husband assured her. "I knew better than to start without you."

"Good." She sipped her coffee. "Go on then."

"Isana, you asked for information about a woman named Marta Bauer," Dr. Silverton said. "May I ask why you wanted to know about her?"

Isana exchanged a glance with Cy, who nodded. As succinctly as possible, she explained the recent happenings—the kidnapping of Cy's mother, her finding Lillian's phone, the attacks, and the deadline to find the list. "We found what we think is the list of names in a book Cy's father left with a close friend and Marta's was the first one.

We tried internet searches but came up empty for her except for a reference in your book."

Dr. Silverton set down his mug. "There's a lot of information that doesn't make into a book, particularly one trying to accurately portray a particular place in a particular time."

The fire popped, making Isana jump as she willed the professor to continue.

"Does that mean you have more info on Marta than you put into your book?" Cy asked.

"Not exactly." Dr. Silverton glanced at his wife. "My dear, would you mind bringing me my laptop?"

Isana rose before Violet could struggle out of her seat. "I'm happy to get it if you'll tell me where it is."

"Thanks." Violet rubbed her belly. "Only seven more weeks, and one of us will be able to get up faster."

Her words broke some of the tension building in the room, bringing a smile to Cy's face.

"Henry's laptop should be charging on the desk in the study. That's the room next to this one closer to the front door."

Isana found the computer exactly where Violet had indicated. Once Dr. Silverton—who insisted being called Henry—had booted it up, he explained his research methods. "I've developed a network of sources in Germany, including many former citizens and government officials, including Stasi agents. Nothing makes it into my books unless I can verify it by at least two primary sources."

"Which means what you had on Marta Bauer couldn't be corroborated." Disappointment crashed through Isana at the realization Henry wouldn't be able to shed light on their mystery after all. Her head ached. A wall clock told her she'd missed her next dose of over-the-counter pain medication. Isana fished for the ibuprofen bottle in her purse. Downing two of the pills with the last sip of her coffee, she refocused on the conversation.

Henry gestured toward his laptop. "I included Marta Bauer as an example of someone who cooperated with the Stasi by informing on her neighbors. Her name is mentioned in numerous reports."

That part he'd written in his book. Isana hoped Henry had more to share than rehashing one paragraph.

"But what I couldn't corroborate was the rumor of her involvement in the black-market procurement of Western products. Several sources pointed to her as one of the leaders of a black market ring—her travel between East and West Berlin appeared to support such a hypothesis—but I could never find definitive evidence of smuggling."

Cy leaned forward, resting his elbows on his knees. "What black-market stuff do you think she was involved with?"

"The usual things. Basics like soap and food, plus luxury items like Western jeans and makeup."

While Cy questioned Henry more about how the black market operated in East Berlin, Isana puzzled over what impact Marta's black-market involvement would have on the women on the list. In a conversational lull, she asked the question.

"None I can think of," Henry admitted. He hesitated, then shook his head.

"What were you going to say?"

"One of my sources said Marta was involved with something more lucrative than the usual black-market items. I pressed him for details, but he clammed up, claiming he couldn't substantiate it so he'd better not say anything."

"What did you think it related to?" Cy clasped his hands together.

"My instinct says she was smuggling people out of East Berlin." Henry closed his laptop. "I do have a list of letters with Marta's name at the top, but I haven't been able to figure out the what the letters mean. I think it must be initials of people she helped escape, but that's a wild guess on my part."

Cy pulled out his phone. "Were these any of these initials?" He showed Henry his screen. "These are the women we found hidden in the book."

Henry studied the names. "No, none of the letters on my list corresponds with these names."

Violet heaved herself out of the chair. "You all can stay as long as you like, but this pregnant woman is heading to bed."

"We'd better be going too," Cy said.

Isana sprang to her feet. "Let me help you clear the coffee mugs."

"I won't say no to that." Violet grinned as she stacked mugs on the tray. Isana carried it to the kitchen and loaded the mugs into the dishwasher while Violet put the cream and sugar away.

"Thanks for inviting us over." Isana closed the dishwasher. "You have a lovely home."

"It was Henry's bachelor pad before we married last summer. I only added a few touches here and there."

"It's nice." Isana pulled out her phone. "I'll rejoin the men after I line up our ride share for the trip back home."

Violet exited the kitchen while Isana opened the Uber app. After securing a pickup in fifteen minutes, a news bulletin popped up on her notifications screen. The headline caught her attention. "Woman's body found in botanical gardens earlier today identified as German national." The reference to the woman's nationality made Isana tap the link for more info.

Washington—The woman found with her throat slashed earlier today in the US Botanical Gardens has been identified as Marta Bauer, a 69-year-old German citizen here in the US under a work visa.

"Can't find an Uber?" Cy's voice nearly made her drop the phone.

Mutely, she held the device out to him, unable to put into words the shock at seeing Marta Bauer named as a murder victim. His forehead wrinkled in question, but he accepted the phone. Then his eyes widened. "She's dead?"

Isana nodded, her composure slipping.

"This can't be a coincidence." He pulled her into his arms. She sank into his embrace, sudden tears spilling down her cheeks.

"Cy? What's wrong?" Violet's soft voice behind them somehow made Isana cry harder.

Cy moved his hand on her back in circles, murmuring soft words.

"Oh, no." The distress in Violet's verse signaled Cy must have shown her the news article. "I'd better tell Henry."

Her sobs subsided into hiccups, but she didn't stir from Cy's embrace. The security she felt in his arms was like nothing she'd ever encountered. The world outside was going mad, with names from the past haunting the present. She wanted nothing more than to stay in this warm cocoon, safe and secure.

CHAPTER
TWENTY

y brushed a strand of hair from Isana's face. His heart ached at the pain flickered in her eyes before she dropped her gaze. "Hey, you okay?"

She sniffled. "I think so." She focused on his wet shirt front. "I watered your shirt but good."

"Then I don't have to wash it."

His joke brought a ghost of a smile to her lips. Good, she was regaining control. He hated to see her so fragile, but after all they'd been through the past week and a half, no wonder reading about the murder of the woman they'd just been talking about would push her emotions to a boil.

"How about a glass of water?"

She nodded. He found a glass and filled it with cold water from the tap. She downed the entire contents in one, long swallow. "Thanks. Guess I needed hydrating." She put the glass in the dishwasher. "I'm usually not such a crier."

"I think you've held up remarkably well under the circumstances. It has been a trying week or so."

"Not every day you nearly get bombed, I'll give you that." She sighed. "What are we going to do? Our best lead just got herself murdered."

"Which might not be as dire as you think." Henry moved a little stiffly on his crutches into the kitchen. After sinking onto a bar stool, he slipped his arms free of the cuffs and hooked the crutch handles over a curved piece of wood that appeared to be specially designed for the job.

Cy wasn't sure what the professor meant but figured he'd expound. In his experience, most academics had no trouble filling empty space.

"Because now people might be more willing to talk?" Isana guessed.

"In a way," Henry agreed. "The reason the Stasi were so successful was because they infiltrated every society institution and aspect of daily life, including personal and familial relationships. They were able to attain this goal through their agents, who comprised 1 percent of the workforce in East Germany, and through a huge network of informants and unofficial collaborators who informed on colleagues, friends, neighbors, and family. By the fall of the Berlin Wall, the Stasi relied on 500,000 to two million such informants and maintained files on approximately six million East Germans—more than a third of the population."

Cy digested the facts, delivered in what he privately dubbed Henry's professorial voice, and wondered the connection to Marta Bauer's death.

"Now dear, don't go all history professor on them," Violet teased as she joined them. "Cy and Isana don't need to know the entirety of your knowledge of the Stasi."

Henry pressed his wife's hand to his lips. "In other words, cut to the chase?"

Violet grinned. "Yes."

Cy snuck a look at Isana, where she stood looking at their hosts. The lines on her face had softened, as if she too had been touched by the tender exchange between husband and wife. A longing to have someone to love as deeply as Henry and Violet flooded his senses. This time, he couldn't stuff it back into a box to examine after his mother's return because the accompanying emotions refused to cooperate. Ducking his head, he drew in several deep breaths. He had to stay strong for his mother's sake. She was depending on him to deliver the list to secure her release. The clock ticked ever closer to the deadline. He had no time to contemplate a future with the lovely Ms. Thomas, not when his own was so uncertain.

"Perhaps I can persuade some sources to talk more openly about Marta's dealings now that she's dead," Henry said. "I'll send some emails tonight and might hear back by morning, given Germany is six hours ahead of us."

"Thank you." Some of the tension left Cy's shoulders, but he still didn't feel Marta's murder would bring the break they needed. "We appreciate it."

"Our Uber driver is a minute away," Isana said.

"Thank you again." Cy shook Henry's hand while Violet gave Isana a hug.

"I'll walk them out," Violet said. "You go send those emails."

At the front door, Violet said, "I know it seems dark now, but the truth will come out."

Cy appreciated her optimism but couldn't bring himself to fully embrace it. "I pray it will." His mother's life depended on it.

West Berlin, June 3, 1988, 10 p.m.

LILLIAN RESISTED THE URGE TO CHECK HER WATCH, KNOWING ONLY A FEW minutes had passed since her last peak. Marta was late like usual. In the eight months since she'd met the woman, Marta had never been on time. Lillian always arrived at their meeting spot early, worried she'd miss the woman, and thus ended up a basket of nerves by the time Marta strolled into view. This time, though, Marta would be arriving at her apartment for the final leg in their journey together.

She marveled at the other woman's colorful appearance, her bright clothes and accessories making her easy to spot. Today would be the day, the time when her life would never be the same. Could she really pull it off? She'd fooled everyone, including her husband. It helped that his work kept him at the office early and late, so they'd hardly seen each other these last few months. Lillian shifted on the hard kitchen chair, her back aching from the added weight around her middle. Pretending to be pregnant had been easier than she'd anticipated. Even her husband hadn't realized the growing belly was a round rubber ball hidden under a corset-like body suit. Of course, with his long office hours, he rarely had time for a meal with her, so he wouldn't notice she'd stopped undressing in front of him. No one questioned her news.

Greg's look of pure joy at the news had made her elaborate deception seem worth it. He'd even rubbed her stomach as it grew, not realizing a baby wasn't inside her womb. With Greg on a several-day assignment, the time had come for her to give birth, so to speak. Lillian had everything ready as instructed. Soon she'd have her bundle of joy, and all the sneaking around and lies would be worth it.

The knock at the door startled her. Rising, she peered through the peephole. Marta stood there alone. Disappointment crushed her. It wouldn't be tonight after all. Marta rapped again.

With a heavy heart, Lillian opened the door. "*Guten abend,* Marta."

"Lillian, you're looking well." Marta kissed both of Lillian's cheeks in greeting as she entered the apartment. "Pregnancy agrees with you."

"Where's the—?"

Marta cut her off with a downward slash of her hand. "Hush now. All is in readiness. Trust me. You have everything from the list?"

"Yes." Confusion and anxiety swirled together. This wasn't at all how Lillian pictured the evening progressing.

"Show me."

Lillian did. Marta nodded her approval, smiling a little to herself. Tour finished, Marta indicated they should sit in the kitchen. Once Lillian had taken a chair, the other woman said, "Let me make you some tea. I brought a special blend to calm your nerves. I can tell you're jumpy."

"I can do it." Lillian started to rise, but Marta shooed her back down.

"I know my way around a kitchen." For a few minutes, the only sounds came from of Marta heating water in the electric kettle and pouring the steaming water into a mug. "Here you go. I added some honey, as it can be a little bitter."

Lillian cupped her hands around the mug, the heat warming her chilled fingers. "Thank you."

Marta waved a hand in dismissal. "*Es war nichts.* Drink up." Her eyes never left Lillian's face.

The staring made Lillian uncomfortable, so she lifted the mug and sipped. The brew was indeed bitter, although she could detect the sweetness of honey.

Marta chuckled. "Bitter, yes? But necessary for our plan."

Their plan. The one the two of them had spent months putting together, turning over to ensure nothing had been left to chance. "I don't understand." Lillian took another drink, as a warm feeling spread over her body. "I thought—"

"All in good time. Finish your tea."

Obediently, Lillian raised the mug to her lips and gulped the cooling liquid. Her vision blurred slightly, and her hand holding the mug dipped. Marta rescued the cup before it tipped onto the table.

"What did you put in the tea?" Lillian managed to ask as the world spun. She fought the urge to close her eyes but knew she would lose that battle soon.

"A little something to help you relax." Marta soothed her. "Come on, let's get you to bed."

Lillian was powerless to stop the other woman from lifting her out of the chair and guiding her down the hall to her bedroom. Marta sat her on the side of the bed and removed her shoes. The last thought Lillian had before her eyes slid shut was she shouldn't have trusted an East Berliner.

Isana pried her eyes open enough to check the time on her phone. 6:18 a.m. At least she'd gotten a few hours of sleep, although not as long as she'd hoped. After the Uber had dropped her at her apartment, she'd been unable to unwind. Worry about Cy and his mother, the wedding exhibition at work, and her own bumps and bruises had contributed to a restless night. Sleep hadn't claimed her until after one, and this morning, her body was sluggish. She needed another eight hours of solid sleep, but that wouldn't happen today.

Her phone buzzed. Cy's name flashed on the screen. Her heart racing, hoping he didn't have bad news, she picked up the call. "Hello?"

"Isana." Cy's voice broke.

Her heart sank. *Dear God, don't let it be bad news.* "I'm here."

"It's . . ."

She tossed back the covers and hustled to her dresser. Whatever had happened, Cy would need her there as soon as possible. She slithered out of her pajama bottoms and into a pair of jeans.

"It's my mother," Cy finally said.

She froze, unable to tell from his tone whether the news was bad or worse. "What happened?"

"She's . . ." He drew in a breath, letting it out in a whoosh. "She's in the hospital."

TWENTY-ONE

Hospital?" Isana sank onto the bed, socks in hand. "Is she okay?"

"I don't know."

The despair in his voice made her want to hug him. "Where?"

"Georgetown. I'm on my way there. She was brought in several hours ago. I don't know anything else, but apparently her condition warranted a check with the police, who found the missing person report I'd filed and called me."

"I'll meet you in the emergency department." She tugged on her socks. "Do you need anything?"

"Just your prayers."

"Hang in there and I'll see you soon." She disconnected. Closing her eyes, she prayed for the first time in a very long time. *Please God, keep Cy's mom safe.*

Forty minutes later, she entered the emergency department at Georgetown Hospital, juggling two to-go cups of coffee and a bag of breakfast sandwiches. Scanning the waiting area, her shoulders sagged when she didn't spot Cy.

She found an empty seat next to an end table and set down the coffee and bag just as her phone buzzed. A text from Cy brought a smile to her face.

Are you here?

Just arrived in waiting area.

I'm with the doctor. Be out as soon as I can.

See you soon.

At least neither one had to report into work, as the investigation into the security breach was taking longer than anticipated. The museum director, on the advice of The Heritage's governing board, had decided to close the museum for the remainder of the week. Without access to their work email or files, it created a de facto holiday for them. While Isana shuddered at the work piling up related to the special exhibit, she was glad to have the time to focus on helping Cy.

Sipping her coffee, she once again found herself praying for Lillian Hillam's full recovery. Her mind spun with questions. Had her captors released her? Had she escaped? How badly was she hurt? Would Lillian provide the answers to who the women on the list were?

"Isana."

In her introspection, she hadn't noticed Cy's approach. He dropped into the chair catty corner to her, his expression haggard.

"I brought you coffee and breakfast." She pointed to the cup, then extracted an egg-and-sausage biscuit for him before taking the second one for herself. "You look done in."

"I didn't sleep much last night." He took a small sip of java before unwrapping the sandwich. "Thanks for bringing this."

"Why don't we eat while the sandwiches are still warm, then you can update me on your mom."

He nodded, his mouth already full of biscuit. For the next few minutes, they sat in silence while the busy emergency department traffic flowed around them. Sandwiches finished, Cy sat back in his chair, coffee cup in hand.

Isana brushed the crumbs from her fingers and gathered the wrappers to stuff into the sack. She drank more coffee while she waited for him to tell her what happened.

"About five this morning, a dog walker found my mom lying on the sidewalk on Carrollsburg Place SW, near Nationals Park. She . . ." His voice broke. "She had no shoes and had been badly beaten."

"Oh, Cy." She touched his hand where it lay clenched in a fist on his knee. "How is she?"

He scrubbed a hand over his face, brushing away tears. "I don't know. There's swelling in her brain from several blows to the head with a blunt object. She has cracked ribs, a broken hand, and bruises all over. Her feet are a mess of lacerations."

"But she's alive." She spoke the words quietly but firmly.

"Yes." He tilted his head to look at the ceiling, blinking away more tears, she suspected, given the sheen she'd glimpsed in his eyes. "She's in a drug-induced coma. The doctors are hopeful the brain swelling will dissipate on its own."

"How long will they keep her in a coma?"

"At least twenty-four hours, then they'll assess the situation and see if the swelling has gone down enough to bring her out of it." His bleak gaze nearly broke her heart. "I don't understand. She wasn't supposed to be hurt. We were to exchange the list for her later today. Why did they have to hurt her?"

"I don't know." She nibbled her bottom lip. "But with the office closed today, that gives us more time to figure out who these women are and what their connection is."

"I don't think we need to keep digging." He ran a hand through his hair. "It's over."

"Someone hurt your mother," she pointed out. "Don't you want to find out who that was?"

"The police have all the information. Let them figure it out." He avoided her gaze, his eyes fixed on the floral carpet.

His words didn't make sense. She thought he was as invested in the hunt for the truth about the list as she was. "But we've made such progress. Don't you want to know why her name was on the list? And what that list means?"

He raised his head, the bleakness in his eyes telling her his decision. "I can't. I've got my mom back, and that's all that matters."

"I see." She leaned toward him, anger mingling with hurt at the dismissal in his tone. "Getting shot at and having your car blown to bits wasn't compelling enough evidence someone didn't want us to find the list, let alone investigate those names."

"When we needed answers to find my mom, it made sense to proceed. But now . . .. I appreciate your help, but you don't have to wait with me."

Isana lurched to her feet, overturning her empty coffee cup on the end table in her haste. After stuffing the cup into the bag with the sandwich wrappers, she paused, then plunged in with the question burning a hole in her heart. "Was it all an act to get my help with your mom's disappearance?"

"Isana," he began, regret lacing his words and piercing her heart, "you're a special woman, but I think in the stressful circumstances, we might have rushed things a little."

"Is that really what you think?" She blinked back tears at his noncommittal answer.

"Listen, I can't talk about that right now, not with my mom lying in a coma." He fiddled with his phone. "Maybe I can call you later."

She straightened. Once again, her mom's words spoken when Isana was a young teen rang true. *No one wants you. Don't you ever forget that.* "Sure." Without another word, she whirled and walked as fast as she could to the exit. Once outside, the wind gust swirled dead leaves leftover from the fall while the air held a hint of the spring yet to come. But not in her own heart. Winter had returned with a vengeance when she'd hoped spring was on the horizon.

~

Cy gripped the arms of the chair hard to keep himself from following Isana out of the waiting room. The devastated expression in her lovely eyes nearly made him blurt out he didn't mean it, that he needed her to stop researching the list to protect her and his mother.

But he held his tongue and his seat until the sliding glass doors closed behind her. His shoulders slumped, pulling his body forward. He'd done all he could to keep Isana and his mother safe.

His mother's words to him replayed in his mind like a revolving door. "Danger. The list. Stop. Don't want you hurt. Keep silent." The words no one knew Lillian had spoken in the ten minutes he'd had alone with her before the MRI showed her brain swelling and the medical team deemed a coma would help reverse the injury.

Her pleading look had compelled him to obey, even if that meant pushing away the woman he cared about. Isana's dark, silky hair and slim figure flashed across his mind. She'd understand why, once he could tell her, wouldn't she? *Please God, let her forgive him.*

"Cyrus Hillam, please report to the check-in desk."

Cy started at hearing his name over the intercom system.

"Cyrus Hillam, please report to the check in desk," the message repeated. He tossed his empty coffee cup into a trash can as he made his way to the reception area. A young man wearing suspenders over his white dress shirt motioned him over. "How can I help you, sir?"

"I heard my name being paged. Cyrus Hillam." Cy waited while the receptionist checked his computer.

"Please step over to see one of the greeters in the blue blazers." The receptionist pointed to the right where a group of people in navy jackets directed visitors and handed out passes.

"Thank you." Cy made his way to the area, stopping to give his name to a volunteer.

"Right his way, sir." The elderly woman briskly walked toward the double doors leading into the patient area.

Cy hustled to keep up, catching her as she used her badge to open the doors. Once through, she led him down a short hallway away from the patient cubicles. Halfway down, she stopped at a closed door, knocked once, then opened it. "Here's Cyrus Hillam, as requested."

Cy stepped through the door and into small waiting room with a loveseat and two chairs, A coffee table took up the middle of the floor. A man and a woman rose as he entered. "Thank you for coming, Mr. Hillam." The woman extended her hand. "I'm Detective Kniper, and this is Detective Wynn."

Cy studied their badges, then sat on the loveseat. "Are you investigating the attack on my mother?" He'd already spoken briefly to a uniformed DC Metropolitan police office after his arrival at the hospital. "Do you have a suspect?"

Kniper retook her chair. "We're not investigating your mother's attack. Did Mrs. Hillam ever mention a woman named Marta Bauer?"

Cy probably didn't do a very good job of keeping the shock off his face. "The German national murdered in the botanical gardens?"

"Your mother did mention her?" Wynn's gaze sharpened on Cy's face.

"No, she didn't. I read about the murder online."

Disappointment flashed in the male detective's eyes before he masked it.

"How is your mother?" Kniper asked. "We're sorry to hear about her being attacked."

"She's in a medically-induced coma because someone hit her several times on the head with a blunt object. She also has cuts and abrasions on her feet, several broken ribs, and six bones broken in her right hand." Cy didn't know why the two wanted to question him about a dead woman he hadn't known, but it was obvious they were after something. He couldn't reveal the reason behind his mother's attack, so he must tread carefully. "If you're not here about my mother's assault, get to the point because I need to get back to her bedside."

For a moment, Cy thought the detectives would refuse to answer. Then the female gave a small nod. Wynn said, "Marta Bauer had a piece of paper under the lining of her shoe with your mother's name and address on it."

"What?" Confusion vied with shock at the detective's statement. "I don't understand."

"You're sure your mother never mentioned Marta Bauer to you?" Kniper pressed as she stared straight at Cy, her directness disconcerting.

He replied in the negative a second time, then asked a question of his own. "Who exactly is Marta Bauer?"

"As the media has reported, she's a German citizen here on a tourist visa," Wynn said. "We'd appreciate it if you would ask your mother about Bauer."

Cy blinked back sudden tears as the seriousness of his mother's condition hit home at the detective's simple request. "Her head injuries appear severe, and the doctors can't assess any brain damage until she's awake." He left unsaid the possibility she might never wake up.

"I'm sorry to hear her condition is that serious." Kniper handed Cy a business card. "Please call me when she's able to talk."

He stood and tucked the card into his wallet. "I will. Now if you'll excuse me, I want to go sit with my mom for a while." Without waiting for a reply, he strode off in the direction of the elevators that would take him to the ICU where his mother lay fighting for her life. As the floors flashed by, the thought that Marta Bauer's presence in the area might have directly contributed to his mother's attack wouldn't leave his mind. But what did the woman who probably helped East Germans escape to the West have to do with his mother?

CHAPTER
TWENTY-TWO

Brenner drew on his cigarette, letting the nicotine calm his anger. He shouldn't have relied on Schmidt, knowing how the man hated Lillian Hillam for giving his name to the Stasi all those years ago. The Stasi had known Schmidt was a double agent and had used him to pass along useless information to the enemy. But when Lillian gave his name, it forced their hand.

Stupid man had simply bided his time to make his move until Brenner was preoccupied with the murder of Marta Bauer. Brenner had returned in the early hours of the morning to find Schmidt drunk and bruised and Lillian missing. Leaving the other man, he'd followed Lillian's flight path, but an ambulance's flashing lights told him he was too late.

Grounding out the butt, he pocketed it before re-entering the house. His stomach clenched at the smell of vomit. At the kitchen table, Schmidt sat bleary-eyed, evidence of a recent embrace of the toilet on his rumpled shirt.

"Ah, good. You're awake." Brenner leaned against the counter. "Ready to tell me what happened?"

Schmidt swiped the back of his hand across his mouth. "Nothing to tell."

"Then where's the prisoner?"

The other man's eyes dropped to the table. "Don't know."

"*Du idiot.*" Brenner sighed. "Do you know what you've done?"

"Regained my honor with the *Verräterin.*" Schmidt pointed a finger at Brenner's chest. "You treated her like a queen when she was nothing but *schmutz.*"

Of course, Schmidt would think Lillian was dirt. He thought she'd unveiled his double life to the Stasi. "You're the betrayer."

Schmidt mumbled something Brenner couldn't distinguish. His anger flared again at the man's insolence. "You think we knew nothing of your double dealings until Lillian Hillam uttered your name?"

His question brought Schmidt's head up, surprise evident in his wide eyes.

Brenner smiled. "Oh, yes, we knew. We knew you were passing along secrets to the enemy. We'd known about it for years. We just made sure you passed along the *right* information. We were already getting tired of your games and had a plan in place for your retirement. All Lillian Hillam did was speed up the timetable."

Schmidt's mouth dropped open. "But . . . " he spluttered.

"Enough of the past." Brenner silenced him with a slash of his hand. "I repeat—what happened here tonight?"

The other man's jaw tightened. "She mouthed off, so I hit her."

Brenner held onto his temper with a Herculean effort. "You did more than hit her. She was found with her head bashed in from several blows."

Schmidt's eyes widened. "I didn't do that! I only slapped her lying mouth."

"Then who did this to you?" Brenner gestured to the bruises forming on the man's head and his torn, bloody shirt.

"I don't know. Someone jumped me from behind, knocked me

out." Schmidt's hand went to the back of his head. "The last thing I remember is hearing her scream."

"Don't step foot outside this house until I return. That's a direct order." Brenner didn't wait for Schmidt's acknowledgement. The man was in no shape to stand, let alone leave. He exited the building, turning his collar up against the wind that brought hints of spring but still the bite of winter. Inside his car with the engine running and the heat on full blast, he punched in a number on a burner phone.

"We have a problem," he said when the other man answered.

A string of expletives was the only reply. Brenner let the man vent, then said into the silence, "It wasn't our man. Someone found out where we were holding the woman and attacked them both."

"Will the woman live?"

"My source says she's in a medically induced coma for at least twenty-four hours to see if the swelling in her brain resolves. Her prognosis is fifty-fifty at this point."

"Keep me informed."

"Sir?" Brenner interjected before the man could disconnect.

"What is it now?"

Brenner ignored the impatience in the other man's tone. "I think I know who's been working against us."

"I'm listening."

When Brenner gave the name, the other man stayed quiet for so long, he checked the call to make sure he hadn't hung up.

"That is very interesting indeed. How sure are you?"

"Eighty percent."

"For now, keep an eye on the woman. And take care of Schmidt. His usefulness is at an end."

Brenner grimaced, then dialed another number. "I have a job for you," he said when the other man answered.

After laying out exactly what he wanted, he pocketed the phone and pulled away from the curb. In a matter of hours, any evidence Lillian Hillam had been held against her will at that location would be erased.

~

Isana moved the wet sheets to the dryer and inserted the requisite number of quarters. Living in an older building meant a shared laundry on every other floor. Thank goodness her apartment was on the floor with those facilities at the opposite end. She set the timer on her phone and returned to her condo. She'd have to do her wash in the middle of the week more often, since everyone else was at work and all six washers and dryers sat empty.

10:38. The morning hours had crept by with the speed of a snail since she'd left the hospital. Her heart ached at the silence from Cy. Even her text asking how his mother was doing had gone unanswered. She berated herself for hoping he had liked her, not just used her to rescue his mother. Men like Cy didn't commit to women like her. How could she have forgotten the mantra her mother had screamed at her growing up? That she came from trash, and she'd always be trash, and the sooner she'd realize that, the better. That no one would want her.

She rested her forehead on the kitchen table as the hateful words replayed in her mind like a song on an endless loop. Stupid to think this time would be any different. Raising her head, her fingers touched her lips as the memory of their kiss clawed its way through the words. His mouth on hers had made her believe his feelings matched her own, but of course, that was because she'd had so few kisses in her life to compare. She would assign more meaning to a lip lock than most people her age. But she wouldn't let Cy's actions and words this morning mar the beauty of that embrace. She'd tuck it away to remember on the lonely nights to come.

"You are worthy of God's love." The words from the church service she'd attended with Cy filled her mind. She'd never felt worthy of anything, but hearing those words had touched something deep in her heart. She might not be worthy of Cy's love, but she was of God's. She reached for her phone and opened the Bible app to search for the passage the pastor had read. Finding Ephesians 2, she read from the beginning. Verses four and five stopped her cold. *But God, being rich in mercy, because of the great love with which he loved us, even when we were dead in our trespasses, made us alive together with Christ—by grace you have been saved.*

The thought God would make her alive because of Christ washed over her, easing the ache of her mother's words and Cy's withdrawal. Maybe there was something to this life in Christ after all. She bowed her head and prayed for herself, for Cy, for his mother's recovery, and for them to find the truth.

Her heartache eased, and she rose with purpose. After putting the kettle on to brew a cup of tea to lift her spirits, she fired up her laptop and spent the next hour working on her wedding dress exhibition to-do list. While she couldn't access the files or work email, she could plan out how she was going to get everything ready in time for a June opening.

Satisfied she'd done all she could, she checked her personal email. Amidst the junk, she found one from Lena.

Hey, Isana. My friend in HR came through. She verified all the people on the list except for Marta Bauer were stationed—with a spouse or by themselves—in West Berlin sometime between 1985 and 1989. I've attached the list with dates. Hope this helps, Lena.

She opened the attachment, skimming the list of names with dates. It merely confirmed their suspicions the connection was West Berlin. But not how were they connected to Marta Bauer, a suspected procurer of black-market goods or possible exit from East Berlin. Had any of the women acquired a maid or personal assistant during their time in West Germany? Perhaps Marta funneled escapees to these women's households.

She read through the list from Lena's friend again slowly. In addition to all the dates, there was a set of letters—perhaps an abbreviation—she didn't recognize after each name. RBWG.

Maybe Lena would be able to shed some light on what those meant. Twelve-fifteen. A quick text confirmed Lena's availability to meet at a café near the State Department building in thirty minutes.

Lena waved from a corner table when Isana arrived. She joined her friend, draping her winter coat over the back of the chair. "Brrr. I thought spring was coming, but it's not going to hit forty today."

"That's March in DC for you," Lena returned. "I went ahead and ordered the quiche and soup special for myself, as I'm on a tight deadline at work and need to get back by one-thirty."

"No problem."

A waiter approached the table, setting down two glasses of water. "I'll have the quiche and soup special as well," Isana ordered. After the waiter departed, she jumped right into her questions. "Thanks again for the confirmation about the names being in West Berlin in the mid-1980s. There's a notation next to all of them I can't interpret. The initials RBWG. I tried Google, but none of the suggestions made any sense given the West Germany context."

"When in doubt, phone a friend. Or text, in this case." Lena pulled out her phone, her thumbs flying over the screen. "I asked my source what those letters mean."

The waiter returned with their dishes. "Guess ordering the special meant you didn't have to wait," Lena said.

The two dug into the savory bacon-and-mushroom quiche and piping hot tomato soup.

"How are things going with Cy?" Lena wiped her mouth, a gleam in her eye.

Isana regretted telling Lena she liked her colleague. "I thought well, but he basically told me that since his mother's in the hospital, he's done with the entire thing."

"What?" Lena speared a bite of quiche. "Tell me everything."

Isana hesitated, unsure about how much to say. But Lena was engaged, so maybe she'd have insight into male behavior that could shed light on Cy's. While they two finished their lunch, she poured out the entire story.

Lena scraped a spoonful of soup. "I think he's scared."

"Scared? Of what?" Isana didn't agree with her friend's assessment of the situation. Cy hadn't seemed scared but determined.

"Of you getting hurt. Or his mother." Lena leaned forward, her eyes intent on Isana. "Are you sure his mom didn't tell him something?"

"His mom's in a coma."

"A medically induced coma. Perhaps she told him something before, and he thinks by continuing with this search, he will put you in even more danger."

"What could be more dangerous than getting shot at and having his car blown up?" Isana stabbed her last bite of quiche. "I think he used me to rescue his mom, and now that she doesn't need rescuing anymore, he's cutting his losses."

"I think you have it the wrong way round."

The waiter cleared the dishes and left separate checks, telling them to pay at the cashier on the way out. Shrugging into her coat, Lena stood, receipt in hand. "I'll let you know when my friend answers about the letters."

Isana gathered her own belongings, her heart once again heavy with hurt. Back outside in the sunshine, she buttoned her coat against the stiff breeze and headed to the nearest Metro station. Lena might believe Cy didn't mean his harsh words, but Isana knew better. As her mother had repeatedly told her, Isana would never be the girl who got the guy.

CHAPTER

TWENTY-THREE

Cy held his mother's hand while machines beeped and whirred in a medical symphony, trying to formulate a prayer. *Please heal her. Please heal her.* He couldn't get beyond the heartfelt words.

Rae wheeled in a computer cart. "You should go home and get some rest." The nurse checked Lillian's vitals and recording the info in the electronic chart. "The doctor requested we start stepping down the sedative to bring her out of the coma."

"That's good news, right?" His mother's pale skin underneath the darkening bruises and abrasions attested to her fragile condition.

"It is indeed."

Cy turned toward the door where a woman in a lab coat, stethoscope around her neck, rubbed sanitizer into her hands. "I'm Doctor Jipping, one of the staff neurologists. Your mother's condition is improving, although she probably looks worse due to the bruising. Her four o'clock CT scan showed less severe brain swelling than originally indicated. As Rae said, we will be decreasing the amount of thiopental overnight to bring her out of the coma by morning. Our hope is that as the drug leaves her system completely early tomorrow morning, she'll wake up on her own."

Dr. Jipping checked Lillian over and answered the handful of questions Cy had about her prognosis. "If all goes as planned, we'll be moving her out of the ICU in the afternoon."

Relief coursed through Cy. His mother would be okay. Perhaps the danger was past. He rubbed the back of his neck, stiff from slouching in the guest chair. "Thank you, doctor."

"My advice is to go home, get some sleep and food, and come back in the morning." The doctor nodded to the nurse and Cy, then left the room.

"Maybe I'll grab something to eat in the cafeteria." While his body ached for rest in his comfortable bed, his mother's warning echoed in his mind. No way was he leaving his mother alone for long, not when someone had tried to kill her.

"Stay away from the meatloaf, but the Salisbury steak is surprisingly good." Rae entered more data into her computer. "Shift change will happen while you're gone, so I'll see you in the morning."

"Who will be my mom's night nurse?" It was hard to keep track of all the comings and goings of nurses, doctors, and other hospital personnel.

"Adrian's on the schedule." The nurse pushed the cart toward the door. "Take the doctor's advice and go home to sleep. Your mom won't wake up while you're out."

"I'll consider it." He followed her out of the room, then took the elevator to the first-floor cafeteria for dinner. While worry continued to zap his appetite, he managed to eat most of the food.

Back on the ICU floor, he noted new faces in the nurses' area and checked the wall clock. Six-thirty. He stopped outside his mom's door. Perhaps he would check on her, then head home for the night. Weariness pummeled every inch of his body. He pushed open the door. A figure stood by her bedside, a syringe poised above the IV catheter. Cy clocked the man's navy-blue scrubs, similar in style to the other nurses. The lower half of his face was hidden by a mask.

The man didn't turn at Cy's entrance, but something prompted Cy to speak up. "What are you doing?" He modulated his tone to sound curious and not accusatory. He didn't want the man to make any sudden moves, not when he had no idea what liquid resided inside the syringe.

The man turned, drawing the gloved hand holding the needle away from the tubing. "I'm Connor with the night shift. Just topping off the patient's sedative. Wouldn't want her waking up prematurely."

An alarm clanged in Cy's head. Connor's words directly contradicted the doctor's report forty minutes earlier. Not wanting to spook the man into giving his mother whatever was in the syringe, Cy stepped closer to the bed. "I thought Adrian would be on duty tonight."

Connor raised his eyebrows. "Adrian called in sick, so here I am."

Cy glanced at the syringe. "The day nurse already took care of my mom's medications before she went off shift." His eyes swept the room, but no computer cart had accompanied the nurse. Then what else had bothered him burst into his conscious. The scrubs. The night staff's scrubs were all light blue, not navy like this man's.

"It's in Lillian's chart." The man inserted the syringe into the port near the IV needle taped to the top of his mom's hand.

Cy didn't think. He simply acted. He pushed the call buzzer, then ripped the IV line from the access point on the back of his mother's hand just as the man depressed the plunger. The man's eyes flared wide above the face mask, then he dashed for the door.

Cy lunged for the intruder as the door opened, knocking the man back into Cy. He tried to grab hold of the man's arm as someone yelled for security. The imposter elbowed Cy hard in the stomach. Cy bent over from the blow, struggling to catch his breath. He raised his head in time to see the man shove a nurse into the sink and escape out the open door.

Cy shoved past the male nurse and into the hallway. Connor yanked over a computer cart, spilling its contents into Cy's path as he dashed for the end of the hall. A security guard rounded the corner.

"Stop him!" Cy shouted as the intruder approached the guard.

Connor kicked out at the guard, but the older man countered with a series of martial arts moves Cy couldn't follow. Soon Connor lay on his stomach, his hands cuffed behind him with zip ties. Cy sagged against the wall, adrenaline ebbing from his body.

"Mr. Hillam?" A male nurse in powder blue scrubs stood in front of him. "I'm Adrian. Your mother's okay. Your quick action didn't let any of whatever was in the syringe enter her bloodstream, as far as we can tell."

"She's really okay?" Cy didn't care that a couple of tears trickled down his cheeks. The man hadn't hurt his mother. That was the important thing.

"The on-call neurologist is checking her over to be sure, but she appears to have suffered no ill effects. We've notified the police about the incident."

"Were you able to recover the syringe and whatever was in it?" Cy didn't want the man to get away with trying to kill his mother because evidence had been lost at the scene.

"We bagged everything for the police. As soon as the doctor is finished with his exam, you can return to her room."

"Thank you." Cy leaned his head against the wall and closed his eyes. Immediately, his mind replayed the scene again in slow motion. Thank goodness he'd listened to his gut and questioned the fake nurse's actions. *Dear God, thank you for sparing my mother's life yet again. Please help me keep her safe, and keep Isana safe too.*

At the thought of Isana, he pulled out his phone and opened a text to her, but his fingers hovered over the keyboard without pressing any letters. No, best he didn't initiate contact after pushing her away this morning. An ache in his chest reminded him of how much that had hurt him. But the attack on his mother this evening reinforced his decision as the right one. The more distance he put between himself and the lovely woman who had become so precious to him in such a short time, the safer he'd keep her. Surely, Isana would understand and forgive him when this was over.

~

Gina drew the smoke deep into her lungs from a forbidden cigarette. The old urge to light up had been overpowering of late, probably because she was dwelling on a time in her life when smoking had been as natural as brushing her teeth. The twins had changed that, replacing the need nicotine had filled with their inquisitive blue eyes and dark blond hair.

Another drag brightened the tip of the cigarette. Her nicotine habit had also provided a cover for her meetings with Marta. Gil suspected nothing then or now. She had been very careful. Her eyes had always been on the presidency for her husband. Left on his own, he would have dedicated himself to serving his country in one foreign post after another, eventually becoming an ambassador. But she had seen his skills and abilities could reach beyond that realm with a little nudge here and a little push there. What was the saying about behind every successful man was a successful woman? Some political wives chaffed at operating outside of the spotlight, but Gina reveled in the secret knowledge that without her machinations, Gil wouldn't be poised to run for president next year.

The First Lady had confided in Gina two weeks ago that her husband would fully support Gil's candidacy. Marissa Williams's words echoed in her mind. *And don't you worry a thing about the former vice president. He's had sour grapes ever since James picked Gil to join him on the ticket for his second term.*

Gina never left anything to chance. Incriminating photos from the former vice president's college days were tucked into a safety deposit box at a Virginia bank under her maiden name. If the president reneged on his promise to Gil and backed his first-term vice president instead, Gina had no compunction about blackmailing the

183

man to withdraw from the race. She would do whatever it took to propel her husband into the White House.

Grounding out her spent cigarette, she picked up the butt and carried it into the house, her Secret Service detail following at a discrete distance. Once inside the house, she turned to her shadow. "I'll be in my office. See that I'm not disturbed."

"Yes, ma'am." The man spoke softly into his mic, probably alerting his colleagues to her location.

Locking the door behind her, she crossed to the desk and keyed in the code to unlock the bottom drawer. Picking up a burner flip phone, she dialed.

"Yeah?" The man on the other end barked.

"Any complications?" She drummed her fingers on the desktop, her mind already going to the next step in her master plan.

"Yes."

The unexpected answer took a moment to register. She stilled her fingers. "Tell me everything."

"The son came back and caught our guy in the act."

She tucked away the pack of cigarettes. "Go on," she prompted.

"He tried to bluff his way through, but the son wasn't buying it and sounded the alarm."

"Was the job completed?"

"No, and our guy was nabbed by hospital security."

Gina sagged against the back of the leather office chair. "I thought you hired professionals who wouldn't get caught."

"The operative was one of my most seasoned guys. Sometimes things don't go according to plan. But don't worry. He won't say a word."

"How sure are you?"

"Very sure. He's been in this situation before. He's only dealt with me through burner phones. There's nothing to tie him directly to you or me."

"You better be sure of that." She disconnected the call, removing the battery and SIM card before putting all the pieces in a pouch to dispose of in the morning. Her head pounded, probably from the illicit cigarette and bad news. If only she wasn't so well-known, she could take care of these loose ends on her own. Back in West Berlin, she could move about freely because no one noticed the wife of a low-level diplomat. At times, she missed that freedom and the accompanying excitement as she outfoxed Western and East German agents to achieve her goal.

Maybe she had overplayed her hand in trying to eliminate all possible threats, but she had gone too far to back down now. Someone else was after the list too. She had no doubt the competing person knew her name was on it, but without hard evidence, it would be a tempest in a teapot, as her aunt used to say. Still, any hint about what linked the women on the list would trigger questions from her husband she didn't want to answer. For more than thirty years, she'd kept the secret. If she had her way, she'd take it with her to the grave.

CHAPTER

TWENTY-FOUR

Isana slipped into an empty seat toward the back of the sanctuary at Redeemer Church twenty minutes after the eleven o'clock start time. Delays on the Metro line had made her late. She bowed her head as the pastor continued his prayer. Something had compelled her to attend the service, even though she might run into Cy. The feeling of warmth, community, and fellowship with God that had enveloped her last week spurred her to come.

"We're picking back up with our series through the Gospel of John. This week, we'll be camping out in the latter half of chapter 8, specifically verses 31 through 59. But to orient ourselves, I'll read the entire chapter," Pastor Hyden said.

She opened the Bible app and found John 8, reading along with the pastor.

"Today, we're going to focus on verses 31 and 32," the minister said.

Isana re-read those verses on her app. *So Jesus said to the Jews who had believed him, "If you abide in my word, you are truly my disciples, and you will know the truth, and the truth will set you free."*

The aptness of hearing about God's truth while searching for the truth about the list struck her full force. As the pastor outlined how seeking God's truth, knowing it and hiding it deep in your heart, drew one closer to Christ, she considered how often she ignored the truth in her own life. How she refused to acknowledge her own past and its hurts, and therefore pushed God and his truth away. The Holy Spirit gently whispered she could give those to God and fully embrace Christ, letting the truth of the gospel wash her clean. Tears trickled down her cheeks as she surrendered to the One who could heal and comfort her. Bowing her head, she prayed for forgiveness, for the ability to forgive others the hurts they'd done to her, and for strength to live life as a new creature in Christ.

She blotted her cheeks with a tissue, suddenly aware the sanctuary was nearly empty. She'd missed the end of the service. Shrugging into her coat, she rose in the pew.

"Isana?"

Cy's voice behind her made her jump. She'd intended to exit the building during the closing prayer to avoid running into him, but apparently, God had other plans. Turning, she hoped her nose wasn't red and her mascara hadn't run from her tears. "Hi."

His haggard appearance softened her response even further. Dark circles under his eyes, along with the beginnings of a beard on his lower jaw, told her the stress of his mother's condition must be taking its toll. "How's your mom doing?"

"Better. She woke up yesterday morning."

"That's great news."

"It is." But his tone indicated something about the situation wasn't great. Perhaps his mother had lasting brain damage from the beating.

"Do the doctors think she'll have a full recovery?" Isana didn't want to probe, but his cryptic reply left her unsettled, and she needed to know.

"There doesn't seem to be any lasting effects on her brain, but they'll be running more cognitive and other tests now that she's awake." His gaze moved from her face to over her shoulder.

"I'm glad to hear it." The silence between them grew as he avoided looking at her. She shifted from one foot to another. Maybe she should exit the pew the other way, since Cy blocked her path forward. "Thanks for the update on your mom. See you tomorrow."

"Tomorrow?" A puzzled expression crossed his face, then cleared. "Right, at The Heritage."

She nodded, a crushing sense of sadness weighing her down. She couldn't stand the torture of conversing with him as if they were strangers. Turning, she moved rapidly to the end of the pew and headed for the exit.

"Isana!" Cy's voice halted her in the nearly empty foyer.

She waited until he caught up with her but said nothing. He shoved a hand through his hair. In his green eyes, she detected misery and confusion and fear. Still he kept silent, as did she. The seconds ticked by as the tension between them built like a toddler stacking blocks. After a full minute—she'd counted the seconds off in her head—of continued silence, she tamped down her own growing misery. She was a grown woman who had her dignity and her pride. She didn't have to stand here waiting and hoping for a man to want her. Letting out her pent-up air on a long sigh, she turned and trudged toward the door.

This time, Cy didn't call her name.

CY CALLED HIMSELF ALL KINDS OF STUPID AS ISANA LEFT. HE'D BEEN shocked to see her after the service and had approached her without thinking through the ramifications of his actions. All he'd wanted to do was make sure she was all right. Clearly, she wasn't, with a reddish tint to her nose and mascara smudged under her eyes. When she asked about his mother, the reminder of what had nearly happened Friday evening slammed into him. After the attempt on her life—the syringe was found to have contained some sort of poison, although the police were being cagey about the exact name

—he'd hired a private security firm he'd worked with on a previous job to stand guard. With his mom awake and alert, he'd given in to her urging to leave the hospital to attend church. The worship service had been a balm to his battered soul, but seeing Isana had reminded him of all he had to lose if he didn't heed his mother's warning.

Lillian hadn't mentioned it again, but then, Cy hadn't managed to be alone with her for more than a couple of minutes with all the hospital staff bustling in and out of her room. At least yesterday she'd been moved to a private room off the ICU floor, thus easing his mind about her medical condition. Today he planned to ask her to explain her warning.

"Trouble in paradise?"

Cy brought his attention back to the present with difficulty, smiling at his good friend, Maddox Camire, who stood with a baby car seat looped through one arm. "Why'd you say that?"

Maddox guffawed. "Seriously? I might be sleep deprived because of this little angel," he nodded at the sleeping baby nestled in the car seat, "but I still have eyes. The lovely young woman you made a beeline for after the service ended. I expected to meet her, not see her hitting the front door with the force of a semi."

Somehow, the image pleased Cy. That Isana was upset about his actions likely meant she cared about him. Then his mother's warning screamed across his mind like a ginormous neon sign. "It's complicated."

"No, it's not. You like her, right?"

Cy sighed, but nodded. "You don't understand."

Maddox went on as if Cy hadn't spoken. "Does she like you?"

Might as well play along so he could leave. "I think so."

"And yet you're pushing her away." Maddox raised a single eyebrow, a gesture Cy both admired and hated because he couldn't manage it himself. "Because you're afraid."

The analysis brought heat to Cy's cheeks. "Not of a relationship."

The thought of falling in love did terrify him, but he was beginning to believe he could overcome that. With Isana's help.

The baby stirred, letting out a little mewing sound. Maddox gently swung the car seat back and forth. "Then what's the problem?"

Cy opened his mouth, but Maddox held up a hand. "Don't tell me. It's complicated." The baby's wails cranked up considerably. "I'd stay and grill you, but the princess is getting peckish. Call me if you want my advice on how to win her back." Maddox headed to the door. "Because from what I just witnessed, you're going to need it."

Cy's phone buzzed, distracting him from Maddox's excellent summary of his situation. A text from his mom had arrived.

On your way?

Yes, leaving church now.

He headed outside toward his rental car. His mom replied before he reached the crossover SUV.

Pick me up a chimichanga at Guajillo's?

Sure. Be there soon.

He checked in with Ted Annok, the security guard on duty outside his mother's hospital room. All was quiet. After placing the order for fish tacos for Ted, a chimichanga for his mom, and the mole chicken with rice for himself, he exited the parking lot. A few blocks away, he stopped for a red light across from the Clarendon Metro entrance. Glancing at the light Sunday afternoon crowd heading to the down escalators, he caught a glimpse of a woman in a brown coat. The woman's profile showed it wasn't Isana, but his mind filled in her features anyway. Silky brown hair he longed to run through his fingers. Slightly upturned nose. Clear, smooth skin. Very kissable lips.

A car horn jerked him back to the empty car. The green light attested to his inattention. With a wave at the driver behind him, he pressed on the gas and entered the intersection. All the way to the restaurant and then hospital, he resolutely refused to dwell on a pair of very fine, hazel eyes.

And how much the organ in his chest ached with the separation.

Lillian Hillam set down her fork, her appetite sated after consuming barely a fourth of the chimichanga her son had brought for lunch. On the couch built in beneath the wide window, Cyrus hunched over his Styrofoam takeout container, but though he pushed his plastic fork around, he took no bites. She hadn't missed the distraught look in his eyes, despite his attempts to hide it from her. She'd always known when something troubled her only child.

"Out with it," she commanded, experience having taught her Cyrus needed a direct approach to get him to unburden himself.

His head swiveled in her direction. "What?"

"You're not eating your favorite dish, which tells me you're upset about something." She ticked off reason number one on her right hand. "You're being evasive when I asked about church, and you're muttering to yourself." She eyed him, holding three fingers aloft. "I rest my case."

Cyrus put the food container on the hard plastic cushion beside him. "I've made a huge mess of things."

"With Isana." She laughed at her son's raised eyebrows. "I'm not blind, you know. I might not have met the young woman, but every time you mention her name, your face lights up like a Fourth of July firecracker."

"I'm exploding all over the place?" His words were teasing, but by the way his shoulders slumped, Lillian suspected he didn't find the comparison amusing.

"What happened?" When he dropped his gaze to the floor, she waited. When struggling with an issue or situation, Cyrus often took his time organizing his thoughts before speaking. While she much preferred her late husband's quick responses, she'd learned to hold her tongue to give her son space.

"Do you remember what you said to me when I got to the hospital?"

Lillian frowned. "When I woke up from the coma?"

"No, when you first came in."

She closed her eyes, trying to dredge up memories of that chaotic time. Her injuries had merged scenes together so the sequence of events prior to waking up yesterday morning had become as jumbled as a junk drawer. All she could recall with clarity was the fear she had for herself, Cyrus, and Isana. "I'm sorry, I can't remember. Everything's still a bit of a blur." The police had interviewed her yesterday afternoon, and she'd given as much information as she could, but even though she named her abductors, she couldn't pinpoint the location of where she'd been held, nor could she name the men who'd beaten her.

Cyrus walked to the door and opened it. He stuck his head out, said something to the man guarding her room, then returned to his seat. "You said, 'Danger. Stop. Don't want you hurt. Keep silent.'"

Lillian stared. She'd claimed to have had no idea why the man and Schmidt had kidnapped her, and Cyrus had acknowledged no financial ransom demand had been made. She froze as her son's exact words to the detective came back to her: "No, there was no request for money."

"What did they ask for?" The words came out harsher than she'd intended, but she didn't restate the question. When Cyrus kept his gaze on the floor and his mouth shut, she offered her own guess. "The list."

His head whipped up. In his eyes, she had her answer. The lies of three decades pressed down on her shoulders, but she couldn't share her secret. Not when it would destroy what was left of her family. It had killed her husband, and she wasn't about to let it take her son too.

"What do you know of the list?" Cyrus locked his gaze on hers.

"I overheard Schmidt on the phone with someone, and they mentioned you were searching for some list." The truth, but not the whole truth. "Were you trying to find it with Isana's help?"

He gave a short nod. "I think there's something you should know." Lillian listened in growing horror as he recounted what had happened to Isana after she found Lillian's phone and then the car bomb outside of Mrs. Johnston's house. "What we didn't understand was why try to kills us if we were supposed to find this list for your release?"

She leaned back against the pillows, possibilities tumbling around in her mind like sheets in a dryer. "Because there are two different people after the list." A face, glimpsed only briefly, flashed in her mind. Her stomach churned as she considered who might be the second party. If she was correct, the person had more to lose than she did.

"Why did you warn me?"

"I'm not sure I did." She didn't want to give away what she knew until she had time to think.

"You seemed so sure I was in danger." Her son paced. "I pushed Isana away because I thought she would get hurt if we continued."

His words penetrated her thoughts. While she wanted to explore his relationship with Isana, she had to figure out who was behind the attacks first. "Continued with what?" Fear gripped her with icy dread.

He sighed. "We think we found the list."

Only years of keeping her emotions hidden allowed for Lillian not to overreact to his statement. "Where?"

"In an old John Grisham novel."

She didn't bother stopping the tears at hearing how Greg had hidden the list in plain sight in the book. How she missed him, and how she longed to correct the assumption he'd taken his own life. Hearing how Schmidt had killed him instead had been like a dagger to her own heart but also a salve on years of blaming Greg for leaving her alone. "And it's a list of names?"

"It's the only thing that makes sense. The first name on the list was Marta Bauer."

At Marta's name, Lillian stiffened. "Is that so?" She couldn't give away she knew Marta and had been told the woman was dead.

"That's not all." He paused. "A German national named Marta Bauer was found murdered in the US Botanical Gardens a few days ago."

Her hand flew to her mouth at hearing the confirmation of Marta's murder. Her theory began to make even more sense. "That's terrible. Do they know who did it?"

"I haven't seen any follow up in the news about it. But you haven't said whether or not you think we're still in danger."

A knock on the door prevented Lillian from answering. Ted poked his head in. "The police detectives are back."

Detective Wynn came in, followed by a woman in a plum pantsuit and elegant high heels. "Mrs. Hillam, this is Captain Pritten. We have some good news and some bad news."

Lillian braced herself mentally while Cyrus took her hand in his. "Go on."

"We found one of your kidnappers, Nathan Schmidt."

Relief pulsed through her, but dread wouldn't let go completely. "And the bad news?"

"He's been murdered."

CHAPTER

TWENTY-FIVE

Isana cupped her travel mug of hot cinnamon spice tea as she waited for the director to begin the Monday morning staff meeting. No one had been allowed in their offices until after the nine a.m. meeting. She studiously avoided glancing at Cy, who had taken a chair at the opposite side of the small auditorium used for museum-sponsored lectures.

Director Umbel tapped the microphone attached to the podium in the center of the narrow stage. "Please find your seats so we can get started." He gave the latecomers a few minutes to settle before clearing his throat. "I know you're all anxious to get back to work, so this won't take too long. As you know, we had a security breach of our computer systems last week that resulted in a staff member being locked in the storage area."

Isana ducked her head. Since most of the staff had already departed for the day, she was fairly certain few knew she was the staffer in question.

"That person is okay, but it took our IT department several days to pinpoint what happened and to enact a fix. Tim is to be commended for his work on this tangled mess." The director paused

197

for a smatter of applause from those gathered. "A former staff member had used his insider knowledge of the system to gain access."

Isana straightened in her seat. No one had bothered to tell her.

"We have turned the evidence over to the appropriate authorities and will be pressing charges against this individual and the current staff member who had assisted him," Umbel continued. "Tim also had each laptop thoroughly checked to ensure no spyware or malware resided on the hard drives."

The director went on to remind everyone of the technology rules as outlined in the employee handbook, then dismissed everyone to work.

"Isana?" Faith Gibbons called as Isana stood. "Come by my office."

"Now?" Isana shouldered her messenger bag, her coat draped over her arm.

"Yes. I'll be along in a moment." Faith hurried to catch up with the director.

Isana sighed and headed to the HR manager's office. As it was, she'd have to put in long hours to pull together the exhibition pieces. She didn't have extra time to waste. Faith's office was a few doors down from Cy's office, but with any luck, he'd already be back to work, and she wouldn't bump into him on her way.

But when she turned the corner to the hallway of offices, she spotted Cy talking with one of the office admins. Her breathing hitched. It wasn't fair he could look so good.

Something he said made the blonde throw back her head and laugh. The young woman put her hand on Cy's forearm, her blue eyes sparkling as she leaned closer. Cy smiled in return, the gesture driving a dagger deep into Isana's heart. Blinking rapidly to keep tears from spilling down her cheeks, she turned to go but spotted Faith hurrying her way.

"Sorry to keep you waiting," Faith said when she'd caught up with Isana. "Come into my office. This won't take long."

Faith's words must have drawn Cy's attention because Isana caught him staring in her direction as she followed the other woman into her office. For a moment, she froze as their eyes met, then she shook her head as if to clear the hold Cy had on her heart and went through the doorway.

"Close the door and have a seat." Faith draped her coat over the back of the leather desk chair. "First, my apologies for not telling you the results of our internal investigation before this morning. I was supposed to call you at home yesterday afternoon once we had the report in hand, but our dog decided to eat something weird and kept throwing up all over the house, so I spent the afternoon and evening in the emergency vet office."

"How is he?" Isana glanced at the numerous personal photos Faith had around her office, many of which showed her and a dark chocolate, medium-sized dog.

"Rocky will be okay, but by the time we got home and I cleaned up the house, it was too late to call." Faith swept a strand of hair off her cheek. "Tim found that Carson had kept in touch with one of the admins, Molly—they apparently had a relationship—and talked her into giving him remote access to her computer. From there, Carson was able to manipulate the system to lock you in the basement."

"He must have had help," Isana blurted out, thinking back to previous conversations with Carson about the museum's electronic inventory system and how he seemed to not easily grasp how it worked.

"The investigation traced the computer used for the infiltration to a friend of Carson's. We've turned all the evidence over to the police, and they will be arresting all involved parties."

Isana sagged against the back of the chair. "What will the charges be?"

"We're leaving that up to the police and prosecutor, but we've made it clear we want charges brought against him and his accomplices." Faith caught Isana's eye. "We do not tolerate the kind of treatment you received from Carson."

Isana nodded acknowledgement. "Thank you."

"If you have further questions, I can put you in touch with the detective in charge of the case."

"Okay." Isana gathered her bag and coat but didn't rise. "I can't believe he would be so vindictive."

"Some men feel particularly threatened by women, especially ones who are smarter than they are," Faith said. "I'm just glad you weren't seriously harmed by his actions."

"I won't be visiting the storage area by myself for a while, that's for sure." Isana stood.

"Oh, that reminds me. We will be installing an intercom system in every room on the storage floor and at either end of the hallway to avoid any future malfunctions."

"That's probably a good idea, since cell reception is zilch down there. Now I'd better get on with the exhibition work."

"I have no doubt you will do a fine job."

Isana tugged open the door and headed down the hallway to the elevators. She was glad Carson had been found out but saddened that someone she'd worked with for three years would hate her so much, he'd conspire to lock her in cold storage for hours. Maybe he hadn't meant to kill her, but she had little doubt she wouldn't have survived the night if Cy hadn't realized she was missing.

Entering her office, she hung up her coat and put away her personal belongings while her laptop booted up. She had to stop thinking of Cy at every turn or she'd never get through the mound of work necessary to pull off the wedding dress exhibition. With a firm shake of her head, she vowed to shove all thoughts of Cy into a mental box and to throw away the key. If he could move on with his life and act like nothing had happened between them, so could she.

Even if her heart was breaking into a million pieces in the process.

～

Cy bit into his PB&J sandwich as he read through yet another email. He hadn't had time to make a grocery run after spending all his free time at his mother's bedside, save for going to church yesterday morning, and had cobbled together a pretty sad lunch from the contents of his pantry. He pulled out his phone and added lunch meat and sub rolls to his grocery list.

His mom had seemed in good spirits when he'd talked to her before unwrapping his sandwich. The security guards were keeping a close watch on her, but no other attempts had been made on her life. The doctor said she would be released when Cy came by after work.

He'd arranged for round-the-clock security at her house and planned to sleep in his old room until the danger had passed. When exactly they'd know that, he wasn't sure, but until they caught whoever was behind the kidnapping of his mom, he wasn't taking any chances. The police hadn't given any updates on the death of Schmidt, only that they were investigating it as a murder. The second man, whom his mother could only describe, had yet to be located.

Someone knocked on his door just as he stuffed the last bite of sandwich in his mouth. "Come in," he said around the bread and peanut butter.

To his surprise and pleasure, Isana pushed opened the door. She hovered in the doorframe, not fully entering his office. Her hesitance sent a ping of regret to his heart, but he steeled himself from wavering from his decision to hold her at arms' length until this—whatever *this* was—blew over. If anything hurt her because of her involvement with his mess, he'd never forgive himself.

"How's your mom?"

He held up a finger, then took a swig from his water bottle. "Sorry, finishing my lunch."

A flush stole across her cheeks. "I'll come back later."

"No!" His near-shout froze her departure. "I mean, it's okay."

She turned back around and took one step farther toward his

desk. Her eyes locked on his for an instant before she dropped her gaze. "Your mom?"

Her prompt reminded him of her initial question. "She's doing much better and will be released when I come by after work. I'll stay with her for a while and have hired a security firm to provide, well, security."

"I'm glad she's okay." Isana spoke to his potted plant, a gift from his mother to brighten up his office. "Do the police have any leads on the kidnappers?"

Her question startled him because he'd become accustomed to her knowing his every step, he'd forgotten she had no knowledge of Schmidt. "One of the kidnappers, a man called Schmidt, was found murdered."

Her hand flew to her mouth. "Oh, that's awful."

"As far as we know, no leads about the death, and the second kidnapper is still at large." Once more, Cy had the feeling his mother hadn't shared everything she'd known about her captors or captivity.

"I'm glad you've hired extra protection. The reason I stopped by was that my friend's contact in the State Department HR division got back to me about the abbreviation RBWG."

"What's it mean?"

"'Registered birth West Germany.' It's the designation used when an American gives birth in another country."

"Ah, I see." He ran over the list in his mind. "So all the women on the list gave birth while in West Germany."

"That's correct."

"Makes sense, given the probable age of the women and status as married women." They never seemed to catch a break in figuring out the connection between the women on the list. It was a question he'd pose to his mother once she was safely home.

"What does your mom say about the list? Did she know the women?"

"We haven't discussed it," Cy confessed. "There are always so many people around in the hospital."

"What about Marta Bauer? Did your mom know her?"

"I haven't had a chance to ask her about Marta either." His statement sounded lame to his own ears. His mother had become a stranger to him. He could see in her eyes she knew more than she let on about Marta and Schmidt, but he didn't have the courage to ask her directly. Maybe it was enough his mother was safe, and they should let the past keep its secrets.

"Anyway, thought you'd like to know about the RBWG reference."

"Thanks for telling me." Cy wanted to add more, that he missed her and wanted her to have dinner with him. But the gulf between them widened with each passing second, and he convinced himself she was safer away from him and his mother. Besides, he had no idea how to bridge the divide if he were unwilling to continue seeking the connection between the names on the list. To do so would mean grilling his mother, and from her response so far, he wasn't sure he wanted to know the answers.

"I guess I'll see you around," Isana finally said into the silence.

He could feel her gaze on him, but he kept his head bowed as if fascinated by his keyboard. The air moved slightly, and he snuck a peek as she stepped into the hallway, then disappeared from view. The ache in his chest grew to the size of a boulder, but he'd get over it. He had too. Shoving the hurt deep down, he resolutely returned to work.

TWENTY-SIX

West Berlin, June 4, 1988, 5 a.m.

A baby cried. Lillian searched for the little one, running through a thick forest of trees that grabbed her arms, holding her back. Still the infant wailed, its cries so loud she wanted to cover her ears. Her eyes opened. A baby screamed nearby.

She wasn't dreaming. She lay in her bed, the room in semi-darkness. In another room, a woman's voice soothed the baby. Lillian turned on her side and gasped at the pain shooting through her midsection.

The door opened and someone hurried into the room. A woman laid a hand on Lillian's shoulder. *"Bitte, bleib still. Ich hole den Arzt."* She clicked on the bedside lamp, then left.

Lillian had no trouble obeying the directive to stay still as the ache in her stomach region intensified, but why would there be a doctor in her apartment?

A man entered, carrying a black medical bag. "Mrs. Hillam? I'm Dr. Engel. How are you feeling this morning?"

"My stomach hurts." The truth and the safest answer she could give in her current confused state.

He nodded as if that made perfect sense. "That's to be expected after what happened."

Lillian closed her eyes briefly, marshaling her thoughts to avoid sounding like she didn't know what had happened, which was the truth. "Everything's a little fuzzy."

"Ah, yes, the anesthesia can have that effect on some people." He patted her hand. "Let me get you some pain medicine."

He started to rise, but she snagged the sleeve of his shirt. "Please, I can't quite remember what happened. I thought I heard a baby crying, and . . . " Tears slipped down her cheeks unbidden, lending credence to her emotional turmoil.

The doctor's demeanor changed instantly. "Oh, you poor dear. I'm so sorry. I thought you knew, but of course, given the circumstances, it's probably not very clear."

Lillian stared at him, blinking away the moisture and willing him to make sense.

"You went into labor last night here in your apartment. Your friend Marta called your midwife as instructed, but the baby was breach and wouldn't turn. The midwife contacted Dr. Sauer, who came here."

"I wasn't taken to the hospital?" Lillian asked the question she figured a woman in her condition would have voiced.

Dr. Engel consulted a piece of paper. "According to Dr. Sauer's notes, the hospital advised him it would be an hour wait for an ambulance to arrive. A massive traffic accident across town had tied up most of the emergency personnel for hours. The doctor had come prepared with a portable ether cannister, and the midwife assisted him in performing an emergency Cesarean-section to deliver the baby."

"A C-section here?" Lillian was horrified, her hand flying to her sore tummy. What had Marta done to her?

"I checked your suture, and there's no sign of infection," Dr.

Engel said. "Dr. Sauer is a skilled surgeon. I doubt you'll have much of a scar. I've let detailed care instructions with the nurse."

"Nurse?" Lillian could hardly keep up with all the information bombarding her. She brushed hair off her forehead with trembling fingers.

Dr. Engel peered closely at her face. "The midwife said you'd engaged Nurse Berta to care for the infant after delivery."

The nurse, with her dark eyes and brown hair pulled back into a no-nonsense bun, had been the quietest of the half dozen women she'd interviewed to help with the baby. "Right, I'm sorry." Tears sprang to her eyes again. "I can't seem to catch hold of a thought this morning."

"That happens sometimes after major surgery. Now, I imagine you'd like to meet your son?"

Lillian nodded, unable to speak. The doctor rose and crossed to the door, speaking to someone on the other side. Berta entered, a bundle wrapped tightly in blue blanket in her arms. The doctor helped Lillian sit up, then Berta gently placed the infant in Lillian's arms.

"He's just been fed," Berta said. "The midwife said you would need to bottle feed."

"That's right." Lillian's gaze never leaving the sleeping baby's face. "He's perfect."

"Clocked in at eight pounds, thirteen ounces. A nice, healthy baby boy."

"I'll come by in a couple of days to check on the suture," the doctor said, but Lillian barely heard him. The door closed behind them, as both doctor and nurse left the room.

The rest of the world faded into the background as Lillian drank in the infant's features. His tiny nose, rosebud lips, light blond fuzz covering most of his head. She unwrapped the blanket to count his fingers and toes—the right number of digits on each appendage— then touched the umbilical cord still attached to his abdomen. He was hers, and she loved him fiercely. "Cyrus Gregory Hillam, welcome to our family."

~

Cy assisted his mother out of her coat, hanging it in the tiny closet off the foyer. "Are you sure you don't want to lie down?"

"Cyrus Gregory Hillam, I have been in a bed for several days. I most certainly do not want to return to one right away. I know my limits."

At his mother's accompanying stern expression, he offered a sheepish smile. "Of course you do." He dropped a kiss on her cheek, the relief at her safe return overwhelming him. "I was so scared when you went missing, Mom."

She hugged him tight. "I was frightened too." For a moment, they stood close together, then she pulled back. "What I need is a strong cup of tea. What passed for tea in the hospital was like strained dishwater."

While the words sounded like Lillian Hillam in her prime, her steps weren't as brisk as she made her way to the kitchen. Cy knew better than to offer to make the tea while she rested at the table. Leaning against the door jamb while she filled the electric kettle, the unanswered questions Isana's visit had stirred up wouldn't leave his mind. But how to breach the subject without putting his mother on the defensive? Perhaps a trip down memory lane would work. "Someone at work was talking about the arrival of their nephew who was born in the hospital parking lot, but mom and baby are safe. That made me realize I'd never asked you about being born in West Germany. Which hospital was I born in?"

She plugged in the kettle. "You were born at home on a rainy night in June."

He hadn't heard that before. "Why not a hospital?"

"In Europe, it wasn't unusual to have home births with a midwife in attendance, even in the 1980s." She spooned looseleaf tea into a ball, hanging it into the teapot. "You were breach, so the midwife called the doctor and an ambulance." The kettle whistled and she poured. "But a bad traffic accident had snarled the roads, and it would have taken too long to get to the hospital, so the doctor performed the C-section right there in our apartment."

"What?" Shock had him stepping into the kitchen and closer to his mother. "Wasn't that dangerous?"

"I'm here, you're here, so everything turned out okay." She touched his cheek, her fingers cold.

"Is that why you didn't have more kids?" He recalled longing for a sibling when he was younger.

"We didn't think we'd even have you." His mother finished fixing her tea and carried it to the kitchen table. "Why all these questions about your birth?"

He joined her. "It's something Isana told me today."

Lillian's eyes brightened. "You apologized for being such an idiot?"

He winced. As usual, his mother was spot on when diagnosing his faults. "No, she told me the abbreviation RBWG after all the American names on the list stood for *registered birth West Germany.*"

His mother stirred sugar into her cup.

"Meaning all the women gave birth while in West Germany."

His mother's cheeks whitened, making the bruises stand out in stark relief. "All the names?"

"Yes." He peered closer. "You don't look so good. Should I call the doctor?"

"No." She stared down at the kitchen table. "I think I will go lie down now after all. I seem to have overdone it."

"Sure." Cy held her chair as she rose, but she waved off his help. Watching her shuffle down the hall toward her bedroom, the niggling feeling he was missing something obvious wouldn't leave him. That the conversation had upset his mom was apparent, but what part exactly had concerned her, he wasn't sure. The urge to call Isana to puzzle it out together had him reaching for his phone, but he stopped before connecting with her. Until the other kidnapper had been apprehended, it was better to forget the entire list to keep her safe.

❧

Isana rotated her shoulders to ease the strain of being hunched over her computer the past five days. She had put in long hours to prepare the wedding dress exhibition. Her laptop clock read 8:57 p.m. Nearly nine o'clock on a Friday night, and she was still at work. Not that she had anyone who would care.

Cy's face flashed in her mind, an accompanying ache familiar in her chest. How had he become so important to her in such a short time? She was a stupid girl, as her mother had always said. Believing a few kisses and longing looks meant anything special. She'd read about emotions being heightened in times of war or stress. Being shot at and nearly blown up certainly counted. Cy probably would have kissed any woman in those circumstances.

She wished she'd ignored his mother's ringing phone under the cherry trees. If she hadn't answered it, she could have happily continued to admire Cy from afar and not had her life upended by a search for a list while getting to know her secret crush. Once again, her heart did a little flip at the memory of spending time with him. Her fingers itched to brush against his jawline and to tangle in his hair. She closed her eyes to block out the recollection of his lips on hers. A tear squeezed past her closed lids, trailing down her cheek.

Wiping it off with a swipe of her fingers, she tried not to think about Cy. After stuffing the binder with photos of the dresses under consideration for the exhibition into her bag, she locked her office and headed upstairs. Tomorrow she'd make the final selections and send the paperwork to the director for his stamp of approval.

On the main floor, she nodded to the cleaning staff and buttoned her coat against the cool March wind. Stepping out into the brisk evening, she slung her messenger bag strap over the opposite shoulder. Her Metro app showed a train arriving at the L'Enfant Metro Station in seven minutes. If she hustled, she'd make it.

The crowded platform meant she had to dodge other passengers to secure a spot close to the edge. Experience taught her to be aggressive when a train was approaching or she'd get left behind on the platform if the train cars were crowded.

The lights under the platform blinked on and off to signal the train's imminent arrival. Isana slipped her hand under the strap of her messenger bag slung across her torso as the train's headlight flashed in the tunnel. People pressed in behind her as the screech of brakes ricocheted off the brick and tile station.

Then a hand shoved hard between her shoulder blades, sending her sprawling toward the incoming train.

TWENTY-SEVEN

Isana pitched forward as fear paralyzed her vocal cords. Someone grabbed her left arm, yanking her back and onto her butt as an out-of-service train whipped by without stopping.

"Hey, are you okay?" The creased face of an older man peered down at her. "I thought for sure you'd tumble onto the tracks."

She accepted his help to gain her feet, her limbs shaky from the near miss. "Thank you for your timely assistance."

"Didn't think you meant to . . . " His voice trailed off but she caught his meaning.

Heat infused her cheeks. "Oh, no! It wasn't deliberate at all." She glanced around before lowering her voice. "I felt someone push me."

Confusion washed over his countenance. "Why would anyone do that?"

The platform lights blinked again. "I don't know." The orange line train pulled into the station, braking to a stop.

"This is my train," the man said. "Will you be all right?"

She nodded, and he entered the closest car. She hurried down the platform to slip into another car, wanting to be alone to process what had just happened. Sitting by the window, she closed her eyes and relived the experience in her mind. Definitely a hand pushed hard against her back to propel her forward into the path of the oncoming train. If the older man hadn't grabbed her arm, she'd be splattered all over the station. A shudder ran through her at the thought, followed by the realization of how few people would come to her funeral. Her mom was busy trying to find a man to take care of her. Her father was busy with his new family in South Dakota. Lena, who had recently become a good friend, might miss her, and maybe Mrs. Jameson, who lived across the hall, since Isana looked in on her cats when she visited her grandkids in Nebraska.

Cy would probably show up, but he would soon forget about her, if he hadn't already. A tear slipped down her cheek, followed quickly by another. Soon, an entire waterfall fell from her eyes, but she didn't bother to wipe them away. The train pulled into her station stop, and she rose, ducking her head to keep from meeting the gazes of her fellow passengers. Outside in the cold March evening, she hurried along the sidewalk to her condo building.

A bowl of homemade chicken noodle soup restored some of her equilibrium. After washing out the pan she'd heated the soup in, she snuggled down on her couch, TV remote in hand. Twenty minutes later, she clicked off the television. Nothing appealed to her, and the incident had revved her internal engine instead of making her sleepy. Might as well see if she could turn up any other info on the women on the list. Now that she knew all had given birth in West Germany, she wanted to see if there were any more connections.

She started with Virginia Sanders, the current vice president's wife. Rumor had it her husband would be announcing his candidacy for president early next year. She Googled *Virginia Sanders and children.* Several articles populated the screen. Isana scrolled down to the oldest one, a video interview which originally aired in 1997 when her husband was running for governor of Maryland.

The segment had appeared on a Maryland public broadcast station and was basically a puff piece about the candidate. The footage showcased the family home, which had been in Virginia's family for more than a century, along with their twin boys, Lyle and Logan, who were thirteen at the time. The gangly identical boys tossed a football with their father on the green expanse of lawn in one scene. The interview portion of the story involved the basic questions of Gil's candidacy before devolving into how the couple met in college, then segueing into his early diplomatic career with the State Department.

"You had your twins while Gil was stationed in West Berlin, isn't that right?" Stacy Maguire, the interviewer, asked.

"Yes." Virginia reached for her husband's hand. "They were actually born at home during a snowstorm while Gil was in another part of West Germany on business."

"That must have been scary, especially with twins," Stacy said.

"It was, but I had a wonderful midwife, who was able to fetch a doctor to assist. The boys were nearly full term and healthy."

"They were delivered by Cesarean section right there in our bedroom," her husband put in. "And I didn't know a thing about it until I came home three days later because the storm had knocked out the phone lines and power in parts of the city."

"You must have been so relieved, given your history of infertility."

Virginia's mouth tightened at the interviewer's statement. Gil squeezed her hand, then looked straight into the camera. "As with any couple who want to have a baby and can't, we were thrilled when Virginia did conceive. And to have the surprise of twins, well, our cup overflowed."

The interviewer leaned toward the couple. "When did you realize you were having twins?"

"Not until they were born, isn't that right?" Gil smiled at his wife. "You could have laid me out flat when I came home and found not one, but two babies and a tired wife."

"Wow, that's quite a story." Stacy segued back to Gil's transition from diplomacy abroad to running for governor.

Isana watched until the end but gleaned no other information about the birth of their twins in West Germany. What a strange story, one that bordered on the unbelievable. A C-section at home in the middle of a snowstorm? The not knowing about being pregnant with twins bothered her too. She Googled ultrasounds in the 1980s and found the practice wasn't commonplace in the United States and even rarer in other countries. So it was conceivable—ha!—Virginia Sanders could be unaware of carrying twins until their birth.

Her phone buzzed. Hope blossomed but plummeted when the caller was Lena, not Cy.

"Hi." Isana could hear the disappointment in her voice.

"Not the caller you were expecting?" Lena's tone held sympathy.

"I'm not expecting any call, but hoping . . ."

"Had a falling out with Cy?"

"You could say that. He's basically said he has no time for me since his mother's return." Isana choked back a sob.

"I'm so sorry. You really liked him."

"I did." Isana drew in a breath to keep the tears at bay. "For the first time, I thought I'd found someone who liked me too. But once more, my mom has been proven right. I'm not worthy of a man's attention."

"Brew some coffee because I'll be there in half an hour."

"What?" Isana asked but Lena had hung up. Swiping the wetness from her cheeks, she shuffled to the kitchen to turn on the Keurig. Last year, Lena had had her own ups and down with her handsome doctor, so she'd understand.

BRENNER FLEXED HIS GLOVED HANDS. IT HAD BEEN A WHILE SINCE HE'D BEEN on surveillance, and he'd forgotten how cold one got standing in place for hours. His perseverance was paying off as he spotted small gaps in the Secret Service patrols around the vice president's residence on the northeast grounds of the U.S. Naval Observatory in DC. Naturally security was tight, but he'd observed enough to come up with several plausible ways of gaining access to the house without drawing attention to himself.

Tracing Lillian Hillam's attackers had taken a few days, but he'd managed to find them in the end. Applying special techniques acquired as a former Stasi agent had loosened their tongues enough to lead him to the one who'd hired them. From there, he easily obtained the name of the woman behind it all—Virginia Sanders, the vice president's wife. Once he'd read her official bio, he'd known why she'd risked everything to silence Marta Bauer and Lillian Hillam. With this knowledge, the reason his boss wanted the list became even more apparent. Possession of evidence implicating the man who would likely become the next President of the United States of treason would be priceless.

His phone buzzed insistently. The boss himself calling. Brenner thought about ignoring him, but changed his mind, answering right before the call rolled to voicemail.

"Hello?" He walked briskly down the sidewalk toward his vehicle, which he'd parked on Whitehaven Street NW, a good distance from the observatory grounds.

"You've been freelancing."

The statement sent a chill down Brenner's back. He'd known the risks involved in ferreting out information not requested by the boss. He stayed silent, neither confirming nor denying the accusation.

"I don't like it when my underlings go off script."

Brenner bit back a caustic response. The man may have hired him, but they weren't supervisor and subordinate like in the old days. "Why are you calling?"

"The list."

Now he understood the man's obsession with finding it. What he couldn't figure out was how having such a list would benefit him. The names meant nothing on their own and would hardly constitute evidence in a court of law. "Why is the list so important to you? You already know three of the names on it."

"Are you questioning my reasons?" The words exploded in Brenner's ear, the harsh tone leaving no doubt he'd stepped on a land mine.

Brenner waited a beat, then replied in a calm voice, "After everything I've done for you, I think I'm owed an explanation, given it's my neck on the line."

Silence greeted his statement. He waited. The man hadn't hung up, which meant he was either considering his answer or his punishment for Brenner's insubordination.

"Meet me at the Udvar-Hazy Air and Space Museum near the Earheart Lockheed Vega plan exhibition at eleven tomorrow."

Before Brenner could agree, the call disconnected. He pocketed his phone, unease twining around him like a slithering snake. He'd make the meeting, but he would make sure certain contingencies were in place in case of a trap. Brenner hadn't stayed alive this long by leaving anything to chance.

CHAPTER

TWENTY-EIGHT

Isana handed Lena a mug, then carried her own into the living room.

"Your apartment is quite cozy." Lena slipped off her shoes before dropping onto the loveseat.

"That's one way of looking at the tiny footprint." Isana settled into an overstuffed chair. She glanced around the one-bedroom condo she called home. "It's small, but since it's only me, it works."

"No, I like how you've divided the open space." Lena nodded toward the corner where floor-to-ceiling dark, velvet curtains hung. "What's that for?"

"My darkroom." Isana was very proud of her ingenuity in devising space for her to develop her own photos. "I was using the bathroom when I first moved in eight years ago, but it was a pain to keep moving all the stuff in and out. A photographer friend suggested blackout curtains might help create the space necessary for the work. So far, it's working well."

"What about the fumes?"

"I have a fan I place in the window to draw out the smells and an air purifier I run as well." Isana sipped her decaf coffee. "Now tell me about the wedding plans."

For the next few minutes, Lena brought Isana up to speed on the details for her late June wedding to Dr. Devlin Mills.

Her own heart ached with Cy's rejection. After all these years, to have finally met someone who seemed to like her, only to have him push her away, brought all of Isana's insecurities to the surface.

"And we'll have dancing elephants perform at the reception," Lena said.

Isana blinked, then offered a sheepish smile. "That obvious I wasn't paying attention, huh?"

Lena held up her forefinger and thumb close together. "Just a smidge. It's okay. I do tend to get carried away when talking about tulle and flowers." She eyed Isana. "But I didn't come over to talk about my wedding. Spill it. What happened with Cy?"

That was all the encouragement Isana needed to relate the entire, sorry mess. At the end of her tale, Isana shrugged. "When I stopped by his office during work to update him on what the RBWG next to the names meant, he acted cold and disinterested, like he couldn't wait for me to leave." She twisted a tissue in her hands, not wanting Lena to think she was seeing boogeymen around every corner. But the train incident still rattled her, so she drew in a breath. "There's more."

Her friend leaned forward, her eyes intent on Isana.

"Coming home today, I nearly fell in front of an incoming train."

"What? Are you okay? Why didn't you say so first thing?"

"I'm fine. A man next to me grabbed my arm in time. I was only shaken." Isana eyed the now shredded tissue. "You'll probably think I'm crazy, but I could have sworn someone pushed me toward the tracks."

"Pushed you?" Lena frowned. "Was the platform crowded?"

"It was at the tail end of rush hour, so the platform was full but not packed. I'm sure I felt someone's hand between my shoulder blades and a hard shove." She shivered. "If the other passenger hadn't noticed me pitching forward, I'd have been on the tracks as the train arrived at the station."

"And you're pretty sure there's no way it was an accident." Lena's statement eased some of the tension in Isana.

She nodded. "But why would someone try to push me onto the tracks?"

"Because someone doesn't want the truth about those names to come out."

Isana threw up her hands. "That's the thing. What truth? All these women have in common is they were in West Berlin in the 1980s."

"No, there's one more thing," Lena said. "They also gave birth while living there."

Isana finished her coffee. "What's the significance of having a baby while overseas? It must happen all the time."

"Have you tracked down the whereabouts of the other women on the list?"

"No." Isana sighed. "But I have the feeling that's your next suggestion."

CY QUIETLY CLOSED THE STUDY DOOR. SETTING HIS MUG OF CHAMOMILE TEA on the corner of the desk, he sank into his father's old office chair. The familiar squeak of the ancient leather brought a fleeting smile to his lips. The old-fashioned mantel clock chimed one-thirty, reminding Cy he should be sleeping, not wide awake in the middle of the night.

His mother had retired early, citing exhaustion. The dark circles under her eyes and the droop to her shoulders attested to her tiredness. Cy had let her go with a gentle kiss on her forehead, despite wanting to grill her about the list and what those names meant. He'd told Isana he wouldn't pursue that line of inquiry with his mother home, but the idea Mom knew something about those names wouldn't leave his mind.

All his life, he'd thought his mother was an open book. She'd overcome the devastating loss of her husband when Cy was in kindergarten and had given him a good childhood despite her own grief. But lately, Cy realized she had her own secrets, ones that might have directly led to her being kidnapped and beaten.

The hurt in Isana's eyes flashed across his mind. His heart ached at his stupidity in pushing her away. At the time, he'd convinced himself it was for her safety, but now he wasn't so sure. Yes, his mother's warning had prompted him to distance himself as a way of protecting Isana. But he was also protecting himself. Isana had become very dear to him in such a short time that it scared him. He had always kept a part of himself back with the women he'd dated over the years, letting them in only so far in order to keep his heart solely his. Seeing his mother's protracted grief over his father's death had made him wary of falling in love.

But Isana had broken through the barriers he'd erected around his heart without him even knowing until it was too late. While waiting for her to come to the hospital, he'd realized he'd fallen in love with her wholly and completely. That scared him more than his mother's warning, although he'd used that as his internal excuse for cooling things off.

He sipped his tea, grimacing at the lukewarm liquid. Seeing Isana earlier today had re-awakened his feelings, making him clumsy in his interaction. The memory of her soft lips under his only made his decision more painful. When had a kiss so discombobulated him? Never. Kissing had always seemed so pedestrian, an expected ending after a nice dinner with a lovely woman. But those chaste pecks on the mouth had nothing on the kiss he exchanged with Isana. His toes tingled as he relived the sensation of kissing her.

A soft thud jerked his thoughts back to the present. Perhaps his mom had stumbled getting out of bed. He was halfway to the door when the sound of footsteps headed toward the study halted him.

The firm steps had a steadiness unlike his mother's earlier pace. Flattening himself against the wall near the door frame, he waited.

Someone turned the handle and pushed open the door. The movement blocked Cy's line of sight temporarily. The figure moved deeper into the room, giving Cy a glimpse of a person dressed in dark clothes, gloves, and a hooded sweatshirt. The bulky clothing obscured the person's gender. Cy concentrated on breathing slowly in and out as the intruder rummaged through the desk. The hood covered enough of the person's face to shield their identity.

After searching each drawer, the figure scattered the papers on the desktop, knocking Cy's mug to the floor. The person glanced around the room. Cy stepped from his hiding place to accost the intruder.

The figure rounded the desk, then lashed out at Cy with a well-placed kick to his groin. Pain exploded, bringing Cy to his knees as the intruder slammed a fist into the side of his head. The room spun as the assailant raced out of the house. The sound of the front door slamming shut told Cy he wouldn't catch the intruder tonight.

Cy stayed on the carpet as waves of pain cascaded throughout his body.

"Cy?"

His mother's voice, laced with uncertainty, penetrated the haze of pain. "In . . . the . . . study," he ground out as he rolled onto his back, drawing in gulps of air to clear his head from the ringing blow.

His mom flicked on the overhead light, her gasp indicating she'd seen the mess made by the intruder. "What's going on? Why are you lying there on the floor?"

"Intruder," was all he could get out.

"Are you hurt?" Lillian dropped to her knees beside him, her hand gently touching his shoulder.

"I'll be okay." He lifted himself up as if moving through mud, each movement calculated and slow. Resting his back against the desk, he took inventory of his body. His head ached but no more pulsating pain. His nether region would recover. "We should call the police."

"No." She crossed her arms. "I don't want more questions. Nothing was taken. You said you'll be okay."

He sighed. "Mom, are you going to tell me what's really going on?"

His mother pursed her lips, a gesture he knew only too well. "I have no idea why someone would break into my home and ransack my desk."

When she had that stubborn look on her face, it was no use arguing. "If you say so." He stood, glad his head didn't swim. He glanced at the mess of papers on and around the desk. "I'll check the doors and windows, then I'm going to bed. We can clean up in the morning."

She nodded, then shuffled back to her bedroom. Cy examined the front door, noting tiny scratches where the intruder must have used a lock pick to gain entry. He engaged the deadbolt and front door chain before double checking all the windows and back door were secured. Then he went to his own room. Despite his exhaustion, his mind twisted the facts over and over again, but no new solutions surfaced. One troubling thought kept rising to the surface.

His mother knew more than she was saying.

CHAPTER
TWENTY-NINE

Isana shielded her eyes from the bright morning sun as she waited on the sidewalk outside her building for Lena. The light breeze carried the promise of spring while birds twittered in the evenly spaced trees along the edge of the walkway. A couple pushing a baby stroller passed, insulated drink containers in hand. A woman jogged by, her black labradoodle loping beside her. Last night, she'd tracked down as many of the names on the list as she could. Online searches had turned up two still residing in the metro DC area. A little more digging uncovered home addresses, one in northeast DC and one in Arlington, Virginia. This morning, she would drop by unannounced with Lena.

A car horn honked, bringing Isana's attention to the road. Lena waved from her sky-blue crossover vehicle. Isana slipped into the front seat, setting her camera case on the floor before buckling up.

Lena pulled into traffic. "Ready for our adventure?"

"I guess." Isana wished she could have Lena's optimism of finding more answers than questions today.

"We don't have to go."

Isana sighed. "It's not that I don't want to find out, but . . . " She struggled to find the right words to express her *meh* feeling about the whole thing but couldn't.

"But you would rather be sleuthing with Cy," Lena finished for her.

"Maybe."

"You can always update him after we talk to the women." Lena turned off Nebraska Avenue NW onto Utah Avenue NW. The scenery changed from commercial to residential, with stately brick homes, manicured lawns, and mature trees. "Wow, these are some big mansions."

"I'd bet my entire apartment would fit into the living room of one of these houses."

Lena slowed to make a right turn onto 32nd Street NW. "We're looking for number 6334."

"There," Isana pointed to a brick house set back from the other homes, with a long, asphalt driveway. "Looks like you can park on the street."

Lena wedged her car into a space between two SUVs and cut the engine. "Ready?"

Now they had arrived, second thoughts assailed Isana. "Maybe this is a bad idea."

"Nonsense." Lena opened her door. "We've got the perfect cover story, so grab your camera and let's go."

Isana shouldered the camera bag strap and caught up with Lena as they crossed the quiet residential street. All too soon, Lena had pressed the doorbell.

The door swung open to reveal an attractive woman in her mid-60s, her shoulder-length hair a lovely silvery gray. "Hello, may I help you?"

Lena stepped forward. "Good morning. I'm Lena and this is Isana. Are you Mrs. Jennifer Blandings?"

"Yes." The woman glanced from Lena to Isana, her hand pushing the door a bit as if to close it. "If you're selling something, I'm not interested."

"Oh, no, ma'am. We're hoping you can help us with our graduate school project," Lena put in. "For our cultural history degree. We're writing about what it was like working and living in West Berlin in the mid-to-late 1980s."

The woman's shoulders didn't relax as Isana had expected. If anything, Lena's explanation had heightened the tension.

"Jen, who's at the door?" A man's voice from somewhere in the house called, then he joined her at the door. "Hello, can we help you?"

Lena repeated her story. "You must be Harold Blandings. I'd love to hear from you both about what it was like to live in West Germany during that time."

Mr. Blandings put his arm around his wife. "We have a lunch date but can spare a little time this morning. Come on in."

Isana followed Lena into the house and to a pleasant living room with several groupings of chairs and sofas. Once everyone found a seat, Lena began. "Thank you for being willing to chat with us. We apologize for showing up unannounced, but frankly, we find we get better results when we come in person rather than trying by phone or email."

After Mr. Blandings offered coffee and was declined by all, he said, "What do you want to know?"

Isana held up her phone. "Do you mind if we record this? Makes it easier than trying to scribble down notes while we talk."

"Sure, go ahead," the husband said. Beside him on the loveseat, Mrs. Blandings firmed her lips but said nothing.

Lena dove into a list of prepared questions, mostly about when they arrived in West Berlin, how it was to work for the embassy during that time, where they lived in the city. After fifteen minutes, Mrs. Blandings appeared more relaxed. Lena looked at Isana and nodded, their prearranged signal for Isana to take over the questioning.

"While Lena will be focusing more on the work and culture of living in West Berlin, I'm more interested in the family life." She smiled at both the Blandings but noted the wife's posture stiffened. "We've read about how difficult things were behind the Iron Curtain in getting staples like flour and sugar. Did you have any trouble with that in West Berlin?"

Mrs. Blandings shook her head. "No, for the most part, the shops were well-stocked."

Isana asked about procurement of various household items and the overall living conditions in the city before segueing to more personal questions. "Your daughter was born in West Berlin, wasn't she?"

"That's right," Mr. Blandings said. "In the middle of a summer thunderstorm that snarled traffic so bad, she was born at home, rather than the hospital."

Isana hoped her face didn't show the shock at hearing such a similar story to Virginia Sanders. "Oh? Mrs. Blandings, that must have been quite an adventure."

"It was."

"Oh, come, now. Tell them what happened." Mr. Blandings glanced at Isana and Lena. "I wasn't there at the time. We thought the baby wouldn't come for another three weeks, so Jen insisted I go out of town on a three-day trip to Munich. When I came home, she greeted me with a daughter."

Mrs. Blandings gave in to her husband's request, but her shuttered expression told Isana she didn't want to. Her story sounded eerily similar to the Sanders' tale, right down to the C-section and unnamed doctor.

"You must have been terrified," Isana said to Mrs. Blandings.

"I was." Mrs. Blandings touched her husband's arm. "We need to be at the club by eleven-thirty."

"Right you are." He stood. "I'm afraid that's all the time we have this morning."

Isana turned off the recording and stood as well, hefting her camera. "May I take a quick photo of the two of you? I'll be putting photographs in with my text as part of the final project."

"I look a fright," Mrs. Blandings said, her hand smoothing back her hair.

Mr. Blandings dropped a kiss on her temple. "You look as lovely as always, my dear."

Isana focused the camera and snapped the photo quickly. "Thank you."

"May I have your phone number in case we need to follow up on anything?" Lena asked. Mr. Blandings provided a number, then waved goodbye as they left.

Back in the car, Lena started it and drove a little way down the block before parking again. "That was interesting."

"It was indeed." Isana hadn't told Lena about the second lady's interview, and somehow, it didn't feel right to share it with her friend before she told Cy.

"Wonder why Mrs. Blandings got so uptight about her daughter's birth?"

"You picked up on that too?" Isana checked the recording, the voices coming through loud and clear on the replay.

"Who knows." Lena shrugged. "Maybe she was still mad at hubby for missing the birth. It does sound traumatic to give birth at home with a strange doctor in attendance."

"Perhaps." Isana closed out of the recording app. "Where to next?"

"Peggy Stratton." Lena put the car in gear and executed a U-turn. "Mind if I listen to a podcast?"

"Be my guest." During the drive to Arlington, Isana tuned out the podcast and thought through the similarities in the birth stories from Virginia and Jennifer. The desire to talk over the coincidence of both women having C-sections at home while their husbands with Cy had her reaching for her phone. But she quelled the impulse. He didn't want her help. If it hadn't been for Lena's push and offer to drive, Isana doubted she would have even bothered to visit the two local women on the list. If part of her hoped whatever they discovered would mean she'd have an excuse to talk with Cy again, she didn't dwell on it.

~

LILLIAN WAVED AS CYRUS DROVE OFF, LENGTHY GROCERY LIST IN HAND. A twinge of guilt pricked her spine at sending him off on an errand so she could slip out of the house undetected, but she ignored it. Some things you couldn't explain to your son. Shrugging into her coat took more effort than she'd expected. Maybe she should take one of the pain pills to keep a clear head. Checking her phone showed she had time to down a pill before the Uber driver arrived. Five minutes later, she buckled her seatbelt and settled back for the trip into DC.

The car dropped her at the intersection of Washington Avenue NW and Independence Avenue NW near the US Botanical Gardens' Bartholdi Park. With the temperature hovering in the low 40s, the park had no lingering patrons. Lillian meandered toward the center where a solitary woman faced the Fountain of Light and Water, still winterized and not flowing.

When Lillian approached, the woman said, "Did you know the fountain's creator also designed the Statue of Liberty?"

"Frederic Auguste Bartholdi created some of the world's most beautiful cast-iron statutes." Lillian stopped beside the woman, her gaze on the waterless fountain. "It was originally made for the 1876 Centennial Exposition in Philadelphia."

"Amazing how works created more than a century ago still have the power to charm us today." The woman put her hands in the pockets of her peacoat, keeping her face—shielded by a hood—in profile. "Some would say the past has no relevance on the present, but I'd disagree, wouldn't you?"

"Yes." Lillian chose her next words carefully. "I also think what was done in the past shouldn't be discussed today."

Gina Sanders turned her full attention to Lillian, her famous blue eyes glittering in the morning sun. "Exactly."

"Then why are you trying to hurt my family?" Lillian didn't miss the slight narrowing of Gina's eyes. "I have just as much to lose as you do."

Gina nodded. "I thought as much when you were missing." She returned her gaze to the fountain, with its dozen lanterns dangling from a mural crown upheld by three sea nymphs. "I have no wish to harm anyone."

Lillian sensed a *however* lingering on the light breeze. When the other woman didn't expand on her statement, she changed tactics. "Someone broke into my house last night and ransacked my office."

Gina swung her gaze back to Lillian, her eyes widening a fraction, but again, she kept silent.

"Nothing was taken that I could see because there's nothing there to find." She fished a coin out of her purse and tossed it into the fountain's drained basin, the metal clinking in the empty bowl. "I remember doing the same in the Neptunbrunnen fountain while living in West Berlin. How many coins I dropped into those waters, each with the same prayer—for a child."

Lillian held out a penny to Gina. "Want to toss it in for old time's sake?" She didn't let her hand waver, her eyes on the other woman's face.

"Thank you." Gina accepted the coin, lobbing it into the basin. "I haven't thought about the Neptunbrunnen in years. I much prefer to live in the present."

"There's not many fond memories of those days, except, of course, the birth of my only son. With all the moves we've had since, there's little I kept from my time in West Germany."

"I was the same way." Gina wrapped her arms around her waist.

In the distance, Lillian spotted a tall man in an overcoat, probably her Secret Service detail. Somehow, the man's presence eased some of the fear she hadn't known she had. "I've already lost so much. I have no intention of jeopardizing my son's life."

"Ah, yes, I'd forgotten about your husband's . . . death."

The slight pause cut deeper than if Gina had simply said "suicide.

The knowledge Greg hadn't taken his own life but that Schmidt had murdered her beloved husband absorbed some of the pain. She'd never be able to tell Cyrus the truth, not without revealing why Schmidt had killed Greg.

Something of the inner turmoil must have shown on her face because Gina winced. "I'm sorry, Lillian."

Lillian waved her hand in acknowledgement. "It was a long time ago."

For the next couple of minutes, neither woman spoke. Then Gina said, "I must go, but I appreciate your discretion."

With what, the vice president's wife had no need to put into words. Gina pivoted and walked briskly from the park, the man in the overcoat following her.

Lillian made her way to one of the benches scattered throughout the park, her mind turning over the conversation. She hadn't even been sure Gina would come when she'd left the message with her personal secretary using the code Marta had taught her more than thirty years ago. But she was certain she had done what she could to ensure Cyrus's safety. Maybe now, she could push him to bring Isana home for dinner so she could meet the woman who had captured her son's heart—even if Cyrus himself protested otherwise.

Her phone buzzed, alerting her to an incoming text. Cyrus, home from his grocery run, worried about her whereabouts. She let him know she'd be home soon, then called an Uber. She'd spent so much time and energy keeping her secret. Maybe it was time to tell her son the truth. Her heart constricted.

Part of the truth he'd understand. It was the other part, the reason Gina Sanders met her today, she couldn't bear to share. Cyrus wouldn't understand, and he probably wouldn't forgive her, especially when he realized it was her actions that indirectly led to his father's death. She buried her face in her hands, sobs shaking her body. She'd already lost her husband. She wasn't about to lose her son too.

CHAPTER

THIRTY

Cy heated chicken noodle soup on the stovetop, his mind not on lunch but his mother. She'd returned home in an Uber from visiting an old friend, and immediately went straight to her room. When he'd peeked in on her an hour later, she was snuggled under an afghan, fast asleep in her bed. Now the clock edged toward one. His stomach growled as the scent of chicken wafted throughout the kitchen.

"Got enough for two?" His mother came into the kitchen, one of his dad's threadbare cardigans over her fleece pants and flannel shirt.

"Yes, be ready in a minute." He poured her a glass of milk, then put cheese slices and crackers on a plate before dividing the soup into two bowls.

"Would you say the blessing?" Mom asked.

Cy complied, then the two ate in companionable silence for a few minutes. Always a fast eater, he'd finished his soup before his mother had consumed half her bowl. Layering cheese onto a cracker, he popped it in his mouth.

"Just like your dad, you know." She pointed to his empty bowl. "I remember when we were first married, if I got up to get the salt from the counter, Greg would have finished his entire plate of food." She shook her head. "Came from growing up in a household of five older brothers. He had to eat quick, or he wouldn't get seconds."

"I remember wanting to beat Dad by cleaning my plate first, but I never did." He loaded another cracker with cheese.

His mom put down her spoon. "I think I've done you a disservice."

Cy paused before eating the cracker. "What do you mean?"

"I was so angry after Greg died. How could he leave us like that without any warning? The stigma of suicide coupled with the stress of raising a child on my own fueled my grief and anger for years. I couldn't let go, didn't want to move on."

His heart twisted at the anguish on her face. He reached for her hand. "It's okay, Mom. You did the best you could in very trying circumstances."

She squeezed his hand. "I'm not sure I did. I think I gave you the impression that love, true love, isn't worth the effort because of the pain it caused when the one you loved is no longer with you."

He opened his mouth to refute her statement, but she ploughed on before he could get a word out.

"You're thirty-five years old and have never had a serious girlfriend." Her eyes stayed steady on his. "And you've cut ties with the lovely woman you've fallen in love with because you're scared."

He pulled his hand free, leaning back in his chair. The need to justify his actions loosened his tongue. "You warned me in the hospital we were still in danger. I didn't want anything to happen to Isana."

"Oh, Cyrus. You were already looking for an excuse to distance yourself from Isana because she was becoming too important to you."

"No, that's not true." He crossed his arms. "It's for her protection. The intruder last night shows I was right to be cautious. As long as we're not investigating the list, she'll be safe."

His mom dipped her spoon into her bowl. "How do you know she's not continuing to look into the names on her own?"

His heartrate sped up at the thought.

"Since you've made it crystal clear she's not to contact you, how will you know if she's safe or not?"

He locked eyes with his mom's, worry gnawing at the edges of his nerves.

"I know you care for her deeply. Stop letting your fear get in the way of exploring this relationship." She ate a bite of soup, then pointed her spoon at him. "Call her. Now."

Cy snatched up his phone and pulled up Isana's number, but he hesitated before hitting the call button. Maybe he should text first, in case she didn't want to talk to him. Having the call roll to voicemail would mean leaving a message. He had no idea what to say to elicit a callback.

"What are you waiting for?"

He jerked his gaze from his phone to his mom's face.

"You're overthinking this. Call her. If you get her voicemail, tell her you were an idiot and ask her forgiveness for not coming to your senses sooner. Then invite her out for coffee or dinner or whatever you young people do for fun these days."

His mother's admonition propelled him to his feet. She was right, like usual. Dropping a kiss on the top of her head, he headed to the study for some privacy. When one groveled, better not to have an audience.

Isana tucked a strand of hair behind her ear, unable to keep from fidgeting as she waited for Cy to join her at Misha's Coffee in Old Town Alexandria. He'd called a couple of hours ago, saying he was sorry for shoving her away and asking for another chance. The sincerity in his voice made her agree to late afternoon coffee, but now that he was officially ten minutes past the meeting time, she was second-guessing her eagerness to see him.

For the third time in as many minutes, she glanced at her phone screen. No texts from Cy. Maybe he'd emailed her instead. A swipe pulled up her email, but no new messages popped up. She put the phone face down on the round tabletop and sipped her coffee, her gaze straying to the entrance every few seconds. A siren blared in the distance. By the time she'd finished her coffee, the disappointment of Cy's absence filled her stomach like lead balloons. Thirty-five minutes past the appointment time. He wasn't coming. Rising, she carried her mug to the dish return tub, then trudged toward the door. Before she could exit, a group of teenagers tumbled inside, pushing her farther into the café's interior with their exuberance.

"Did you see the accident?" asked a boy with shaggy blond hair as Isana sidestepped him.

"It was scary," a girl said, shivering for effect. "I could have sworn the SUV headed straight for him."

"The poor guy never had a chance," a boy wearing a Washington Commanders team hoodie agreed.

Unease pricked at the back of Isana's neck. She inserted herself into the conversation. "Did you say there was an accident involving a vehicle and a male pedestrian? Where was that?"

The teens fell silent at her question, the trio staring at her with closed expressions. She hastened to explain. "I was supposed to meet my friend and he never showed up, so I wondered . . . " She hoped by not finishing her thought, one of the teens would jump in with more details.

The girl's hand flew to her mouth as she gasped. The boys exchanged a glance, then the blond teen shrugged. "He was tall, with blond hair cut shorter than mine. We were on the opposite corner when it happened."

"The guy was crossing," the teen with the hoodie consulted his phone, "Union Street with the light and this SUV comes roaring down Prince and hangs a right."

"The driver barely slowed down enough to make the turn," the blond teen said. "The guy saw it coming and nearly made it to the sidewalk, but the SUV swerved and clipped him."

Isana's heart pounded so loudly, she could barely hear the hoodie teen's follow up.

"The SUV took off, but I snapped a pic." He held out his phone to her. In it, a slightly blurry SUV roared off down the street.

"Did you show this to the police?" She could make out a U and a B on the license plate, but little else.

"Nah, there were closer witnesses." The hoodie teen shifted on the balls of his feet.

Isana sensed the group was eager to get to their coffee. "Would you mind texting me that photo? In case it's my friend, it might help to find the driver."

The teen's eyes lit up. "Wow, I didn't think I might have taken the only photo of the unsub."

Isana suppressed a smile at the teen's use of police lingo and rattled off her number. The teen thumbed it in, and her phone vibrated with his text. "Thanks."

The boys headed for the ordering counter, while the girl lingered a second. "Hope your friend's okay." Then she joined the group.

Isana pushed out the door and turned left, the flashing lights at the intersection less than a block away sending her pulse into overdrive. *Please, God, let Cy be okay.*

An ambulance pulled away from the curb as she reached Union Street. A motorcycle policeman stood talking to a couple wrangling an exuberant puppy on a leash. Isana paused to take in the scene. A police cruiser idled at the curb, its blue lights flashing. An officer sat behind the wheel, her attention directed toward the console computer.

She moved toward the vehicle but was intercepted by a female officer. "Can I help you?"

"I hope so," Isana said, surprised at how shaky her voice sounded. "I was supposed to meet my friend at Misha's, but he didn't show up." She drew in a breath. "Then I heard some teens talking about a hit-and-run and thought maybe it was my friend."

The woman's gaze turned sympathetic. "What's your friend's name?"

"Cyrus Hillam." Isana blinked back tears as she waited for the woman's answer.

"Give me a minute." The cop stepped back, then spoke into her shoulder mic.

Isana hugged herself against the light breeze. A prayer spilled over in her heart for Cy's safety and health. Her faith, which had been dormant for so long, had blossomed during her time with Cy. She didn't think it could be all attributed to the danger their discoveries had engineered. His ease with praying and talking about God had prompted her to open her Bible app and read a Psalm on the Metro on her way to work and give thanks at night for the day's events.

"Miss?" The police officer wore a neutral expression, not letting Isana know whether or not she would provide the information she sought. "May I have your name?"

"Isana Thomas." *Please tell me Cy's okay.*

"May I see your ID?" The officer's name tag read *C. Smith.*

Isana slipped her license from her phone's case wallet and handed it to the officer, who studied it before giving it back.

"Thank you. I was heading to the coffeeshop when you stopped by," Officer Smith said. "Mr. Hillam asked we tell you what happened."

Isana put her hand over her mouth to stop sobs from escaping. *Tell me!*

"Mr. Hillam was in an accident. A vehicle struck him in the cross-walk." The officer consulted a notebook. "Two witnesses claim the car swerved to deliberately hit him. He sustained an injury to his left leg and ankle but was conscious when emergency personnel arrived on scene."

Relief that Cy's injuries didn't appear extensive flooded her system, and she nearly collapsed onto the sidewalk. However, knowing Cy needed her strengthened her muscles enough to keep her upright. "Did you get a description of the car?"

The officer rattled off a generic description. "No one got the license plate." She glanced over her shoulder at the intersection. "And the red-light cameras wouldn't have caught the vehicle either, since he was executing a legal right turn."

"Until he hit Cy." Isana started to slip her phone into her pocket when she remembered the teen's text. She pulled up the photo, enlarging it before flipping her phone around to show the cop. "One of the teens at the coffee shop took this photo."

The officer accepted the phone, pinching her fingers to enlarge the photo even more. "That's a good image of the plate. Would you forward this to me?"

"Of course." Isana keyed in the officer's number, then sent the pic. "Which hospital did they take Cy?"

"Inova Alexandria Hospital on Seminary Road."

Isana nodded. Not near a Metro. She'd have to call an Uber.

"Do you need a ride?" Officer Smith offered.

"Yes, please." Isana waited while the cop spoke briefly to her motorcycle colleague, then returned to the cruiser where her partner waited. During the short ride to the hospital, she prayed for his swift recovery and the apprehension of whoever had tried to kill him.

CY ACCEPTED THE CRUTCHES FROM THE NURSE, STANDING ON HIS RIGHT LEG while she adjusted the height to fit him. She held a packet of discharge papers in her hand.

"Ah, I see your ride has arrived." She eyed his struggle with maneuvering the crutches to take a step. "You have someone waiting for you?"

"Yes." Cy had been relieved to receive Isana's text about being in the hospital waiting room.

"Good." The nurse nodded, then called over an older man wearing a maroon blazer and dark blue slacks pushing a wheelchair. "Neil, would you please escort Mr. Hillam to the waiting room? Here are his discharge papers."

Neil accepted the papers as Cy eased into the chair, laying his crutches across his lap. "Ready to go, young man?"

Cy thanked the nurse, then Neil guided the chair toward the bank of elevators. Fifteen minutes later, the automatic doors to the waiting area came into view. "Is your ride here?"

"I hope so." Cy let Neil push him through the doors. Cy's first sweep of the groupings of chairs and loveseats didn't reveal Isana. She hadn't left, had she?

"Looking for me?"

Cy swung his head around to see her.

"So that's a yes?" A smile flashed across her face, but she quickly sobered at the sight of his bandages. "Let's get you home."

"You look like you're in good hands." Neil handed Isana the stack of papers. "I'll wait here with him until you bring your car around."

Isana tucked the papers into her purse. "Where to—your condo or your mom's house?"

"My mom's. She won't rest easy until she sees with her own eyes I'm okay."

Isana typed something into her phone. "An Uber driver will pick us up in five."

Neil pushed the chair to wait outside, Isana walking beside him. Seeing Isana made his heart happy. There was no other way to describe the warm feeling coursing through his veins. He had been all kinds of a fool to have told her to leave.

During the ride to his childhood home, they talked about the weather and other banal things. His mother met them at the door. "Cyrus! What on earth happened?"

"Hi, Mom." He kissed her cheek as he passed her in the foyer. "This is Isana Thomas."

"Hi, Mrs. Hillam," Isana said.

"No need for formalities, my dear. Call me Lillian." Mom closed the front door. "Now, a cup of tea and some fresh scones will be just the thing."

Cy winked at Isana behind his mother's back as he followed her into the kitchen. Once everyone had hot tea and cranberry scones before them, Lillian caught Cy's gaze. "What happened?"

He broke off a piece of warm scone, popping it into his mouth to buy time to formulate his answer. He didn't want to alarm his mother, not after what she'd been through, but he also didn't want her and Isana unaware of the continued danger.

"Quite stalling," his mother said.

"You know me too well. I think someone tried to run me over."

Mom covered her mouth. "Oh, no."

Isana's expression was more thoughtful than shocked. "That's what the kids said."

"What kids?" Cy sipped his tea.

"I was waiting at Misha's Coffee for our, er, meeting."

"I'm so sorry about that," he interjected, but she waved her hand to hush him.

"After half an hour, I decided to leave, but a trio of teenagers came into the café, and I got tangled up in the group at the door. One of them was talking about a black SUV nearly running someone down at the nearby intersection." Isana cupped her hands around a mug adorned with seashells. "I asked what they meant." Her eyes met Cy's. "Somehow, I knew it was you."

He wanted to touch her hand to reassure her he was okay, but his mother's presence made him shy.

"One of the teens snapped a pic of the departing vehicle, which he sent to me." She showed him a photo, slightly out of focus, of a Ford Explorer. "I hustled to the corner and asked a police officer about the accident. You had given permission for them to tell me where you were, so I headed to the hospital after sending the photo to the police. You must have been terrified."

The fear at hearing the roar of an engine, then a screech of tires as the vehicle took the turn at speed, coursed through his body again. "The driver aimed right at me, didn't slow down, didn't hit the brakes. I don't know how I managed to get out of the way, but I did." He nodded toward the crutches propped against the wall. "I cut my leg on the jagged end of a storm drain."

"I don't understand." Mom's gaze was troubled. "This shouldn't have happened." She stood. "Please excuse me. I need to lie down."

"Mom? Are you okay?" Cy started to rise as well, but she waved him down.

She touched his shoulder. "I'm glad you're okay, but I think I've had enough excitement for the day."

He frowned as she left the room, not speaking until he heard the bedroom door close. The feeling his mother was hiding something returned full force with her abrupt departure.

"How's she doing?"

Isana's question drew him back to the beautiful woman sitting across the table from him. "I don't know. Physically, she's healing, but mentally, something's troubling her." He hadn't meant to share his concerns over his mother's state of mind, but he suddenly wanted Isana to understand. "She's been more secretive than before."

"What do you think she's hiding?"

He ate another piece of scone while considering her query. "I think it has something to do with my father and possibly their time in West Berlin."

"Have you asked her for more details about your birth?" The change in topic surprised him.

"Yes, but she only reiterated what I'd already known." He finished the scone, brushing his fingers off on a napkin.

"At home by C-section?" Isana's eyes met his, her gaze direct and steady.

"I think so, yes." Cy's heartrate accelerated. "What are you getting at?"

"The Sanders and the Blandings both have similar stories."

"I'm confused."

She blew out a breath. "I found an old TV segment of Virginia and Gilbert Sanders when he was running for governor of Maryland. In the interview, they were asked about the birth of their twins while in West Germany. The story is similar to yours. The father was away, there was a storm, and the mom had an emergency C-section at home by a traveling doctor the midwife found. Dad comes home to a recovering wife and babies."

"Things were different in a foreign country back then, especially West Berlin. I don't think there's anything—"

"Lena and I visited Mr. and Mrs. Blandings, another name on the list, and heard nearly the same story. Electrical outage tangled up traffic. Emergency C-section at home by a doctor the midwife found while the husband was out of town on an extended trip." She shrugged. "I'm not sure what it means, but it's certainly strange all three women had eerily similar birth experiences while living in West Berlin."

He rubbed his forehead. "I'm sure it's not at all an unusual story. Besides, weren't these births spread out over several years?"

"Yes." She drained her mug, her eyes intent on his. "You don't find it the least bit odd, these nearly identical birth stories?"

He shook his head. "I can't say that I do."

Her face fell.

"Hey, we'll figure it out."

"Will we?" Tears shimmered in her eyes.

"Don't cry." He scooted his chair closer to hers.

"I don't know why I'm crying." She sniffled, using her napkin to wipe the wetness from her cheeks. "I was so scared you were really hurt."

"I know. Thank God I wasn't."

"I've never prayed so hard in my life on the ride to the hospital."

He gave into the impulse to thumb away a tear from her face. "I'm glad you did." Her eyes closed as he continued to brush tears across her smooth skin. "Isana, I've been all kinds of a fool."

Her eyes opened to stare into his own. "You have?"

"You're not going to make this easy on me, are you?" He leaned closer, wanting to be nearer to her. "I'm sorry. I was scared for your safety but also of my growing feelings for you."

"You have feelings for me?" Her eyes sparkled, the last vestiges of tears receding.

"I do," he said. "I'm falling for you. Hard."

"You are?"

"I am." He tugged her closer until their lips were millimeters apart. Desire to put his mouth on hers nearly overrode his control, but he wanted her to confess what she felt for him first. "What about you?"

"Oh, I think I'm falling for you too." Her eyes dropped to his lips. "Do you think you could kiss me now?"

"With pleasure." His lips claimed hers in a kiss that drove all other thoughts from his mind. Mingled with the passion came a feeling of coming home, of finding where he belonged. If he had any say in the matter, he'd never be so foolish as to let Isana go again.

CHAPTER

THIRTY-ONE

Seated at her dressing table, Gina smoothed lotion across her still flawless complexion. Her nighttime routine hadn't varied much since the day she turned twenty-two and realized she needed to take care of her skin or it would sag like her Aunt Milly's before she hit forty. A strict regime of creams and lotions, along with a discrete trip or two to the plastic surgeon for a little assistance in keeping age at bay had given her the face of a much younger woman.

"Turning in?" Gil dropped a kiss on her head, his eyes meeting hers in the large, lighted mirror.

"I thought I'd read some of the Hayley Mills autobiography in bed." Gina recapped the lotion bottle. "It's still a little chilly. Think we could have a small fire?"

"Excellent idea." He knelt by the fireplace, putting a match to the kindling already in place. Soon flames licked the dry wood and paper. He fed it some larger sticks, then replaced the screen. "I'll put on a log or two in a few minutes."

Gina crossed to their king-sized bed, the covers turned down and the pillows plumped. Slipping underneath the sheets, she picked up her reading glasses and book. Her husband disappeared into the adjourning bathroom, the sound of his electric toothbrush faint behind the half-closed door. She lost herself in Hayley's childhood, barely noticing Gil feeding the fire, then slipping into bed beside her.

When he didn't pick up his own book—a treatise on foreign diplomacy in the twenty-first century—she glanced at him over the top of hers. His eyes searched her face. "Gil? What is it?"

"You know I love you."

Her heart beat faster, the seriousness of his countenance scaring her. "And I love you." She leaned over and kissed his cheek, wondering if his declaration was a prelude to further intimacy.

But rather than kiss her back, he touched her hand with his. "Why did you meet with Lillian Hillam today?"

"She's an old friend from our West Berlin days." She marked her place in the autobiography, then closed the book.

"What did she want?"

Gina relaxed. Gil's question indicated he was on a fishing expedition. She'd become an expert at deflecting queries with enough truth to satisfy the asker without giving away the true reason. "What most old acquaintances wanted—to renew our friendship. I'm sure she'd heard the rumors about your potential candidacy and wanted to make sure I'd remember her and her son. You have no idea how many people from our past I have to be courteous to without promising anything."

Her husband studied her face. "Did she tell you about being kidnapped?"

"Kidnapped?" She affected surprise. "No, she didn't say a word." Technically true. "When?"

"She was found pretty beat up on the street last Saturday after being held for more than a week. One of the kidnappers was found murdered but the other man—the one Lillian said was in charge—has yet to be located."

"That's terrible. Poor woman." Gina shook her head. "She looked pale, and I thought I detected bruising, but one doesn't ask such personal questions. She wasn't at all like the woman I knew briefly in West Berlin."

For a while, the crackling fire was the only sound in the room. Gina peeked at her husband, who stared at the ceiling, his lips in a grim line. He knew. No, he suspected something. But what? She couldn't risk pressing him without giving away her secrets.

"I know my political success is largely because of you." He didn't look at her but continued to gaze upwards. "I know what you've done, you've done for me, for us, for our future."

Her breath hitched, but she steadied her breathing and relaxed the muscles in her face. He couldn't know. She'd been too careful. Time for a little distraction. She bridged the distance between them, snuggling closer to his side. Her fingers played with his still-thick head of hair. "My whole life has been for you and the boys."

"That's what makes this so hard." The anguish in his voice hammered on her heart.

"It doesn't—"

"Stop." He captured her hand in his, stilling her caresses. "I know about Marta Bauer."

The name cracked like a whip across her body, jerking her away from him. She scooted back to her side of the bed. She had to know what he thought he knew. "That's a name I haven't heard in a while."

"Then you don't deny knowing this woman?"

She met his gaze with a steady look. "Of course not. I met her during our time in West Berlin. We had coffee together a few times."

"How did you meet her?"

Her heartrate slowed at the benign questions. He wanted to believe in an innocent explanation for whatever he'd heard. She would give him one. "Through a mutual friend. Lillian Hillam." She had no qualms about bringing Lillian's name into it. After all, the woman knew Marta too.

"You never mentioned Marta or your meetings before."

"Darling," she cooed in her sweetest voice, "if I told you about every acquaintance I had coffee with, you'd be bored out of your mind. You were working a lot, and I had to fill my days somehow. I went out to lunch and dinner and drinks with a lot of people, some only a few times and others more frequently." She shrugged, seeing the tension ease a bit in the hard lines of her husband's face. "Are you asking about Marta because some woman with that name was found murdered in DC recently?"

His gaze sharpened. "What do you know about that?"

"Nothing except what I read in the paper." She widened her eyes as if a thought had just occurred to her. She had to play this with the right amount of hurt and indignation to make Gil buy it and stop asking questions. "Wait a minute. You didn't think I had something to do with the poor woman's demise, do you? Because she was a German national?"

For a moment, she thought she'd pulled it off, that he believed her story and all would go back to normal. Then he blinked, and she spotted moisture in his eyes. Rising, he crossed to the wall safe hidden behind a painting of Siberian dogs by Franz Marc on loan from the National Gallery of Art.

"I don't understand." She climbed out of bed, her eyes unable to look away as he opened the safe and pulled out a brown mailing envelope.

Without a word, he moved back to the bed and upended the envelope. Onto the rumpled bedspread tumbled her collection of burner phones. Gina barely glanced at the devices. Instead, she raised a trembling hand to her lips and forced tears from her eyes, a trick she'd mastered in childhood. "Oh, darling. I wanted to tell you, but she said she'd hurt you if I did."

Confusion flashed across his face. "What?"

She pressed her advantage, rushing around the foot of the bed to his side. "Marta. She contacted me a few weeks ago. She threatened me, saying she would scuttle your campaign before it even launched if I didn't help her. She kept referring to some mysterious event that happened during our West Berlin time. I had no idea what she was talking about or what she wanted help with. She sent me the burner phones, said someone would be listening. I think the woman was paranoid, maybe suffering from dementia."

"Why didn't you tell me?"

The question sent a shiver of relief up her spine. He wanted to believe her. She would help him to do so. "Because I thought I could reason with her, find out what she wanted, and get her help. She was obviously a sick woman, spouting all kinds of nonsense. I only spoke with her a couple of times." She laid a hand on his arm. "She wanted me to meet her at the botanical gardens, but I couldn't make it. Had a luncheon with the Daughters of the American Revolution that day. When I read she'd been killed, I didn't want to worry you that I could have been hurt too, if I'd gone like she asked."

Her husband's expression softened. Elation raced through her, but she ducked her head to hide her satisfaction. She'd always known how to handle Gil, how to make him see her side of things. Burying her head in his chest, she sobbed. "I was so scared, but I knew I had to be strong for you."

He hesitated a fraction of a second before enfolding her in his arms, his hand stroking her hair. "I'm sorry you had to go through that alone. Next time, please tell me."

"I will." She hiccupped, raising her tear-stained face to press her lips on his. "Forgive me?"

"Always." He dipped his head to claim her mouth again. As he deepened the kiss, Gina smiled inwardly at how easy it was to distract a man from digging deeper into matters he had no business messing with.

"Is this the house?" Isana pulled to the curb in Cy's rental car in front of a small bungalow in a Maryland suburb.

Beside her, Cy consulted his phone. "Yep, number 3942."

A late model SUV sat in the driveway. The porchlight hadn't

been turned on, but light shown through the filmy curtains covering a large front-facing window. "You're sure it's not too late to call?"

"It's only seven on a Sunday night." He unbuckled his seatbelt. "No one goes to bed that early."

"True." Isana watched him open the door. "Do you need any help?"

"Stop hovering like a mother hen." He heaved himself up using the door frame for leverage, hiding a wince of pain. No way he wanted her thinking he couldn't participate fully in this investigation. "I can handle a short walkway and a couple of stairs."

"If you say so." She got out and stood back while Cy wrestled his crutches out of the back seat, then shut the car door. "Ready?"

He nodded and they made their way to the front door. She pressed the buzzer, hearing the chimes ring somewhere in the house. "A real doorbell instead of one of those electronic ones."

The porchlight flicked on before Cy could respond, and the door opened slowly. An elderly woman wearing a purple bathrobe and fuzzy pink slippers peered at them through thick glasses. "We aren't buying."

"We're not selling," Isana countered quickly before the woman could shut the door in their faces. "Are you Heather Edwards?"

The old woman scrunched up her nose. "Maybe. The name sounds familiar."

"Mom!" A woman in her late thirties bounded up behind the older one. "You're not supposed to answer the door."

"Then tell people to stop ringing the doorbell!" The old woman glared at her daughter. "They're looking for Heather Edwards."

Pain flashed across the younger woman's face. "Mom, that's you."

Heather shook her head. "Not me, must be confusing me with someone else. My name's not Heather Edwards." She frowned. "Can't recall what my name is, but I know it's not Heather." Heather turned and shuffled off toward the back of the house.

Isana's heart dropped. Another dead end. "I'm sorry to have bothered you."

The daughter offered a tired smile. "Alzheimer's. It's gotten worse since my dad died last fall. I thought she'd be okay once I moved in. Or maybe my dad hid her condition from me longer than I realized."

Isana exchanged a glance with Cy, who nodded to explain why they were on her doorstep. "We thought your mom might be able to help us with some information about her time living in West Berlin."

"West Berlin?" The daughter's eyes brightened. "I have some questions of my own about her time there. Won't you come in?"

"Sure." Isana followed the daughter into the house, Cy at her heels.

"I'm Christy Edwards, well Lam now," the woman said. "Let me settle Mom with her game show, and we can talk in the kitchen." She eyed Cy's crutches. "Go on down the hallway, and you can sit the kitchen table."

"Thanks," he said.

The yellow kitchen with green cabinets, their once vibrant color faded, still exuded cheer. Settling at the table, neither one spoke until Christy returned. "She'll be okay for half an hour or so. Loves 'Wheel of Fortune.' One blessing about Alzheimer's is even the reruns appear new to her."

"Again, we're so sorry to barge in like this," Isana said.

Christy waved her hand. "It's okay. I'm moving Mom to a home at the end of the week and then getting the house ready to put on the market. I had to take a leave of absence from my job." She sighed. "Don't know why I'm telling you all of this."

"It's okay." Isana couldn't imagine what the other woman was going through with her mom.

"Do you want anything to drink? I can make coffee or tea, or there's water in the fridge."

"We're okay," Cy said

Christy pulled a can of carbonated water from the refrigerator.

Returning to the table, she popped the top, then asked, "What did you want to ask Mom?"

"About your birth," Isana said. On the ride over, she and Cy had decided to cut directly to the heart of the matter.

"My birth?" Christy's brow furrowed. "I don't understand. Do you know my mom?"

Isana shook her head.

"Then why are you asking about my birth?" Christy's demeanor shifted from friendly to wary.

Exchanging a quick look with Cy, Isana said, "I know this sounds strange and maybe even a little intrusive, but it's important. Cy's mom was kidnapped recently."

Christy's eyes widened. "Your mom was kidnapped? Is she okay?"

"She managed to escape and is recovering," he said. "But we need your help to figure out who did this."

"The kidnappers wanted a ransom of sorts. Not money but a list of names they thought Cy's father had hidden." The words sounded far out even to Isana, but she plunged on. "We found a list with twenty names. One of them was Cy's mom's name."

Christy covered her mouth with her hand. "And one name was my mom's."

"That's why we're here." Isana drew in a deep breath, letting it out slowly. "The only connection we can find between the women— and they were all women—on the list was each spent time with their husbands in West Germany, specifically West Berlin, and each gave birth to their only children there."

Isana let her words sink in, knowing it was a lot for someone to process. What she didn't expect were the tears in Christy's eyes. "What is it?"

"It explains so much." Christy dabbed at her cheeks with a paper napkin.

Isana glanced at Cy, who reached for her hand under the table and squeezed. "What does it explain?" she prodded when Christy stayed silent.

"My father died of myeloma," Christy said. "When he was first diagnosed three years ago, the doctors wanted to try a bone marrow transplant. I was eager to get tested to see if I might be a match, but my mom was dead set against it."

Isana's stomach churned as she sorted through why a mother wouldn't want her daughter to even be tested for such a procedure. When Christy paused to take a sip of water, she interjected. "But you weren't a match."

"Nope." Christy twisted the napkin around her forefinger. "But it isn't unusual for a parent-child not to be a match."

Isana sensed a big *but* coming.

"But the test uncovered something unexpected. I wasn't related to my father."

THIRTY-TWO

Cy gaped at Christy, her words not at all what he had expected. "Your mom had an affair?"

"Let me check on her." Christy made her way down the short hallway to the living room. The theme song for *Jeopardy!* blared from the TV.

"This is taking a strange turn," he said.

Isana caught her upper lip between her teeth. "Hmm."

Before he could ask what she was thinking, Christy returned. "Mom's asleep." As she settled back into her chair, she fiddled with the tab on the fizzy water can. "Mom doesn't know I know."

"We won't say a word," Isana said. "But we need to figure out what the kidnappers wanted before someone else on the list gets hurt."

Christy nodded, as if coming to an internal decision. "When the bone marrow showed I wasn't biologically related to my father, I didn't tell either one of my parents. I couldn't ask my mom if she'd had an affair, and I couldn't ask my father either. For all I could tell, the two had a very loving and close relationship. If I was the product of a slipup, it had been long been forgiven and forgotten."

Cy threaded his fingers through Isana's, enjoying her closeness while hearing a love story.

"But I had to know for sure." Christy sighed. "I kind of stole my mom's DNA from a paper coffee cup and sent it off along with mine and my father's to one of those genetic companies."

"Like 23AndMe or AncestryDNA?" Cy had friends who'd submitted DNA to one of those companies to see where their fore-bearers had come from.

"It was a little more specialized in determining maternity and paternity, but yes, similar concept."

"What did you find?" Isana asked when Christy didn't continue.

"That I wasn't related to either one of my parents."

It took a moment before the import of what Christy said sunk in. He couldn't keep the shock from his voice. "You were adopted?"

"Yep, with Slavic and German ancestry." Christy fisted her hands together. "When I tried to confront my mom about it, she told the strangest tale, one I attributed to her Alzheimer's."

"She didn't deny you were adopted?" Cy clarified.

"Not at all. Mom said I was born during a summer wind storm that knocked out power to the hospital where she was scheduled to give birth."

"Wait a minute," Isana interjected. "Your mother told you the story of your birth? But she clearly couldn't have given birth to you?"

"I told you it was strange." Christy stood. "I think this might help to explain it. Be right back." She headed out the kitchen's other door, away from the front of the house.

"Have you noticed how similar this is to the other birth stories?"

Cy didn't respond, not likely the direction this conversation was going.

"It can't be a coincidence, right?"

Before he could answer Isana's question, Christy re-entered the kitchen carrying what appeared to be an old scrapbook. "I found them." She set the book on the table and flipped through the pages. "Here we go." She turned the book so Cy and Isana could see. Her finger pointed to a snapshot of Heather Edwards as a young, very pregnant woman.

"She faked her pregnancy." Isana leaned closer to the book. "Did she supposedly give birth by Caesarean section?"

"How did you know?" Christy sank into her chair.

"It tallies with other birth stories from several of the women on the list."

Cy stared at the photo of a smiling Heather, presumably her husband beaming beside her. Her rounded belly protruded from under her maroon-colored dress. "She certainly looks pregnant."

"There's more." Christy pulled loose papers from the back of the book. "I found these when I went through a desk drawer." She handed them to Cy.

The words *adoption agency* adorned the top of the page. "They were trying to adopt?"

"They applied for adoption prior to my father's oversees assignment. Based on the application, the reasons for adoption included their apparent inability to conceive a child."

Cy flipped through the pages, his heart aching at the hopes and dreams represented on the agency's paperwork. Then on the final page, a red stamped REJECTED ended those dreams. "Why were they not approved?"

"It's not spelled out, but I suspect my father's age. He was fifteen years older than my mother, and at that time, deemed too old at forty to be a father."

"How devastating." Isana touched the papers with her fingers. "Your poor parents."

"Then I found this." Christy laid another piece of paper on top of the failed application.

Cy picked it up, his eyes skimming the medical form. The words *malformed fallopian tubes* leapt out at him. "Your mother couldn't have children."

"Not a chance." Christy restacked the papers.

Isana tapped the photo of the "pregnant" Heather. "She faked pregnancy and giving birth."

"There's no papers about a secret adoption?" Cy asked, the alternative even more troubling.

"Not that I've found." Christy closed the album. "Two things bother me. First is where I can from. Was I stolen from my parents? Sold by my parents? I have no idea. Second is that my mother couldn't have pulled this off by herself. Who helped her?"

Isana gripped Cy's hand. "Did your mother ever mention someone called Marta Bauer?"

"I can't believe it." Christy's eyes widened as she looked from Cy to Isana. "How do you know these things?"

"She has talked about Marta Bauer," Cy pressed.

"Lately, often. She's very agitated, saying she'll be late to meet Marta. Then she'll beg my father's forgiveness, saying she did it so they could be a family." Christy swiped fresh tears from her cheeks. "Who's Marta?"

Cy deferred to Isana, as he was still trying to fit all the pieces together. Isana had told him what she and Lena discovered, that the women on the list pretended to be pregnant and illegally adopted babies. He'd pushed aside the thought his mother had done something similar. Surely, she'd have told him if he was adopted, right?

"We think she was someone who helped these women get babies," Isana said in a soft voice, her eyes filled with compassion.

Christy's mouth dropped open. "What?"

Isana repeated her statement as Cy's uneasiness about his own origin wouldn't quiet. He'd taken his mother's assurances she did not know anyone named Marta or anyone on the list as the truth, but hearing Christy's story meant he needed to re-examine his own. He would demand answers from Mom as soon as they returned home.

"Are you saying it was a secret adoption?" Christy shoved her hands through her shoulder length hair.

"That's one explanation," Isana agreed.

Christy latched onto it, but Cy could see Isana had an alternative theory. He'd ask her later, after his conversation with his mother.

"I'm still going through their papers, so maybe I'll come across the documents." Christy sighed. "I'll try to ask Mom, but she has trouble recalling my name, so I doubt she'll be much help."

"All of this is supposition on our part," Isana said.

"Help!" Heather shouted from the living room. "Help!"

Christy stood. "Mom needs something." She pulled a wry smile. "That's her way of calling for me."

Isana and Cy rose too. "Thank you for talking with us," Cy said. "We appreciate it."

"You helped fill in a few of the missing pieces." Christy moved toward the living room. Her mother shouted for help again. "Would you mind seeing yourselves out? Mom's getting agitated."

"No problem," Isana said.

Christy hustled off, disappearing into the living room while Cy followed Isana down the hallway to the foyer and into the cool night. Isana started the car and activated the navigation system to return Cy to his mother's house. "I'm sorry."

"For what?" Cy settled back against the seat as she pulled away from the curb.

"For not remembering this is your story too."

He looked out the window at the bright lights of a strip mall. On the parallel side street, a dark Hummer revved its engine as it picked up speed. Idiot. Probably thought the empty stretch of asphalt gave him license to drive too fast.

"Cy?"

"Sorry." He sighed. "I have the feeling my mother hasn't been forthcoming about why she was kidnapped and what she knows about the list."

"And you've never had an inkling you might have been adopted?"

Isana's question irritated him. His parents hadn't lied to him. There had to be another, perfectly reasonable explanation to Lillian Hillam's name being on the list. "You haven't proved anyone but Heather Edwards faked her own pregnancy and secretly adopted a child," he snapped. "All you have are similar delivery stories."

"I know, but it's the only explanation that makes sense." She halted for a red light.

"No, it's not." He crossed his arms. "It's the only one you're interested in pursuing."

The light turned green. Isana gave the car gas, leaving his comment hanging in the air like wet laundry on a clothesline. He directed his gaze out the passenger side window. The Hummer he'd seen earlier barreled down the access road. He considered other reasons for his mother's name on the list of women who'd given birth while living in West Berlin. Perhaps she'd helped facilitate the adoption of a few babies. That was a good thing, right?

The Hummer blew past a stop sign, the aggressiveness of the driver pulling him from his thoughts. "Isana, watch out for the—"

The Hummer swerved onto the main road, smashing into the right back bumper of the rental.

Brenner yanked the wheel of his SUV to swerve around a pickup truck, his eyes on the Hummer racing through the intersection. Horns blared as he narrowly missed sideswiping a Lexus sedan. The Hummer rammed into the rear passenger side of the crossover vehicle carrying Isana Thomas and Cy Hillam. Metal screeched as the larger SUV swung into the driver's side, forcing the smaller car to the right.

Ahead, a giant excavator paralleled the road on the shoulder, its huge bucket dangling. All at once, the Hummer driver's intent became clear. He was aiming the crossover toward the construction vehicle.

Brenner had a checkered past, but he justified his former actions with the knowledge the men and women he'd encountered were professionals who knew the risks involved in playing the spy game. Thomas and Hillam were civilians caught up in a web not of their making. He'd started following them after Lillian had escaped from

Schmidt, knowing their lives would be in danger the more they pursued answers about the list.

Pressing on the gas, he shot through a gap between vehicles, straddling the broken white line. Sirens blared in the distance, but help from that quarter would come too late for Thomas and Hillam. Bracing for impact, he mashed the gas pedal to the floor and hit the Hummer's rear bumper. His SUV's slightly lower bumper locked underneath the Hummer's. Brenner wrenched the wheel to the left, forcing the Hummer away from the crossover.

The other driver wrestled with the wheel, moving the Hummer —and Brenner's SUV—back and forth on the four-lane road. He eased his foot off the gas, putting more strain on the Hummer to pull his SUV along behind him. A few more feet, then he stomped on the brakes. The sudden stop jerked the Hummer hard enough to raise the front wheels off the ground a couple of feet before it slammed onto the asphalt.

Police cars raced up from behind and left, effectively boxing in the two linked vehicles. Brenner cut his engine and placed his hands carefully on the wheel. In the rearview mirror, he couldn't see whether Thomas and Hillam had managed to safely stop their vehicle. Multiple cars, trucks, and delivery vans had crumpled fenders, smashed in doors, and missing side mirrors from their encounter with the Hummer and his SUV. Closing his eyes, he breathed in and out slowly. He was much too old for this. His doctor would have a coronary if he knew. Of course, Brenner had no intention of telling his physician about the incident.

The boss would not be pleased, but soon he'd have other things on his mind, like how to combat the truth of his own role in this mess. That was Brenner's security—his knowledge, along with hard evidence, of the man's complicity in the scheme. It had taken Brenner many years to gather proof, but the last pieces had fallen into place. Brenner would walk away a rich man, never to worry about looking over his shoulder again.

CHAPTER

THIRTY-THREE

Isana couldn't stop her hands from shaking. Even wrapped around a mug of hot tea, her fingers trembled. Across the table, Cy sipped decaf coffee, while Lillian pulled a tray of blueberry scones from the oven. The sweet scent of baked pastries usually made her stomach leap for joy. Tonight, she nearly gagged as the smell filled her nostrils. The stress of the accident triggered unpleasant memories of coming home from school and seeing the kitchen transformed into a bakery, with cookies, brownies, cakes, and pastries covering every surface. Her mother, wearing a splatter-covered apron, danced about the kitchen to an oldies radio station. The scent of sugar and desperation mixed together to make Isana's stomach clench. When her mother baked, things were about to turn ugly. Turning her head, she breathed through her mouth until the nausea passed.

The deliberate vehicular incident had shattered her nerves. She appreciated Lillian's attempt to soothe them with homemade baked goods, but Isana couldn't forget the terror behind the wheel as the Hummer driver tried to kill them. The black SUV roaring up to fend

263

off the Hummer attack had been so unexpected, Isana still felt she'd dreamed it.

"Isana?"

Cy's voice broke into her thoughts. She met his concerned gaze. "I'm sorry. Wasn't paying attention."

"No need to apologize," Lillian said as she joined them at the table, her own mug of chamomile tea in hand. "Would you like a scone?"

The sugary scent overwhelmed her, pushing her nausea to the forefront with a vengeance. With a violent shake of her head, she shoved back from the table and dashed for the hall bathroom, making it just in time to empty the meager contents of her stomach into the toilet bowl. She sank to the cool tile floor, resting her head against the wall until her stomach settled down. After rinsing her mouth and splashing cold water on her face, she returned to the kitchen. The scones had been removed from the table.

"Oh, my dear, I'm so sorry." Lillian held out a fresh mug of tea. "I made you a cup of green ginger tea for your upset tummy."

"Thank you." Isana retook her seat, her limbs weak. The hint of baked goods still clung to the air, but the smell wasn't as strong as before. She ducked her head, her eyes on the wooden tabletop, but she felt the weight of their gazes on her. An explanation was in order, but she never knew how to explain her mother. "The stress of everything . . . "

Cy touched the back of her hand. "It's okay. The tea will help."

Relief at his not pressing her for answers she wasn't ready to give deflated some of the tension still swirling around inside. The ginger tea, with a little sugar, did tame her stomach. The quietness of the kitchen soothed her tattered nerves. When she finished the tea, she found her hands had stopped shaking.

"Better?" Cy gathered her mug, along with his own and his mother's.

"Yes, thank you." She sighed. Lethargy pulled at her limbs as a headache pressed against her temple. She wanted nothing other than a warm bed in a quiet room but couldn't summon the energy to call an Uber to take her home.

"Cy, you can sleep on the pullout couch in the study," Lillian said briskly. "Isana, I put clean sheets on the guest bed."

Isana met Lillian's gaze, the compassion and understanding nearly undoing her fragile hold on her composure.

"Thanks, Mom." Cy leaned back against the counter. "I didn't want Isana to be by herself tonight."

She didn't want to be alone either, and gratitude for his mother recognizing that filled her.

"I also put some flannel pajamas and a fresh toothbrush on the dresser." Lillian stood. "I'm off to bed." She touched her son's cheek. "I'm so thankful you're okay."

He held her hand against his face. "Me too."

"See you two in the morning." With a wave, Lillian left the kitchen.

A different kind of tension radiated between them. Cy turned and loaded the mugs into the dishwasher. "I hope you will stay."

"Frankly, I'm too tired to go anywhere else." She rose on surprisingly unsteady legs.

"Whoa, there." He slipped an arm around her waist. "I've got you."

She sagged against him, letting his strength be enough for them both. "Point me in the direction of the guest room before I fall over."

"Right this way." Using one crutch, he kept his other arm around her as they made their way to the bedroom. "I'd better say good night here."

She smiled, his gallantry increasing the warm, fuzzy feeling being near him engineered. "See you in the morning."

He dropped a quick kiss on her lips. "Sweet dreams."

Her hand touched her mouth. "I will now." Her cheeks heated at his grin, and she ducked into the room, shutting the door quickly before she lost all sense of decorum and kissed him back with all the love in her heart. She quickly changed into the borrowed PJs and brushed her teeth in the adjoining bathroom. Snuggling into the bed, she prayed again they would find the answers they needed and for their safety. Sleep crowded her mind, pushing all thoughts at bay save one—Isana's hope Cy would still want to kiss her after they confronted his mother about his birth.

~

"Are you anxious?" Pastor Hyden paced a few steps from the pulpit. "Are you living in fear?"

Cy shifted in the pew beside Isana. His mother hadn't attended church with them this morning, citing a poor night's rest. The dark circles under Mom's eyes and the paleness of her cheeks attested to the validity of her claim. His rest hadn't been peaceful either, as his brain kept replaying the terrifying moments before the SUV had intervened and drew the Hummer away from his rental. Stifling a yawn, he refocused on the sermon.

"So many of us choose fear, allowing our anxiety about the past, future, or present become all-consuming," Hyden said. "But what's the cost of that fear and anxiety? Fear damages relationships. Anxiety immobilizes us from living the life God has called us to live for him."

Of all the sermon topics, today's had to be on anxiety and fear. Cy resisted the urge to squirm as the minister read Philippians 4:6-7. "Do not be anxious about anything, but in everything by prayer and supplication with thanksgiving let your requests be made known to God. And the peace of God, which surpasses all understanding, will guard your hearts and your minds in Christ Jesus."

The words dug deep into Cy's heart. Don't be anxious. Pray with thanksgiving. Peace from God will come. He'd allowed fear to push out peace. His prayers of late hadn't been peppered with thankful-ness but anxiety. *Dear God, forgive me for not giving my fear over what my mom may or may not have done to you. Help me to rest in you.*

His heart lightened as he tuned back into the sermon, rejoicing in how the Holy Spirit works in hearts to chastise and renew. By the closing hymn, he had firmed his resolve to confront his mother about his birth and felt a peace that no matter the outcome, everything would be okay.

"The sermon touched close to home, didn't it?" Isana shrugged into her jacket.

He buttoned his against the March wind, which still carried a sharpness underneath spring's warmer overtone. "A little too close but needed."

"I've let fear paralyze me when it comes to relationships," she admitted as they joined the crowd headed for the exit. "My dad left when I was a teenager. I think he'd had enough of my mom. I think she has an undiagnosed and untreated mental illness, but she's refused to see a doctor about it. She's able to keep things together just enough to avoid being institutionalized, but she's far from well."

"That must have been hard." He couldn't imagine how difficult her growing up years had been. "Do you ever see your father?"

Isana shook her head. "He sends the occasional birthday card with a check, but he remarried two years ago and has a new family now. She probably has bi-polar, given how manic she can be at times. I used to think she was on drugs, but now I realize it was probably just the disease. My dad didn't notice until he'd stopped traveling so much for work because she was able to cope so well."

"Where is she now?" Cy wanted to squeeze her hand, offering what comfort he could, but he couldn't let go of his crutches.

"Florida, I think." She stayed close to his side as they weaved through the crowded narthex. "She stuck around until I graduated from high school, then disappeared. I haven't seen her in years, although she calls me whenever she needs money."

"Isana!" Lena pushed through the crowd, her fiancé, Devlin Mills, at her heels. "How are you?"

"I'm okay." Isana returned Lena's hug.

"What happened to you?" Lena's eyes widened as she took in Cy's crutches.

Quickly, Cy recounted the accident that resulted in thirty stitches on his left calf. "I'll follow up with my doctor on Monday."

"I'm glad you weren't hurt worse. Are you ready?" Lena smiled expectantly, glancing from Isana to Cy.

Cy looked at Isana, who raised her eyebrows as if saying she didn't know what Lena meant either. "Ready for what?"

Lena's smile dropped. "For lunch with the Silvertons, of course."

"With Henry and Violet?" Isana sounded as puzzled as Cy felt.

"You didn't get my message?" Lena withdrew her phone. "I sent you a text yesterday saying they wanted to get together. Henry said he'd found something about Marta."

"I didn't get a text." Isana glanced at her own phone as Lena checked hers.

"Well, that explains it." Lena turned her phone screen to face Isana and Cy, where the message registered as undelivered. "I know it's last minute, but can you come?"

The thought of putting off the confrontation with his mother made Cy answer in the affirmative without consulting Isana. "We didn't have any firm lunch plans." Then he realized how presumptive he'd been and quickly added, "Unless Isana has someplace to be?"

Isana nudged him gently with her elbow. "I will need to go home eventually, but that can wait until after lunch."

Lena looked from one to the other. "I think there's a story there. Spill it."

As they exited the building into the sunshine, Cy recounted what happened yesterday, from their conversation with Christy Edwards about her mother and the Hummer driver smashing into their vehicle. "The rental company wasn't happy with the damage, but since the police report backs up our version of events, they hauled away the damaged one and replaced it this morning." By the time he finished, they were on the sidewalk outside the church.

"I'm so glad you weren't hurt," Lena said.

"We'd better get going or we'll be late to the Silvertons." Devlin put his arm around his fiancée's shoulders.

"Of course." Lena snuggled closer to Devlin. "See you there."

Cy used to envy the close relationships of married and engaged couples, but since Isana came into his life, he began to hope to have such a relationship with her.

"They look so happy together, don't they?" Isana touched his shoulder before moving toward the rental.

"Yes, they do." Cy waited while she unlocked the car doors. "I find I'm not as jealous these days when confronted with marital bliss or a couple in love."

"You're not?" She settled behind the driver's seat as he stowed the crutches and swung into the car.

"Nope." He leaned over and dropped a quick kiss on her cheek. "Not when I have the potential for my own happily ever after."

"You do?" Isana touched the place where Cy's lips had been.

He gave into the impulse to thread his fingers through her hair and tug her upper body toward him. "I do." He sealed his declaration by capturing her lips with his.

CHAPTER

THIRTY-FOUR

Lillian twisted the wedding band around her left ring finger, the gold circle a little looser than usual after her kidnapping ordeal. Relief had coursed through her when she'd read Cyrus's text about their grabbing lunch with friends before returning to the house. She'd known by his expression last night she wouldn't be able to avoid the conversation she'd been dreading for more than thirty years. How she wished Greg was beside her. Surely he would have forgiven her by now. As it was, she'd never hear the words of forgiveness from her husband's lips. He'd died before they'd had a chance to reconcile after his discovery of her secret.

The doorbell chimed. Lillian glanced at the stove clock. 11:30. Her friends would be at church, and door-to-door salespeople generally didn't stop by on a Sunday morning. The bell donged again. She made her way to the front door. The shadow of a man passed by the narrow window to the left of the door.

She punched in 9-1-1 and placed her finger over the connect button. Keeping the chain engaged, she pulled open the door enough to ask, "Yes?"

The man turned. "Mrs. Hillam?"

Lillian said nothing. The sliver of space between the door and the jamb gave her enough of a glimpse to show she didn't recognize the him.

He spread his hands, then slowly opened his jacket. He lifted each pant leg, displaying only socks. "See, no weapons."

She didn't reply, certain she'd heard his voice before.

He added, "I think we have a mutual goal."

Something about the man's speech patterns nudged her brain to recall an overheard conversation while she was being held by Schmidt. Her heart pounded as she placed him as the man who'd come to the house where Schmidt had held her. After his departure, Schmidt had treated her better, so this man must have been in charge of her kidnapping. She started to close the door, not wanting to experience the horror of captivity again.

"I have no intention of harming you."

Lillian couldn't let his statement go unchallenged. "You kidnapped me."

"That was Schmidt."

"You were there."

"I was."

His bald acceptance flummoxed her temporarily, but she quickly recovered. "There's nothing I want to say to you. I'm calling the police."

"You and your son are still in danger, along with your son's pretty co-worker."

The words reignited the fear simmering in her bones. "If you harm them . . . "

"Not me, but someone else."

"Who?" The hard countenance of Virginia Sanders flashed across her mind. Surely the vice president's wife wouldn't . . . But as soon as the thought surfaced, Lillian realized she knew the answer.

"*Um die Vergangenheit in der Vergangenheit zu halten.*"

The German phrase—to keep the past in the past—convinced her to listen to the enemy before her. Maybe he did have the solution she sought to keep Cyrus from finding out the truth. Her fingers trembled as she undid the chain, a prayer winging heavenward. *Please, God. Help me.* She couldn't pray the rest, knowing God required her to tell her son the true circumstances about his birth. But the stakes were still too high. She'd lose everything if she did and face prison as well.

Pulling the door wide, she stepped back to allow the tall man to enter. "Come in."

He followed her to the kitchen, where she sat at the table without offering him coffee. "What can I do for you, Mr . . . .?"

"Lorenz. Brenner Lorenz." He took the chair opposite. "Mrs. Hillam, you have the list."

His calm statement sent a prickle of unease skittering across her back like tiny spider legs. She said nothing, sensing he had more to add.

"Your name is on that list."

Still she kept her expression blank and her lips sealed.

"Also on the list are the names Heather Edwards, Jennifer Blandings, and Virginia Sanders." Mr. Lorenz folded his hands on the table. "I think you know exactly why those names are on the list."

Lillian shrugged, the gesture at odds with her pounding heart.

"Your son and his girlfriend are getting close to figuring it out as well."

At the mention of Cyrus and Isana, she clenched her hands together on her lap.

Mr. Lorenz's eyes bored into hers with a knowing stare. "And you haven't told him the truth. Not about his birth or exactly what you did."

"What do you want, Mr. Lorenz?"

"What did Virginia Sanders say to you?"

The question stunned her, and her face must have given away a flash of surprise because he nodded. A slight smile creased the corners of his mouth. "Let's just say I have a vested interest in the outcome of this, as do you." He steepled his fingers. "What I'm proposing is that we help each other."

"Why should I believe you want to help me?" Lillian might be older than him by at least a decade, but she was no fool.

"Because we do want the same thing—for interest in the names on the list to fade into the background, never to see the light of day."

"Why should I believe you, after what Schmidt did to me?"

"I apologize for Schmidt's overzealous nature."

"You apologize." Fury grabbed her by the throat. "That man killed my husband."

"Yes."

The simple agreement siphoned off some of the anger, but she still fought to retain control. The hurt and anger over Greg's death assailed her afresh, making her body tremble.

"We knew he had the list but didn't realize the extent of Schmidt's fury."

His serene explanation did nothing to calm her. "I don't think we have anything left to discuss."

He studied the tabletop, one finger tracing a pattern only he could see. "For the sake of your son, I'm asking you to hear me out."

"What does Cyrus have to do with this?"

His green eyes met hers. "Everything."

"Thank you so much for inviting us to lunch." Isana carried her cup of decaf coffee into the pleasant living room after dining on an eggplant parmesan lasagna, spinach salad, and warm, crusty bread. "It was delicious."

Violet smiled as she waddled into the room, her hand resting at the small of her back. "You can thank Henry for the main course. It's his specialty."

"Really?" Lena set down the tray with an assortment of cookies and a stack of cocktail napkins. "I had no idea you cooked."

Henry maneuvered himself into his easy chair, laying the crutches on the floor beside him. "My mother taught us to cook as kids, mostly to keep us out of trouble, I think. As a bachelor, I preferred to keep things simple in the kitchen."

"I didn't discover the full extent of my husband's culinary arts until I got pregnant." Violet took a seat beside Isana on the couch. "For the first three months or so, the sight and smell of most foods made me want to puke."

"My dear, let's not upset anyone's stomach," Henry admonished gently.

His wife threw him a withering look. "He's only saying that because his tummy couldn't handle my morning sickness."

Lena held up a hand. "Whoa, TMI. My stomach might rebel too."

Devlin set Cy's mug on the end table while Cy dropped into the seat on the other side of Isana.

"I don't know how you do it with such ease, Henry," Cy said. "I'm exhausted walking with these things." He waved a hand at his crutches, now propped against the end table.

"Practice," Henry replied, "and I'm using them to help me walk with both legs,not using them to take pressure off one leg, like you are."

"Maybe that's the difference." Cy leaned back, casually laying his arm along the back of the couch behind Isana.

She shifted slightly closer to Cy, hoping he'd get the hint and put his arm around her, as the conversation drifted to the finicky Virginia weather and the delayed arrival of spring. A warm hand settled on her shoulder. She glanced at Cy, who winked at her before squeezing her. Isana wished she felt brave enough to put her head on his shoulder and snuggle closer, but while she might do such a thing in private, it seemed too bold a move before others.

During a lull in the conversation, Henry said, "After you visited, I was curious about Marta Bauer, and decided to do some more digging into her background."

"What did you find?" Isana reached up and took Cy's hand in hers.

"Marta was a survivor. She'd grown up an orphan of the state—there's nothing about what happened to her parents—and trained to be a nurse and midwife. As I mentioned during your last visit, I suspected her of smuggling black market goods into East Berlin and potentially people out."

"But you couldn't find any collaboration of either of those," Cy said.

Henry exchanged a glance with his wife, then returned his gaze to Cy and Isana. "When I was writing my book, that's correct."

Isana's pulse accelerated. "You found something out, something you can prove."

Henry nodded. "I went back to a couple of sources. It's been several years since I'd talked to them, and sometimes time will loosen tongues."

"What did you find?" Devlin asked the question on the tip of Isana's tongue when Henry didn't immediately continue.

"Evidence that Marta Bauer was heavily involved in the black market, bringing Western goods into East Berlin. One of my sources shared with me a marriage certificate showing Marta Bauer had secretly wed one of the checkpoint guards along the Berlin Wall."

"How could you secretly wed anyone in East Germany?" Lena's voice sounded as confused as Isana was.

"With great difficulty," Henry said. "She and her groom found an old priest to perform the ceremony. I don't think it was legal in the eyes of the state, but since they wanted to keep it under wraps, I suppose that didn't matter."

"She used him to cross the border without being concerned about searches," Isana said.

"That's probably correct," Henry agreed. "One source directed me to someone who knew someone—it's like playing the game Six Degrees of Separation—who could tell me exactly what Marta was up to."

Isana clutched Cy's hand tighter. She snuck a glance at his face, which had a blank expression as he stared in Henry's direction. She had a terrible idea of what Henry would say and prayed Cy would be able to weather the coming storm.

"Just tell them, Henry," Violet urged when her husband once again paused.

"I couldn't believe it, but I have been able to confirm the truth of what I'm about to tell you." Henry's eyes softened behind his glasses as he met Isana's gaze, then shifted his attention to Cy. "For a period of time in the mid-1980s, Marta Bauer smuggled babies out of East Berlin."

CHAPTER

THIRTY-FIVE

Are you okay?"

Cy bit back a sarcastic reply as Isana pulled into the driveway at his mother's house. He'd appreciated her not talking about Henry's revelation during the ride home. The bombshell that Marta had smuggled babies out of East Berlin hit him square between the eyes, a stunning blow he couldn't wrap his mind around. He barely said a word after Henry revealed what he'd found out. He'd have to ask Isana to tell him the details he'd missed. His mind circled around and around the devastating conclusion his mother and his father weren't his biological parents. This bit of information, coupled with what they'd learned from Christy Edwards, cemented the truth, at least in his mind.

"Cy?"

"How much?" The question spilled out before he'd even realized he wanted to know.

"How much what?" Isana punched off the engine.

"How much do you think my parents paid for me?"

"They must have wanted a child very much."

Her soft reply only fueled his anger at the years-long deception.

He wanted to run into the house and shake his mom until she spilled the truth. He didn't want to think about how desperate they'd been for a baby. "Yeah, well, that didn't mean they could buy one."

"Your mom's been through a lot lately." Isana put a hand on his shoulder. "Maybe we should pray before we go in?"

Shame washed over him at his arrogance in forgetting both God and the pain his mother had suffered recently from her kidnapping. He grabbed her hand and met her gaze. The compassion and acceptance in her eyes gave him the strength to nod in agreement with her suggestion to pray.

"Dear Heavenly Father, please comfort Cy as he confronts his past. Please be with Lillian too. Help her to get this secret out into the open at last so healing may begin in her life and in her son's. Amen."

He squeezed her hand. "Thanks."

For a few minutes, they sat in silence. Birds chirped. Dogs barked. A runner flashed by the house, followed by a pack of kids riding their bicycles. A normal Sunday afternoon. Cy's heart was still heavy, but the anger had faded. With his emotions more under control, he could think beyond his personal circumstance. "Do you think someone wants the list to confirm who paid for their children?"

"Perhaps," she said slowly. "Some people might be willing to pay for continued silence."

"Another question for my mom." Cy brought her hand to his lips and pressed a kiss on the back. "Ready?"

"If you are, I am."

"Let's go in."

Once inside the house, the stillness registered immediately with Cy. "Mom?" He went down the hallway, his crutches slipping a bit in his haste. The study's door stood slightly ajar. He pushed it open and went in a few steps to ascertain the room was empty.

Isana appeared in the kitchen doorway. "She's not in the kitchen, living room, or dining room."

His breath hitched. *Please God, not again. Let my mom be safe.* "Maybe she's lying down in her bedroom."

"I'll check." Isana moved down the hallway toward the two back bedrooms faster than he could on his crutches. She reappeared with a shake of her head. "Empty."

He hobbled into the kitchen and sat in a chair to check his phone. No missed calls or texts. "I'll send her a text."

Mom, we're at the house. Where are you?

Out with a friend. I'm okay.

Relief poured over him at her immediate response. "She's all right. Says she's out with a friend."

"That's good news." Isana laid a hand on his shoulder. "You look tired."

He summoned a smile. "I guess hearing your parents probably bought you on the black market can take a toll."

"You don't know that's what happened in your case."

"But given the information we've been gathering, it's highly likely." He rested his weight on the crutches, wanting nothing more than to lie down on the guest bed and sleep until his world returned to normal. "I wish we'd never heard of the blasted list."

Sympathy flooded her eyes. "This hasn't been easy on you, I know."

Not wanting to wallow in pity, he decided action would stave off the feeling of uncertainty. "While my mom's out, let's take a closer look at my birth certificate."

"Are you sure you wouldn't rather rest your leg first? I could make you a cup of coffee or tea."

He shook his head. "I have to know."

She nodded once. "I would too." Then she stepped closer, fitting her body against his and wrapping her arms around his middle in an embrace that warmed him from head to toe. He leaned his head down, breathing in the slight hint of cherry blossoms in her hair and wishing he was steady enough to stand without his crutches so he could fully enjoy her embrace.

Pulling back, her hands lingered at his waist while her eyes met his. "Remember, whatever we find, it doesn't change who you are now. It only changes who you were in the past."

Then she planted her lips on his mouth, and all thoughts about the past faded from his mind. All he could think about was kissing this wonderful woman who cared for him despite his unknown birth. If he had his way, he'd stay here, kissing Isana, for a long time.

BRENNER HANDED LILLIAN HER COFFEE CUP, THEN JOINED HER AT THE SMALL round table. He watched her fiddle with the cardboard sleeve before removing the lid and taking a sip.

"How did you find out?"

Her question was one he'd been expecting. "She died, you know."

Lillian's face whitened. "I didn't."

Brenner shrugged, the gesture at odds with the pang of grief, still sharp after all these years. "We weren't married, and I was . . . working a lot." No need to share details of his position with the Stasi. "We were careful to keep our relationship secret, so everyone thought she was alone."

Guilt, his constant companion, poked him. He could have saved her life and their child if he had ignored her request for secrecy. Only later did he realize she'd done it to protect him.

"Marta," Lillian began, then swallowed the rest of her words along with another sip of coffee.

"Ah, the intrepid Marta Bauer." He leaned back, leaving his own coffee untouched. "She was a master at saying exactly what her clients needed to hear."

"I was foolish to believe her."

"You were desperate." He held no animosity for this woman who had stolen his heritage. She had been caught in a trap without even knowing it, snared by Marta's promises. "I don't blame you. You gave him a good life."

Tears filled Lillian's eyes. "I tried." She blotted her face with a paper napkin. "It wasn't easy after Greg died."

Anger at Schmidt's revenge threatened to derail his thoughts, but he tamped it down. Schmidt had been dealt with. "What does Cyrus know about all this?"

"Nothing."

Her quick reply told him fear still had her in its icy grip. "You realize you'll have to tell him the truth."

"About everything?" She wouldn't meet his gaze.

"Lillian." He spoke her name softly, as if talking to a frightened animal. "Don't you think it's time to make a clean slate of things, as you Americans like to put it?"

"I can't." She choked back a sob. "He'll hate me. Then I'll lose him. He's all I have."

Brenner sighed at the woman's stubbornness. Time to try another tactic. "His life is in danger."

"What?" His statement had rattled her. "But I was assured—"

"And you believed her?" He shook his head. "You really are too trusting."

She covered her mouth. "She promised."

"She has more to lose than you."

Lillian's eyes widened. "You mean . . . "

"Oh, yes. Marta had the same deal with everyone. She was no one's fool."

She stood. "I must go."

He detained her with a hand on her arm. "We'll go together."

"No, please," she begged, but he refused to be moved by her tears.

"It's for the best. Enough lives have been ruined because of this lie." He wasn't sure his words would be enough to convince her. He determined to tell Cyrus if Lillian didn't, but it would be better if Lillian did.

Her shoulders straightened. "Okay, but I'll explain."

"As long as you say everything." He didn't have to spell out the rest of the warning. He could see in her eyes she understood he would step in if she whitewashed the truth. As they left the coffeeshop, a tiny seed of hope sprang in his heart. The feeling, so long suppressed, took him by surprise.

At his age, with his checkered past, to have an optimistic view of the future was not something to take for granted. He even found himself wanting to pray to the God he'd been told all his life was dead for a blessing on their conversation. But old habits die hard, and he ignored the impulse, preferring to rest in the surety of his own actions. Finally, after more than thirty years, he would meet his future face to face.

THIRTY-SIX

Gina Sanders smiled and waved at the crowd gathered on the sidewalk outside the restaurant where she'd had lunch with the current First Lady. Reporters shouted questions about their meeting, but Gina kept smiling and waving without answering. Her favorite Secret Service agent, Jasmine, held open the door of the Lincoln Town Car. Gina gave the tall, black woman with long braids a genuine smile as she slid inside, the agent closing the door before joining the driver in the front seat.

"Home, ma'am?" her long-time driver, Amir, asked.

"Yes, please." She settled back against the leather seat. The meeting had gone well. The President would endorse Gil for their party's nomination when the time came.

Her phone vibrated. Probably Gil wondering how the luncheon went, but the caller was from a blocked number. She ignored it and flicked her phone off silent mode. A soft ping alerted her the unknown caller had left a voicemail. Curiosity pushed her to listen to the message.

"How much do you love your family?" a mechanical voice said. "Hard to put a price on that, isn't it? I'm willing to discuss it. Oh, and next time, answer your phone, or I'll call Lyle and Logan directly." The caller rattled off each of her sons' cell numbers. "I'm sure they'd love to hear the true story of their birth."

Gina deleted the message with a trembling finger. She would not let this person destroy all she and Gil had worked for. She would not allow him to turn her sons against her. Perhaps she would be better off riding out the storm. After all, she was the vice president's wife. No evidence existed to prove whatever claims the caller made.

The more she turned the problem over in her mind, the more she leaned towards not ignoring the caller. She had adequately plugged potential leaks. Everything would be okay.

Her phone signaled a text had come through. She smiled at the sight of her son Logan's name flashing on the screen.

Hi, Mom. We need to talk.

Sure, what's up?

Not over text. I'm at the house.

Her smile faded. Logan never dropped by unannounced. Maybe something happened to Marissa or the baby. Her heart stuttered as her fingers composed the question.

Everything okay with Marissa and the baby?

M and baby are fine. Will you be home soon?

She glanced out the window to gauge their location. They were passing the British Ambassador's residence.

Nearly there.

I'll be waiting in your office.

She closed the text, slipping her phone into her handbag. The final ten minutes of the drive seemed to take three times as long. Finally, Jasmine opened the door. "Welcome home, Mrs. Sanders."

"Thank you." Gina hurried up the stairs and into the house. Her assistant met her in the foyer, but Gina waved her off with a flick of her hand as she beelined for her first-floor office.

Logan stood with his hands clasped behind him as he stared out of the large window overlooking the side gardens.

"Logan?" Gina slipped off her light coat, draping it over the back of a sofa.

He turned, his dark brown eyes meeting hers. The hardness in them made her grip her hands together, but she pasted a welcoming smile on her face. "What's so urgent, darling?"

"This." He nodded toward a plain brown envelope resting on the desk blotter.

"What is it?" She crossed to the desk, her fingers hovering over the item without touching it.

"Open it."

His refusal to explain sent her pulse racing, but years of practice in hiding her emotions allowed her to affect a nonchalance as she picked up the packet. "You sound so mysterious." She slid out the contents onto the desk surface. With an effort, she picked up the top photograph of her wearing a hideous 1980s maternity dress that billowed out over her protruding stomach. She moved the top photo aside to see a half dozen more photos of her pregnant self on the streets of West Berlin. "Where did you get these?"

"They arrived by messenger to my office."

His implacable tone jerked her eyes from the photos to her son. "I'm not sure why you're upset about some photos showing I'm pregnant." She halted at the pinched look on his face.

"Stop lying."

Gina heard pain behind the anger in Logan's words, but she was not going to be harangued by her own son. A good defense sometimes meant going on the offense. "I think you'd better explain yourself."

"You want an explanation?" Logan moved closer, giving Gina a glimpse into how tightly he was hanging onto his control.

The level of anger made her uneasy, but her only recourse was to brazen it out and see what he thought he knew.

"Dad's not our father."

She nearly laughed with relief. This she could counter easily but she wouldn't let him off the hook quiet yet. "What do you mean?"

"I mean he is not our biological father."

"How do you know?"

"Mom, stop it! You know what I'm talking about. Does Dad know?"

"Does Dad know what?" Gil stood in the doorway.

Gina had been so focused on Logan, she hadn't registered the door opening. Now she turned to her husband. "You'd better come in. Logan has some questions about his birth."

Gil closed the door, then came to stand beside Gina, slipping his arm around her waist. "We should have told you, but honestly, we didn't think it would matter."

"Of course it matters!" Logan looked at his father, then Gina. "You're telling me you know you're not our biological father?"

Gil nodded. "Of course, I do."

Logan's shoulders slumped. "I don't understand."

Gina rushed to his side, slipping her arm through Logan's. "My darling, maybe we should have told you and Lyle, but like your father said, we didn't think it mattered because you're our sons in every sense of the word."

"So who's my father?"

"We don't know." The ring of truth in that statement should convince Logan. "We learned early in our marriage we couldn't have children."

"Correction," Gil said. "I couldn't father children. Something wrong with my sperm."

"We tried invitro fertilization with a sperm donor, but I couldn't carry a baby to full term." Sadness overtook Gina at the memory of those dark days. The West Berlin posting was supposed to be a fresh start for them after the heartache of losing several babies.

"We decided to adopt when we returned to the states," Gil said, "but then your mother met a young, pregnant woman in West Berlin who didn't have a partner and was desperate for her baby to have a better life."

"Wait," Logan extracted his arm from Gina's and took a step back. "The note with the photos said something about the black market in Berlin. Are you saying you bought us?"

"It wasn't like that." Gina fluttered her hands to create the helpless female she often impersonated. "We helped with her medical and living expenses. That's all."

"But these photos." Logan pointed to the glossy pictures on her desk. "You appear pregnant."

"Your mother had to pretend to be pregnant," Gil said. "We weren't going through the proper channels, so everyone had to think the baby was hers."

"At the time, we didn't know she was carrying twins. That was quite a surprise," Gina added, hoping Logan would be satisfied with their explanation. "The moment I held you and Lyle in my arms, you were ours."

Logan scrubbed a hand over his face. "This still doesn't negate the fact you bought us."

Even angry, Logan sounded like the prosecuting attorney he was. Gina turned to Gil, hoping he'd be able to convince Logan his parents weren't terrible people, just a couple who desperately wanted a child.

"Son, your mother explained." Gil laid a hand on Logan's shoulder. "We were given an opportunity to help a young woman out of a very sticky situation. Even in the 1980s, having a child out of wedlock in West Germany was frowned upon. Her parents kicked her out. We helped her by giving her a place to live when otherwise she would have been on the streets."

"How did you find her?"

Logan's question gave Gina hope he was gradually accepting their explanation. Like father, like son. Both men preferred to have a simple explanation that checked all the boxes. In Gina's experience, the truth rarely fit those qualifications.

"It was a chance meeting at a café where the girl worked," Gil said. "Your mother befriended her, and after learning of her condition, offered to help. When the girl expressed her intention of giving the baby up for adoption, Gina came to me."

Logan glanced from one to the other, his eyes lingering on Gina's. The sadness in her son's caused Gina's heart to lurch. He knew. Panic tumbled her insides like sheets in a dryer, but she tamped it down from long practice. Or he knew this story was a lie.

The office door opened. "I said we weren't to be disturbed," Gina snapped as she turned to face the interloper. Instead of a member of staff, Lyle Sanders stood in the doorway dressed in a rumpled suit and tie. He swayed, bracing his hand on the door frame. A silver hip flask dangled from his left hand. "I see you started the party without me."

His slurred words indicated he had been drinking. Gina wrinkled her nose. "Lyle, come in and sit down before you fall over."

"Yes, ma'am." Lyle gave her a two-finger salute and staggered toward one of the chairs grouped in front of the fireplace.

Logan crossed to close the door, while Gil addressed his twin. "You've been drinking."

Lyle raised the flask to his lips, tilting his head back to swallow the last drop. He let it fall to the floor. "I have indeed been drinking." He pointed a finger at his mother. "And I didn't drive. Took an Uber."

At least they wouldn't have to worry about a driving under the influence charge levied against Lyle ahead of her husband's big announcement. Lyle pushed to his feet and crossed to the desk, jabbing a finger at the photographs. "I see you got the same ones I did."

Logan joined his brother at the desk. "Yes."

Lyle pivoted to face his parents, nearly falling over with the effort. "Did she tell you the sob story about the unwed mother?"

Gina froze at the venom behind Lyle's words. Lyle pointed a shaking finger at her. "Lies, all of it lies."

"Son, I think you should—"

Lyle shook his head, the movement sending him crashing into a chair. He braced his hands on the back, managing to keep his feet. "No. I know. Ask her about Marta Bauer."

Gina's brain kicked back into gear. She spread her hands in a supplicating gesture. "Gil, I told you, I knew Marta in West Berlin. We had coffee together a few times."

"No, no, no." Lyle raised his head, the anguish in his eyes slicing Gina's heart into ribbons. "Another lie. Marta wasn't a friend."

Gina affected a puzzled expression. "We weren't friends, more like friendly acquaintances."

Gil rested a hand on Lyle's shoulder. "Your mother and I have already discussed Marta."

Lyle shook off his father's hand. "You mean she convinced you she barely knew the woman." He met Gina's gaze. "Are you going to tell them the truth or am I?"

"The truth about what?" She plastered a caring expression on her face. "I didn't think you'd started drinking again. Does Zoey know?"

"Leave my wife out of this!" Lyle's knuckles turned white as he gripped the back of the chair. "You'd drink too if you found out you had been purchased like a piece of meat."

"It's not like that," Logan said. "Mom and Dad explained about they only helped our birth mother with living expenses and stuff like that."

"And you believed them?" Lyle snorted. "Of course you did. You always were more gullible than me."

Gina needed to take control of the conversation before it was too late. "I don't know what you think you know—"

"I know you wanted a baby," Lyle cut across her words. "That I can forgive you for. You loved us, and we had a good life."

Gina relaxed slightly. He didn't know. It would be okay. Everything would turn out like she'd planned. She'd have the life she'd been working towards and the freedom to enjoy it.

Then Lyle stared straight into her eyes and her heart stuttered at the anguish and certainty there.

"Why don't you tell them, Mother." He slurred her name. "Tell them what price you paid for us."

CHAPTER

THIRTY-SEVEN

Arlington, Virginia, October 12, 1993

What have you done?"

Her husband's question cracked across the kitchen like a whip. Lillian turned off the burner under the skillet with half-browned ground beef before facing Greg. His cheeks flushed with anger, he stood in the kitchen doorway.

"You're home early." She managed to stay calm, but her body trembled.

"Why didn't you tell me?" The anguish behind the anger told her he'd uncovered the secret she'd carried for five long years.

But she'd not make the rookie mistake of answering the question without clarifying what he knew and what he only suspected. "Tell you what?"

He shot a hand through his dark blond hair, sending the strands every which way. "That Cy is not my son."

With effort, she kept her face as neutral as possible. "He's as much your son as he is mine."

Greg closed his eyes briefly, pain etched in every line on his face. Meeting her gaze, he said in a soft tone, "But he's not related by blood to either one of us, is he?"

The moment of truth had arrived. There was nothing but to confirm what he already knew. Lillian had always known this time would come, but she'd hoped it would be when Cyrus was older. "No."

Her husband pulled out a chair at the small kitchen table and sank into it like a man twice his age. "Tell me everything."

Crossing to the table, she sat in the chair opposite him. "I didn't see any other way for us to have a child." She begged him with her tone and expression to understand. "The infertility treatments weren't working, and none of the adoption agencies would even consider us given your heart condition."

Even now, her anger burned at the rejection because Greg had bicuspid aortic valve disease, a condition that required continual monitoring by a physician but didn't impact his day-to-day living. However, because people with BAVD can experience heart failure or aortic aneurysm, Greg was considered high-risk and therefore not eligible as an adoptive parent.

His closed expression didn't alter as she explained about being contacted by a woman named Marta who could get her a baby from an unwed mother in East Berlin who wanted her child to have a better life outside of the German Democratic Republic. How Marta coached her on how to act and appear pregnant, how the woman took care of all the details, even going so far as to have a doctor cut Lillian as if she'd had a C-section giving birth to Cyrus.

"You were away so much during the last three months of the pregnancy, it made it easy to pretend."

"And that made it all right to fool your husband?" he spat back, angrier than she'd ever seen him.

"No, but Marta said the fewer people who knew the truth, the better." What had seemed so logical six years ago now sounded like the lame excuse it was.

Greg bowed his head, as if he couldn't stand to look at her another second. "What exactly did this Marta want in return for procuring a baby?" His voice held a weary tone that chilled her more than his previous anger had.

The question hung in the air between them like an undetonated bomb. Once she answered it, the explosion would hurt them all.

"I know it wasn't money, because we didn't have that kind of wealth."

Yet another reason adoption through the normal channels had been closed to them. She hung her head, fighting to keep the tears at bay. Since he did the finances, she couldn't hide any funds from him. That's why she had to use an alternative method to pay Marta.

"Lillian?" His hands reached across and grasped her cold fingers. "Tell me."

Tears slipped down her cheeks despite her best effort. She opened her mouth but couldn't force the answer out. Instead she said, "You'll hate me."

His thumb rubbed the knuckles of her hand. "No, I won't. But you can't carry this secret by yourself any longer."

She sniffled and nodded. He was right. Despite her happiness in raising their son, the secret between them had created a distance she only now saw had hurt their marriage. Instead of protecting Greg, she had driven a wedge into their lives by cutting him off from the most intimate part of herself.

"A name," she whispered.

Color leached from his face, and his fingers on hers stilled. "What name?"

"Nathan Schmidt."

Isana dried her hands, then opened the bathroom door. Voices in the kitchen alerted her that perhaps Cy's mom had returned home. She sent a quick prayer for the difficult conversation ahead. Cy's birth certificate listed Lillian and Greg Hillam as his parents, with place of birth as West Berlin, West Germany, leaving him more confused than ever.

Entering the kitchen, she noted a man had accompanied Lillian, who sat at the kitchen table with her head bowed.

"Isana." Cy crossed and took her hand in his. "This is Brenner Lorenz."

She nodded at Mr. Lorenz. Cy gave a slight shake of his head as if letting her know he didn't have a clue as to why the stranger was in his mother's kitchen. The tension in the kitchen hovered near the boiling point.

Lillian looked older than her sixty-odd years, her hands clasped tightly together. "Sit down, everyone. Please."

Lorenz took the chair to the right of Lillian, leaving Cy and Isana to complete the square. She was grateful to be next to Cy rather than across from him. Cy scooted his chair a little closer to hers, draping his arm along the top. If she leaned back, she would feel his arm against her shoulders. The closeness calmed her nerves.

Lillian cleared her throat. "I'm sure you two have a lot of questions, but I ask for your patience, as this story has many facets, and the telling might take some time."

"We're listening," Cy said in a gentle voice.

His words must have eased some of the tension from his mother because her shoulders relaxed a little.

"I had six miscarriages early in my marriage." Lillian's voice broke a little as she recounted the grief and loss of those days. "After we lost the last baby, Greg and I decided to adopt. But because of Greg's heart condition," she turned to Cy, interrupting herself. "You might not know your father had bicuspid aortic valve disease."

"I didn't."

As Lillian explained what that meant for adoption, Isana grieved for the couple who so longed for a child.

"When we arrived in West Berlin for your father's posting, we were at the end of our rope. We knew we couldn't adopt stateside, and we didn't have the funds to adopt internationally. We thought we were out of options. Then I met Marta Bauer."

"The woman who was murdered here a few weeks ago?" Isana wanted to be sure it was the same Marta Bauer and not just a woman with the same name.

"Yes, but I had nothing to do with her death," Lillian said. "I never even knew she was in America until I read about her murder."

Isana believed her, but if Marta hadn't contacted Lillian, who had she contacted? It seemed too much of a coincidence Marta would be in the US during the same time as Lillian's kidnapping and the attacks on her and Cy.

Lillian continued her story about how Marta said she could get her a baby from an East German woman who wanted her child to have a better life.

"The photo albums show you pregnant during your time in West Berlin." Cy furrowed his brow. "You pretended to be expecting a child?"

Lillian exchanged a quick glance with Lorenz, then said, "Yes, that was part of Marta's plan."

"Did Dad know?"

Lillian flinched at her son's question. "Not at the time. His work had him traveling all over Germany, and he was gone a lot during the last three months." She drew in a breath. "Then Marta showed up one night in June during a storm to say it was time. She drugged me, and the next thing I knew, I woke up, and you were there."

Isana suspected there was more to the story but didn't press Lillian for details.

"You never asked where I came from? Who my biological parents were?"

Lillian shook her head. "I was so thankful that at long last I had a baby of my own, I didn't ask a lot of questions."

"Did you ever find out?"

Isana reached out for Cy's hand, hearing the anguish in his question. He grabbed hold of her fingers as if grasping a lifeline.

"It's time for me to tell my story," Lorenz said.

CHAPTER

THIRTY-EIGHT

Cy couldn't wrap his mind around what he'd heard. His mother essentially took another woman's baby and raised it as her own. Now this stranger had something to add.

"Rather than *um den heißen Brei herumreden*, I'll get straight to the point," Lorenz said.

"He means he's not going to talk around the porridge," Lillian translated. "Or, as we Americans put it, he won't beat around the bush."

The ease with which she interpreted the German idiom reminded Cy how much of his mother's life he didn't know.

Lorenz offered a tight-lipped smile, then continued, his English inflected with a slight German accent. "As you might have guessed, I grew up in the German Democratic Republic, what you lot called East Germany. I moved to East Berlin in the late 1970s and decided to make the police my career after I finished school. I excelled at my training and was plucked from the ranks to join the Stasi."

At the mention of the country's secret police, Cy wondered if

Lorenz was still involved in espionage, but now wasn't the time to probe deeper into that question.

"Then I met Nikoletta Otto." Lorenz's eyes took on a faraway expression, as if seeing this woman again in his mind's eye. "She was so beautiful, so full of life. She also was running a black-market scam and got caught."

Cy listened as Lorenz gave a few more details about how he and Nikoletta fell in love, as he began to think Lorenz might be discussing Cy's biological mother.

"We fell in love, but Nikoletta refused to marry me, saying I shouldn't throw away my career by linking myself permanently to someone with a record like her. I didn't care, but she stood firm." Lorenz sighed. "Months went by without my seeing her, and even then, she obscured her pregnancy from everyone, even me."

Lorenz seemed to guess the question Cy had. "It was a cold winter, and she could get away with wearing bulky sweaters and coats. A huge surveillance case kept me too busy to notice any changes, since we only spoke on the phone or met for a quick cup of coffee. When I did ask to spend more time with her, she put me off with excuses. In late May, I'd had enough and refused to leave until she let me in."

Cy could see how much Lorenz had cared for Nikoletta in his tone of voice—as much as he cared for Isana. What a fool he'd been to push her away when he should have been holding her close.

"Nikoletta said she wanted nothing to do with me and I should stop coming around harassing her. That she'd moved on to someone else. She even told me the baby wasn't mine, so I shouldn't worry about her." A flash of pain crossed Lorenz's face as he relayed her words. "It worked. I left and resolved to forget her."

"Did you find out what happened to her?" Isana asked when no one spoke for a few moments.

Lorenz sighed. "Someone called the police about a bad smell coming from her apartment. Someone from the Stasi usually accompanied the *Volkspolizei* on such calls."

Cy imagined the probable reason being to ensure nothing sensitive could be leaked.

"My superiors sent me because they knew I'd known Nikoletta." A shadow crossed Lorenz's face and Cy braced himself for what came next. "Nikoletta was dead. Those *Der Mistkerls* had left her to bleed to death after she'd given birth."

The four of them sat in silence for a time. Cy mourned the woman who was probably his birth mother.

"How did you find Mrs. Hillam?" Isana threaded her fingers through his, holding his hand on her lap. The gesture brought comfort Cy didn't know he needed.

"She'd left me a letter." Lorenz ran a hand over his face. Cy suspected he might have been wiping away a few tears. "In it, she asked my forgiveness for pushing me away and for giving away our baby. She told me how she'd cut a deal with Marta Bauer to give the baby a better life outside of the GDR and had been afraid I'd persuade her to change her mind."

The import of Lorenz's words sunk in slowly. Cy met the other man's eyes. "Are you saying—"

"I believe I'm your biological father," the other man said. "It's taken me years to track down what happened to Nikoletta's child. Marta was very good at leaving no trail behind. If you're willing, I'd like to do a DNA test to see if we're a match."

Cy glanced at his mother, who had tears streaming down her cheeks. "Mom, it's okay. It was a long time ago. I don't know why you didn't tell me sooner I was adopted."

"Because it wasn't done legally. I have no official adoption papers, only a birth certificate that's not real." She swiped tears from her cheeks. "I didn't want you to hate me for stealing another woman's baby."

"It doesn't sound like you stole her child. She gave you her baby because she wanted a better life for him, for me." Cy squeezed Isana's hand, then released it to take his mother's into his. Lillian cried softly.

"It took me years to track down those responsible," Lorenz continued. "But eventually, I found Marta Bauer."

The doorbell rang, intruding on the private moment. Isana stood. "I'll go see who it is."

Cy nodded his thanks, then returned his attention to comforting his mother. He couldn't quite believe the man opposite him was his biological father. The undercurrent of some other emotion permeated the room, leaving Cy to wonder about Lorenz's motives in coming forward now.

Isana appeared in the doorway.

"Who was at the door?" Lorenz voiced the question.

Cy half-rose as Isana's pale cheeks registered, steadying himself against the tabletop. "What's wrong?"

A man stepped out from behind Isana, his features hidden behind a facemask and hoodie. A black handgun rested against Isana's ribs.

THE COLD METAL DUG INTO ISANA'S SIDE. *DEAR GOD, PLEASE KEEP ME SAFE. And Cy and his mother and the man who may be his biological father.* She refused to let the fear rising inside her win. With slow, deep breaths, she managed to hold onto her emotions. The man jabbed the gun deeper into her flesh. Isana couldn't keep the gasp of pain from escaping.

Cy moved a half step toward her, but the man ground the weapon harder into her side, and Cy eased back into the chair.

"Phones turned off and in the middle of the table," the gunman barked, his voice muffled slightly by the surgical mask. "Now."

Cy, Lorenz, and Lillian all powered off their phones, placing them in the center. Isana moved her hand toward the back pocket of her jeans, meaning to add her phone to the mix, but the man jerked her elbow. "Stay still."

She let her hand fall to her side, glad she'd put the phone on silent mode. With any luck, the man would forget she might have one.

"What do you want?" Lorenz crossed his arms, his tone mild and his posture relaxed.

"Shut up!" the man growled. He leaned closer to Isana. "Find me a plastic bag for the phones."

She began opening cabinets, deliberately working her way around the kitchen in the opposite direction of the drawer with the aluminum foil, cling wrap, and plastic bags.

"Hurry up!" He pressed the gun hard into her side.

"That's not helping," she snapped. "I'm going as fast as I can."

At her response, the gun's pressure eased slightly. She opened the drawer with the bags. "Found them." Selecting a gallon sized, zipper-top bag, she held it out.

"Put the phones in the bag." The man walked with her to the table, one hand still tight on her elbow while the other kept the gun in place.

Isana gathered the phones, sliding them into the bag, then closing the top.

"Drop it on the floor."

She did as instructed.

The man stomped his heel onto the phones until they broke into metal and plastic pieces. Then he kicked the bag away from him. "Give me the list and the book."

"I'll get it," Cy said. "It's in the study."

"No, your mother will," their captor responded. "You have two minutes. And leave the door open. No funny business."

Lillian hurried from the kitchen. The gunman dragged Isana to the doorway, which gave him an unobstructed view of the study entrance.

How did he know about the book? Isana latched onto the question as it distracted her from the fear of being shot. The man's cold tone told her he wouldn't hesitate to pull the trigger if his demands weren't met, but if she let herself dwell on that, she'd fall apart. Only she, Lillian, and Cy knew the significance of the book. She couldn't stop the gasp from releasing but thankfully, no one noticed. The widow. *Please God, don't let Mrs. Johnston be hurt because of us.* Someone must have visited her and asked what she'd given Cy.

Lillian reappeared, the Grisham book in her hands along with a piece of paper. She tucked the paper inside the book as she returned to the kitchen. The man stepped aside, tugging Isana with him to allow Lillian to enter clutching the book.

The man nudged Isana with the weapon. "Take the book."

Isana grasped it from Lillian's hand, hugging it to her chest.

"Sit back down, Mrs. Hillam." The man stepped back toward the doorway, his grip on Isana's elbow tightening. "You'll all stay there for an hour. Do not call the cops." He paused. "And because I know you'll be tempted to deviate from my instructions, there are hidden cameras and microphones throughout the house. We'll know, and she'll die."

Isana yelped in pain as the gun slammed deeper into her ribs. The man didn't give her time to react, merely rapidly moved toward the front door, hustling her along in front of him. "You'll do exactly as I say, and I won't blow the entire house to smithereens."

"There's a bomb in the house?" She couldn't help voicing the question.

"Do you want to take the chance there's not?" They'd reached the front door. "Open it."

Visions of Cy's car exploding filled her mind as she fumbled for the door handle.

"Hurry up!"

Tears stung her eyes, but she opened the door, then pushed open the storm door. The man hurried her toward the street as a dark SUV pulled to the curb. "Get in back and lay down on the seat."

She complied, scooting on the bench seat and ducking her head. Something slammed into the back of her skull and darkness fell like a curtain over her eyes.

CHAPTER

THIRTY-NINE

Cy jumped to his feet the second the front door closed. "We have to go after her."

"Steady there," Lorenz said, his tone too mild for the circumstances in Cy's opinion.

"How can you say that?" Cy shoved a hand through his hair. "She's, she's . . . " He couldn't say the words out loud, as if uttering them would make the situation even worse.

"The woman you love." Lillian wiped tears from her cheeks. "I know, son. She's a lovely young woman. I couldn't have asked for better daughter-in-law."

Cy blew out a breath in an attempt to bring his roiling emotions under control. "Isn't that a little premature?"

Lillian shook her head. "I don't think so, but there'll be plenty of time to contemplate the future once we've rescued Isana."

The surety in his mother's voice calmed him. He returned to the table, glancing at the stove clock to check the time. Only five minutes had passed since the gunman had taken Isana out of the house. Another fifty-five before they could leave themselves.

Lorenz rose, his eyes sweeping the kitchen. Lillian reached out a hand toward Cy and he took it.

"I'm so sorry," she whispered. "This is all my fault."

"No, it isn't," he countered as Lorenz continued to examine the room. Cy leaned across the table. "What's he doing?"

"Looking for cameras."

His mother's answer reminded him they were trapped in this house for forty-nine more minutes. Each passing second he couldn't look for Isana felt like an hour. There was nothing he could do for her now. Except pray. He bowed his head. *Dear God, please keep Isana safe. Please let there be an end to this soon. Please.*

Lorenz retook his earlier seat. "There are two cameras in the kitchen, so he wasn't lying about those." His voice was so low, Cy could barely hear it. "Don't look, but one is near the stove clock and the other is on the top of the cabinets directly behind me."

Cy nearly turned his head reflexively when Lorenz pointed out the cameras location but managed to keep his eyes on his mother's face. New lines of worry had etched themselves on her face, making her seem older than she had before her kidnapping.

"Where does that leave us?" Cy asked in a similarly quiet voice.

"Stuck here until the hour is up," Brenner replied. "Do you have a deck of cards?"

Cy frowned at the request, then saw the wisdom of having something to occupy their time. "Sure." He hobbled over to the kitchen junk drawer and grabbed the card box. Back at the table, he shuffled them. "Rummy?"

Both Lillian and Lorenz nodded. Cy dealt the cards, half his mind on the game and the other half praying endlessly for Isana's safe return.

~

GINA FORCED A SMILE AT LYLE'S QUESTION. "I TOLD YOU, DARLING, WE didn't buy you. We paid for your mother's care and housing. That's all." She reached out a hand toward her husband, needing him beside her while she weathered this latest storm.

Gil tucked her hand in the crook of his arm, drawing her closer to his body, still lean after forty years of marriage. "I don't like your tone, Lyle. Please speak to your mother more respectfully."

Lyle snorted, his eyes flicking toward Logan, who still studied the photos of Gina pretending to be pregnant. "If I found out the truth, don't you think others will too?"

"I've told you the truth." Gina kept her voice patient, her expression caring, even while her pulse raced. She wouldn't allow herself to fail, not when so much more was at stake beyond hurting her sons and husband. If her secret came out, it was bye-bye White House, hello jailhouse. "Why don't you tell me what you think you know?"

Lyle turned to his twin. "Do you remember Zoey threatened to give me one of those DNA home test kits for Christmas?"

"You said you'd rather not rattle any family skeletons by seeing your DNA profile," Logan replied. "So she didn't."

"That's what I thought," Lyle said.

Fear pricked Gina, like a needle delivering a drug to her bloodstream.

"What do you mean?" Logan prompted when Lyle didn't say anything else.

Lyle sighed. "She swiped my DNA without asking me and submitted it. As a surprise."

"That's illegal." Logan, ever the attorney, cut to the heart of the matter.

"It's a little too late to worry about that." Lyle looked toward Gina and Gil. "She also took samples from you two." He drew out a folded envelope from his back pocket. "That's how I found out about the adoption."

"Sweetheart, I'm so sorry. We should have told you, but it never seemed like the right time." Gina glanced at Gil for assistance.

"Zoey also uploaded the results to Ancestry.com to see if there were any long-lost relatives rattling around the Sanders line," Lyle continued as if Gina hadn't spoken. "Boy, did that open a can of worms."

He handed the envelope to his brother. "Go ahead, Logan. Read what our dear parents did to get us."

Logan unfolded the envelope and pulled out the contents. In the sudden silence, the muffled sound of a phone trilling, it's ringtone unfamiliar, permeated Gina's conscious.

Gil cocked his head. "Is someone's phone ringing?"

The twins checked their phones, answering in unison in that uncanny way of theirs. "Not ours."

Gil removed her hand from his arm and strode toward her desk, cocking his head as if listening for the phone. The ringing stopped, only to begin again immediately. He bent and tugged at the locked bottom lefthand drawer. "I think it's coming from this drawer. Gina?"

The timing couldn't have been more awful. She pasted a concerned look on her face. "I can't imagine . . . " She hurried to the desk, gently maneuvering her husband out of the line of sight for when she opened the drawer. The ringing ceased. She hesitated, key in the lock, to see if the ringing would continue. "Oh, well. False alarm."

She straightened, tucking her keyring back into her pocket. "Must have been one of those spammers. I'll check later." She eyed the twins, her heartrate skyrocketing at Logan's furrowed brow, his head bent over the papers from the envelope.

Best to play ignorant, her default act throughout her life. When people thought you were stupid, they discounted you. She'd realized in her teens she would get further if she hid her brains behind a sunny disposition and a fashionably dressed body. And she had, nearly all the way to the White House. Soon, the sitting president would announce his endorsement of Gil, with the official party nomination coming next year. In the meantime, Gil would begin fundraising to build his war chest. Her husband would make a fine president, one of the best, she was sure.

"Mom?" Logan's voice had a little-boy-lost-quality to it.

Instinctively, she crossed to him, laying a hand on his arm. "What is it?"

He sidestepped away, sidling up to his twin and handing the pages to Lyle, who tucked them back inside the envelope. Her boys exchanged a long glance. Their ability to communicate without saying a word had bothered her during their childhood. They shared a bond she would never be able to understand.

A knock on the study door startled her. Gil crossed to open it. One of the new Secret Service men stood there. Whatever he said to Gil must have been important because her husband moved aside and allowed the man to enter. Behind the Secret Service man came a young woman and two men, both wearing facemasks and hoodies pulled low. A fourth man brought up the rear.

The Secret Service man immediately stepped back into the hallway, closing the door behind him.

"We're having a family discussion. You need to leave." Gina projected strength in her voice.

"I don't think so, Mrs. Sanders," said the unmasked man.

His response, spoken in a tone of someone used to getting what they wanted, told Gina she needed to re-evaluate her initial impression. She swept her eyes over the man again, this time his more formal attire registering. While the two masked men wore jeans, the spokesman had on a custom-made, pinstriped charcoal gray suit with a lighter gray dress shirt and a bold gray-and-red tie. The entire ensemble screamed of his power. She'd spent a lifetime living among powerful men and bending them to her will. She could do the same with this man.

"We have much to discuss," the leader continued. "Please, take a seat."

The young woman whimpered. Gina flicked a glance her way, barely managing to keep her face expressionless as she recognized Isana Thomas—and the Glock pressed into her side.

"I've had enough." Lyle headed for the door.

The unmasked man nodded, and the masked man not holding Isana punched Lyle in the jaw. He crumpled to the floor in a heap. Gil leaped forward, but the masked man holding Isana swung the gun toward her husband, halting him a few feet from Lyle.

"As I said, let's all sit down before someone gets seriously hurt." The unmasked man swung around one of the desk chairs, dropping into it as if he'd been invited for a cozy chat. "Phones turned off and on the desk first, please."

Everyone shuffled forward, dropping their phones on the gleaming surface of the desk. The masked man who'd decked Lyle checked each phone, then nodded to the leader. Gina waited until Gil chose a seat, wanting to be close to her husband. Instead of picking the couch, Gil picked the other club chair, isolating himself from the family. Typical of her husband, wanting to play a lone hand to save the world. Gina sank onto the sofa on the opposite end from Logan, who stared in the direction of his fallen twin.

The man holding Isana shoved her onto the love seat and took up a position behind her, his gun visible to everyone. The other masked man stood somewhere behind Gina.

"Good. Now that we're all settled, we can begin." The man crossed his legs. "For simplicity's sake, you can call me Bob."

"What do you want, Bob?" Gil snapped.

Bob withdrew a piece of paper from his inside pocket. "Since I now possess the list, I hold all the cards, don't I, Mrs. Sanders?"

Gina swallowed hard, clenching her fingers together to stop them from shaking. She could do this. He was fishing. He couldn't possibly know for sure. "What list?"

Bob shook his head. "The time for playing games is past. Unless you want to lose everything, I suggest you listen closely."

Gil didn't even glance Gina's way. "Leave my wife out of this. She has nothing to do with whatever this is."

Bob's eyes glittered as a smile crept across his face like a cat burglar sneaking out a window. "He doesn't know. I'm surprised you kept it a secret all these years." He flicked a glance toward Logan. "He knows something, probably his brother too. Interesting."

Gina found it decidedly uninteresting as she struggled to keep her outward demeanor calm. Her mind raced to figure out how to stay ahead of Bob and whatever he thought he knew or had.

Bob pulled a sheaf of papers from his inside coat pocket. "This is what I want in return for my silence on the list."

"What list?" Her husband's famous control neared the cracking line.

"Why the list of embassy wives from the West Berlin days, of course." Bob tapped the papers against his leg. "Doesn't ring any bells?"

No one moved or offered an explanation. Gil frowned as if trying to figure out the significance of such a list. She schooled her own countenance into blank interest, a look she'd perfected over the years and used during those endless rubber chicken dinners she'd had to attend as Second Lady.

Bob met her gaze, his smile growing. "I think we'll let Gina explain exactly what these lovely wives did to acquire their babies."

CHAPTER

FORTY

As the tension rose like flood waters in the room, Isana hugged her aching ribs, thankful the man no longer jammed the gun into her tender side. Pain laced her ribs, so she shallowed her breathing, which helped a little. Her head still hurt from the blow in the car, muddling her thinking when she needed to concentrate on what was happening. *Please, God, keep Cy and Lillian safe. Let me be able to track this conversation. Give me the words to say if an opening presents itself.*

By closing her eyes and drawing in slow breaths, the pain in her head and ribs receded enough to allow the words to filter into her mind. Better than thinking about whether or not the men who'd grabbed her had rigged Lillian's house with a bomb. Isana hadn't been too surprised to see the Sanderses, not with knowing Virginia Sanders's name was on the list. As the most prominent person named, it made sense for Bob to come here to negotiate the truce. If that was indeed what was happening. She hadn't quite followed the entire conversation.

Gina Sanders ignored Bob's statement that she would explain, crossing her arms and firming her lips.

"Very well, we'll move on for now." Bob smoothed the papers in his hand. "I think you'll find my requests manageable."

The masked man closest to Bob took the papers and handed them to Gilbert Sanders, who accepted them with a steady hand. Silence built in the room as Vice President Sanders studied the documents. Near Isana's feet, one of the twins—Lyle, she thought—stirred, redness from the punch the only color on his face.

As Sanders bent his head over the documents, Isana's thoughts returned to Brenner. She sensed he'd been working behind the scenes for a while but not behind the attempts on her and Cy's life. Something about the way Lillian had looked at him made Isana think he might have been involved in her kidnapping. Brenner was holding something back, but she believed he thought he could be Cy's biological father based on his relationship with Nikoletta, who both he and Lillian named as Cy's bio mom.

"This is impossible." Sanders raised his head, his face chalk white. "What you're asking me to do could be construed as treason."

An expression that reminded Isana of a lion licking its paw after feasting on a fresh kill crossed Bob's face.

"I wouldn't be too worried," Bob said. "What's one more treasonous act in the Sanders family?"

"What are you talking about?" Sanders blurted the question, his face a mask of confusion.

Bob steepled his fingers. "Why don't you ask—"

"What's happening?" The injured twin twisted his body into a seated position, bracing his back against the loveseat to the right of Isana.

"You okay, Lyle?" Logan half rose from his seat, but one of the masked men shoved him back down.

"Let's all keep our seats," Bob said. "Lyle, you can stay there or join Ms. Thomas on the loveseat."

Lyle didn't reply. He simply cradled his head in his hands and stayed on the floor.

"Now, I think Mrs. Sanders was going to explain exactly what she's done to keep the origin story of the twins a secret." Bob nodded toward Mrs. Sanders. "Go on, Gina. Don't be shy. Your audience is waiting."

Mrs. Sanders opened her mouth, then snapped it closed without uttering a word.

"Not one to brag about your exploits?" Bob pointed to Mrs. Sanders. "Your mother is as cutthroat as they come. I must admit to being impressed with the swiftness and the ferocity of her response to the perceived danger to her family."

"Gina?" The vice president's voice shook as he gazed at his wife. "What have you done?"

"See?" Bob rubbed his hands together. "Even her husband believes her capable of doing whatever it takes to protect her family."

Mrs. Sanders angled her body away from Bob, her face devoid of expression.

"Come now, Gina," Bob said. "I'm sure Ms. Thomas would like to know why you have been trying to kill her, her boyfriend, and her boyfriend's mother."

Isana gasped, unable to keep her shock contained. "You were behind the car bomb? Tried to shoot me by the Tidal Basin?"

"I'm afraid the Tidal Basin incident was partly my fault," Brenner said as he stepped into the room through French doors, a handgun pointed straight at Bob.

"Are you sure we can trust Brenner?" Cy crossed his arms in a futile effort to contain his anxiety. He stood with his mother in the lobby of FBI headquarters in downtown DC. Brenner had dropped them off half an hour ago with a sealed envelope with *urgent* written on the front along with the words *West Berlin 1980s* for FBI Director Harold Channing. The front desk receptionist had taken the envelope and invited them to wait.

"I don't know." Lillian faced Cy, her eyes troubled. "I've always known this day would come, but I was too much of a coward to confess on my own. Please believe me when I say I didn't know—didn't want to know—what really happened behind the scenes. I truly thought I was helping a poor East Berlin mother by giving her baby a chance for a better life."

"It's not true?" He'd fitted more pieces together during the ride to the FBI building. Marta Bauer had run a baby selling ring in which she smuggled infants out of East Berlin and sold them to desperate American women living in West Berlin.

"It's true, but it's not the whole truth."

"Mrs. Hillam, Mr. Hillam?" A tall black woman wearing a tailored navy suit stood a few feet away. "I'm Special Agent LaTasha Burns. If you'll come this way, the director will see you now."

Cy followed his mother and Burns to the elevator bank. No one spoke during the short ride. Why would the FBI be concerned about a baby-selling ring from forty-odd years ago in a country that no longer existed? His mother's earlier words rang in his ears. *I didn't know what really happened.*

His musings came to a halt as the elevator slid to a stop. They trailed Burns through a maze of cubicles and offices until she arrived at a less cluttered corner of the building.

An older woman with silvery hair and a bright floral shirt smiled as they approached. "Go right in, Agent Burns."

"Thank you, Ms. Perkins." The agent knocked once, then opened the door marked FBI Director Harold Channing. "Director Channing, I have Mrs. Hillam and her son, Mr. Hillam."

"Thank you, Agent Burns." Channing came around his desk. "Please shut the door as you leave."

"Yes, sir." Burns closed the door with a soft click.

"Mrs. Hillam, Mr. Hillam, have a seat." The director crossed to a small conference table and pulled out a chair for his mom.

Cy took the seat to the left of her, while Channing sat opposite.

Channing tapped the envelope Brenner had given them on the table. "Do you know what's inside?"

Cy shook his head, but his mother answered, "I think so."

When the director didn't continue, Lillian squared her shoulders. "It's a list of names, including my own and the vice president's wife. Every one of those names, except for Marta Bauer's, were American women living in West Berlin during the 1980s." Her voice broke on a sob.

"Mom, you don't have to do this." Cy placed his hand on her shoulder.

"Yes, I do." Lillian turned to the director. "May I have a glass of water?"

"Of course." Channing reached for a filled pitcher resting on a tray with four glasses. He poured water into a crystal glass. "Here you go."

She took the glass and drank deeply. "The Americans wanted a baby but couldn't have one on their own. Marta somehow found this out and convinced each of us she could find a baby from an unwed mother in East Berlin who wanted her child to have a better life. I learned later Marta also supplied many Western goods for East Berliners. My husband, Greg, and I couldn't have children, and US adoption agencies wouldn't consider us as potential parents because of Greg's chronic heart condition."

Cy shifted in his seat. All of this he knew, but the sense of foreboding grew with every word his mother uttered.

Channing listened without comment, his gaze never shifting from Lillian's face.

His mother took another sip, then continued. "Part of Marta's plan was for us to pretend pregnancy. That would give the baby a US birth certificate without question. She coached us on all aspects of pregnancy, bringing us bigger 'stomachs' as we supposedly progressed. She grilled us on when our husbands would be out of town so we could time the 'birth' of the babies." Lillian glanced at Cy. "Your father didn't find out until shortly before he died. He thought we'd finally been successful in getting pregnant against all odds."

"Oh, Mom." He covered her hand in his. No matter what happened, she would always be his mother.

She straightened her spine, the words tumbling out faster. "I didn't question how Marta could be so sure about the timing of the birth, how nearly impossible it would be to know exactly when a baby would arrive." Drawing in a breath, she exhaled slowly. "Everything went off without a hitch. Marta even had a doctor give each of us a mock C-section incision to pretend we'd had emergency Caesareans in case anyone ever asked. It was good enough to fool my OB-GYN."

The extent of the lie shocked Cy. He'd assumed it had merely been a clandestine baby swap, not an elaborate hoax.

Lillian drained the last of the water, setting the glass down with a trembling hand.

"Mrs. Hillam, the note mentioned you had urgent information for me. What you've told me is a crime but not one worth prosecuting at this stage for various reasons."

Cy had been so focused on his parentage, he hadn't considered what his mother had done was illegal.

The director's words should have soothed Mom, but instead sobbed quietly.

"It's okay." Cy rubbed her back as if he were the parent and she the child. "You shouldn't be in any trouble. But if what you know can help us find Isana . . . "

Lillian raised her head. "Right, we must rescue Isana."

"Is Isana the missing young woman referred to in this note?" Channing tapped the envelope.

"Yes, she was kidnapped." Cy succinctly recounted the circumstances. "Brenner Lorenz, the German man who wrote the note, said he knew where she was but told us it was important for you to know the whole story immediately."

Channing's body language, which had been more indulgent as he listened to Lillian's story, tensed slightly. "Then I think you'd better tell me the rest, Mrs. Hillam."

Lillian nodded, wiping the tears from her cheeks with the handkerchief offered by the director. "I'm ashamed to say I didn't think twice about the payment. At the time, it was worth it to get a baby. Now I see how easily Marta manipulated me, and I assume the others, into giving her what she wanted."

Cy had assumed Lillian had paid cash for him, a straightforward business transaction of goods—the baby—for money. But his mother's words puzzled him.

"Marta didn't want cash for the baby?" Channing gave voice to the question rattling around Cy's brain.

"No." Lillian sucked in a breath, moving forward enough to make Cy drop his hand from her back. "I wish it had been money, but Marta was smarter than that."

When Lillian didn't go on, Channing prompted, "What was the payment?"

"A face." Lillian almost smiled. "Sounds so simple, doesn't it?"

Channing abandoned all pretense of not being interested. "What do you mean?"

"Marta said she needed the identity of a double agent, one who switched to working for the Americans. When I protested I didn't know any double agents, she said she would show me some photographs. All I had to do was let her know which one I saw in the embassy. That was all." She drew in a ragged breath. "See? It didn't feel like a betrayal."

Cy worked to keep his thoughts to himself as the implication of what she'd done skittered around his mind like a marble in a pinball machine.

"Who was the double agent?" Channing's voice was soft.

"Nathan Schmidt. But she also asked for the name of the person who met with Nathan."

"The American's name?" Channing's gaze never deviated from Lillian's.

"Yes."

"And did you give it to her?"

Cy held his breath as his mother answered, knowing her next word could brand her a traitor. And there was no statute of limitations on betraying your country.

FORTY-ONE

Brenner enjoyed the shock on Bob's face as he emerged from behind the heavy floor-to-ceiling curtains in front of the French doors. Really, the man could have thought of a more suitable alias. Brenner had been listening at the door for a while to time his entrance for maximum effect. "Isana, you okay?"

The young woman nodded, her face pale but her jaw firm. He moved his concentration back to Bob. "Decided the personal touch would be best to convince the Sanders family to do your bidding, eh?"

Bob shrugged, then straightened his shirt cuffs under the tailored suit jacket. His former boss had always been a sharp dresser. His need for haute couture had been part of the reason behind his extracurricular activities. He needed lots of cash to fund his wardrobe and other luxuries.

The hoodlum behind Isana pointed his weapon at Brenner, as did the masked man behind Gil Sanders. "Gentlemen, it's probably best to keep our weapons out of sight, don't you think?" Brenner re-holstered his Sig Sauer, knowing Bob would instruct his men to follow suit. "The last thing we need is a shootout to bring in the Secret Service."

Bob nodded, and the two masked men's weapons disappeared from view. Brenner stayed put with his back to the French doors. No need to give them a chance to circle him from behind. "Now that we're all more comfortable, we were discussing what Mrs. Sanders has done to protect her secret."

Gina lifted her chin, defiance pulsing off her like a strobe light.

"The truth will come out, Mrs. Sanders," Brenner snapped, his patience at an end. The woman had nearly destroyed innocent lives because of her need to keep quiet.

"They already know the truth," she replied.

Bob's eyebrows rose. "Do they indeed?"

Brenner allowed Bob to regain control of the conversation. Better to let the man think he was back in charge.

Bob turned to Logan. "What exactly do you know about your entrance into the Sanders family?"

Logan kept his gaze directed at the carpet. "While my father was stationed at the US Embassy in West Berlin, she pretended to be pregnant and stole another woman's babies to pass off as their own. She said they paid the woman's living expenses and the mother wanted us to have a better life than she could provide."

"Bravo, Gina. An excellent cover story." Bob clapped his hands slowly. "Now tell them what really happened."

"But that is what happened," Gil said.

"Two names." Bob directed his gaze toward Gina.

Gina pressed her lips together so firmly, Brenner detected a white circle around them. Close-mouthed to the end. He glanced at Isana, who had a hand to her head. One twin sat on the floor, a blood smear across one cheek. The other's rigid posture contradicted his hung head. The vice president wore a troubled expression as he too looked at Gina.

"Stefan Jung and Randall Brooks," Bob said.

No one reacted but Gina, who flinched as if struck. Bob pointed a finger at her. "Aha, so you do remember those two men."

Gil's brow creased, then his mouth dropped open and his eyes widened. Brenner almost felt sorry for the vice president as the man clearly recognized the names. And likely, their significance.

"Randall Brooks was found dead in West Berlin near the Wall, his throat slashed, three weeks before the babies came." Gil spoke softly, but his words carried throughout the suddenly silent room. "Stefan Jung had German immigrant parents, spoke the language like a native, and had successfully brought out numerous defectors to the West, including several prominent scientists. He too had his throat cut. Their murders were never solved."

The unhurt twin jumped to his feet, his cheeks flushed. "You bought us with names?" He glanced at his father. "I don't understand . . . " His voice trailed off as Brenner surmised the meaning of his mother's betrayal sunk in.

"Your darling adoptive mother decided being a mother meant more than loyalty to her country," Bob said. "Randall Brooks was a CIA agent working in West Berlin. Stefan Jung was an East German spy turned double agent. Brooks was his Western contact."

The injured twin raised his head, speaking for the first time since Brenner's appearance. "So dear mom is a traitor."

"And there's no statute of limitations on prosecuting traitors." His father's shock and sorrow aged his face.

"It wasn't like that!" Gina rose, her entire body trembling. "I was helping that mother by taking her babies. She wanted them to have a better life." She turned to her husband. "It was just a couple of names. I didn't know what Randall was doing. Marta showed me photos, lots of photos. All I had to do was point to anyone I'd seen in the Embassy."

Gil didn't look away from his wife, so Brenner couldn't read the vice president's expression.

"I did it for us," Gina pleaded. "I did it so we could have a family."

She gestured toward the twins, who both weren't looking in their mother's direction. "And we have a lovely family."

"Did you even ask what Marta would do with the names?" Gil's voice was gentler than Brenner expected.

Gina shook her head. "No. I was thinking of the baby we'd have. What were a few names in comparison to becoming a mother?"

"And Marta?" Brenner inserted, hoping Gina would confess her more recent misdeeds. "Why did you have her killed?"

"She was always a money grubber." Gina added a few spicier names for the dead former East German. "When she contacted me saying she was here in the US, I knew what she wanted, and I knew I would never be free from her and her insinuations."

"Why try to hurt this young lady?" If Gil thought his wife would be repentant about her actions, he had sadly misjudged her.

"Because she and Lillian's son were snooping around looking for the list Lillian's husband had found and secreted away." Gina's tone was entirely reasonable. "As soon as I'd heard about Lillian's kidnapping, I knew it had to do with our time in West Berlin. I'd heard rumors Marta had compiled a list of the women she'd helped and who each had paid for her services by identifying double agents."

The matter-of-fact way Gina spoke told Brenner the woman had compartmentalized her actions years ago. She spoke of sending men and women to their deaths as if discussing the weather.

"I couldn't let such a list come to light, not without harming Gil's presidential candidacy." She smiled at her husband, her earlier tremors gone. "I did it because you'll make a wonderful president."

"Indeed he will," Bob agreed, "which is why you'll be keeping quiet about what Mrs. Sanders did."

"At what cost?" One of the twins—Logan, Brenner thought—re-engaged in the conversation. "You came here to exact a price for not revealing what she'd done. What are you asking?"

Gil picked up the piece of paper he'd let fall to the floor during his wife's revelations. "As president, he wants me to push certain pieces of legislation to benefit his financial holdings."

"Money?" Lyle spat out the word as if it tasted bad in his mouth. "This is all about getting more money?"

"With money comes power," Brenner interjected. "That's what Bob is after." While his intentions weren't any nobler, he at least had peace his search for Nikoletta's and his child had come to an end.

The study door burst open. Brenner immediately raised his hands while the two masked men reached for their weapons.

Three men entered, their guns drawn. "Freeze! FBI! Get your hands where we can see them!"

Lillian twisted her hands together as she waited in a small interview room at FBI headquarters. A female agent sat in the corner, her attention on her phone. The director hadn't placed her under arrest yet, but she'd been told to stay here while other agents took Cyrus out of the room. His anxiousness concerning Isana's safety had been growing by the minute. Not that Cyrus said as much. She was his mother and could tell by the way his body twitched a bit.

Cyrus had insisted on going with the agents when they confronted the vice president's wife, saying he'd take an Uber to the residence if he had to. The director must have seen how serious Cyrus was because he'd agreed without demur as long as Cyrus obeyed FBI instructions.

Now Lillian was left with her thoughts. Part of her felt sorry for Virginia Sanders, knowing how the woman had felt all those years ago when faced with getting her heart's desire at long last. Giving up a name or two must have seemed like a small price to pay for a child of her own. However, Lillian could not condone the woman's more recent actions, given they nearly killed her son and the woman he cared for.

Brenner must have messengered over proof of what Virginia Sanders had done because Channing had asked them about the car bomb and Marta Bauer's murder. Lillian also recounted her meeting with Gina in which the other woman promised to stop trying to harm Cyrus and Isana, although not in so many words.

As the revelations continued to pour in, Cyrus hadn't said much. Lillian reflected her actions might have cost her his love. *Please, God, don't let me lose my son.* Her faith had never been strong, more of a this-is-what-we-should-teach-our-son kind of thing. Lately, though, she'd been feeling a stronger tug on her heart, a yank really, to confess her sins, namely what she'd done to get a baby. But instead of listening to the still, small voice when it first began to whisper, she'd ignored it, letting fear of what Cyrus would think of her flourish enough to choke out any inclination toward redemption.

In the end, she'd been forced to lay it all bare and now faced charges of treason. Somehow, though, her heart didn't feel as leaden but lighter, as if a great burden had been lifted. She didn't know what would happen to her, but releasing the secret she'd carried for more than thirty years had eased something inside her very being.

To distract herself from worry about Cyrus and Isana, Lillian pictured the vice-presidential mansion. She'd attended a function with Greg there before his West Berlin posting. Greg, who'd been horrified at what she'd done to create their family and who had died trying to put it to rights. *I'm sorry, my darling. You were right. I should have come to you when Marta first approached me.* But she hadn't, and her failure to do so had resulted in the deaths of Marta and Schmidt.

A light sweat broke out over her body. Lillian struggled to catch her breath as pain stabbed her heart. Was this what Greg had felt over her betrayal? His heart breaking?

"Ma'am? Are you alright?" The agent lightly touched Lillian's arm.

Lillian gasped for air as the discomfort intensified.

"I need an ambulance! Possible heart attack in progress." The agent eased Lillian out of the chair and onto the carpeted floor.

As she lay her head on the floor, Lillian hoped it wasn't too late to make amends for the past.

HARD STEEL JABBED AGAINST ISANA'S TEMPLE AS FBI AGENTS SURROUNDED the room's occupants, guns focused on the masked men, Bob, and Brenner. The masked man who'd grabbed Isana in Lillian's house wasn't going to give up without a fight, if his actions were any indication of his frame of mind. She held as still as she could with a gun pressed to her head, one silent prayer looping over and over. *Lord, please protect me and the others. Don't let any more blood be shed.*

Vice President Sanders raised his hands, as did his wife and sons. Brenner did again as well after laying his weapon on the floor and kicking it away.

"Sir, put your weapon down!" a male agent shouted at the masked man holding Isana hostage.

The man behind Isana didn't move his gun.

"I said put your weapon down!" the agent repeated, his voice firm and sure. "It's over."

Isana caught a glimpse of the other masked man being led away in handcuffs and Brenner being cuffed too. Bob hadn't moved from his seat, his hands in the air.

The masked man stayed still, his gun against Isana's head. Directly across from her, Bob smiled, as if enjoying the chaos he'd created with his thirst for money and power.

"Everyone, get back or I shoot her." The man's muffled voice carried into the stillness of the room.

Tension rose like steam from a boiling kettle as the agents, weapons still trained in Isana's direction, stepped back.

"I'm FBI Director Channing." A man with an air of authority in his tone spoke from a position to Isana's right. But she couldn't turn her head to see, given the gun against her flesh. "We're going to remove the vice president and his family. Is that okay?"

"Make it quick," the gunman replied.

This time, Isana caught the faint sound of an accent. German? Did this man have a connection with Marta and her baby-stealing-for-names scheme? Agents escorted the vice president's family from the line of fire. Now no one stood between herself and Bob.

The man must have dropped to a crouch because his breath now tickled the hairs on Isana's neck. The gun stayed firmly in place.

"When I reach a count of three, fall sideways to the left."

She blinked at the words. What he suggested seemed to indicate he wanted her out of harm's way.

"Touch your left ear if you understand."

Isana swallowed hard and reached up to place her fingertips along her left ear. She clung to the hope his words gave and prayed once more for safety and to see Cy again.

"One."

Her body tensed.

"Two."

She released a breath.

"Three."

Isana flung her body to the left as the man removed the gun from her head. She squeezed her eyes shut, her hands going to cradle her head. Two gunshots echoed in the room. The thud of a body hitting the floor wrenched a scream from her.

Someone touched her shoulder, and she screamed again.

"It's okay."

At the unfamiliar female voice, she opened her eyes to meet the woman's concerned gaze. "I'm FBI Special Agent McCathy. Are you hurt?"

Isana shook her head. As she pushed herself to a seated position, the room spun, then righted. "What happened?"

McCathy hesitated, then said, "The man holding you hostage shot the man sitting in the chair opposite him."

"Dead?" Isana didn't want to see what happened to Bob. Agents swarmed the chair, making it impossible for her to gain a glimpse of the man who'd orchestrated so much pain and suffering for his own gain.

"Right between the eyes," the agent replied.

"And the shooter?" Isana feared she knew the answer. Another causality.

"He should live," McCathy said. "Shoulder wound from one of our agents."

"Please, I want to know if she's all right!" Cy's voice permeated the room's hubbub.

Isana couldn't believe it. "That's my . . . " She wasn't sure how to finish the sentence, but if the gleam in McCathy's eye was anything to go on, the other woman understood.

"Let's get you out of the crime scene." The female agent rose. "Can you stand?"

"I think so." Isana got to her feet with some assistance from McCathy, since her legs behaved as if they were made of Jello instead of bone. After a couple of wobbly steps, she regained her strength and moved unassisted through the chaotic room and through the door.

Cy paced at the far end of the hall, arguing with a pair of agents in dark blue suits. McCathy called to one of them, and Cy spotted Isana.

"Isana!"

Within seconds, he'd reached her and pulled her into his arms. "I thought I'd lost you when I heard the shots."

"I'm okay." Isana slipped her arms around his waist and laid her head on his chest. His heart beat fast under her ear. The solid form of him eased more of the tension from her body. Tears of relief trickled down her cheeks, wetting the front of his shirt.

He leaned back and tilted her chin up with gentle fingers. "Hey, it's over."

"I know." She sniffled. "I was so scared."

"Me too." Cy dried her tears with a handkerchief. "I never prayed so hard in my life."

"Me either." She drew in a deep breath, letting it out slowly as the tears subsided. "Where's your mom?"

"She had to stay with the FBI." He wrinkled his forehead and dropped his hands to her waist. "She might go to jail for giving an enemy agent the names of one of our agents. I can't believe what those women did to get a baby."

Isana wished she could erase the hurt in his heart over his mother's treasonous act. Perhaps reminding him of how God brought good out of the situation would help. "I'm not condoning what she did, but if she hadn't, we never would have met."

His expression brightened a little. "True."

She had one more distractive measure up her sleeve. Rising on tiptoes, she planted a kiss on his mouth. Cy deepened the kiss, his hand moving to play with her hair.

"Mr. Hillam?"

Isana broke the kiss, heat flooding her cheeks as she turned to meet McCathy's gaze. The agent's compassionate expression brought back the tension kissing Cy had erased.

"Yes?" Cy kept his arm around her waist as he faced the agent.

"Your mother's been taken to the hospital for a suspected heart attack."

FORTY-TWO

Five weeks later

Isana depressed the shutter on her Leica, then adjusted the focus again before snapping another picture. The late April sun cast a brilliant hue of colors as it sank behind the Jefferson Memorial. She framed a third photo to include a cherry tree branch, a single blossom still hanging onto the limb amidst the green leaves.

The warm spring air and clear sky soothed her soul after the events of March. She tucked the camera back into its case and slung it across her body before moving along the paved trail circling the Tidal Basin. Joggers huffed past, weaving around moms pushing strollers. Couples walked arm-in-arm, sometimes stopping to steal a kiss or two under the trees.

She'd thought she would be among those who found love this spring. Hope, which had blossomed during their search for the list and the dramatic ending at the vice presidential mansion, had slowly faded with each subsequent abbreviated conversation or text exchange with Cy. She was more than willing to give him space after his mother's unexpected death following a second heart attack while in the hospital. The media frenzy with the arrest of Gilbert and Virginia Sanders had only briefly mentioned Lillian and Greg Hillam, as well as some of the other names on the list. The Blandings she and Lena had gone to see had also been taken into custody related to what the press dubbed "The Baby Stealgate." In Germany, several women testified to having their newborns snatched by Marta Bauer, some willing, some not.

Brenner Lorenz turned out to be a rather big deal in the former German Democratic Republic, and a DNA test proved he was Cy's biological father. While working for Bob, aka Joerg Horn, Brenner compiled a damning list of evidence linking Horn to kidnapping and murder. A former Stasi higher up, Horn transferred his skills to building an empire funded by blackmail and intimidation in the US.

Mrs. Sanders confessed to hiring thugs to scare Isana and Cy off their search, but she denied ordering Marta's death. However, as the investigation continued, the media reported a strong link between Marta's murder and the vice president's wife.

Isana exited the path, heading toward the West Basin Drive bus stop to catch a ride to her quiet apartment. This was the first evening since she went back to work she'd been out of the office before eight. Getting the wedding dress exhibition ready in time for June had meant long hours. While she still had a lengthy to-do list, the major tasks had been checked off ,and she had itched to photograph a spring sunset.

Cy had been equally busy, both with work and his mother's estate. Her offers to help sort through the Falls Church house had been gently rebuffed, as he explained his need to focus on tying up the numerous loose ends. When they texted, it was about mundane things. She missed their previous closeness and couldn't help thinking he was having second thoughts about their relationship. The bus lumbered up to the stop, its air brakes whooshing as the doors opened. She climbed on, choosing a seat in the back next to the window. Maybe no one would notice her crying there. Thinking about Cy brought on the tears. The busyness of work distracted her enough she could keep her emotions in check at the museum. On her own like this gave her too much time to remember the feel of his arms around her. The touch of his hand in hers. The softness of his lips on her mouth.

Using the backs of her fingers to wipe away tears, she breathed in and out slowly in an effort to calm her roiling emotions. She'd thought he'd cared for her, had wanted to explore a life together. How had she totally missed the cues he hadn't felt as deeply as she had? Her mother's strident voice echoed in her head, "You're not worth . . . " Cringing at the remembered curse word Mom used to end the statement, Isana reminded herself instead she was fearfully and wonderfully made in the image of God.

One good thing had come out of it. She'd returned to church. She'd purposefully attended the early service to avoid running into Cy but had been going each week. She'd even joined Lena's Bible study, much to the other woman's delight. Learning about her walk with God had given Isana the strength to get out of bed in the mornings when memories of Cy threatened to overwhelm her.

It all circled back to Cy. She sighed and pulled the string to indicate the bus should let her off at the next stop. She supposed with time, she would not feel such a sharp ache each time her mind fixated on his handsome face. At The Heritage, their paths crossed infrequently enough with her office in the basement, she could easily avoid him. Quite a change from when she'd planned her coffee break route to pass by his office in the hope he'd say hello to her.

Swiping fresh tears from her cheeks, she exited the bus and headed toward her apartment building around the corner from the stop. Mentally reviewing her fridge contents, she decided a shopping trip tomorrow needed to be added to the list of chores she'd been neglecting. Having a free Saturday for the first time in a month felt strange, given she'd spent the last four at the museum working on the exhibition.

Inside the lobby, she greeted one of the dog owners whose name she could never remember. "How's Charlie doing?" Isana bent to pet the wiggly cocker spaniel, who rewarded her efforts with a hand lick.

"Much better." The young woman flipped back her long, auburn hair nearly the same shade as her canine's. "I hope she won't be as inquisitive when it comes to eating objects found on the sidewalk."

"Enjoy the walk. It's a nice spring evening." Isana straightened and headed to the elevator. Exiting on her floor, she slipped her lanyard holding her keys and license from her neck. When she turned the corner to her apartment, she halted at the sight of Cy lounging against her front door, his attention on his phone.

She must have made a noise because he looked up and quickly slipped the device into a pocket.

"Hi."

"Hi." Isana hated the way her pulse jumped at his greeting. Why did he have to look good enough to nibble on in his jeans and form-hugging dark-blue Henley shirt? "What are you doing here?"

The question appeared to startle him. She saw it in the way his eyes widened. Perhaps it had come out sharper than she'd intended, but really, what did the man expect after having minimal contact with her recently? She'd just jump into his arms at the first opportunity? She tamped down the little voice that screamed she would and plastered what she hoped was a noncommittal expression on her face.

Cy gestured toward a takeout bag sitting at his feet. "I brought dinner." He shifted, his gaze burning into hers. "I'd hoped we might eat and talk."

Behind her, one of her neighbors exited their apartment. Isana moved closer to Cy, her heart hammering so loudly, she was sure he'd hear it. "I guess you should come in.

He moved aside for her to slip her key into the lock and shove open the door.

Once inside, she led the way to the kitchen. The smells of Mexican food tickled her nostrils, reminding her that a granola bar did not constitute dinner. Without speaking, she dug out plates and forks, then filled two glasses with filtered water. "We can eat at the table."

She brought the dishes to the small table in what the condo literature had optimistically called the dining alcove.

Cy seemed content to let the silence build as he opened containers of sauteed peppers and onions, portabella mushrooms, and thin slices of steak. "I hope you like fajitas."

"I do."

Cy reached a hand toward her. "Shall I say grace?"

Should she acquiesce and hold his hand while he prayed? Isana slid hers into his before she'd consciously thought about the answer to her internal query. He squeezed it gently, then prayed for their food and conversation.

Isana blinked back sudden tears as the memory of other meals they'd had together filled her with sadness. She directed her gaze down to her filled tortilla, her appetite fleeing. If he came to tell her in person they were over, she'd rather hear it first. There was no way she could choke down anything while waiting for the other shoe to drop.

Gathering her courage like an old woman pulling her cardigan tighter around her shoulders, she restated her earlier question. "What are you doing here?" She held up a hand when he started to reply. "And don't tell me dinner. I know you needed space to sort through everything you learned about your birth and your mom's passing, but it's been more than five weeks since that day at the vice president's mansion, and we've only texted."

When he didn't immediately say anything, she shoved to her feet, her movement sloshing the water in their glasses. "I can't do this."

That seemed to loosen his tongue. "Do what?"

Exasperation pushed the words out fast. "I can't pretend we didn't hug, we didn't kiss." She pointed her index finger at him. "You told me you cared about me. But all I get is crickets when I try to connect with you. Was it all a lie? Were you just using me to help your mom?"

~

ALL VERY EXCELLENT QUESTIONS, ONES CY WASN'T SURE HE COULD adequately answer. He'd been in a tailspin ever since learning his mother had committed treason to get a baby—him. Then Lillian had a heart attack, landing her in the hospital. He'd been by her side, hearing how sorry she was and how much she loved him when another attack slipped his mother into a coma from which she never roused. The numbness following her death had allowed him to make it through her funeral and to return to work after the allotted bereavement time off ended.

In the days after Lillian died, Cy hadn't been able to muster the energy to respond to Isana's texts and calls beyond surface details about the funeral arrangements and when he'd be back in the office. In the four weeks since his return to work, it had been easier to ask her for time and then bury himself in catching up with work than examining his feelings for Isana. If he were being honest with himself—and clarity sometimes came along with insomnia—fear held him back from rekindling his feelings for the woman across from him.

How could one contemplate a helpmate when his entire world of who he was and who his parents were had imploded? Unfair to Isana, but he couldn't find a way past it or to figure out how to trust this vibrant woman when his very life was built on a lie.

The hurt glistening in her eyes sliced another ribbon in his own heart. At his delay in replying, she turned away and dipped her cheek to her shoulder as if blotting tears from her face. She stiffened her spine. He admired the lovely curve of her figure, calling himself all sorts of a fool not to fight for her. But his mother's death and revelations had mired him in inertia—he couldn't gin up the energy to explain what had been swirling in his mind.

She spun around, a red flush replacing the paleness of a moment before. Anger sparked in her eyes. "Was my mother right?"

Her apparent change in subject loosened his tongue. "About what?"

"That I'm unloveable, that no man would ever want me."

The starkness of the words and the pain behind them told Cy Isana didn't want to believe them, but his actions of late had made her question the truth. "No. It's not you, it's me. And I don't mean it like I don't want you, because I do." He stopped because the words kept getting jumbled up in his mind and he was terrified he'd say the wrong thing and ruin any chance he had with this incredible woman.

For a moment, she simply stared at him. When he remained motionless, she took two steps. She reached down and tugged his chair out, moving his body to face hers more squarely.

Then she huffed out a breath, took his face in her hands, and kissed him full on the mouth. His body went from feeling lethargic to energized, his brain zinging with all sorts of adjectives. Wonderful. Spectacular. Stupendous. Delightful.

He was on his feet without even realizing he'd risen. His arms wrapped around Isana, their kiss deepening until all his thoughts centered around the woman before him. The fear of the future melted away in the heat of the passion generated by the meeting of their lips.

A warning bell rang insistently in his brain, telling him to back off before things progressed any farther. Reluctantly, he broke the kiss, resting his forehead against hers. The words now tumbled out. "I'm sorry. I'm so very sorry. I've been an idiot. I've—"

"Shhh." Isana placed her fingers over his lips. "Hush now. There'll be time for all of that later. For now, just hold me." She tucked her head against his chest.

His fingers stroked her hair, as his own tears fell onto the silkiness of the strands. Somehow, against all odds, he'd been given a second chance at loving this woman. He silently prayed God would help him be worthy of her love.

EPILOGUE

Two months later . . .

Isana adjusted the veil, admiring the lace as it cascaded around Lena Hoffman's head. "There, you look gorgeous."

Her friend slowly turned and gazed into the full length mirror in the bridal changing room at the church. "Not too bad."

Isana touched the other woman's arm. "As blushing a bride as I've ever seen."

Someone knocked on the door. "I'll get it." Isana stepped around the tall screen that shielded the bride from anyone entering the room. Opening the door, she greeted Violet Silverton, who juggled a squirmy three-month-old baby girl in her arms. "Hello, Iris. Are you behaving yourself for your mommy?"

The baby cooed and waved her chubby hand. "Henry says she's living up to her namesake and being very persnickety," Violet laughed. Henry and Violet had named their daughter after the senator who died trying to expose the man responsible for betraying his country and killing one of Violet's dearest friends. Isana and Cy had enjoyed getting to know the Silvertons, who had become close friends in the aftermath of Lillian's death.

"But as much as I love talking about my daughter, I came to let you know it's time," Violet winked at Lena, who'd peeked around the corner of the screen. "Get her into position."

"Will do," Isana said as she shut the door behind Violet and Iris. "I swear, that baby gets cuter by the day."

"Thinking of your own future children with your handsome boyfriend, are you?" Lena picked up the voluminous skirt of her wedding dress and eased toward the door.

Isana flicked a piece of lint off the skirt of her forest green taffeta concoction and tried to cool her hot cheeks. "Not going to distract me from getting you to the back of the church on time. Let's go."

Lena rolled her eyes. "I'm just saying you and Cy have been inseparable, and it's only natural for you to think about the future."

"Of course we think of the future, but we're not rushing things. Now enough talk about me—you have a groom waiting for you at the altar." Isana gathered the short train at the back of Lena's gown and carried it as Lena walked slowly in front of her toward the designated spot.

Lena halted behind the flower girl, one of Devlin's adorable nieces. Her three other bridesmaids fussed over Lena in her dress before the wedding coordinator hushed everyone and opened the double doors as the sound of "Ave Verum Corpus" by Mozart soared in the sanctuary.

Three hours later, Isana slid into a seat beside Cy, her duties as maid of honor complete. "Whew. Remind me never to be another maid of honor. Way too much stress."

Cy dropped a kiss on her cheek as they eyed the happy couple dancing the "Electric Slide" with Devlin's squealing nieces and nephews. "Your speech was perfect."

"Thanks." Isana slipped off her heels to wiggle her toes. She eyed the appendages. "I think the best man might have injured my toes.

He must have stepped on them a dozen times during the bridal party dance."

As the music from the line dance faded, the DJ announced a slow dance. Cy leaned over and gazed down at her stockinged feet. "They okay to try a spin around the floor with me?"

Isana bit back a groan but slipped the shoes back on. "Only if you promise to keep your feet well away from mine."

He placed a hand over his heart. "I promise." He held out a hand to help Isana out of the chair. Spinning her around with a flourish, he gathered her in his arms. "Isn't this better?"

She sighed, nestling her head against his broad chest. "Much better." For a few moments, she counted his heartbeats while he expertly guided her around the dance floor. When he spun her away from him and back again, she said, "I didn't know you could dance."

"My mom insisted on teaching me in high school." His eyes darkened but the fact he was able to mention Lillian without a flash of pain was a huge improvement. With her encouragement, Cy had been seeing a therapist to untangle his emotions and feelings concerning his mother's actions. She'd also had her own counseling sessions to finally put to rest her mother's hurtful words. He'd also struck up a correspondence with Brenner Lorenz, who was fully cooperating with the Justice Department about a host of crimes related to his time in East Berlin and in the United States. Brenner was being held at an undisclosed location while he spilled his secrets, but had been allowed to send letters to Cy. The two had tentatively connected, as Brenner related details about Cy's biological mother and other family history.

"She did a good job," Isana agreed as Cy neatly maneuvered them around another couple.

Lena and Devlin spun past, their faces alight with happiness. Maybe one day, that might be her and Cy. Isana had been trying to give him space to process and not push him to take their relationship to the next level, but waiting was not easy. Now that they'd found their footing, she was ready to fully commit to the man in her arms.

As the song came to a close, Cy twirled her once more before ending their dance with a dramatic dip. Her breath caught in her throat at the look of love radiating out from his eyes. He lowered his lips to capture her mouth in a searing kiss that made her forget they were on the edge of a dance floor in front of many friends.

Cy broke the kiss and gently raised her to a standing position, his gaze intent on her face. "Marry me."

Isana blinked, not sure she'd heard him over the lively number now bringing more wedding goers to the dance floor.

Cy must have taken her hesitation to mean she needed more of a declaration. "I love you, Isana." He reached into his suit's inner breast pocket and withdrew a sparkling ring. "I've been carrying this around for a month, trying to figure out the right time to ask you, and today I realized I had wasted an entire month without you as my fiancée. Would you spend the rest of your life with me as my wife?"

Isana looked from the ring in his hand to his face. She threw her arms in the air and whooped, her cheer drowned out by those on the dance floor singing along to a popular song. "Yes, yes, yes." She held out her left hand and he slipped on the ring. "I thought you'd never ask, Mr. Hillam."

"I thought you'd never say yes, Miss Thomas." He leaned closer, bringing his lips close to hers. "I love you."

"I love you too." She breathed in the scent of his cologne and bridged the final distance to his mouth. Before her eyes slid closed to enjoy their first kiss as an engaged couple, she caught a glimpse of Lena and Devlin smiling a few feet away, along with Henry, Violet, and baby Iris applauding nearby. God had indeed brought about his own gentle reckoning to give her a new beginning with Jesus and this wonderful man.

THE END

About the Author

Sarah Hamaker loves writing books "where the hero and heroine fall in love while running for their lives." She's written romantic suspense novels and nonfiction books, as well as stories in *Chicken Soup for the Soul* volumes. As a AWSA certified writer coach, her heart is encouraging writers. She's a member of AWSA; Christian Authors Network; ACFW; ACFW Virginia Chapter; and Faith, Hope and Love, as well as the president of Capital Christian Writers Fellowship. Her podcast, "The Romantic Side of Suspense," can be found wherever you listen to podcasts. Sarah lives in Virginia with her husband, four teenagers, a preschool foster child and three cats.

Connect with Sarah!

Website: sarahhamakerfiction.com

Newsletter: https://sarahhamakerfiction.ck.page

BookBub: https://www.bookbub.com/profile/sarah-hamaker

Goodreads: https://www.goodreads.com/author/show/1804799.Sarah_Hamaker

YouTube: https://www.youtube.com/channel/UCzI8JVSzbms6MoQbFc6SiLQ

LinkedIn: https://www.linkedin.com/in/sarah-hamaker-7295a01/

Amazon Author Page: https://www.amazon.com/-/e/B002TIARBS

OTHER BOOKS BY SARAH HAMAKER

The Cold War Legacy Trilogy

A compelling trilogy about ordinary women uncovering extraordinary secrets of the past that could cost them everything.

The Dark Guest (Seshva Press LLC), The Cold War Legacy Book 1

4.5 Amazon Star Rating; 4.59 Goodreads Rating

The Cold War is over, but The Wolf is still at the door.

When Violet Lundy isn't cleaning rooms at Happy Hills Assisted Living Facility, she loves spending her free time with resident Rainer Kopecek. Hearing his stories of the dangerous life he led behind the Iron Curtain in

East Berlin makes her own life seem more tolerable. But when Rainer is found dead and his room in disarray, Violet suspects foul play.

Dr. Henry Silverton lives among his books, teaching and writing about the Cold War. A letter about an East German traitor known only as "The Wolf" propels Henry out of academia and into Violet's life. Together, they embark on a perilous quest to uncover the truth about Rainer's death and the traitor's identity.

Can Violet and Henry uncover the secrets of the past before one of them ends up as The Wolf's next victim?

The Dark Atonement (Seshva Press LLC), The Cold War Legacy Book 2

4.5 Amazon Star Rating; 4.38 Goodreads Rating

A translator and a medical researcher team up to find a long-lost scientist with an innovative cancer treatment.

German translator Lena Hoffman thought her grandfather died years ago. But the unexpected arrival of a cryptic postcard seems to indicate otherwise. As Lena delves into her grandfather's past and uncovers information about him and his cancer research work in East Germany four decades ago, she unwittingly puts her own life in danger.

Dr. Devlin Mills works as a cancer researcher at the National Institutes of Health and lives across the hall from Lena, although they've never formally met. But when Lena is nearly run down by a vehicle, Devlin finds himself thrust into the role of protector. As their lives intersect, the pair find themselves in a race to discover the whereabouts of her grandfather—and whoever wants to silence him—before the past catches up with the present.

Dangerous Christmas Memories (Love Inspired Suspense)

4.5 Amazon Star Rating; 4.38 Goodreads Rating

A witness in jeopardy...and a killer on the loose.

Hiding in witness protection is the only option for Priscilla Anderson after witnessing a murder. Then Lucas Langsdale shows up claiming to be her husband right when a hit man finds her. With partial amnesia, she has no memory of her marriage or the killer's identity.

Yet she will have to put her faith in Luc if they both want to live to see another day.

Deadly Diamonds (Seshva Press LLC)

4.5 Amazon Star Rating; 4.56 Goodreads Rating

The race to find missing diamonds puts a widow in danger.

Three years ago, Dulce Honeycutt's life imploded when her husband died after a robbing a jewelry store and her 18-year-old son, Kieran, landed in prison as an accessory. The uncut diamonds were never recovered, and when rumors fly that she and Kieran know where the gems are hidden, their lives are in danger.

Veteran insurance investigator Miles Sharp believes Dulce knows more about the diamonds than she's revealing. But as the attacks on the beautiful widow's life multiply, he struggles to maintain his professional objectivity. Is Dulce a victim or is her story a sweet web of lies?

Illusion of Love (Seshva Press LLC)

4.5 Amazon Star Rating; 4.61 Goodreads Rating

A suspicious online romance reconnects an agoraphobe and an old friend.

Psychiatrist Jared Quinby's investigation for the FBI leads him to his childhood friend, Mary Divers. Agoraphobic Mary has found love with online beau David. When David reveals his intention of becoming a missionary, Mary takes a leap of faith and accepts David's marriage proposal.

When Jared's case intersects with Mary's online relationship, she refuses to believe anything's amiss with David. When tragedy strikes, Mary pushes Jared away.

Will Jared convince Mary of the truth—and of his love for her—before it's too late?

Mistletoe & Murder (Seshva Press LLC)

4.5 Amazon Star Rating; 4.12 Goodreads Rating

Alec Stratman comes home to Twin Oaks, Virginia, after his Army retirement to contemplate his reentry into civilian life. Instead he's greeted with the murder of his beloved Great-Aunt Heloise.

For Isabella Montoya, the loss of Heloise Stratman Thatcher goes beyond the end of a job. Heloise had encouraged Isabella to follow her dreams and helped fund her studies. Now, accused of her mentor's murder, Isabella is scrambling to prove her innocence.

Since his great-aunt had written glowing letters about Isabella, Alec is unwilling to believe the police's suspicion of the former housekeeper. Instead, he works to help clear her name.

Will Isabella and Alec be able to navigate the secrets that threaten to derail their budding romance and uncover the truth about Heloise's death before the killer strikes again?

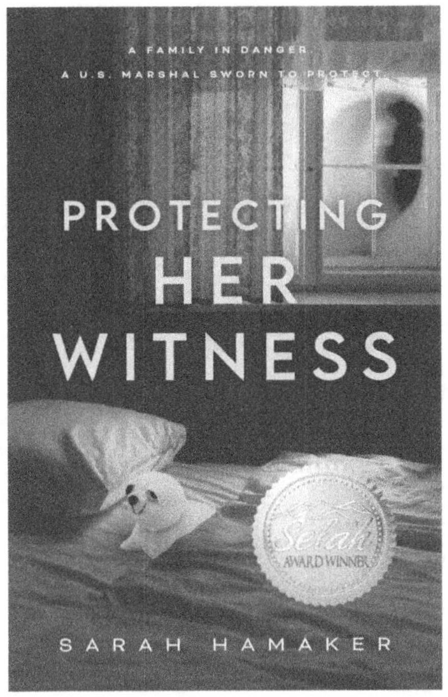

Protecting Her Witness (Seshva Press LLC)

4.5 Amazon Star Rating; 4.49 Goodreads Rating

Winner of the 2022 Selah Award in Romantic Suspense

A family in danger...a U.S. Marshal sworn to protect.

U.S. Marshal Chalissa Manning has been running from her past and God for most of her life. When she meets widower Titus Davis and his son, Sam, her well-built defenses begin to crumble. But someone is targeting Titus and Sam, and it's up to Chalissa to both protect them and to find out who is behind the attacks.

As the threats pile up, will Chalissa be able to keep the family she's grown to love safe?

Vanished Without a Trace (Love Inspired Suspense)

4.5 Amazon Star Rating; 4.50 Goodreads Rating

A missing person case. A new clue. And a fight for survival.

After nine years searching for his missing sister, attorney Henderson Parker uncovers a clue that leads him to Twin Oaks, Virginia—and podcaster Elle Updike investigating the case. Partnering with the journalist is the last thing Henderson wants, until mysterious thugs make multiple attacks on both their lives. Now they'll have to trust each other...before the suspected kidnappers make them disappear for good.